I can only make things up about things that have already happened . . .

— Alison Bechdel

For Mark Warren and Annika

LIBRARY OF CONGRESS CIP DATA ON FILE.
CATALOGUING IN PUBLICATION FOR THIS BOOK
IS AVAILABLE FROM THE LIBRARY OF CONGRESS.

ISBN-13: 978-1-4328-8648-6 (hardcover alk. paper)

Published in 2021 by arrangement with Little, Brown and Company, a division of Hachette Book Group, Inc.

Printed in Mexico
Print Number: 01   Print Year: 2021

HOMELAND ELEGIES

AYAD AKHTAR

THORNDIKE PRESS
A part of Gale, a Cengage Company

GALE
A Cengage Company

HOMELAND ELEGIES

CONTENTS

OVERTURE: TO AMERICA 11
A CHRONOLOGY OF
THE EVENTS 19

FAMILY POLITICS 21
I. On the Anniversary of Trump's
First Year in Office 23
II. On Autobiography; or,
Bin Laden 56
III. In the Names of the Prophet 100

SCRANTON MEMOIRS 157
IV. God's Country 159
V. Riaz; or, The Merchant of Debt . . 210

POX AMERICANA 293
VI. Of Love and Death 295
VII. On Pottersville 376
VIII. *Langford v. Reliant*; or, How My
Father's American Story Ends . . 414

FREE SPEECH: A CODA 547
ACKNOWLEDGMENTS 561

OVERTURE: TO AMERICA

I had a professor in college, Mary Moroni, who taught Melville and Emerson, and who the once famous Norman O. Brown — her mentor — called the finest mind of her generation; a diminutive, cherubic woman in her early thirties with a resemblance to a Raphaelesque putto that was not incidental (her parents had immigrated from Urbino); a scholar of staggering erudition who quoted as easily from the *Eddas* and Hannah Arendt as she did from *Moby-Dick;* a lesbian, which I only mention because she did, often; a lecturer whose turns of phrase were sharp as a German paring knife, could score the brain's gray matter and carve out new grooves along which old thoughts would reroute, as on that February morning two weeks after Bill Clinton's first inauguration, when, during a class on life under early American capitalism, Mary, clearly interrupted by her own tantalizing thought,

11

looked up from the floor at which she usually gazed as she spoke — her left hand characteristically buried in the pocket of the loose-fitting slacks that were her mainstay — looked up and remarked almost offhandedly that America had begun as a colony and that a colony it remained, that is, a place still defined by its plunder, where enrichment was paramount and civil order always an afterthought. The fatherland in whose name — and for whose benefit — the predation continued was no longer a physical fatherland but a spiritual one: the American Self. Long trained to worship its desires — however discreet, however banal — rather than question them, as the classical tradition taught, ever-tumescent American self-regard was the pillaging *patria,* she said, and the marauding years of the Reagan regime had only expressed this enduring reality of American life with greater clarity and transparency than ever before.

Mary had gotten into some trouble the previous semester for similarly bracing remarks about American hegemony in the wake of Desert Storm. A student in the ROTC program taking her class complained to the administration that she was speaking out against the troops. He started a petition and set up a table in the student union. The brouhaha led to an editorial in the campus paper and threats of a protest that never actually materialized. Mary wasn't cowed. After all, this was the early '90s, and the consequences of astringent ideological fire and brimstone — or sexual abuse of power, while you're at it — were hardly what they are today. If anyone had a problem with what she said that afternoon, I didn't hear about it. The truth is, I doubt many of us even understood what she was getting at. I certainly didn't.

Worship of desire. Tumescent self-regard. A colony for pillage.

In her words was the power of a great negation, a corrective to a tradition of endless American self-congratulation. It was new to me. I was accustomed to the God-blessed, light-of-the-world exceptionalism that informed every hour I'd ever spent in history class. I'd come of age in the era of the hilltop city gleaming for all to see. Such were the glorified tropes I learned at school, which I saw not as tropes but as truth. I saw an American benevolence in Uncle Sam's knowing glare at the post office; heard an American abundance in the canned laugh tracks on the sitcoms I watched every night with my mother; felt an American security and strength as I pedaled my ten-speed Schwinn past split-level and two-story homes in the middle-class subdivision where I grew up. Of course, my father was a great fan of America back then. To him, there was no greater place in the world, nowhere you could do more, have more, be more. He couldn't get enough of it: camping in the Tetons, driving through Death Valley, riding to the top of the arch in St. Louis before hopping a riverboat down to Louisiana to fish for bass in the bayou. He loved visiting the historic sites. We had framed our photos of trips to Monticello and Saratoga and to the house on Beals Street in Brookline where the Kennedy brothers were born. I recall a Saturday morning in Philadelphia when I was eight and Father scolding me for whining through a crowded tour of rooms somehow connected with the Constitution. When it was over, we took a cab to the famous steps at the museum, and he raced me to the top — letting me win! — in homage to Rocky Balboa.

Love for America and a firm belief in its supremacy — moral and otherwise — was creed in our home, one my mother knew not to challenge even if she didn't quite share it. Like both Mary's parents — as I would later learn from Mary herself — my

14

mother never found in the various bounties of her new country anything like sufficient compensation for the loss of what she'd left behind. I don't think Mother ever felt at home here. She thought Americans materialistic and couldn't understand what was so holy about the orgy of acquisition they called Christmas. She was put off that everyone always asked where she was from and never seemed bothered that they had no idea what she was talking about when she told them. Americans were ignorant not only of geography but of history, too. And most troubling to her was what she thought connected to this disregard of important things, namely, the American denial of aging and death. This last irritation would yield a malevolent concretion over the years, a terror-inducing bête noire that saw her to her grave, the thought that growing old here would mean her eventual sequestering and expiration in a "home" that was nothing like one.

My mother's views — however rarely voiced — should have prepared me to understand Mary's dyspeptic take on this country, but they didn't. Not even my Islam prepared me to see what Mary saw, not even after 9/11. I remember a letter from her in the months following that terrifying day in

September that changed Muslim lives in America forever, a ten-page missive in which she encouraged me to take heart, to learn what I could from the trouble ahead, confiding that her struggles as a gay woman in this country — the sense of siege, the unceasing assaults on her quest for wholeness, the roughness of her route to autonomy and authenticity — that all these had been but fires beneath her crucible, provoking creative rage, tempering sentimentality, releasing her from hope in ideology. "Use the difficulty; make it your own" was her admonition. Difficulty had been the flint stone against which her powers of analysis were sharpened, the how and why of what she saw, but which I still wouldn't see truly with my own eyes for fifteen years to come, my deepening travails as a Muslim in this country notwithstanding. No. I wouldn't see what Mary saw until I'd been witness to the untimely decline of a generation of colleagues exhausted by the demands of jobs that never paid them enough, drowning in debt to care for children riddled with disorders that couldn't be cured; and the cousins — and the best friend from high school — who ended up in shelters or on the street, tossed out of houses they could no longer afford; and until the near-dozen suicides and overdoses of fortysomething childhood classmates in a mere space of three years; and the friends and family medicated for despair, anxiety, lack of affect, insomnia, sexual dysfunction; and the premature cancers brought on by the chemical shortcuts for everything from the food moving through our irritable bowels to the lotions applied to our sun-poisoned skins. I wouldn't see it until our private lives had consumed the public space, then been codified, foreclosed, and put up for auction; until the devices that enslave our minds had filled us with the toxic flotsam of a culture no longer worthy of the name; until the bright pliancy of human sentience — attention itself — had become the world's most prized commodity, the very movements of our minds transformed into streams of unceasing revenue for someone, somewhere. I wouldn't see it clearly until the American Self had fully mastered the plunder, idealized and legislated the splitting of the spoils, and brought to near completion the wholesale pillage not only of the so-called colony — how provincial a locution *that* seems now! — but also of the very world itself. In short, I wouldn't see what she saw back then until I'd failed at trying to see it otherwise, until I'd ceased believing in the lie of my own redemption, until the suffering of others aroused in me a starker, clearer cry than any anthem to my own longing. I read Whitman first with Mary. I adored him. The green leaves and dry leaves, the spears of summer grass, the side-curved head ever avid for what came next. My tongue, too, is homegrown — every atom of this blood formed of this soil, this air. But these multitudes will not be my own. And these will be no songs of celebration.

A CHRONOLOGY
OF THE EVENTS

1964–68 My parents meet in Lahore, Pakistan; marry; immigrate to the United States
1972 I am born on Staten Island
1976 We move to Wisconsin
1979 Iran hostage crisis; Mother's first bout with cancer (with recurrences in '86, '99, and 2010)
1982 Father's first attempt at private practice
1991 Father's private practice folds; he declares bankruptcy, returns to academic medicine
1993 Father first meets Donald Trump
1994 Dinner with Aunt Asma; reading Rushdie
1997 Father's final encounter with Trump
1998 Latif Awan killed in Pakistan
2001 The attacks of September 11
2008 Family trip to Abbottabad, Pakistan
2009 Car breaks down in Scranton

2011 Bin Laden killed

2012 First opening of a play in New York City; meet Riaz Rind; Christine Langford and her unborn child die

2013 Awarded Pulitzer Prize for Drama

2014 Join the board of the Riaz Rind Foundation; meet Asha

2015 Diagnosed with syphilis; Mother dies; Trump declares his candidacy

2016 Trump elected

2017 Sell my shares in Timur Capital; *Merchant of Debt* opens in Chicago; Father tried for malpractice

2018 I begin to write these pages

FAMILY POLITICS

I.
ON THE ANNIVERSARY OF TRUMP'S FIRST YEAR IN OFFICE

My father first met Donald Trump in the early '90s, when they were both in their midforties — my father the elder by a year — and as each was coming out from under virtual financial ruin. Trump's unruly penchant for debt and his troubles with borrowed money were widely reported in the business pages of the time: by 1990, his namesake organization was collapsing under the burden of the loans he'd taken out to keep his casinos running, the Plaza Hotel open, and his airline's jets aloft. The money had come at a price. He'd been forced to guarantee a portion of it, leaving him personally liable for more than eight hundred million dollars. In the summer of that year, a long *Vanity Fair* profile painted an alarming portrait not only of the man's finances but also of his mental state. Separated from his wife, he'd decamped from the family triplex for a small apartment on a lower floor of Trump Tower. He was spending hours a day lying in bed, staring up at the ceiling. He wouldn't leave the building, not for meetings, not for meals — subsisting on a diet of burgers and fries delivered from a local deli. Like his debt load, Trump's waistline ballooned, his hair grew long, curling at the ends, ungovernable. And it wasn't just his appearance. He'd gone uncharacteristically quiet. Ivana confided to friends she was worried. She'd never seen him like this, and she wasn't sure he was going to pull through.

My father, like Trump, binged on debt in the '80s and ended the decade uncertain about his financial future. A doctor, he'd transitioned into private practice from a career in academic cardiology just as the hostage crisis began. By the time Reagan was in office, he'd started to *mint money,* as he liked to put it. (The playful attack of his Punjabi lilt always made it sound to me more like he was describing the *flavor* of all that new cash rather than the *activity* of making it.) In 1983, with more money than he knew what to do with, Father took a weekend seminar in real estate investment at the Radisson hotel in West Allis, Wisconsin. By Sunday night, he'd put in an offer on his first property, a listing one of the

instructors had "shared" with the partici-
pants on a lunch break — a gas station in
Baraboo just blocks from the site where the
Ringling brothers started their circus. Just
what it was he needed with a gas station
was the perfectly reasonable question my
mother flatly posed when he announced the
news to us later that week. To celebrate, he'd
mixed a pitcher of Rooh Afza lassi — the
rose-flavored squash beverage was my mother's favorite. He shrugged in response to
her question and held out a glass for her to
take. She was in no mood for lassi.

"What do you know about gas stations?"
she asked, irritated.

"I don't need to know the day-to-day. The
business is solid. Good cash flow."

"*Cash* flow?"

"It's making money, Fatima."

"If it's making so much money, why did
they need to sell? Hmm?"

"People have their reasons."

"What reasons? Sounds like you have no
idea what you're talking about. Were you
drinking?"

"No, I wasn't drinking. Do you want the
lassi or not?" She shook her head, curtly.
He tended the glass to me; I didn't want it,
either; I hated the stuff. "I don't expect you
to understand. I don't expect you to sup-

25

port me. But in ten years, you'll look back on this, you both will, and you'll see that I made a great *investment.*"

I wasn't sure what I had to do with it.

"Investment?" she repeated. "Is that like when you buy a new pair of sunglasses every time you go to the store?"

"I'm always losing them."

"I can show you fifteen right now."

"Not the ones I like."

"What a pity for you," she said, her voice dripping with sarcasm as she headed for the hallway.

"You'll see!" Father cried out after her. "You'll see!"

What we were to *see* were the subsequent "investments" in a strip mall in Janesville; another in Skokie, Illinois; a campground outside Wausau; and a trout farm near Fond du Lac. If you don't see the logic in the portfolio of holdings, well, you're not the only one. It turned out the haphazard purchases were all the advice of the seminar instructor, Chet, who'd sold him the first. All were financed with debt, each property operating as some form of collateral for the other in some bizarre configuration of shell corporations Chet came up with — for which he would be indicted in the aftermath of the S&L crisis. My father was lucky to dodge the legal bullet. Oh, and yes, we did have our obligatory copy of Trump's *The Art of the Deal* on the shelf in the living room — but that wouldn't be for a few years yet.

My father has always been something of a conundrum to me, an imam's son whose only sacred names — Harlan, Far Niente, Opus One — were those of the big California Cabernets he adored; who worshipped Diana Ross and Sylvester Stallone and who preferred the poker he learned here to the *rung* he left behind in Pakistan; a man of unpredictable appetites and impulses, inclined to tip the full amount of the bill (and sometimes then some); an unrepentant admirer of American pluck who never stopped chiding me for my adolescent lack of same: If he'd had *my* good fortune to be born here?! Not only would he never have become a doctor! He also might actually have been *happy*! It's true I can't seem to recall him ever looking as content as he did for those few middle Reagan years when — on the promise of the system's endlessly easy money — he awoke each morning to find in the mirror the reflection of a self-made businessman. It would prove a short-lived joy. The market crash in '87 initiated a cascade of unfortunate "credit events" that, by the early '90s, reduced his net worth to less than nothing. I'd just started my second year of college when he called to tell me he was selling his practice to avoid bankruptcy and that I would have to leave school that semester unless I could secure a student loan. (I did.)

If not fully reformed by the reversal of fortune, Father was certainly chastened for a time. He returned to his position as a professor of clinical cardiology at the university and threw himself back into a career of research, for which, despite his misgivings, he was clearly suited. Indeed, after just three years back in the academy, he found himself once again at the top of his field and on an awards dais, handed a medal for his recent studies of a little-known disorder known as Brugada syndrome. It was the second time he'd won the American College of Cardiology's Investigator of the Year award, making him only the third physician in its history — and likely the most insolvent — ever to be honored twice in a career.

It was Father's work on Brugada, a rare and often fatal arrhythmia, that led to his first meeting Donald Trump.

In 1993, Trump's troubles were still legion. He'd gone to his siblings to ask if he could borrow money from the family trust to pay bills. (He would go back for more a year later.) He was forced to give up his yacht, the airline, and his stake in the Plaza Hotel. The bankers overseeing the restructuring of his holdings put him on a strict monthly allowance. And in the press, there was no relief: his mistress, Marla Maples, was newly pregnant, and his press-canny, now finally ex-wife was destroying him in the court of public opinion.

In short, he was going through a lot. So it wasn't entirely surprising to either Trump or his doctors when he started to experience heart palpitations. As Trump described it to my father, he first felt the alarming sensation while golfing on an unusually hot morning in Palm Beach; he felt something strange in his chest, like a pounding on a distant drum; then he felt faint. When he sat down in the golf cart to rest, the pounding neared, grew more intense: "It felt like my heart was being slammed around inside that big empty drum."*

* I found Trump's description oddly poetic. Father always said he found the man sharp. It was a measure of how far Trump had finally fallen in his eyes by the fall of 2019 that, when I told him I was writing these pages, he offered to get me into the office where he no longer worked — at that

29

A few days after the palpitations on the golf course, Trump was having dinner at the Breakers, then the premier luxury resort in Palm Beach. He hated the Breakers — or so Father recalls him explaining at some length during their first patient exam — but had to go to the dinner there because he was meeting a member of the city council who, Trump thought, knowing how much he hated the Breakers, had probably scheduled dinner there on purpose. Trump's application to turn Mar-a-Lago into a private club was still pending, and he needed all the support on the Palm Beach city council that he could get. So the Breakers it was, even though he said the food was gross and overpriced. "Just wait 'til I get my club running. We're going to bury the Breakers." He'd ordered a bone-in rib eye — "Always well done, Doc. Because I don't know the kitchen, and I don't know what filth they've got back there. Who's cooking what. Touch-

point, he was retired — so I might be able to peruse Trump's medical file. Though tempted, I didn't see the need. Father remembered so much of his time with "Donald" and remembered it so well; he could call up details of even the most trivial exchanges with a vividness usually reserved for the recollection of a great romance.

ing the food. The only way to be safe —
steak, fish, whatever. Well done. Unless it's
my kitchen, and we're gonna have a great
restaurant at Mar-a-Lago, the greatest, but
see . . . I'll still have it well done there, too.
I just think it's better that way" — and just
as the food came to the table, Trump said
he started to feel faint. He got up and
excused himself to go to the restroom,
where he couldn't believe how pale he
looked. Once again, he felt that sensation
he'd felt on the golf course, his heart rattling around as if inside the skin of an empty
drum. He knew something was wrong. He
knew he needed to get home.

It was a short distance to Mar-a-Lago —
just three miles — but as soon as the car
pulled out of the parking lot, he started to
feel worse. Along Ocean Boulevard, he
asked his driver to stop the car, and that
was it. The next thing he remembered was
lying on the sidewalk, hearing the waves.
His driver would later tell him he collapsed
facedown into the rear footwell. The driver
would get out and turn him over, finding
Trump's eyes rolled back into his head. He
couldn't find a pulse on Trump's wrist or
neck, couldn't hear a beating in his chest.
The driver shook him hard, and then, just
as abruptly as he'd fainted, Trump came

back to. Color rushed into his face; the veins in his forehead started to pulse. Dazed, he got out of the car and lay down on the sidewalk along the beach. Listening to the steady rhythm of waves washing onto the shore, he would later tell my father, seemed to make the strange beating in his heart subside.

Doctors' examinations over the following days and weeks pointed to a cardiac event, but Trump's heart muscle itself was healthy, his coronary arteries clear of any occlusion. A further battery of tests resulted in a pile of EKG strips that showed an occasional pattern the specialist in Palm Beach had never seen before. It had the vague contour of a shark fin. Even as late as 1993, most cardiologists didn't know that this is what Brugada syndrome looks like.

The strips were sent to Mount Sinai Hospital, in New York, where a cardiologist on staff referred them to my father, in Milwaukee. Considered the leading special- ist in Brugada in the States, second in the world only to the Brugada brothers, who had identified the syndrome at their labs in Belgium, Father was accustomed to EKG strips and patients pouring into his lab from across the country — and, later, from the Far East. Indeed, Trump wasn't even the first person of some fame whose case had come his way. The year prior, Father was flown first class to Brunei, where he examined the sultan himself in a lab that had been outfitted to Father's specs by the time he'd touched down in Bandar Seri Begawan. Though Trump was no monarch — at least not yet — he wasn't about to get on a plane for Milwaukee, either. So Father was flown — again, first class — to Newark, where Trump's helicopter was waiting for him. He flew into a heliport along the Hudson River, where a car picked him up and drove him to Mount Sinai. Ushered into one of the exam rooms, where the equipment was set up for a battery of tests — the usual twelve-lead EKG, followed by a stress test, and if neither induced the Brugada arrhythmia, there was an option to inject an alkaloid through an intravenous line — Father waited for his patient to arrive. But Trump never showed.

That night, in the room at the Plaza Hotel that had been arranged for him, Father's bedside phone rang just as he was falling asleep. It was Donald himself. What follows is my approximation of their conversation, shaped by Father's recollection of, above all, the man's solicitousness:

"No one seems to know how to say it,

Doctor."

"Nothing new there."

"How do *you* say it?"

"*Ak*-tar."

"So *Ak,* like in *Oc*-topus."

"That works."

"But is that how *you* say it? Where you're from? — Where *are* you from?"

"Pakistan."

"Pakistan —"

"And we pronounce the name differently there."

"I'm talented. I can say it right."

"So we say A*kh*tar." Father reverted to the native *kh* guttural sound that no white American in his experience had ever been able to master. There was a moment's silence on the other end of the line.

"Oh, that sounds hard. I don't know about that, Doctor."

"*Ak*-tar is fine, Mr. Trump."

They both laughed.

"Okay, okay. *Ak*-tar it is. And you call me Donald. Please." Trump then proceeded to apologize for missing his appointment. Disarmed by his warmth, Father demurred. Trump asked if his room was big enough: "It's New York City. Hard to feel like you ever have enough space. But I had them put you in a nice suite. Do you like it? We redid

34

those rooms when I bought the place —"

"Mr. Trump —"

"That hotel is a masterpiece, Doctor. The *Mona Lisa*. That's what it is."

"Mr. Trump —"

"Call me Donald, please —"

"Please excuse me, Donald, but I didn't come to New York to stay in a nice hotel. I came here to help you. I'm not sure you understand how serious this problem with your heart could be. If you have Brugada, I'm not exaggerating when I say you are a walking time bomb. You could be dead tomorrow." There was silence. Father continued: "I'm flattered to receive the royal treatment from you, Donald. I am. But I just came from Brunei, where I treated the sultan of Brunei. He is a king, and he was on time for his appointment. Because he understood that if he doesn't get it taken care of, he might be dead tomorrow."

"Okay, Doctor," Trump said blankly after a short pause. "I'll be there. What time?"

"Eight a.m."

"I'm sorry I missed it today. I'm very sorry, Doctor. It wasn't respectful of you. Or your time. I apologize. I mean it."

"It's fine, Donald."

"You forgive me?"

Father laughed.

"Okay, good. You're laughing," Trump said. "I'm sorry about today, but I will be there tomorrow. First thing. I promise."

Early in the campaign for the 2016 election, when there was all the anatomizing of Trump's character and his style — and the speculation about his *real* chances — one thing much repeated was that Trump did not know how to apologize. As he careened from one lie and ill-advised faux pas to another, it was endlessly remarked that the man seemed incapable of saying he was sorry, even when it might have helped him. To admit you were wrong meant to show weakness, and this, it seemed, ran contrary not only to his every business instinct but also to the very rule of his being. An unmistakable contempt for weakness is what I gleaned from every boardroom firing of *The Apprentice* I ever saw. Invariably, the contestant who ended up on the other side of Trump's jab-and-sack signature line, spat out onto Fifth Avenue, forlorn, ferried — via black limousine — far from the Olympian suite near the top of Trump Tower, where the remaining aspirants sipped Champagne and celebrated the wisdom of Mr. Trump's choice; invariably, that contestant was the one too willing to share blame, too willing to admit that a team failure was probably just that, failure of a *team,* not of a sole individual. In his on-screen role, Trump's bewilderment over such displays of levelheadedness and camaraderie struck me as bizarre. Was it really possible he believed blaming someone else to save face was a legitimate business strategy? Of course, we now know it to be much more than that, something closer to the summum bonum of the Trumpian Weltanschauung. It's likely that the real *role* he played was with Father that night on the phone — and the next morning, when he showed up to his examination on time with two cups of coffee and a small white gift box containing a LOVE LIFE! lapel pin, which he hoped Father would accept as a token of his contrition. My father would never forget the gesture.

To think: all it took was a worthless trinket Trump probably pilfered from the gift shop at Trump Tower for Father to feel justified, years later, in dismissing all that chatter about the man's not knowing how to apologize: "If they only knew him," he would hiss at the pundits on TV — and usually by way of yet another reminder about that lapel pin: "If they knew him, they wouldn't say these things. They would know they were wrong."

■ ■ ■

It would take years to get to the bottom of Trump's malady. Though Father still thought Brugada was possible, he wasn't sure. There was little margin for error: Brugada, untreated, was usually fatal. But the only treatment was an implanted defibrillator, which Trump didn't want unless Father was absolutely certain it was necessary. Father couldn't give him that assurance, for the shark-fin form characteristic of Brugada hadn't recurred on any of the Holter monitor strips or during the biannual exams Trump flew Father to New York to perform. There were no further fainting episodes, though Trump did continue to report feeling that strange empty rattling in his chest from time to time. He would feel it, get winded, then sit down and wait for it to pass. Certain that these were incidences of arrhythmia, but perhaps not of the Brugada variety, Father prescribed a mild beta-blocker and a daily hydrating regimen. For four years these seemed to keep the troubling symptoms at bay.

By 1997, innovations in gene testing made it possible to know for certain that Trump did *not* have the life-threatening heart condition that his earliest EKG strips had been thought to reveal. With a diagnosis of Brugada off the table, the rationale for Father's trips was gone. The visits stopped. Trump never called again. In truth, Father never had all that much face time with the man outside the exam room at Mount Sinai. Apart from the morning heart tests, there'd been the occasional lunch or dinner, the comped suite at the Plaza, the one trip to Atlantic City, where he sat at a baccarat table and lost $5,000 in ten minutes while Trump looked on over his shoulder. It wasn't reasonable for Father to feel as close to Trump as he did, but such things are rarely reasonable. He went into a kind of withdrawal — mourning, really. The simple mention of Trump's name — on the nightly news, or in the daily paper — could conjure his gloom and send him into brooding silence.

Eventually, though, the trips to New York resumed. Under the pretext of attending some medical conference or other with only the most tangential connection to his field, he would fly himself first class; book a room at the Plaza; have dinner at Fresco by Scotto (where he and Donald once slurped spaghetti and meatballs); head to a fitting at Greenfield Clothiers in Brooklyn, where

Trump's suits were tailored and where the staff still referred to Father as Mr. Trump's doctor; and call the person I would later gather he missed even more than Trump himself — a hooker by the name of Caroline. I wouldn't learn of her existence until after my mother died, and when I did, I admit I was taken aback. Not that he'd been unfaithful but that he'd been paying for it. I grew up with the image of my father as an oversize Boy Scout, a feckless if well-meaning *puer aeternus,* bumbling along on the force of his natural gifts. He was not, I'd have said, much interested in the seedier side of life. I was wrong. Father's first visit to a prostitute required little more in the way of goading than some "locker-room talk" between procedures one afternoon, which had Trump waxing jubilant about the surpassing solaces of professional sex. Noting Father's saucer-eyed interest and divining his lack of experience, Trump gave him a number. I don't doubt Father probably hung up a few times before he replied to what I imagine was a silken greeting from the other end of the line, a madam's voice at a private club in the East 40s — a brownstone not far from the UN — where, on the second floor, Father picked his poison, a petite, buxom blonde with a long face

40

whom Trump, too, had apparently "known" and who was reputed to have a mouth of velvet. Father fucked Caroline for fifteen years — *exclusively,* I would later gather (aside from my mother, of course). I would learn of her existence when I discovered I had a half sister in Queens, though this is not the moment for that Pirandellian tale. Suffice it to say Trump's faux largesse — or, rather, Father's longing to live in a tawdry, gilt-and-gossamer penumbra that masqueraded as largesse — this has had an outsize effect on the Akhtar family. And it accounts for something no one understands: my father supported Trump's election, and he supported him well past the point that any rational nonwhite American (let alone sometime immigrant!) could possibly have justified to himself or anyone else. And, yes, the blow-by-blow of Father's enthrallment with candidate Trump, first nascent, then ascendant, then euphoric, then disappointed, then betrayed and confused, and finally exhausted, a gamut of intensities whose order and range are proper to the ambit of all addiction — yes, a granular account of Father's *addiction,* his ceaselessly shifting emotions, his evasions and avowals and disavowals, the steady shedding of his civility, the daily obsession, the ad hoc

41

rationalizations — all this might be of value to note, to show, and, in the process, through this unlikeliest of American Muslim lenses, to reveal the full extent of the terrifying lust for unreality that has engulfed us all. Yes, it might be of value, but I don't know that I can bear to pen it. I love my dad. I think he's a good man. I can't bear to invest a writer's weeks and months — let alone years! — on a portrait of my father as menacing dolt. And so an afternoon's glancing views will have to do.

To wit:

A breakfast place in Waukesha where we were the only nonwhites enjoying brunch the weekend after Trump entered the race with those infamous remarks about Mexican immigrants being rapists and murderers. "I don't know what you're so worked up about. He's a showman. He's drawing attention. He doesn't really mean it." "Then he shouldn't say it." "You're not a politician." "Neither is he." "That remains to be seen." "You're not telling me you think this is a good idea." To which Father didn't respond, only gestured at the busboys in their Mexican football team jerseys: "Anyway, these people need to learn English."

And:

His avid, mounting glee during the primary debates, as Trump insulted the other candidates. "Look at them. Wax dummies, every one. Empty suits, empty words. They deserve every bit. He's just saying what everybody already thinks."

And:

Trump's proposal for a Muslim database, for which, oddly, Father didn't believe he would have to register. "I don't pray; I don't fast; I'm basically not Muslim; you're the same; he's not talking about us. And anyway, I was his doctor, so we don't have anything to worry about."

And:

The mental contortions he performed to make sense of Trump's nonsense, which made me wonder if he was going senile. "Everything he says about the media is right. It *is* rigged. Rigged to make money. Think about it. They don't *report* news. They *sell* it. And what do you think they're selling? Hmm? That Donald can't win. That he *won't* win. But the more votes he gets, the more that story isn't true. Everybody knows this is a lie. He's rising. They're trying to keep him down. He's a fighter. You know what a fighter does? He fights. That's why we love him!" (Huh?)

And:

The eruption of bigoted views I'd never

43

known he'd espoused. That whites were lazy, and all they really cared about were their weekends away and their summer vacations; that blacks didn't like to pay their medical bills because they still had a slave's mentality and saw the system as a master to be rebelled against; that women had a deeper understanding of life because they had to give birth and were built to suffer, which is also why they wouldn't care that Trump said nasty things about them — they ultimately expected it; that Muslims were backward because the Quran was nonsense and the Prophet was a moron; that Jews were neurotic because their fathers didn't know how to shut their wives up so the mothers drove the children crazy; and that's just what I remember without having to think too much about it.

For a thoughtful man — at least one who'd evidenced *instances* of thoughtfulness with reassuring frequency over the years — the man seemed to be turning into an imbecile, his hodgepodge views like mental flatulence, one fetid odor after another. To push the metaphor: it had the logic of dysentery, an infection of his political consciousness occasioning wanton noxious discharge. And further: a child shits on the floor and sticks its finger in the feces, delights in the odor, and relishes the disgust in everyone else. Puerile pleasures, that's what Father was learning again — we all were — and Trump was our tutor. I really can't imagine that my father, this man I know and love, whom I still admire in so many ways, I can't imagine he didn't sense something was amiss. But somehow, he just kept looking the other way, seeking some worthwhile reason for the widespread abasement. Like others, Father started to wonder if this coarsening of our national life might not be a liberation, a required caustic, the dawn of some new era of political truth telling. Even during the unfathomable October of 2016, which saw the release of both the pussy-grabbing audio and Comey's letter to Congress, weeks that cemented our status as the world's laughingstock; even by late October, when Father's faith in the man appeared to be faltering, finally tempered by Trump's unremitting intemperance, the haplessness, the evident bad faith, the disgusting comments about women and their genitalia; even as late as a week before the election, I remember him telling me on the phone that Trump, flawed as he was, might still be the better choice. I couldn't bear it.

"Dad. I don't understand. I mean, what

do you keep looking for in this guy? He's a liar. He's a liar and a bigot, he's incompetent —"

"He's not really a bigot."

"Well, he's got everyone fooled. I don't understand what you see in him."

"I told you before. He's a *wrecking* ball."

"You were on Facebook and you read a letter some kid wrote his teacher. I read that, too."

"Made sense, didn't it?"

"Dad! You're not some coal miner's son from West Virginia, or wherever the fuck that kid was from —"

"Language, *beta.* You need to calm down."

"I'll calm down when I understand why you don't care that this guy, who is going to make our lives miserable if he's president, why that doesn't matter to you —"

"It's not real. It's all bluster."

"How do you know that?"

"You know how I know. I know him."

"You haven't spoken to him for twenty years!"

"Eighteen. And would you calm down —"

"You're counting?!"

"He's looking for attention. That's all. They're saying he wants to start a new television channel."

"Just answer me this, Dad. Just one thing.

Just one. Doesn't it matter to you that your children might be affected —"

"You'll be fine —"

"Your sister in Atlanta, the aunties, the cousins —"

"Relax."

"No, Dad. I want to know what you think. I know you don't think you'll have to sign up for a registry —"

"There'll be no registry. You'll see."

"What about the travel ban he's talking about? Hmm? What about when Mustafa and Yasmin can't get on a plane to see us anymore?"

"I said, *relax.*"

"And after that? What comes next? How much longer before they tell *you* you're not a real citizen because you weren't born here?"

"Not happening —"

"Or me? Because I'm the son of someone who they decide should never have been given citizenship?"

"You're famous. Nobody's going to do anything to you."

"I'm not *famous.*"

"You're in the paper all the time."

"Being in the paper in Milwaukee doesn't make me famous. And I don't see what that has to do with anything —"

47

"Besides. He's not going to win."

"Besides?"

"You're smart enough to know that. He doesn't even *want* to win. He's trying to send a message."

"I thought you said he was trying to start a channel."

"Same thing."

"He's running for an election he doesn't want to win so he can start a channel to send a message?"

"Exactly."

"What's the message?"

"The system is broken."

The maddening thing about this sludge of self-involved sophistry was that it all made perfect sense to him.

"I have no idea what you're saying, Dad."

"I'm saying he won't win. So you should calm down."

"And how do you know that?"

"Nate Silver."

"What if he does?"

"He won't."

"What if he *does*?! I mean, *you're* still saying he's the better choice."

"He is."

"Better how?"

"Lower taxes."

"You've got to be kidding me —"

"If you made more money, you would understand."

"I made more than you did last year."

"It's about time."

"It sounds like you're gonna vote for him."

He paused. "No."

"Sounds like you are. And I gotta say, I still don't understand what your problem is with Hillary."

"No problem. We need a change —"

"Is it that she's a woman? I mean, she can't get pregnant anymore, so that shouldn't be a problem for you —"

"I don't like your tone."

"What would Mom say? If she was here?"

"About *what*?"

"How do you think she'd feel about having her pussy grabbed, too?"

"Out-of-bounds!"

"Is that how *Caroline* liked it? Did she love it when you grabbed her pussy?!"

"You are not talking to me like that, goddammit! Do you hear me!? I am still your father!!"

My heart was pounding. He was right. I'd crossed a line. I was in pain. I was trying to hurt him. I hated what was happening. To him. To the country. To me. I wanted to tell him I was sorry. That it hadn't been me speaking. Not really. That this was what

Trump was doing to all of us. But I didn't.
I knew he wouldn't understand.

On Election Day, I was in Chicago. I'd been
invited to teach a class at Northwestern, so
I voted a week early, at the church in
Harlem where I'd cast my vote for a Demo-
crat four out of the last five presidential
elections. I remember the almost ebullient
buzz on campus that day, the thrill of knowing the madness with Trump would finally
be over. I didn't admit to anyone my lingering fears that he might not lose. I'd observed
a change in myself in those last few weeks
before the election, a new, narcotic dependence on my phone, an aching that wasn't
even for the phone itself but for the daily
clatter of outrage about Trump it delivered.
I remember feeling — through that last
fortnight before Election Day — a hunger
to be haunted. Night after night, I dreamed
of the man. I'd ejaculated in a nightmare
about the Trump wives and daughters, a
cabal of buxom blondes who took turns
putting lipstick on my penis. Every morning
I awoke and reached for my phone. I'd
never experienced such pervasion. I felt
Trump as closely as I felt myself, medium
and message all in one. I worried it wasn't
only me. If others were feeling as I did, I

worried that boded ill. The improbable saga of this campaign, its whiplash reversals, its perverse pleasures — didn't a story this insane require an ending commensurate with the madness? The writer in me knew that stories are made of movement, not morality; demand conclusion, not consonance; and often conjure into being the very terrors they are written to wish away. As a writer, I knew this. But there was the needle at the *Times,* and the winding-path ribbon at *FiveThirtyEight.* Both assured me I was wrong.

Until they didn't.

As I watched the returns, Wisconsin alarmed me. I knew it well and knew that the already reported precincts were where most of Hillary's support would come from. I couldn't understand why the commentators continued to pretend that the swelling numbers for Trump in Wisconsin were anything other than decisive. It would be another hour before that *Times* needle swung in the opposite direction and Nate Silver's ribbon turned bright red.

I called home at 10:30, once it was clear to me Trump was going to win my home state and likely the election. Father picked up. He'd been drinking. I couldn't gauge his mood.

"Are you watching?" I asked.

"Looks like he's gonna win," he said, slurring. On the television, John King was showing the tally from Sheboygan County, where Father had a clinic. "Sheboygan, too?" I heard him ask, confused.

"Did you vote?"

"What?"

"Did you vote, Dad?"

"What business of yours?"

"I don't know. We've talked about it enough."

"Goddamn right we talked about it enough."

"You sound upset."

"Huh?"

"You sound upset."

"He's winning. Don't you see?"

"Didn't you vote for him?"

"I told you, goddammit, I'm not talking about this."

And then he hung up on me.

He never would tell me how he voted, but the shame I heard in his voice was unmistakable. I think he was admitting to me, that night — in the only way he could — that he'd done it. Despite knowing better, he'd voted for Trump.

I've wondered what he might have been thinking as he stepped into the all-purpose

52

room in the quaint town hall of the suburban enclave where he lives, a room likely
filled that day mostly with the whites he
thought too concerned with their summer
vacations; I've wondered, as he walked into
that room and showed his ID and took his
place in line — did he know yet? Or when
he stepped into the voting machine, drew
the curtain, and stared at the cleft column
of names — what was he feeling? What
moved him to lift his hand for the tiny lever
on the red side and press down on it? I've
wondered if some part of him didn't really
believe he was doing it, or believed it
wouldn't matter — for wasn't it a foregone
conclusion at that point that Hillary would
win? And if he voted for Trump only because
he really thought *she* would win, what was
he really trying to say? What private thought
or feeling was he honoring? What fidelity
did he not want to betray? I don't think it
was misogyny; he loved Benazir Bhutto, was
gutted by her killing. No. I think it was his
enduring love of Trump.

What was this attachment to the man? Was
it really just the memory of the helicopter
rides, the spacious suite, the hooker, a
tailor's tape, a lapel pin? Could it really be
so banal? Or were those things standing in
for something else, something more encom-

passing and elusive? Father always called America the land of opportunity. Hardly original, I know. But I wonder: Opportunity for whom? For him, right? The opportunity to become whatever *he* desired? Sure, others, too, but only insofar as *others* really meant *him*. And isn't that what Mary was saying all those years ago? That our vaunted American dream, the dream of ourselves enhanced and enlarged, is the flag for which we are willing to sacrifice everything — gouging our neighbors, despoiling our nation — everything, that is, except ourselves? A dream that imagines the flourishing of others as nothing more than a road sign, the prick of envy as the provident spur to *one's own* all-important realization? Isn't this what Father saw in Donald Trump? A vision of himself impossibly enhanced, improbably enlarged, released from the pull of debt or truth or history, a man delivered from consequence itself into pure self-absorption, incorporated entirely into the individualist afflatus of American eternity? I think Father was looking for an image of just how much more his American self could contain than the Pakistani one he'd left behind. I think he wanted to know what the limits were. In America, you could have anything, right? Even the presidency? If an idiot like Trump could get hold of it, couldn't you? Even if you didn't want it? After all, the idiot apparently didn't want it, either. He just wanted to know he *could* have it. Or maybe the emphasis there needs to shift: he wanted to know he could *have* it.

Yes. I think that's right.

Elsewhere, I've referred to Trump's ascendancy as the completion of the long-planned advent of the merchant class to the sanctum sanctorum of American power, the conquering rise of mercantilism with all its attendant vulgarity, its acquisitive conscience supplanting every moral one, an event in our political life that signals the collapse not of democracy — which has, in truth, enabled it — but of every bulwark against wealth-as-holy-pursuit, which appears to be the last American passion left standing. De Tocqueville would not be surprised. My father is no exception. Trump is just the name of his story.

II.
ON AUTOBIOGRAPHY;
OR, BIN LADEN

Not quite ten years after 9/11, I wrote a play in which an American-born character with Muslim origins confesses that as the towers were falling, he felt something unexpected and unwelcome, a sense of pride — a "blush" is how he describes it — which, he explains in the play's climactic scene, made him realize that, despite being born here, despite the totality of his belief in this country and his commitment to being an American, he somehow still identified with a mentality that saw itself as aggrieved and other, a mind-set he's spent much of the play despising and for which he continually uses, to the chagrin of those onstage (and many in the audience), the term *Muslim.* Later, the play's only other character of Muslim origin refers to the 9/11 attacks as something America deserved and a likely harbinger of more to come. When the play went on to win a Pulitzer and be performed around the country, and then the world, the one question I would be asked more than any other — and which I'm still asked fairly often — is how much of me is in it. Over time, I've gleaned that what I'm usually being asked is whether I, too, felt a blush of pride on September 11, and, if so, whether I believe America deserved what it got; and finally, if I, like my character, think that further Muslim attacks on America are likely. When they ask if the play is autobiographical, what people are really asking me about is my politics.

For years, I deflected. Had I wanted to write an autobiography, I could have done so; had I wanted to write an anti-American screed, I could have done that, too. But I hadn't done either. Wasn't that enough? Apparently not. To most of my questioners, I discovered, my demure evasions were really affirmations. My choice not to disavow having had such feelings myself was taken as a tacit confession of guilt. Why else would I stay silent? In other words, while those asking couldn't identify with having feelings like this, they certainly could identify with not wanting to admit them if they did. As ever, interpretation has more to do with the one interpreting than the one being interpreted.

Realizing my reticence was proving counterproductive, I tried a different tack: For me to indulge the question — I would say — and point *away* from the work back to the life of the one who created it only undermines the particular sort of truth that I believe art is after. Art's power, unlike journalism, has little to do with the reliability of its sourcing, I would say. Finally, I would quote D. H. Lawrence: "Never trust the artist. Trust the tale." For a time, this seemed to work well enough.

Then, in November of 2015, some four months into his candidacy, Trump announced he'd seen Muslims celebrating in Jersey City on the day of the attacks. My agent's phone started ringing. I turned down a request to appear on Bill Maher's show to discuss the claim, and two days later, I declined a similar invitation to appear on *Fox & Friends*. But the questions kept coming as people now cited my play as proof of a deeper, alarming truth about the American Muslim response to 9/11. My evasions started to seem irresponsible to me. Wasn't it important for me to say *something* substantial? But what? The sentiments expressed in the play had, of course, come from somewhere, but how to express the complex, often contradictory alchemy at

58

work in translating experience into art? The only thing I could put simply was that there was no simple way to put it. There was no straightforward way to speak of the tortured vein opened up in my family by the killing of the man I believe my mother was in love with most of her life — not my father but one of his best friends from medical school, Latif Awan. It was during my mother's grief over Latif's murder that she would make comments that led to the lines in my play, comments in which I would educe not only the startling depth of my mother's divided loyalties but also the contours of the deepest fault line, I believe, separating so much of the so-called Muslim world from the so-called West. Just a few words, but ones for which I had a lifetime of context. I'd buried both context and tale inside the play I wrote, masking its true source from the audience. I didn't believe a more obvious rendition would meet with greater understanding. I still don't. But I suppose we're about to find out.

FIRST THINGS, OR PARTITION

To have heard my parents reminisce about medical school in Pakistan in the 1960s was to be treated to the aureate tones and hues common to most reports of halcyon days, though the lengthening view on Pakistan's subsequent turbulent history has certainly made its '60s era look like a never-again-to-be-seen high-water mark. In 1964, when my parents met — the same year my mother met Latif — one could have imagined that the rivers of blood spilled to found the Pakistani nation had finally dried, that the ghosts of India's partition had wreaked their last havoc and finally decamped for the brighter beyond. It was not to be. For Pakistan's late-twentieth- and early-twenty-first-century obsession with terror-as-tactic — learned of course from the CIA — was the paranoid calculus born of partition's trauma, a self-corroding defense that speaks to the still desperate, still feverish Pakistani fear of its Indian progenitor. There's no good reason to give short shrift to the story of partition, still too little known to most, of how India was sundered and Pakistan created by the beleaguered, ever-duplicitous British in the wake of the Second World War; there's no good reason not to tell the tale in its epic amplitude, except that it's been well told many times, and because these pages are not the place — and I am not the person — to attempt any such full account. My tale is entirely American. But in order to understand it, you'll need to know at least this much: by 1947, Britain's long-practiced imperial strategy of divide and conquer resulted in the to some ill-conceived, to others God-ordained decision to carve off zones of the Indian motherland so that Hindus and Muslims would not have to live side by side any longer. Little matter that Muslims and Hindus had lived together for hundreds of years in India; after a century of British policies pitting them against each other, stoking a constant conflict for which the British Raj offered itself as the only containing force, the king's empire could no longer ignore the fact that the social fabric was on the verge of coming apart.

Before the Second World War, the British paid ample lip service to the idea of self-government in India, but granting full independence was never a serious option. The Raj was the jewel in His Majesty's crown; giving it up was unthinkable. But by 1947, the British nation was exhausted and traumatized by German bombing; discouraged by the loss of so many of its soldiers; shocked by the desertion and mutiny of its Indian servicemen; benumbed by unprecedented winter cold and an energy shortage that had the population shivering and its factories shuttered; broke, owing not only the Americans for the money that was keeping its economy afloat but India, too; and disgusted by the growing violence between Muslims, Hindus, and Sikhs for which it took no responsibility, violence that would shortly lead to a bloodbath of historic proportions. Overwhelmed by these troubles at home and in its disintegrating colony, Britain concluded that exit from the subcontinent was the only option.

This standard reading of the history was one Father hated. He called it the "blame game" and found faulting the British for partition's violence particularly difficult to stomach. Who had done all the senseless killing? Was it the British hacking apart their former schoolmates limb from limb, beheading their Muslim or Hindu neighbors, roasting their infants on spits? Was it the British who had done all that — or had we done it? Sure, fine, yes, they had perpetrated evil and enslavement in their endless plunder of the Indian motherland since the early 1600s — but so what? Were we robots? Did we *have* to keep repeating the violence? And since *we* were the ones repeating it, what sense did it make to blame *them* for it? What was the value in it? Wasn't the history clear? We'd long sued for independence; the British had finally conceded; we were the ones who couldn't make it work without the bloodshed — so how exactly were *they* to blame? And if we hated them so much that we couldn't see the facts for what they were, why, then, were we still speaking their language when we had so many of our own? Why were we quoting Shakespeare and playing squash and eating cucumber sand-wiches? And why didn't we tear up the roads they'd built and pave our own? Or fill the canals they'd dug to transform dusty Punjab into the most fertile land on the subcontinent? Why didn't we complain about all this, too?

Father's reading of the history had a particularly derisive view of the Muslims of prepartition India, a besieged minority, yes, but deeply deluded in their besiegement, still dreaming of the pre-British Mughal era, when Muslims ruled the land. He thought this a recollection of useless glory, one that echoed the even more futile Muslim exercise of celebrating the Islamic Golden Age, a long-concluded chapter of history that had Muslims ruling much of the then known world by the turn of the last millennium. We — and now the referent would slip, as it often did when he was on a first-person-plural rampage, "we" no longer pointing to *all prepartition Indians* but to "we" *the Mus-*

63

lims — liked to spend our time yowling for a past that helped us not a whit, a past that only fortified our loftiest delusions and encouraged excuses instead of the work required of us if we were ever to catch up to the rest of the world. I remember a particularly violent tirade in late 1979, two weeks into the hostage crisis in Iran, when a mob of Pakistanis — after hearing (false) radio reports of an American military attack on the holiest of Muslim sites in Mecca — marched on the US embassy in Islamabad and burned it down. In fact, there *had* been an attack in Mecca, but the United States had had nothing to do with it — the perpetrators turned out to be Saudi. To Father, the knee-jerk violence was typical: "Blind and stupid! Caught up in the past! Can't even tell the difference between their anger toward the British and their anger toward the Americans! Litigating crimes of history in a courtroom of fools! When are they going to understand the only ones they're hurting are themselves?!?!" The referent would slip again, a new "we" — now referring to us as Americans — as opposed to the older one, which was now the "them" he wanted nothing to do with, namely, Muslims: "It makes you wonder, *beta*. Maybe that's what they really want. To fail.

Not up to the challenge, not interested in change. The whole Muslim world. Expecting failure, so failure they get. Pouring all their creativity into finding new people to blame for old problems." It was during that very same fall of 1979 — when my third-grade class was studying the American Civil War, and as he leafed through the pages of the textbook dealing with the American South's agrarian economy one Saturday afternoon — that he would make the following memorable analogy: "Imagine, *beta,* the South had won. Alabama, Tennessee, all that backward nonsense down there. What did they have back then? Just like your book is saying — slaves and cotton. No manufacturing. No transportation. No navy. If they had won the Civil War and were on their own? It would have been a disaster for them. If they didn't have the North to depend on? To hold them up like we've done for more than a hundred years? What do you think it would be like down there today? Hmm? A shithole even bigger than it is now," he said with relish as he snapped the book shut. "That, my boy, is Pakistan in a nutshell. As pathetic as the South would be today if its every wish came true."

With me, Father disparaged his native country often and without reservation, but he didn't speak that way about it in front of his wife, my mother. She loved Pakistan, or at least was bound to it in a way that reached as deeply into her as anything could. Years after 9/11, she, too, would sour on the Pakistani experiment, saying she didn't recognize the country she'd grown up in, but by then, battling cancer for the fourth time in thirty years, there were reasons for this shift in her feelings deeper than just the war on terror. Unlike Father, she'd grown up close to the line through Central Punjab that divided the Indian nation and had been old enough during partition to have seen horrors she would never forget. One of her earliest memories was of being in Lahore station the summer of the bloodshed, when fifteen million people were uprooted and migrating with their belongings, Muslims leaving India, Hindus and Sikhs fleeing what is now Pakistan. She'd strayed from her father briefly onto a quay where workers were pulling what looked like long brown heavy bags from a train. The workers were having difficulty tossing them as far as they seemed to want to. It wasn't until she approached that she saw they were not bags but naked bodies. The heaps were of the dead. A woman's corpse tumbled from the pile, her long hair falling away to show a face with a hole where there should have been a nose and two pink bloody circles on her chest. Her breasts had been cut off.

It was a summer of horrors. In their neighborhood — close to a Sikh holy site in Wah, where thousands of Sikhs had been maimed and raped and killed in their homes and in the streets — she came across dismembered limbs, hands and feet poking up from shallow graves along the road. She saw dogs gnawing at human heads. She found a Sikh mother in a blood-splattered shawl holding a disemboweled child. She was barely five years old when she saw this. And she wasn't just a witness. Her family, too, had lost many to the violence. Her dear favorite aunt, Roshina — her mother's younger sister — was living with her in-laws on the other side of the border and didn't make it back alive. Set upon by a Hindu mob while hiding in the family home, Roshina was pulled through the living-room window and gang-raped in the front yard, then beaten to death. Her husband had already made it to Pakistan, and when he heard the news, he gathered a mob of his own and went into the streets. They brought a bloodied Hindu boy back to the house; Mother thought the boy somehow responsible for what had happened to Roshina; she pressed her face to the bedroom window facing the driveway and watched them chop the child down with an ax.

To have lived through events like these so young was to know that murder is not an abstraction or something perpetrated only by evildoers. Good people could kill and be killed. It also taught her a fear for her life, a fear her body would never forget. It was no surprise she was as paranoid as she was about India. Even as she sat in her suburban American kitchen sipping Sanka, a quarter century removed from the sights and sounds of trauma, even as she stared out at a quiet backyard hedged by protective cornfields half a world from any Hindus who might have wished her harm, even there, even then, she worried about them coming to destroy her. Like Pakistan itself, she'd been forged in the smithy of that mortal fear. And it wasn't just Hindus. Lethal danger lurked everywhere, and any reminder of it could overwhelm her. She didn't watch the news. She couldn't bear any corporal image of atrocity, current or past, a difficulty especially pronounced when it came to the Holocaust. Even the mention of Auschwitz or Treblinka brought on a peculiar rush of mourning and resentment it would take me a long time to make sense of. Though she never directly suggested an equivalence between what happened to the Jews in the Second World War and partition, she implied it. And what seemed to bother her most was that it reminded her not of what she'd been through but of how little anybody in this country — by comparison — knew about it.

She rarely talked about all this. Much of what I know comes, as so much does to children, by learning the unspoken family rules, the assumptions gleaned from frowns of disapproval, shifts in mood at the mention of the wrong thing. I would piece together a better picture of her inner life from the dozen diaries she left when she died, diaries in which I would also discover that what she'd seen as a child during partition, she believed, was at the root of her recurring cancer. She wrote of her body being riddled with affective scars, buried feelings she'd never known how to feel, emotions she still didn't know how to make sense of, a baleful store she worried was metastasizing into the tumors threatening her life every seven or so years. The picture my aunts — her sisters — conveyed to me of my mother as a child seemed to support at least the assumption of an early, powerful repression at work in her makeup. They remembered an often bold, always curious, lighthearted girl who bore little resemblance to the quiet, tense, reserved woman I knew, though I did spy that eupeptic person peeking through her eyes from time to time. The oddest things — polka music, Reese's peanut butter cups, tea roses, and (later, in the era of TiVo) David Letterman — could conjure a softened, playful mien that made her look like a different woman entirely. The other thing that always did the trick was seeing Latif.

ZAKAT

By the time Mother met Latif, during her first year of medical school, he was in his third year and already betrothed. I don't know the exact circumstance of their meeting — likely through the man who would eventually become her husband, my father, Latif's best friend — but I do know what she wrote in her diary two days after Latif was shot to death, in 1998:

We knew when we met. But what could he do? He was already promised to Anjum. I thought if he loves S so much, there must be something more to him. Give him a chance. I didn't realize it was nothing

70

but selfishness. (You did know.) Quite the opposite of L. I still remember my hand in his hand, as big as a giant's. That gentle smile. "I've heard so much about you, Fatima." What he heard I never asked. And now he's dead.

The S was my father, Sikander, whom she chose — according to more than one bitter entry in her diaries — on the grounds that Latif loved him.

Latif was big. Very big. A half foot taller than my father — who is almost six feet himself — and a hundred pounds heavier. His forehead, too, was tall, defined by a hairline set farther back on his head than seemed to make sense for a man still so young. His eyes were slim and brown, his face long, his mouth wide. He looked not unlike a Punjabi version of Joe Biden, which mostly accounts, I think, for my mother's enduring love of the Delaware senator and eventual vice president. A big man with a big head and very big hands, but she was right: he was so gentle. It endeared him to me as a child, too. Sure, it was thrilling to be lifted aloft, to tower above everything nested on those massive shoulders, but it was the tender grip of those massive hands on my ankles as we walked that I recall most vividly, the pleasure of feeling such power so completely corralled, and not as a mitigation of the threat his size implied to others but as an expression of kindness — a kindness that, yes, you could absolutely see in his smile.

Latif and Father graduated from medical school two years before Mother did and were among the first recruited by American hospitals in the States under a new program that offered young foreign doctors visas, jobs, plane tickets, and apartments. Father found a position in cardiology in New York City, and Latif ended up as a resident in internal medicine not far from Trenton. (By then, Latif had married Anjum, the fair-skinned second cousin he'd grown up always knowing he would have to marry; Mother and Father had also wed, but she wouldn't join him here in America until she graduated.) Trenton was close enough for Father to make a quick trip down for biryani with his friends on a homesick weekend but far enough for him to live his new American life unobserved, unimpeded. Latif was religious — always had been — and Father didn't want him to know just how much fun he was having with whiskey and cards. Which isn't to say Latif had ever been one to hector others about their faith, at least not back in Pakistan. But being here worried him, as he saw his fellow classmates taking the American lifestyle too much to heart. Remember the British, Latif would say. They mingled with us back home for centuries, but never too closely. They were careful to safeguard what was theirs. The lesson was one worth heeding, Latif thought, lest they forget who they were and where they really came from.

Whereas to Father, not forgetting who he was would have meant not forgetting he was Punjabi, to Latif it meant never forgetting he was Muslim. Land was an earthly tie; faith a celestial one. But if Latif never missed prayer, or a fasting day in Ramadan, it was not only — or even mainly — out of concern for his eventual entry into heaven. Heaven above, he would say, was an image from which to build a life here below. It's true that my recollections of him — loping gracefully through his backyard (or ours) in *shalwar kameez,* exuding an inner quiet, in whose presence discussion of the higher things felt not only natural but also necessary — so many of my recollections are marked by something angelic, by which I mean nothing fey or diaphanous or otherworldly but potent, light-giving, concerned with helping others in the here and now.

When he spoke about what it meant to be Muslim, he didn't refer to the afterlife tomorrow but to the lives of those around him he wanted to make better today. Above all, it meant a commitment to *zakat.* The term usually refers to the yearly Muslim tax paid from one's assets and distributed to the poor, but in his family it had come to mean not just the redistribution of their (considerable) wealth but also active service to those in need — the Muslim version, if you will, of Christian charity. Latif's *zamindar* (landowning) grandfather in North Punjab had started an orphanage — the care of orphans being a particular involvement in the Muslim world, as the Prophet was allegedly orphaned at the age of six — which his father continued to maintain. Latif grew up spending Sundays there, playing with the kids as his father did the rounds. It must have felt natural to him, later, in medical school, to give up what little free time he had on the weekends to volunteer at a local clinic for the poor. In Trenton, he would do the same through his residency and internship, and five years later, when he left New Jersey to join a practice in Pensacola, he initiated a free Sunday morning clinic at his office. Latif's aggressive and entirely unselfconscious Samaritanism provoked leery reluctance in his new partners, but when word got out about the generous new doctor in the heavily churchgoing community, it started to bring in patients who could pay their bills, too.

I remember his office on one of those Sunday mornings. We were on our yearly visit to the Florida Panhandle to spend time with the Awans. It was one of two weeks a year that our families spent together. They would come to Wisconsin in the winter; we would visit Pensacola in the spring. I was breathlessly involved in a game of tag with the Awan kids that morning — there were four of them, twin sons followed by two daughters, all within five years of one another — when I fell to the ground and felt something pierce my knee. I looked down and saw a slim silver shank emerging from the fleshy bump just beneath my kneecap. A fishhook. I pushed at it, following the bend of the shank, thinking I could dislodge the barb. That's when the blood started to bubble up and spurt. Soon, my knee and ankle were covered in it.

Mother panicked. She tied my leg in a kitchen-towel tourniquet, and Anjum drove us both to her husband's office. I limped up the driveway between them and into the long, flat building that looked more like a construction-site trailer than a doctor's office. The waiting room was completely filled. There must have forty people there to see Latif. Almost everyone was black. What I remember most about that afternoon — other than the odd experience of feeling nothing in my knee as I watched Latif cut it open with a surgical knife and release the barb from the fleshy pink-and-white tendon in which it was embedded — the thing I most remember is his face as he emerged from the hallway, before he knew that we were there. He looked like a different man. Not gentle, but absorbed; not soft, but resolute; the usual ineffable inwardness now visible and thrust outward, pushed to every edge of his considerable frame, as if the sleeves of his soul — if you'll forgive the awkward metaphor — had been rolled up in preparation for the real work of his life. Even his eyes looked rounder to me, more awake. It was clear he was at home here, surrounded by those who needed him, his true kin, the kind to whom he belonged, I think, more than he ever would to us.

DECEMBER 1982

The Soviets had been in Afghanistan almost three years. I was ten. Latif and Anjum's twin boys were twelve, the two daughters nine and seven. They showed up at our house a week before Christmas break, and I was surprised to find Ramla, the older daughter, wearing a hijab. I'd never seen any of the more restrictive forms of head covering — hijab, burka, purdah — on any of the women or girls I knew. Both Anjum and my mother would sometimes wear loose-fitting *dupattas,* for the sake of fashion, I always supposed, more than religion. Maybe that's what was so surprising about seeing Ramla's face tightly framed by that dull forest-green cloth: just how stark and severe it made her look. She didn't like it, and she told me so more than once on that trip. I'd always thought her the most "American" of her siblings, more American, certainly, than I was. That December, she'd come to Wisconsin knowing the lyrics to most of the songs on Michael Jackson's *Thriller* — no matter that the album had just been released or that her father wouldn't let her buy it. She'd made a secret tape at a friend's house and carried the cassette with her everywhere, always ready to pop it into a tape deck for a song or two when her father wasn't around.

Latif was getting stricter, not only with his kids but also with himself. He'd taken now to wearing — when he wasn't in scrubs — a loose-fitting white *jalabiya*. To a non-Pakistani, the nuance would have been lost. The long, free-flowing gown was Arab attire and tended to signify a deepened commitment to the faith. The battle with the Soviets in Afghanistan was transforming him, shedding new light on a more frivolous life in the West than perhaps he'd expected, more frivolous than he felt he could bear. Fellow Muslims were being slaughtered daily in their battle against an evil empire, and here he was raising children who complained there were not enough marshmallows in their bowls of Lucky Charms.

For us, the true Soviet evil wasn't socialism — as it was for most Americans — but atheism. Even the least religious of us couldn't imagine a fate more abhorrent than subjugation to those who imagined there was no God at all. And if the mujahideen fighters of Afghanistan were enacting a great American myth of demanding liberty or demanding death, it was in the service of a freedom uniquely creedal, a distinction ignored by Ronald Reagan a few years later, when he extolled the fighting Afghans — precursors to the Taliban — as freedom fighters, comparing them to the Contras and others, who were, in his words, "the moral equivalents of our founding fathers."

To us, the founding fathers had nothing on these holy warriors. Sure, those men in hoary wigs had fought, too, but not for God. They didn't want to pay taxes to a king who they felt exploited them, so they took up arms. Where was the nobility in this? More apposite would be the future example of those first responders walking into the second burning tower knowing their attempts to save trapped souls were likely to end in an avalanche of fire and steel from which they wouldn't return. This is what we saw in those Afghan fighters, an unflinching, inexpressibly noble willingness to die for something more important than their lives, or their liberty, or their happiness.

On the first night of the Awans' visit that winter, the meal was long and splendid. Though she was a wonderful cook, Mother hated the kitchen except for those two weeks a year, when, on the contrary, she seemed, happily, to pass hours there alone (or with Anjum) absorbed in the preparation of what could only be called our feasts. For that first night, she'd prepared a sumptuous reminder of the Lahori past the adults at the table all shared — paaya, or hoof stew, which, as students, they would seek out on weekend mornings from street vendors in Mozang, Old Anarkali, along Jail

Road, and even in the red-light district, where Father said it was best. The stew took a long time to make well, and Mother had had it simmering on low heat in the kitchen since sunrise the day of their arrival. When I saw her scrubbing the short goat legs the day prior, scraping the hooves clean in the sink, I couldn't imagine putting anything like it in my mouth. But at dinner, Father and the Awans were all in a state, unaware how silly they looked as they sucked at the marrow and scooped fingerfuls of dripping, fatty paaya and naan into their mouths; I succumbed to curiosity. The rich flavor — round with familiar hints of clove, garlic, coriander seed, bay leaves — was astonishing.

As Latif served himself a second helping, he and Father traded news about their families back in Pakistan, bantering in the fluid admixture of Punjabi and English that was my parents' usual lingua franca. It was while talking about his brother (Manan) in Peshawar — a city close to the Afghan border — that Latif first alluded to wanting to go back to Pakistan:

"They've been fighting Russian tanks and missiles with pistols, Winchester rifles. But Manan says the Americans are helping now. Bringing money, bringing weapons. Finally.

They see that if Afghanistan falls, Pakistan will be next. That won't be good for anyone. On Sundays, Manan said Americans are pouring out of the church in Peshawar. The city is filled with them. They're opening camps to train *jihadis* — in Swat, in Waziristan." Latif's sons — Yahya and Idris — were listening, rapt. "It makes you wonder what we're doing here when there's so much more we could be doing back home."

"Doesn't make *me* wonder," Father said, an ankle bone to his mouth. Anjum, too, seemed less than impressed.

"I don't know why you keep harping on all the work to be done *there,*" she said to her husband. "There's work to do here, too."

"It's not enough just to send money anymore."

"I'm not talking about the mujahideen, Latif."

"Right. But I am."

"So the only solution is to go back?" She sounded exasperated; it was clearly not the first time they'd had this conversation.

He didn't answer. Beside him, his daughter Ramla was looking down into her plate.

Anjum turned to my parents: "We've been here twelve years now. I don't know how it is for you, but it's just not the same when

81

we go back. It's not home for us in the same way." She turned to her husband again: "Even you say the same thing every time we're home. How much you miss it —"

"Air-conditioning, Anjum. Air-conditioning. That's all I miss."

"The fishing, the ocean . . ."

"They have ocean in Karachi."

"Karachi?" Anjum snapped. "Is that near Manan in Peshawar?"

"No ocean in Peshawar. Other end of the country," Father gibed gently.

Latif sighed, and all at once, his defensiveness was gone. He looked almost fragile: "The longer we're here, the more I wonder . . . who I'm becoming."

"You're not the only one," Mother said with a consoling tone. I could feel she was taking his side against the others. "It's not our home. No matter how many years we spend here, it won't ever be our home. And maybe this brings out things in us that were never meant to be brought out."

"Like what?" Father asked.

"Like regret."

"You're saying people back home don't have regrets? Is that it?"

"I'm saying you can only regret what you chose not to do." Her eyes stole a look at Latif. Anjum noticed. Latif looked away.

"When we leave home, there are so many things we don't have the luxury not to choose anymore. That's a different kind of regret. A sadder, more hopeless kind."

"Speak for yourself," Father said. "I love it here. Like I never loved being in Pakistan."

"They have whiskey in Lahore, too, Sikander."

Father's reply was swift and curt: "Fatima. Please. We have guests."

I looked at Latif. He was chuckling. My parents' testy dynamic was nothing new; it wasn't even the first time I'd seen him appear to enjoy it. "Of course there are the comforts here," he said, looking at his own wife now. "The freedom, above all — if you have money."

"It doesn't hurt to have money here," Father said.

"Doesn't *hurt*?" Latif repeated. "This country makes you a criminal for being poor. I see how the blacks are treated here. I see what they have to go through. It gives you a different picture of this place."

"It's true. It's not easy if you don't have money, but at least you're free to make it here. As much as you can. As much as you want. And without cheating anybody to do it."

83

"When I see what's happening to our brothers in Afghanistan, freedom to be rich is not enough."

"It's not *only* money," Father said. "The work I'm doing here I can't do back home, you know that. We don't have the labs. We don't have the mentality. Back home, if it's not already in a book, people don't think it exists. No creative instinct."

Latif nodded: "But I'm not in research. The only good I'm doing is for those poor people in Pensacola."

"What about your children?" Anjum asked with sudden intensity, releasing the question like a rock from a slingshot.

Latif held his wife's gaze for an uncomfortably long moment before replying, calmly: "They'll do as well in Pakistan as they would do here. Better, even. Less confused." Anjum looked away, her tongue playing along the inside of her pursed lips.

The younger daughter, Hafsa — who was nibbling at the plate of Kraft macaroni and cheese Mother had made for her — piped up: "I like Pakistan. Everybody looks the same. They look like us." My parents laughed. I looked over at Ramla. A thin tuft of her brown hair was poking out from one side of that green head scarf. She was sitting back in her chair, away from the table.

Father turned to her as well: "What about you, Ramla, *beti*? What do you think? How do you feel about living in Pakistan?" Her face filled with alarm, her lower lip now trembling. She looked at her mother, helpless, and suddenly erupted, screaming: "I hate it, I hate it, I hate it!"

Then she leaped from her chair and bolted up the stairs.

In the ensuing silence, Anjum shot Latif an angry look. Latif held her gaze, then quietly rose, stepped away from his place at the table, and went up the stairs after his daughter. Years later — long after the Awans had left America and relocated to Peshawar — I would learn from Mother that the head cook at Latif's family's estate back in North Punjab had been caught in the pantry with his mouth on the girl's private parts. I don't know when this discovery took place, though I suspect Ramla's outburst was a sign that the molestation had already begun. I don't know what happened to the cook, though I can certainly imagine Latif snapping a man's neck like a twig.

JIHAD

We never saw them again in America. The fight with the Soviets got worse that winter, and in the spring of 1983, Latif moved his family, as promised, to Peshawar. They stayed with his brother for a time, then took a house in the western outskirts of the city. The United States was doubling down on its support for the Afghans that summer, and Peshawar was awash with dollars. The Americans offered to pay, soup to nuts, for Latif's new clinic, on the condition that it would also be used to treat wounded mujahideen fighters from across the border. CIA money, Father said. Latif was given enough to set up a facility without precedent in those parts, where he could help the poor, tend to wounded mujahideen, and train young field medics to care for ailing soldiers on the front lines. But apparently, the clinic would function as more than just a medical center. Rumor had it that a back room on the second floor of that two-story concrete-brick building operated as the Pakistani army's preferred meeting point in Peshawar for exchanges between American intelligence and the Afghan tribal powers waging the war against the Soviet forces. Clearly, Latif was finally doing all he could — save picking up a gun and heading for the Afghan mountains — to battle back the Russian infidels.

He never picked up arms himself, but his twin sons eventually would. In 1989, when

— to much of the world's surprise — the mujahideen prevailed, the Soviets withdrew their troops. But the battles wouldn't end; Russia and the United States continued to fund a proxy war for another three years through various intermediaries, and Latif's sons would both join the fight under the banner of the Americans. It was a conflict being paid for by opium grown under the logistical guidance of American intelligence, and one of the twins, Idris, would get deeply involved in the production of the drug; by the mid-1990s he was dead of an overdose. The other, Yahya, would work his way up a complicated chain of command, eventually forging close relationships with militia leaders who found their way into power during the Taliban era. When we visited in 1990, Anjum traveled south from Peshawar to see us; I barely recognized her. It had been only seven years since I last saw her, but her youth was gone. Under the white wool shawl draped around her torso and covering much of her head, her once russet hair was fully gray, her face gaunt and drawn. Ramla and Hafsa were with her — both wearing hijabs — and seemed to be flourishing. Ramla had been accepted to medical school and would be starting in the fall. Hafsa, then fifteen, aspired to do the same.

If the girls missed America, they didn't say it, though it was clear from Ramla's avid queries about New Kids on the Block and *Honey, I Shrunk the Kids* that she was still plugged into the American experience. (This was well before the era of the internet.)

Anjum was worried about her sons. She didn't recognize them. They'd dropped out of college to become vigilantes out of some B movie, racing about on motorbikes with assault rifles slung over their shoulders. Latif, too, had changed, she said. His tenderness had hardened; he was more unforgiving now. He had no patience for her misgivings about their new life. Instead, he expected an attitude of sacrifice equal to the occasion, which, as he saw it, was warfare. He thought it a defect in her character that she couldn't see the battle for Afghanistan as her own.

But wasn't the war over? Hadn't they won?

The only thing that annoyed Latif more, Anjum said, than her dismay over the endless fighting was her inability to understand the supposed complexity of it. "What's complex?" she mused out loud over tea and sweets that afternoon. "Maybe it's all very simple. Men love to fight. They want to fight. They need to fight. And what's complex are the reasons they come up with to do the thing they really want, which is just to keep killing each other." I remember Mother offering every sign of sympathy, but it's clear from the entry she made in her diary that evening that she'd actually been thinking mostly about herself:

Anjum came to see us today. L is too busy with jihad. No message from him. Not even hello. The marriage is fraying. She never loved him. Foolish to think it would have been different for me — but you've always been foolish.

In the days after Anjum's visit, I heard Mother tell her sisters she thought Anjum would leave Latif and return to America. She was wrong on both counts: Anjum would stay with her husband until his death, in 1998; then, when she tried to return to America, she would discover that she couldn't. Her naturalized citizenship had been revoked.

THE ABUNDANT IDYLL DESPOILED
I've held off long enough. Here's what happened to Latif:

Once the Soviet empire collapsed — and with it, the covert war with America in

Afghanistan — the United States discontinued its support for its partners in the region. Robert Gates, then deputy director of the CIA, would later confess the mistake the United States made in walking away from the groups it had funded all those years, a mistake that would lead directly to the first World Trade Center bombing and eventually to 9/11. The straight line from the American-backed mujahideen to Al Qaeda is still a story little told, little understood; in his way, Latif's fate is emblematic of it. For once the American money dried up, like everyone else who'd depended on that cash, Latif pivoted. His allegiance didn't change. His fundamental loyalty had always been to the Muslim rebels fighting the irreligious onslaught of the Soviets, not to the Americans. Now their wrath had turned from the Soviet empire to imperialism of the American variety. How this substitution took place is not particularly complicated. It was 1991, and George H. W. Bush made a fateful decision to intervene in the affairs of a regime the United States had put into place and supported for the better part of almost thirty years. Since the ayatollah's ascent to power in Tehran, the Americans built up Saddam Hussein even further to keep the Iranians weak on their western flank. Iran and Iraq warred for eight years, and Iraq would eventually prevail in this proxy war on behalf of the Americans — so, of course, it was now time for America to get rid of its "friend" in Baghdad.

The abandonment of Afghanistan and the first war in Iraq sent a clear message: whatever the Americans said meant nothing; whatever they promised was a lie. If you paid in blood to help them manage their interests, they poured money down your throat and invited you to Washington to fly your shawls and head scarves like flags of freedom; when you tried to manage your own interests, then your Islam was backward, unruly, oppositional, an excuse to kill you. Warnings about American influence were nothing new for Muslims of the Levant and its eastern beyond, and some had long been advocating resistance, violent or otherwise; for many more, the first Gulf War was a moment of truth and gave fresh, decisive life to the old argument that the West's welcome was predatory and that Westernization would cost Muslims their land, their beliefs, and their lives. Osama bin Laden was only the fiercest, most partisan spokesman for such views, which had (and continue to have) deep support in much of the Muslim world. Case in point: above the

91

patients gathered daily in the waiting room of Latif's Peshawar clinic, a framed photograph of the holy mosque in Mecca hung, and alongside it, a portrait of bin Laden.

How do I know this? Because I saw it on CNN.

In late June of 1998, my father was traveling home from a medical conference in Key West. He had a layover in Atlanta and some time to kill before his flight to Milwaukee. As he settled in at a bar near his gate, he looked up at the screen, where he was as shocked as you can imagine to see the name and the picture of his dear friend from medical school. TERRORIST SPIES KILLED was the title running under the story. Father asked the bartender to turn up the sound. Then he pulled out his cell phone and called Mother back home. After that, he called me.

The story reported that two brothers allegedly operating as spies for a Muslim terrorist network — the media had not yet taken to calling the group by its chosen name, Al Qaeda — had been killed in a pair of raids that were creating diplomatic complications with the Pakistanis. It wasn't clear who had carried out these so-called raids, which — Father was to learn — consisted of nothing more than a bullet in the temple for Latif and Manan as each left home on a morning in early May. (Father said it was widely rumored in Pakistan that this was the CIA's preferred method for local assassinations.) The CNN piece showed the nondescript two-story exterior of the clinic as well as the faded pea-green walls of a waiting room full of Peshawari poor — mostly women with children — where the camera lingered on the portrait of bin Laden. For CNN, clearly, this was the salient detail that conveyed the essential meaning of the story: poor brown ignorant hordes flocking to a malign manipulator who was stoking their rage against the forces of freedom and hope.

The report failed to mention that Latif was an American citizen.

Mother was distraught at the news. She took to bed, and she didn't leave her room for days. Father was worried and asked me to come home. I obliged, but my presence did nothing to comfort her. She didn't want comfort. I date my mother's intensifying anti-Americanism to that summer, the summer when, in response to attacks on two US embassies in East Africa, Bill Clinton bombed a Sudanese medicine factory. When Mother — herself a doctor trained in the Third World — learned that the factory had been responsible for producing every ounce of Sudan's tuberculosis medications, she was particularly incensed. She already despised Clinton for his indiscretions with Monica Lewinsky, and the attack on the factory came three days after Clinton's disastrous address in which he admitted he'd been lying about the affair all along. She saw in this sequence a murderous cynicism: an American president under political siege distracts the nation by killing Muslims.

In the last weeks of summer that August, she wrote in her diary of America as a foreign place, a place she didn't recognize, didn't like. She wrote in bitterness, even rage, and when writing about it wasn't enough she picked up the phone and unloaded to me:

"Doesn't know what 'is' means. What kind of nonsense is that?"

"That's not exactly what he said."

"That is *exactly* what he said."

"He meant he was referring to the present tense. That technically, at that time, when he was speaking, he was not in a relationship with her."

"I'm not an idiot. I know what he *meant.*"

"I wasn't implying you were an idiot, Mom."

"Legal nonsense."

"He *is* a lawyer. They both are."

"With his fat nose and his fat wife."

"I'm not sure what that has to do with anything —"

"Clinton is a liar. If he wants to lie about putting cigars where they don't belong, that's one thing. To kill people around the world to distract everyone from his lies, that's another."

"I don't know if that's what he was doing —"

"Of course it's what he's doing."

"They just bombed our embassies, Mom."

"You think that came out of nowhere? Hmm? When you push people and push them, and take advantage of their goodness and hope, when you use them for your own goals and throw them away, what do you expect? Do you expect them to send you roses?"

"That's one way of looking at it."

"What is the other way?"

"It's politics. Nobody's anybody's friend. Everybody is using everyone else."

"What's your point?"

"Pakistan took the money. For years they took it. What do you always say to me? Don't ask anyone for money and don't take it if they offer. It always comes with strings."

95

"The only strings were to beat the Russians."

"Apparently the strings also included not bombing US embassies."

There was silence on the line. "You're different," she said.

"Different from what?"

"From the child I raised."

I had never heard her say this. But the resignation in her voice made me think this was not a new thought.

"Maybe that's because I'm not a child anymore. I'm twenty-five."

"Latif was right. The longer we stay, the more we forget who we are."

"Uncle Latif is dead."

"You think I don't know that?!" Her tone was sharp, wounded.

"I just mean, maybe it's better to still be alive, Mom."

"When we used to take you to the *masjid* back during the war, you were the first to put your allowance into the box for the mujahideen."

"I always thought it was going to help Uncle Latif."

"And that essay you wrote in class . . ."

"Essay?"

"About Gaddafi."

"Mom. I was in middle school —"

"You called him a hero."

"Because I didn't know any better."

"What you knew then is better than what you know now."

"Do we have to talk about this?"

"He was the only one speaking up to the West."

"Is that why he bombed the plane to Scotland? Killed all those passengers? To speak up to the West?"

"You don't think they kill our people every day? Look at what they did to Latif. Who was doing their dirty work. He was *their* citizen! Can you believe that? They kill one of their own citizens who was fighting for them?"

"Maybe he wasn't anymore, Mom."

"Wasn't anymore what?"

"Fighting for them. Maybe that changed. Maybe that's the reason —"

She cut me off, her wounded tone intensifying: "They don't have the courage to face death themselves, so they make us face it. Then they throw us away when they get what they want." She paused; I stayed silent. When she spoke again, it was quietly; she was seething: "That man is not wrong. Our blood is cheap. They run around telling everyone else about human rights. But not for them. Look how they treat their own blacks."

"Mom."

"Turning us against each other. Making us spill each other's blood. Just like the British."

"Mom."

"Taking what we have. Oil, land. Treating us like animals."

"Mom."

"He's right. They deserve what they got. And what they're going to get."

These last words were the lines that would end up in my play.

The man she was referring to being right was, of course, bin Laden.

Later, after the attacks in 2001, she would never admit to having said anything of the kind. Understandably. I think most of the Muslim world could not have imagined how terrible redress would feel, when it came. Not only to Americans but to those in the Muslim world as well. For despite our ill usage at the hands of the American empire, the defiling of America-as-symbol enacted on that fateful Tuesday in September would only bring home anew to all the profundity of that symbol's power. Despite the predations on which it was predicated, the symbol sustained us, too. Many have disdained the

American response to the attacks as child-ish, have seen these years of vengeful war as the murderous tantrums of a country too young, too protected from the world, too immature to understand the inevitability of death. But I think the matter is more complicated. The world looked to us — and now I speak as an American — to uphold a holy image, or as holy as it gets in this age of enlightenment. We have been the earthly garden, the abundant idyll, the productive Arcadia of the world's pastoral dream. Between our shores has gleamed a realm of refuge and renewal — in short, the only reli-able escape from history itself. It's always been a myth, of course, and one destined for rupture sooner or later. Yet what an irony: when history finally caught up to us, it wasn't just we Americans — or even mainly we Americans — who would suffer the disastrous consequences.

III.
IN THE NAMES OF
THE PROPHET . . .

Di qui nacque che tutti i profeti armati vin-
sero, e i disarmati rovinarono.*
— Niccolò Machiavelli

1.

I have an uncle named Muzzammil, who,
for a fair stretch of my childhood, went by
"Moose" — the least rejected of the countless attempts to simplify the phonetic
conundrums of his name to those with no
working knowledge of Punjabi. Since he immigrated to the San Diego area, in 1974,
there'd been periods lasting from minutes
to months when he was called, in no particular order, Muz, Muzzle, Mazz, Muzzy,
Musty, Sammel, Sammy, Maury, Marty,
and Marzipan, which led to Al, and then
Alan — I kid you not — and, of course,

* Thus it is that armed prophets succeed where
unarmed prophets fail.

100

Moose. The last was coined by a fellow biochemist newly appointed at the lab in La Jolla where Muzzammil worked, an Italian named Ettore, who'd dealt with his own travails in New World pronunciation of an Old World name and came up with the moniker that would stick. There was certainly something apposite about it. Moose was a plain, largish man with a flaring Roman nose that drooped to a bulbous end; his shoulders drooped, too; and, yes, there was a kind of homely, even lumbering majesty about him. We, American-born kids of our Pakistani-born parents, also struggled with saying his name, for though of course he was never Moose to us, our parents said his name one way, and he offered it to us — native American speakers with our own varying levels of Punjabi incompetence — in the bizarre, labored accent he'd come upon to make himself sound more American, his diphthongs flattened by ever-widening contortions of his lips, his affricates shoved so far forward he couldn't seem to get through a sentence without baring unnecessary teeth. It wasn't just hard to gather a coherent, repeatable sense of what he was saying when he said his name — I always thought it sounded a little too much like the brand-name laxative fiber my father used to take, Metamucil — it was also sometimes hard to understand what he was saying at all through that tortured soup of bizarre signs and sounds.

I loved him. All the kids did. He was like one of us, willing to lose himself in our games, our worlds. I'd met him first in Pakistan, in my father's village. He'd just been married, and he and his new wife, Safiya, had come to pay their respects to my father's parents. I remember him showing me how to use a laundry basket to catch birds. We practiced on the chickens in the compound, then took it out to the village square to try it on the parrots. Magically, we entrapped a kingfisher. Muzzammil took hold of the bird from under the basket and handed it to me, its electric blue and blazing orange a wonder in my palms. Later, we saw much of Muzzammil in Wisconsin, as his work in pharmaceuticals brought him to Chicago for business. One year, he visited us around Halloween. Some of the neighborhood kids were over, and Muzzammil snuck into the fort of sheets we'd built in the basement, where he regaled us with a tale about a half lionfish, half child his biochem lab concocted for the military, which creature, he claimed, escaped from its tank and was now wreaking havoc on the local mouse population in La Jolla. I'm not sure we were particularly terrified by any of this, but he did a convincing impersonation of the creature eating a mouse that would remain a mocking motif — always reenacted with some attempt at his strange accent — among the crew of neighborhood kids for the months that followed.

Muzzammil's name came from the Quran's seventy-third surah (or chapter), entitled Al-Muzzammil, or, literally, the Enfolded One. The chapter is short and at the outset paints a picture of our Prophet enfolded in his bedsheets, exhorted by God's voice to resist sleep and rise to spend part of the night studying the Quran:

O thou enfolded one!
Rise. Stand in prayer the night, at least a
 little,
Half — less or more; and recite the
 Revelation with care.
We will send you the Word.
For rising is hard and good, and night a
 time for study,
The day consumed by your duties.
Remember the Name of your Lord. To
 Him, devote yourself complete.
To the Lord of the East and West; there is

* When I was in college, Surah Al-Muzzammil would end up on my reading list for the Meccan unit of my Islamic Studies class in the history of the Quran. I recall sitting in the first-floor reading room of the university library, looking up from the pages of the translation we'd been assigned, catching hold of the image of my uncle turning in our guest-room bed mixed and mingling with the picture of the person who, since childhood, had always been the Prophet to me. That image was, itself, some version of a person I'd known who had no connection to the Prophet whatsoever. He was a man I'd seen as a very young boy in my father's village whom my father seemed to love. We were by the village well; they were laughing; then they hugged. I remember the green scarf tied to this man's head, a long black mustache above his lip, a booming laugh his joy released. I remember looking up to see a metal pail pouring water into an earthenware jar as large as I was. For some reason, this man I would remember being called Tafi, though my father recalls no such person. I can't tell you why Tafi somehow became the Prophet in my mind, but he did. Whenever my mother — or her sisters, or her mother — would tell me tales of the Prophet, I saw Tafi in the role, which meant my every thought of the Prophet was dressed in some version of that green scarf

Though he was named for the Prophet, Muzzammil was in no way religious. As a chemist, he thought when you got down to the basics — to the molecules and their constituent atoms, that is — there really was no need for a God, Muslim or otherwise. Safiya, his wife, wasn't so sure. I remember her making a case for faith at Thanksgiving dinner one year, an argument I would later discover was the same wager Pascal suggested one might want to make sure one got right. Safiya's name, too, was drawn from the Prophet's life. Her namesake was the seventeen-year-old daughter of a Jewish tribal leader in Medina whom the Prophet — after killing her husband in battle — would take as his eleventh spouse. The Prophet's Safiya was supposedly a very beautiful woman, which is not exactly what I would have said of the Safiya I knew, at least not before saying other things about her: she was short; she was plump and calm; she brimmed with what seemed to me to be well-being. In opposition to the underlying, fractious despair of my parents' hurly-burly, Safiya and Muzzammil seemed blessedly stable. I heard no sharp retorts, felt no

and handlebar mustache, not to mention ringed with a liquid, unbridled joy.

wounded silences, saw two people who genuinely seemed to feel that life was better with the other in it. The looks of love between them would surprise me, discreet (or not-so-discreet) glances and half smiles exchanged over nothing, as he mixed sugar into his tea, say, or as she brushed flour from her cheeks while mixing and making chappatis, or as they held hands and shuffled along in their sandals on our summer walks through the neighborhood. He picked roses for her in the evenings from my mother's bushes when they were in bloom. She would clip a blossom from the stem and wear it in her hair at dinner. On our living-room couch, they nestled much closer than I ever saw my parents do, their own alleged *love marriage* notwithstanding. Indeed, I saw enough of whatever was working between Safiya and Muzzammil to recognize, as I got older, all the unknowing American ado about the unconscionable injustice of arranged marriage as exactly that, a lot of ignorant fuss. Their marriage had been arranged. The first time they saw each other was the afternoon before they were engaged, when Safiya was marched into a living room to clear the tea setting so that she and her prospective groom could each catch a glimpse of the other. There was no reason for it to work, except that it did — though Safiya did seem to believe their union was emblematic of some more enduring truth about love. It was from her that I first heard the analogy comparing love and arranged marriages to kettles of water pitched at different temperatures: the former already boiling, with no chance to get any hotter; the latter cold at the outset, requiring steady application to be sure but with ample room to heat up over the years.

They had one child, whom they would name Mustafa, a beloved patronymic on Safiya's side of the family meaning "chosen one" and another of the Prophet's many epithets. I have two cousins and an uncle named Mustafa. Indeed, of my twenty-two first cousins, fifteen have names taken from the Prophet or his circle; among my eight immediate aunts and uncles, the number is five. My mother's name, Fatima, owes its stupendous popularity in the Muslim world to being the given name of the Prophet's only daughter with his first wife, Khadijah — which is also the name of one of my mother's sisters.

I have two cousins named Ayesha. The first, Ayesha G, is a consultant for McKinsey who lives in Connecticut. She has three daughters with her husband, who is ten years older than she is and on his second marriage. He's white and works in finance but converted to Islam for her sake, and so, instead of getting disowned by her parents for marrying outside the faith, Ayesha G is that rare conquering hero who's succeeded in bringing one of *their kind* over to our side for a change. The other, Ayesha M, is a stay-at-home mom of five who splits her time between Islamabad and Atlanta, miserably married to her childhood sweetheart. Ayesha was the name of the Prophet's favorite of his many wives, a woman — as we are taught in our tradition — of great heart and intellect. She was the daughter of the Prophet's right-hand man, that pillar of staid, unquestioning support, Abu Bakr, the first outside of the Prophet's family to convert to Islam in its earliest days and the first to lead the community after the Prophet's death. The Prophet's Ayesha is the subject of much love and lore, called the Mother of the Believers, and of course her betrothal to the Prophet at the tender age of six — the consummation of their marriage delayed until the onset of her puberty, at age nine (when the Prophet would have been fifty-three) — has been a subject of debate and derision for centuries. This story caused no undue compunction in my community until after 9/11, when we all started to realize how backward it made us look, idealizing what people here could only conceive of as child rape; we weren't just risking derision but also bodily harm. Only then did the arguments about the reliability of the early sources go mainstream enough to become a subject of dinner conversation in my extended family. Which sounds about right. You don't go looking to change a story that's been working for you for a thousand years until you have a damn good reason to change it.

Ayesha M is six years younger than I am, the second daughter of my father's youngest sister. I remember a waif of a girl, gangly and game — at least when her domineering older sister, Huma, wasn't around to step on her impulses — who grew up into a lithe, lovely woman with more than just a recognizable portion of the offbeat gamine that she was the summer I was thirteen and back in Pakistan with my folks, visiting their various siblings and their families. One afternoon, when we were over at Ayesha and Huma's house for tea, the girls persuaded me to play Ken to their respective Barbies in the living room. Huma was ten. Ayesha was seven. The play veered, perhaps inevitably, into the question of marriage. Would my Ken marry Huma's Barbie or Ayesha's? (Only their outfits distinguished the two blond dolls, this being well before the era of anything like Brown Barbie — let alone Hijarbie.) The question led to an argument between the sisters about which one of them would marry their father. The claim went back and forth, Huma increasingly irritated at Ayesha's insistent desperation to be included in the quartet of their father's possible wives, until the older sister announced to the younger with finality that it would be their mother and her, and no one else. By this point, Ayesha was ready to cry, but before she did, she blurted out a surprising rejoinder:

"I don't care, because, anyway, I'm going to marry Rasool-e-Pak."*

Huma snickered. "I already told you. You can't. He's dead."

"I don't care. Mom said Rasool-e-Pak married Ayesha when she was nine, and she became his favorite wife."

"I said he's dead, dumbhead."

"I don't care. I'm going to do the same."

"You're so stupid."

"*You're* so stupid."

* Urdu for "Holy Messenger" — commonly used to refer to Muhammad.

110

"No, you are."

"*You* are."

And on and on, until Huma finally snatched her sister's Barbie and smacked it against the fireplace tile, putting a crack in its face. That's when Ayesha broke into tears and stormed out.

Everyone in Ayesha and Huma's family had green cards, but it wasn't until two years later that their parents would decide to sell their Islamabad home and relocate to Atlanta, where their father, after working for Coca-Cola in Pakistan since the late 1970s, had been offered a job at the US headquarters. They bought a house in Decatur, east of downtown, where they were delighted to find a vibrant (though small) Muslim community. That first year, Ayesha met Farooq, a ten-year-old whose Pakistani family had emigrated from Kenya. I didn't hear about Farooq until they were in their midteens, and I wouldn't meet him until he and Ayesha were in their midtwenties and getting married, at which point I found him slick and insincere and mostly neglectful of his fiancée in ways that would have shocked me even if I wasn't seeing them on the eve of their "special day." When I later heard from my mother that Ayesha was unhappy back in Islamabad — where they moved after the wedding, Farooq thinking his American MBA would get him further there, faster — I assumed the problem was not Pakistan but Farooq. I hope I won't be taken for trying to prove my deductive capacities by sharing what the family would all find out in due course: Farooq was abusive, sometimes physically, and Ayesha had taken (and been hiding) it for years. For all his forward American thinking, my father would address his niece's predicament in true Punjabi style: he called a cousin in the village, the sort of fellow who could round up a crew and pay someone a visit that wouldn't easily be forgotten. Last I heard, Ayesha had decided to stay in Atlanta with the children year-round; Farooq was spending most of his time in Islamabad.

But well before any of this would happen:

During the rehearsal dinner the day before their wedding, Ayesha gave a speech in which she told a story. (Celebratory rehearsal dinners replete with roasts and speeches and, usually, with the bride and groom in Western garb are a new and still uncommon custom in Pakistani American weddings; the time for public palaver of this sort is at the end of the sequence of wedding events, during the *walima,* when the bride and groom host their guests as a newly married couple.) Ayesha was wearing a stunning emerald-green column gown, her thin-as-stick forearms each covered with rows of golden bangles that murmured as she moved. Her hennaed hands unfolded the paper on which she'd made notes as she lifted her lightly trembling lips to the microphone to speak. In a quavering voice, she told us that since she was a very little girl, she'd always had the feeling she was going to meet her husband when she was nine. She didn't know why she thought that, but she did. What happened when she was nine? That was how old she was when her family found its way to Decatur. "Goooo, Bulldogs," she added with a fist pump for the sizable contingent of fellow Decatur High grads in the audience. And nine was how old she was when her family ended up sitting next to another local Pakistani family at a Fuddruckers one Friday night during their first few months in Georgia. That night, she shared pickles with the boy who would end up as her husband, Farooq. Looking back now, she said, her voice breaking as she teared up, she knew that meeting him then was kismet. Meant to be.

Of course, it's impossible to know for certain if her mother's telling her that the

Prophet had married his favorite wife at nine was the decisive early prompt that led to Farooq. What is certain, though, is that the story Ayesha told us during her rehearsal dinner was one she'd told herself countless times, and that this story was if not inspired, then certainly legitimized by that oft-told tale of the Prophet and his child bride, and that all this made it somehow easier for her to stay in a relationship — and, later, a marriage — that might not have been the best thing for her. The Prophet's relationships with women, however progressive and egalitarian some of them might have been for those medieval times, can hardly be taken as exemplary today. This might seem obvious — it certainly is to me — but so many I love very dearly don't see it that way at all.

2.

The Prophet's beloved Ayesha had two half sisters, Umm Kulthum — a name some will recognize as belonging to the most famous Egyptian singer of her era — and another named Asma. I had an aunt Asma — a great-aunt on my mother's side. Asma taught literature and critical theory at UConn until her untimely death from a stroke in the early aughts and was the first person to tell my parents, after hearing that I wanted to be a writer (and after she read a story I sent her when she wrote to ask me if what she was hearing from my parents was true), that writing was not quite so far-fetched a career as they might think.

That, anyway, is what she told my parents; what she said to me was different.

We met in Providence in the spring of '94, a few months after our exchange of letters and weeks before I was to graduate from Brown. She took the train up from New Haven, where she lived, and we met for dinner at a swanky seafood restaurant not far from the station. I found her in a booth overlooking the river in a dark brown *kameez* with a cream-colored *dupatta* slung across her shoulders. She was reading, her head tilted down, the angled edges of her gray bob falling forward and anchoring her thinking face to the page. Her large brown eyes looked even larger and browner through the lenses of her thick black-framed reading glasses, which she pulled off as she rose up and enfolded me in her arms. I was surprised by the welcome. Though we'd met many times — she and my mother had grown close when we lived in New York City during the 1970s — I'd never been treated to anything like this display of either affection or familiarity.

We sat, and she asked what I wanted to drink: "Because if you want wine, I'm happy to get a bottle and we can drink it together. Do you like red or white?" Her accent was strong and sonorous, the rounded vowels and pointed consonants shaped with ease and sophistication, an aural marker not only of her education — Kinnaird College, in Lahore, and Cambridge after that — but also of her lingering pride in the glories of the Raj, under which her family had produced a slew of journalists and university professors. I noticed the not entirely empty martini glass at the edge of her setting.

"I don't drink," I lied.

She smiled wryly. "I won't tell your *ammi*. What do you like, red or white?"

I shrugged. "Whatever you want, Auntie."

"Red it is, then. And I know the one," she said, slipping her glasses back on to peruse the wine list. "This Saint Emilion from Tertre Roteboeuf is brilliant. Rich and racy." She waved over a waiter and indicated her selection. He nodded, eyeing me briefly, then cleared my salad plate and left the wineglass. "Always better just to point it out," she said once he was gone. "Half the time they don't have the first clue what they have on the list. If you had any idea how many times they've brought out the wrong bottle!" She reached for a bag on the seat beside her and pulled out a stack of books tied together with twine. "These are for you. This is where you need to begin if you're going to be a writer."

"That's so nice of you, Auntie. Thank you."

"It's a hard life. It's thankless. If you can do anything else with yourself, anything more certain, you owe it to yourself and to everyone you love to do that. But if you can't, if you need to be writing, well, then, one of the joys of the lonely journey ahead, *beta,* is the comfort of reading. A day spent reading is not a great day. But a life spent reading is a wonderful life."

I thanked her again as I picked up the stack and read the bindings:

Orientalism.
Pride and Prejudice.
The Muqaddimah.
Death Comes for the Archbishop.
The Wretched of the Earth.

"It's a hodgepodge, I know. And I'm sure somebody has made you read the Jane Austen already. But I do think it the most wonderful novel ever written. I don't think

117

you can read it enough times. And not just for the pure, unending delight. Her analysis of the world is not to be underestimated. You'll find more wisdom about the way the world really works in those pages than in a million more pretending to tell you. Money, money, money. That's all it ever comes down to." She looked up with a smile at the waiter who'd returned and stood now, pulling the cork, a napkin draped over his forearm. He poured briefly for her to taste. She swirled and smelled, then brought the glass to her lips. "Hmm, it's good. But it needs to breathe. Pour us both half glasses, and we'll wait. Thank you." Once he was gone, she resumed: "Of course, before you read or write another word, you must read Edward Said. What a brilliant man. And gorgeous. He moved like a leopard. I met him at a conference ten years ago. If I hadn't been married, *beta,* what I would have done to get into that bedroom! Anything. Anything! Don't tell your *ammi* I said that. You don't tell her about me and Edward, I won't tell her about you and this Saint Emilion." She sipped from the glass again. "Better, but it needs time. Edward's book is indispensable, Ayad. There are very few books you can say that about. But *Orientalism* is one. You won't know who you are until you've read it. Whatever you *think* you are now, when you finish that book, you will be something different. What are you reading currently?" she asked as she bit on a piece of bread and started to chew.

"Rushdie."

"*Midnight's Children?* Brilliant book. Just brilliant."

"No. *The Satanic Verses.*"

She coughed. She reached for her water and sipped to clear her throat, staring at me, the taut lines on her forehead now crossed and furrowed. "Why are you reading *that?*"

The Rushdie was the final reading assignment in my ongoing independent study with Mary Moroni, the professor I mentioned earlier (and of whom there will be more said in the pages ahead). "I've made you read too many white people," she'd said to me as we sipped tea in her office one afternoon earlier that spring. I laughed, but it was clear she wasn't joking. I'd been curious about Rushdie's book since its publication five years prior. My mother bought a copy during the commotion, tried reading it, and soon gave up. She couldn't make heads or tails of it was what she said. For more than a year, the book had lain on the side table in our living room, where she'd set it down

119

never again to pick it up, dog-eared some thirty pages in. That copy I'd brought to school, hoping I would get to it at some point.

Mary hadn't read it, either, and was curious to do so as well.

It took me three days to read Rushdie's book, three days that remain singular in my reading life. I'd never before encountered so much of myself on the page — my questions, my preoccupations, the smells and sounds and tastes and names of my family — a potent form of self-recognition that bred a new certainty: I existed. There was also the dizzying thrill of formal discovery: I hadn't read Gárcia Márquez yet or the postmodernists — so *The Satanic Verses* was my first experience of both magical realism and metafiction. Most thrilling was the book's unapologetic parody of the Muslim mythology I'd grown up with as a child. To write a book filled with so many unthinkable thoughts, and to do so with such joyous abandon. I didn't know anyone could do such a thing.

As I sat across from Asma that evening in downtown Providence, I wouldn't have time to find the words to explain how significant an event Rushdie's book was in my life. She interrupted my hesitating silence and began

120

her attack: "I never thought I would be saying this about him, after that brilliant first novel, I mean, *brilliant* — look, I knew he never came up with anything on his own, borrowing everything, and, of course, what crime is there in that? Everyone knows there's not a *new* idea to be found anywhere under the sun. Shakespeare stole from everyone. So what's the issue with Salman doing the same thing? The problem, *beta,* is that you have to do it well. You have to do it *better* than the ones you're stealing from. He's not. Not anymore. It's *used* now. *Tired.* And worst of all — and this is what really bothers me — it's the *malice.*"

"Malice?"

"The sickening, ad hominem attacks on the Prophet, peace be upon him. Picking through that disgusting orientalist history, disgusting tales the Christians told to make the Prophet out as some sex-crazed cult leader, God forbid. I mean, *this* is what we have to expect? From *Salman*? From one of *us*?"

"He says he's not a Muslim, Auntie."

She snorted. "Please. I read that idiotic essay. Even more pathetic than how derivative he's become is his cowardice. He knew what he was doing when he was writing that book. I know for a fact. We have friends in

121

common. He was going around talking about sending the mullahs a message they won't forget. Well, message received. But guess what? He didn't *like* how they received it. So now? *It's not about Islam,* he says. *I'm not Muslim. How can it be blasphemy if I don't believe in it?* He's a coward. He's a coward and a hypocrite."

To tell her I didn't agree would have implied that I understood what she was getting at. I didn't really. I, too, had felt shocked reading the famous dream sections of the book set in the fictional Jahilia, depicting the Prophet as a mostly unremarkable man, maneuvering and money-minded, confused about his calling; I'd experienced shock, but not that of blasphemy. Instead, I'd wondered why it had never occurred to me that the Prophet might just be as mythic a construction as I considered Jesus and Moses to be. I didn't see anything malicious about Rushdie's portrayal of the Prophet. I found it brilliant. Terrifyingly so. In fact, the book worried me in a way far more as one who wished to write than as a Muslim: I worried I would never write anything remotely as powerful.

"Does he think any of this is *new*?" my aunt went on. "Calling him Mahound? Really? That's been around since the Middle

Ages, Salman. We all know what it means."
She stopped, with a sudden thought. "I
hope you're doing your homework, *beta*. I
hope you know what he's saying when he
uses that name. He's calling the Prophet an
impostor at best, a daemon at worst."

"I know, Auntie. But it's a dream sequence. And there's the writer, Salman, in
the book, writing it, who —"

"Dream sequence? More creative cowardice if you ask me. Hiding behind *dreams*.
It's clear as day what he's doing. He's trying on his own Nero complex to see how
well it fits." She drank again, this time
pleased. "It's good we waited. Try it now."

I drank. It tasted bitter to me.

"Wonderful, isn't it? Such a rich body."

"What's a Nero complex, Auntie?" I
asked.

"Right. That's something Albert Memmi
talks about in his book *The Colonizer and
the Colonized*. I'll send it to you. He says
that when you come to power through having usurped it, you're never free of the
worry that your claim to power is not
legitimate. And this fear of illegitimacy, this
sense of being haunted, it causes you to
make those from whom you stole power suffer. Fits Richard the Third and Rushdie
both to a tee. He thinks he's one of *them*

now. He's usurped the place he wanted, and now he's terrified he doesn't fit the part. So he puts his own people down just to prove himself. What other reason does he have to bring all this medieval nonsense back? To rub our noses in this filth about the Prophet being a fake and his wives no better than prostitutes? And then you want to pretend it's not about the Prophet, it's not about Islam — because it's some *dream sequence?* And you go around saying it can't be blasphemy because you don't fast and you don't pray? What is this garbage? *He's* the prostitute. *He's* the impostor. Not the Prophet. Frankly, it's surprising a man like that had a book like *Midnight's Children* in him. But it goes to show you. Every era has its Boswell."

Most literary Muslims I would meet in the years ahead seemed to share the broad outlines of my aunt's feelings about Rushdie and *The Satanic Verses.* Some of it was driven by envy, no doubt. Rushdie's travails made him the most famous author alive. But there were those with no real basis for envy who still objected to the work. Naguib Mahfouz, the great Egyptian novelist and Nobel laureate — himself no stranger to fundamentalist attacks — told the *Paris Re-*

view in 1992 that he found Rushdie's novel insulting:

> Rushdie insults even the women of the Prophet! Now, I can argue with *ideas,* but what should I do with insults? Insults are the business of the court . . . According to Islamic principles, when a man is accused of heresy he is given the choice between repentance and punishment. Rushdie was not given that choice. I have always defended Rushdie's right to write and say what he wants in terms of ideas. But he does not have the right to insult anything, especially a prophet or anything considered holy.

Mahfouz's response pointed to an enduring fact of so much Muslim intellectual life, a lasting sense that the Prophet is sacrosanct, that his status as a model of holiness and virtue in all things is not to be disputed; and therefore, that the demonstrable pruning and cherry-picking of the sources in support of what, on greater study, could only be seen as a fiction, curated for effect, that this process of "constructing" the Prophet's identity is not an acceptable subject of public discourse; and finally — and most odd to me — that time spent on the thorny matter of the Prophet's historicity is taken as evidence not of one's interest in truth but rather of one's craven dependence on *the West,* which — one is summarily scolded — does not itself have left any sacred symbols of its own and therefore mars and makes a mockery of the only such symbol still unsullied by the destructive cynicism and faithlessness of the European Enlightenment. Some version of a similar argument is offered in support of the eternity of the Quran and its status as the preeminent voicing of the Godhead in human language. I find both positions only more and more perplexing with the years, especially as, with each successive reading of the Quran, it's become only clearer to me how indebted it is not only to the time and place in which it arose but also to the psychology of the one whom I cannot but see as its author, Muhammad. (For Muslims, to speak of Muhammad as the author of the Quran is a surpassing blasphemy; only God could have authored such a miracle, we are told; Muhammad was just a holy stenographer, if you will, taking divine dictation.) My own journey from childhood faith to adult certainty about the very human contingency at the heart of Islam's central narratives is a tale beyond the scope of these pages but one that, someday, I will try to tell in all its tortured entirety. When I do, I will attempt it without an ounce of malice and may still not survive its publication. For now, let me try to stay alive and just say these three things: as Muslims, (1) we are more affected by the example of the Prophet than we realize; (2) we are shaped by the stories we tell about him in ways that elude our daily understanding; and (3) there will be no meaningful philosophical shift in the sociopolitical substratum of the Muslim world until the example of the Prophet and the text of the Quran are exposed to a more robust interrogation of their claims to historical truth. This may all sound both reasonable and unsurprising to you, non-Muslim readers, and may strike some of you, Muslim readers, as uncomfortably close to the sorts of calls for a reformation of the faith that so many have found historically ignorant at best, mortally insulting at worst. And yet the fact that I can barely say it all without some fear of reprisal is, ignorance and insult notwithstanding, a true measure of how far we, Muslims, still have to go.

3.

A rondo, then, whose recurring leading theme leaves my aunt Asma dangling midthought and drops us now in Abbottabad for its culminating recapitulation. The year is 2008. The setting is the home of my father's middle sister, in the northeastern suburb of this almost-mile-high city in North Pakistan, where in three years' time, Osama bin Laden will be found and killed. To anyone who knew much of anything about Pakistan, the fact that bin Laden was living in Abbottabad when he was killed signaled the obvious. Abbottabad is a military town, a kind of Pakistani West Point, filled to the brim with soldiers, cadets, officers. My aunt Ruxana — a name without any connection to the Prophet's circle, although her only son is one of the two Mustafa cousins I alluded to earlier — lived there for most of her adult life, married to a colonel in the Pakistani army who was also a lecturer at the military academy. I'd been to Abbottabad many times when I was growing up, and what always struck me about the place was its histrionic sense of order, reflecting the civic ideal I heard so much about whenever I was in my parents' homeland: stability and prosperity guarded and ensured by the armed forces. Abbottabad was like a commercial for martial law, the sort of place not only where the trains ran on time but also where the call to prayer didn't sound either as loud or as persuasive as it did elsewhere. To me, the notion that bin Laden had been living there for six years without the direct support of the Pakistani military was utterly implausible.

My father and I were in Abbottabad visiting Ruxana in October of 2008. She was then still alive, though already sick with the leukemia that would eventually kill her. It was my first time back in Pakistan since 9/11, and I found a country very different from the one I remembered. Any love or admiration for America was gone. In its place was an irrational paranoia that passed for savvy political consciousness. Looking back at that trip, I see now the broad outlines of the same dilemmas that would lead America into the era of Trump: seething anger; open hostility to strangers and those with views opposing one's own; a contempt for news delivered by allegedly reputable sources; an embrace of reactionary moral posturing; civic and governmental corruption that no longer needed hiding; and married to all this, the ever-hastening redistribution of wealth to those who had it at the continued expense of those who didn't. There was much talk of conspiracy on that visit in 2008, the usual stuff I'd been hearing for years — about 9/11 being an inside job, perpetrated now by American intelligence, now by the "Jews"; or the 2005 earthquake in Swat caused by American bombings; or the convoluted attempts to construe Bhutto's assassination as the result of US meddling — but I'd resolved no longer to argue with my relatives or storm out of family dinners.* During that trip, I resolved to stay calm through the crazy talk, to stanch my outrage, to listen for an emotional logic driving the thoughtless and obsessive suspicion. What I heard as I

* By the time Malala was awarded the Nobel, in 2014, the conspiracy paranoia in my parents' home country had started to show symptoms of widespread social psychosis — that is, wide-scale diminishment of any sense of reality, the rise of mass delusions impairing functional operation of the social body and state — with talk of Malala staging her own shooting for a visa to America, or being the Hungarian child of Christian missionaries or an agent working for the CIA, opinions espoused by more people in my family and in the country at large (and by those with a greater level of education) than you would ever believe possible.

listened with new ears was fear. I heard the worry of a world treated to seven years of military and political bullying under the cover of "fighting the terrorist threat." By 2008, it was clear there would be no end to the bloodshed that the Bush administration had started based on pure fabrications, and it was easy to understand the terror that motivated the infuriating stupidity of my Pakistani relatives: that they might find themselves next up in the round of imperial slaughter, future victims of this new era of unending American vengeance.

But I digress.

To resume: the setting is my aunt Ruxana's home in Abbottabad, a bungalow-style construction dating from the Raj, its spacious rooms appointed with flourishes of British style. In the living room, the cherry wainscoting gives way to a fading William Morris wallpaper of boughs and branches; over the various fireplaces scattered through the house are mirrors and candelabra and mantel clocks; and, in the guest room where my father and I are staying — my mother isn't feeling well and opted to stay back with her parents in Rawalpindi — the taxidermied head of a blackbuck mounted over the bed. Ruxana has made us an extraordinary dinner of shaami kebabs and okra masala and tandoori naan baked in the clay tandoor oven out back. Her head is covered with a shawl, but not for modesty's sake. She has no hair left. Her light brown skin is turning yellow-gray. She moves with the labored effort of one summoning strength she doesn't really have.

Ruxana returns from the kitchen, drops a new round of hot naan into the bread basket, takes her seat alongside her husband, Naseem, a short, stout man with a straight, strong back. His speech, like his mustache, is clipped and confident. I have never not seen that scowling smirk on his face, not a look of contempt but of a man enamored with control. Even his arm as he lifts the cup of lassi his wife has prepared bears the self-curtailment of a life made sense of through military drill. My cousin Mustafa, twenty-nine, a bank teller, is here. His sister, Yasmin, thirty-two, a pediatrician, is not. The conversation has turned to the bombings that have become a fact of daily life in Pakistan. In his usual peremptory manner, Naseem explains the dilemma in brief, declarative sentences. The problem is simple, he says, though no one wants to admit it. Pakistan created this cancer in its fight with India; now the cancer has turned on its host. I ask him for clarification, and this leads to a vigorous lesson in Pakistani foreign policy, circa 2008:

"We are stuck between two enemies. Afghanistan to the west. India to the east. The history of politics in this country is defined by our borders. India, through Kabul, has meddled in our affairs from the beginning on the western front. I hope I don't need to explain to you what they've done to us along the northern and eastern fronts." He paused, waited for me to respond. I shook my head, affirming that, of course, I needed no explanation of the existential threat Pakistan has always felt along its Indian border. "So what are the means of control? The militants were willing to fight our fight in the north. We befriended them along the western front to keep our influence alive in Afghanistan. But when you feed a monster, it grows. When it attacks you — because it always will — you have only yourself to blame."

My father was hunched over his plate on the other side of his sister, her arm resting on his shoulder as he ate. She gazed at the side of his face and brought her finger to his cheek. Feeling her caress, he looked like he was going to cry.

"The problem is the children," Naseem continued. "The madrassas are filled with

133

them. Filled! Madrassas teach them, feed them, fill their heads with talk of jihad from the time they're four and five. By the time they're ten they want to fight! We're filling the country with boys like this. That's where this endless supply of young men is coming from, young men happy to blow themselves to bits." As Naseem stopped on a thought, I reached for a kebab from the plate at the center of the table; I broke up the patty into pieces as he continued: "Tactically, I understand it. It makes sense why we did what we did. In theory, it's a playbook taken from the Americans. Terrorism worked well for them in Central America, El Salvador, Nicaragua. What *we* didn't account for was the difference in proximity. Using a strategy like this so close to home was bound to have an effect it would never have had for the Americans."

"That's not true, Abu." It was my cousin Mustafa, who sat on the other side of the table. He was holding an apple from which he'd yet to take a bite. The assertion had been softened by an upturned, halfhearted interrogative tone. Like his father, Mustafa was short and stout, but there was nothing rigid or severe about him. He cowered in the shadow of his father's carefully groomed imperiousness. Since the onset of his late

134

adolescence, I'd suspected Mustafa was gay. For the better part of the following decade, I hoped — arrogantly, no doubt — to find some way to broach the subject with him, somehow to convey that, should he need support from within the family to live his truth, whatever that might be, I could be counted on. No such conversation ever transpired. Two years ago, I heard from someone in the family that he'd left Pakistan and was living in Holland with a male partner.

"How so, *beta*?" Naseem asked.

"The Americans put off the payback. But it came, sooner or later." He shrugged as he spoke, seeming almost to retract the thought as he offered it. When he was finished, he took a bite of the apple in his hand and studied his father's face as he chewed.

"But you see — *that* was tactical *genius*. September eleventh was an act of war that changed the history of how war will be fought as long as there is fighting to be done." He looked at me, then at Father, whose gaze — now glaring — had lifted from his plate. "I'm not saying it was a good thing, Sikander. I'm talking tactics. From a pure *military* point of view. You have to be able to see the genius in it."

"Genius? What genius, Naseem-*bhai*?"

135

Father's tone was sharp, a clear contrast to the affectionate address. "Look at the chaos it started."

"Who *truly* started the chaos we may not agree," Naseem replied just as sharply, though the ensuing silence seemed to give him occasion for regret. "I was talking purely from a battlefield perspective, but yes, you are right to signal the difficulty in managing an entire campaign of such tactics. That is what has failed here in Pakistan. Which is what I was trying to say before. About the cancer we created and that has consumed us."

Father looked down into his plate. His agitation was apparent. Ruxana stood and moved her hand gently along his shoulder. "Anyone want more naan?" She was looking at her husband.

"I'm fine," Naseem said in Punjabi.

"I won't say no, Rux," Father said to her as if to oppose him. "They're too good." She smiled and turned to me.

"I'm still working on this one," I said, showing my plate. Ruxana headed for the kitchen, but stopped at the doorway and looked back at us: "Get the arguments out of your system by the time I get back," she said sweetly.

"No argument here," Naseem said, forcing a smile. Once she was gone, he turned to Father again: "You see, *bhai,* the effects of war are always personal, but in fact, war is the least personal thing there is. Which can make it hard to see objectively." Father was scooping food with his morsel of bread, feigning absorption in his meal. When he looked up, chewing, it was at me. There was a warning in his eyes.

I didn't heed it.

"What would it mean to manage a campaign like this effectively, Uncle?" I asked.

"Do you know Clausewitz, *beta?* The trinity of war?" I shrugged. Clausewitz was only a name to me. "Three parts of war: the individual, the circumstance, the collective," Naseem said, using his middle, ring, and pinkie fingers to count out the categories. "You can reframe each of these in various ways. The individual soldier; the unpredictability of the situation; the state. Or passion, intensity, the emotional case for war; chance — like winter coming too soon for Napoleon's campaign into Russia; and the reasoned, political will to finance the fight. Mastery of the first two parts of the trinity is what we saw on September eleventh. The last part, the collective — that is what has yet to be properly worked out. Al Qaeda is too dependent on the individual, who in

137

turn is too vulnerable to the variations of chance circumstance. What is needed is a state structure flexible enough to encourage the sort of individual agency and creativity we saw on that day. This is what can transform the innovation into a possibility for collective and political action."

"Okay. I understand, but what does that really look like?"

"We've seen it before. The North Vietnamese. Sparta. But the best example is still the sunnah." I stole a look at Father, knowing this was likely to get a rise out of him. *Sunnah* was the word we Muslims used for the customs of the Prophet and his Companions, the traditions outlined by the practices of that first community of believers, whose example was still seen as a viable template for possible utopia in much of the Muslim world. "I'm not referring to it from a religious point of view per se. You can take that or leave it. Here in Pakistan, we tend to take it — but all the same. My point is the vision of a community that does not bifurcate its military and political aspirations. The question of policy will always contain the question of warfare. 'War is just politics by other means,' to bring it back to Clausewitz. Yes, of course, the question of warfare is ultimately always subordinate to that of civil order, but it is wrong to think of it as a *separate* question. You cannot make the world as you wish to see it; you cannot keep it the way you want it, not unless you are willing to fight to do it. That is the meaning of war. And the more a society understands this reality, the better. The human being is a battling creature, *beta.* That will never change. To pretend otherwise is to delude ourselves. We fight as a way to make meaning of our lives. That is why protecting the citizens against war is always a recipe for long-term civil disintegration. The nation must be brought into the military mind-set. Muhammad, peace be upon him, did this better than anyone ever has. Not only was he a good man, the best of men, he was also a great military man, one of the greatest. The fashions come and go, and right now, it's not in fashion to think this way. But history is clear. The real leaders, the ones we remember — they are the ones willing and able to lead their societies straight into the fight." I was tempted by a rejoinder to his mention of Sparta: What had they given the world but their unfortunate victory over Athens? I knew what his reply would be. To him — to so many Muslims — Athens had nothing on Mecca or Medina; for them, Muhammad was Socrates and Pericles and

Themistocles all rolled up into one. They saw the Prophet and his first followers as the wisest, most courageous of our species ever to step upon the earth and imagined their assembly — attendant dramas and all — as a polity without peer, worthy of eternal emulation. I knew no occasion to sing these predictable praises would be forgone. I held my tongue.

Taking my silence for encouragement, Naseem cited the great American presidents as proof of his point about the fundamental military basis of great leadership: Washington, Lincoln, Roosevelt. I recall thinking it was starting to sound rehearsed, as if he'd shaped what he was now saying for other captive American ears before mine. Bear in mind, this was back in 2008, still a full half decade before the eruption onto the international stage of ISIS and its black standard bearing the insignia of the Prophet's personal seal. In returning to all this, in writing it out, I find myself wishing Naseem and I had been able to have *that* conversation, the one about ISIS. The principles Naseem was outlining were, of course, central to the disgusting social and military project that would come to bloom in Syria and Iraq like toxic desert dogbane, a demonic, self-referential refraction of that first Muslim community Naseem invoked, the original Companions of the Prophet recast as sex-crazed purveyors of snuff films whom even Rushdie's satirical genius could not have imagined. That would have been a discussion worth having, but it wasn't meant to be. I would never see him again. By summer of the following year, Ruxana was dead, and Naseem wouldn't outlive his wife by much. While taking a walk in the Shimla Hills above the city three months after his wife's passing, he would succumb to a myocardial infarction. His body, like his wife's, would be buried the same day — per Muslim custom — meaning no one from my family had time to get back to attend either funeral.

Father abandoned us to our conversation shortly after Naseem's mention of FDR. After I went to bed, I heard him talking softly with his sister in the backyard late into the night. I didn't see him again until the following morning at the same dining table, where, after fried livers and parathas, we said our goodbyes. My cousin Yasmin — on two hours of sleep after her all-night duties at the hospital — was particularly moved and having some trouble feeling her arms. Emotions, she said, aggravated her MS symptoms. Diagnosed with multiple sclerosis in her midtwenties, she'd spent four weeks with my parents in Wisconsin in the mid-1990s seeing specialists and depended now on the American medications Father sent her regularly, medications she could neither get in Pakistan nor afford on her own and that had put at least fifty pounds on her otherwise delicate frame. She joked about the weak embrace as she hugged me, then kissed Father, her face slick with loving tears. Father's parting with his sister was especially moving. By daylight, my aunt Ruxana looked even gaunter than she had at dinner, but as she held her brother, her eyes blazed with grave and vivid joy. Naseem watched the siblings touch foreheads, my father's hand to the back of his dying sister's bald head, their eyes filling with tears.

After the crying and the goodbyes, we walked out to the car Naseem had hired to take us back to Rawalpindi, a midnight-blue Mercedes sedan driven by a dark young man with a shawl folded across his shoulder. His name was Zayd, a cognomen of the Prophet's beloved adopted son, Zayd ibn Harithah, whose pulchritudinous wife — Zainab bint Jahsh — Muhammad would marry and make his seventh spouse after his Zayd divorced her, to my knowledge the only instance in which our Prophet married a sometime daughter-in-law. Our Zayd was clearly a religious man, his dark shoulder-length locks fanning out from beneath the strict enclosure of a tight white kufi on his head; every effort he made — opening the trunk, lifting and laying our bags inside, shutting the lid and opening our car doors — was accompanied by a quiet invocation: "Bismillah al-rahman, al-rahim."* Once we were settled in our seats, Zayd took his own in front and paused ever so briefly before turning the key to start the ignition: "Bismillah . . ." he whispered.

Father shot me a look and rolled his eyes.

The drive out of the northeastern part of the town took us past the dirt-road entrance that led to the compound where, at that very moment, Osama bin Laden was residing. We couldn't have dreamed it. After wending our way along the side streets, past fields and houses surrounded by mud-brick walls, we found the main road. We drove until we came upon the military academy where Naseem taught — which Zayd pointed out — and where we paused for a cavalry unit at least forty strong to trot across the asphalt. Once we were moving again, it wasn't long

* In the name of God, most good, most merciful.

143

before we'd left the city limits and were speeding along the Karakoram Highway back south. That was when Father turned to me — irritated — and asked what was wrong with me. I told him I didn't understand the question.

"I don't remember the last time I got a word in without you adding your overeducated two cents —"

"Overeducated two cents — ?"

"For a change you butting in would have been welcome. All that phony military talk, pontificating. I don't know how Ruxana's put up with him for so many years."

"I wanted to let him speak."

"Why?"

"I wanted to know what he thought."

"Thought? Is that what he was doing? *Thinking?"*

"Dad —"

"Ingrates. That's all they are. When he had heart trouble a few years back? What did he do? Came to America. The medication that helps his daughter? Comes from America. It doesn't matter how much money they take from us, how much support —"

I cut him off; I knew this drill: "He wasn't saying anything against America. All he said was that 9/11 was a brilliant tactical strike. That's hard to deny."

Father was incredulous. "So you *agree* with him?"

"Agree about what? I was trying to understand where he was going with it."

"I know exactly where he was going. He was taking a highbrow *shit* on our country. It took all I had to keep out of it."

"I think it was wise you did."

He glared at me, then shook his head. "Unhappy. Both of you. You and your mother. You don't know how to be happy. You don't even want to be happy."

"What are you talking about?"

"You think it's so much better here than back in America?"

"I never said that. I don't know why you're —"

"Trust me, you don't have a clue how terrible your life would have been if I'd stayed here. Not a clue."

"Dad. Stop."

"A writer? Hmm? *Theater?* You think they have that kind of *bullshit* here? Thirty-six years old and still asking me for money? You think anybody here would let you get away with it? You'd get laughed off the streets. If we were *here*?! *You* would be supporting *me*! Do you understand that? Why do you think Yasmin is still living at home? She goes to the hospital, makes her salary,

145

brings it home, and puts it in her father's hands. *That's* how it works in Pakistan." I'd heard it all before: that my mother pined for a Pakistan that no longer existed; that I'd stupidly bought into her nostalgia; that I was avoiding the hard truth about myself as a writer — if I still couldn't make a living doing it, I probably wasn't any good — and of course, above all, that I always failed to recognize just how much I owed my life to his decision to come to America. This last matter was a point of often injured pride with him. He'd been brandishing my supposedly unprecedented privilege and his exclusive role in it — for indeed, my mother had never wanted to leave their homeland — since the moment I could understand language. This line of attack always hurt, and this instance was no exception. But he'd paid for the trip, and I was only too aware that the familiar slights and complaints and his pleas for credit were part of the cost to me. Perhaps what also made it easier to bear with grace was knowing where the emotional strain in his voice was really coming from. He'd already lost one sister — when he was twenty-four — a wound he used to say would never heal. Yes, he'd been irritated by Naseem's pedantry, but at root, even this irritation was about his sister's illness. I

146

knew it the night prior and knew it now as I listened to him go on: "*Roosevelt?* What does that stooge know about *Roosevelt?* What's the use spending all that time reading those books about Roosevelt if you can't be bothered to use the information when it's needed?"

"What books?"

"The ones about Roosevelt you were carrying around every time I saw you."

"Those were about Teddy, Dad."

"Mhm?"

"The first Roosevelt president? Teddy Roosevelt? Not FDR."

A brief pause would be his only acknowledgment of the misunderstanding: "It makes no sense. What's it good for? All the education and you don't say a useful thing when the idiot starts in with the nonsense. A fool like that will never understand the first thing about a man like FDR. *That* was a great man."

"Ronald Reagan wasn't such a fan, Dad."

"*Now* you've got the wisecrack? — That's nonsense, and you know it. Reagan voted for the man every time. I know for a fact."

"And then spent every hour of his political career undoing the man's legacy."

He stared at me now, blankly, then turned away in disgust.

Out the window, the dramatic mountain vistas had given way to the familiar concatenation of sometimes ramshackle roadside constructions, stores and schools and homes, tea stands, food stands, pumping stations; the earlier evergreen of the Hazara steppes now replaced by sundry shades of drying earth, from ecru to umber, mud-brick walls and sand-brown lots and road shoulders, tan trails leading into the darker sunbaked fields beyond, and everywhere around us, clouds of turbid beige kicked up by the chaos of jockeying buses and painted trucks passing, honking, themselves dun with dust; even the late-morning sun seemed to color everything with a straw-taupe hue.

We rode in silence until Zayd's flip phone sounded with a call. He answered in a dialect — Gujarati, Father would later tell me — I didn't follow. But Father did, and when the call was over, he leaned forward to ask — in Punjabi now — for details about Zayd's son. The boy had been burning up with fever since the middle of the night. Zayd and his wife had been trying to get a doctor to see him, but no doctor had shown. Father pressed him for details, and when he realized we weren't far from where Zayd lived — outside the town of Hasan Abdal

148

— he offered to take a look at the boy himself. In the rearview mirror, I saw Zayd find Father's eyes, his hooded gaze bouncing from the road to the mirror and back. He seemed to be working through his surprise at Father's kindness. There was no need for that, he finally said; the doctor they knew would eventually come and the boy would be fine, of course. Zayd was clearly moved by Father's offer but didn't seem to know how he could possibly accept it; the gap between us — poor rural driver in front, wealthy urban American expatriates in back — was not a gulf easily bridged.

But Father was insistent, and finally Zayd relented.

It was another ten minutes before we slowed and turned into a steep dip off the National 35. The bottom of the car's front end scraped against the pebbled shoulder, and its wheels now searched for new purchase on a pockmarked path in the dirt. We sped up again, moving past a row of stores selling cell phones, wicker beds, fried fish. The road — if you could call it that — narrowed as it passed through a grove, and beyond it was what could only be described as a shantytown.

We slowed to a crawl as we entered. Everywhere around us were makeshift one-story structures built from soiled cloth, worn straw, broken bricks, rusting tin, plastic sheets, cardboard. They were tied with twine, bound with mortar, wrapped with ribbons of duct tape. Dogs rummaged and children played in eddies of debris — paper, plastic, rags, bags, bottles, the discarded appurtenances of modern, disposable life. From within these poorest of poor houses, families looked out at us as we passed, dozens at a time crowded into the tiny threadbare rooms. I'd been to my parents' homeland many times but not once to a place like this.

As we crept along, our car wheels sloshed through a runnel of thick black standing liquid on the left side of the road — from the smell, clearly human waste — and children started to gather around us. They pressed their smiles into the glass. Two of them, a boy and girl, mounted the back fender, and the girl stood and waved like a festival queen on a parade float greeting her onlookers. Zayd honked lightly, and the children spooked — but not for long. Soon there were more of them than before, some now holding sticks they used to urge us along. Their heads were tousled, their clothes smudged with dirt, their faces lit up with a joy particular to each — the half-held smile of one, the crow's-feet already forming at the edges of another's eyes, the dimples, the delighted gazes. They were singing now, a song whose words I couldn't follow, and as they sang, more faces appeared in the open doorways and windows with only hanging cloths to keep the heat and cold and fetid odors out. More children appeared, dozens and dozens of them, their gathered voices ringing out with a melody everyone knew.

And then, all at once, the singing stopped. They scattered and were gone.

I looked over at Father. His eyes were wet. "So poor, but still so happy," he said with a sniffle. I wasn't sure what he was crying about, really. I doubted it was the children.

We'd turned off the main artery onto a path just wide enough for the car, and shortly Zayd stopped before a large rusted box — what looked like the severed back third of a shipping container — with a clean green curtain mounted at the mouth, drawn shut now, the whole structure lifted from the ground and perched on a set of concrete blocks. The elevation, the simplicity of the single window treatment, set this shanty apart.

Zayd hopped out and pulled the door open for Father, muttering his *bismillah*. At

151

the curtain's edge, a woman's small face appeared. Like Zayd, she was dark; her nose was pierced. As Father and I emerged from the car, she adjusted her *dupatta* to ensure her hair was fully covered. Zayd spoke to her in Gujarati and lifted himself up — there was no step — then reached back to help Father up as well. As they disappeared inside, I peered after them. The single room was spare, a faded red carpet covering much of the floor, shelves bolted into the walls, holding clothes and pans, a mattress barely large enough for two in one corner and, next to it, another much smaller one where their boy lay inert. Father's fingers were already on the child's neck, checking his pulse, prying open his sleeping eyes to inspect. There was a small box fan mounted on the right wall, and it kept the air inside the container surprisingly cool. Zayd saw me and approached. He kneeled at the opening and asked if I wanted tea.

"I'm fine," I said in Punjabi. "But thank you."

He pulled his cigarettes and held them out to me. I took one and let him light it.

In the alleyway, I smoked as I waited. It was cleaner here, the sickening odor of human waste easier to ignore. Across the way, an old man with a thick henna-red beard squatted against a plywood wall, a hookah to his lips. I nodded a greeting, which he didn't acknowledge. Farther on, a trio of women leaned over a metal basin, washing clothes. From afar, I heard the children singing again, their motley chorus riding the breeze. Zayd appeared in the alleyway, lighting a cigarette as he joined me. His demeanor was different from the way it had been earlier — warm now, nervous, talky. He asked if what Naseem told him was true, that my father was a famous doctor in America.

I told him he was.

"Mashallah,"* he said. "Are you a doctor, too?"

"Oh, no," I said with a laugh that visibly perplexed him. "I'm a writer," I said, which only seemed to confuse him more. My Punjabi was iffy at best, indulged and gently mocked by my extended family, most of whom had good English of their own. And though I'd been in Pakistan now for three weeks, it was only in speaking to Zayd that I truly realized just how bad my Punjabi was. "Yes. He's a very famous heart doctor where we live in America. But he's a good

---

* Another common Muslim invocation, meaning: "As God has willed it."

doctor for everything; very good with children who are sick. He loves children."

"Mashallah," Zayd said again. "Osama always has luck on his side." Seeing my surprise, Zayd laughed. "My son, I mean. Not bin Laden Sahib." I noticed him watching for my reaction as he took another drag. Exhaling, he brought his hand to his chest to indicate himself: "I'm Zayd. The Messenger of God, peace be upon him, had a Zayd, too." He spoke now in a more formal, Urdu-inflected register, and his demeanor changed: "The Prophet's Zayd had a son — and his name was Osama. Hazrat Ali was one lion of God. Osama is the other. A baby lion," he said with a smile as he tapped away the ash at the end of his cigarette. Across from us, the old man was still squatting, lips affixed to his pipe as he watched us talk. The children's melody sounded closer now, as if they were approaching from the alley's other end. "It's a beautiful story. Can I tell you?"

"Of course."

"When Zayd's Osama was ten years old, he started praying. One day he asked the Prophet, peace be upon him, if he could join the men in battle. 'I am old enough to stand alongside you, the Prophet of God, in prayer, so why am I not old enough to join the war against the enemies of our Lord?' Can you believe it? He loved our Messenger, peace be upon him, loved him so much that he wanted to be by his side even in the fight. Of course, he was too young. So the Prophet, peace be upon him, said no. But every year Osama would ask, and every year the answer was no — until he turned seventeen. And then our great Messenger, peace be upon him, said yes! And what a great fighter Osama became! *So* good that he became the youngest general in the army. Can you believe it?"

I offered a quiet *mashallah* of my own in response, not knowing what else to say.

Just then, the gaggle of children raced past us — no longer singing now — chased and chasing, slamming the Mercedes with their palms and sticks as they passed, screeching with unbridled glee. Zayd shouted at them as they disappeared down the alley. Across the way, the old man smoked, watching.

As Zayd inspected his car, I burned with a question, mentally framing it in my meager Punjabi, searching for the proper measure of deference in my word choice to be sure I didn't give offense. By the time I'd settled on the form my question would take, he'd returned to his place alongside me, satisfied, it seemed, there were no new scratches.

"Do you hope your Osama, too, becomes a great fighter one day?" I asked. My worry had been needless; he was visibly pleased. And I couldn't have expected how uncomplicated his reply would be:

"If he can give his life to make the world a better place, *inshallah,* if he can live up to the name he has — what more blessing could a father ask for?"

SCRANTON MEMOIRS

IV.
GOD'S COUNTRY

A BLOWN GASKET

A decade ago, while driving back to Harlem from upstate New York — where I'd spent the weekend with my parents at the Finger Lakes resort they visited every few years, an excursion memorable not only because it was then my father announced I'd been conceived on the resort's second floor, in a room on the "lake" side (he couldn't remember any longer exactly which one), but also because it was the last time I would see my mother before she was diagnosed with the recurrence of the cancer that would eventually take her life — it was while driving back along I-81 that my Saab 900's exhaust started sending out white smoke, or so a Pennsylvania state trooper would inform me once he'd pulled me over to ask if my engine had overheated. That was when I first noticed that the needle of the car's temperature gauge was pointing in the

159

wrong direction. We popped open the hood to take a look inside, and foul-smelling steam nearly singed our faces. He laughed as he pulled out a handkerchief and wiped his cheeks and forehead; I wiped mine on my sleeve. The trooper's earlier approach to the car had put me at ease — his slow, deliberate movements; his measured, cheery tone intended, I'd thought, to announce he was just there to help — and his reaction now only reinforced the message.

He was bone-white, his features boyish, though there was something ancient about his vaulted cheekbones and the Tartar slant to his eyes. Polish or Serbian, I thought, though the last name on his tag betrayed no obvious ethnic origin: MATTHEW. As we stepped away from the car, he pointed ahead at an exit. We weren't far from Clarks Summit, he said, where there was a garage. He suspected that was where AAA would take me, though he had to admit he'd only ever heard bad things about the service there. "I know a garage in Scranton where I always go. It's a little farther, but they'll come get you with their own truck. I know the owner. They do great work. I'd be happy to call him for you."

It was a bright, mild day in late October. The surrounding hills were ablaze with autumn color. As Trooper Matthew and I waited for the tow truck, his cruiser between us and the traffic's noisy ebb and flow, he turned to me and asked — entirely benignly, I thought — where my name was from. I knew from experience that an honest answer to this not infrequent question could raise suspicions where there might otherwise have been none, my well-intentioned interlocutors suddenly beclouded by some reflexive evocation of terror. In the trying months after 9/11 — when the simple act of mounting the city bus and paying my fare had become a provocation, met with fearful, watching glares — I'd settled on a prophylactic strategy: "India," I would say. It was a lie. The name wasn't Indian. But I knew the question usually masked a curiosity about my origins, and as you already know, my parents were born in what was then India. This answer had the obvious advantage of connoting not the referents of terror, murder, and rage that most associated with Pakistan but rather the bright colors and spicy tastes of delightful dishes like tikka masala, gyrating flash mobs in Bollywood movies, and yoga pants. To complicate all this further, my name is actually Egyptian, and depending on the political moment — in the wake of attacks like those on tourists at Luxor and Sharm el Sheikh, or two years later, during the misleading months of the so-called Arab Spring — mentioning Egypt can become a prompt to more questions, each riddled with a particular pitfall that often leads to the very sort of mistrust I am ever keen to avoid in the first place. If all this sounds somewhat paranoid, I am happy for you. Clearly you have not been beset by daily worries of being perceived — and therefore treated — as a foe of the republic rather than a member of it.

Standing alongside Officer Matthew, surrounded by the painted hills, grateful for his charitable interest in my vehicle's proper repair, disarmed by gratitude, I opted for the complicated truth. "The name is Egyptian," I said.

"Really?"

"My parents aren't from Egypt, but when my father first came to this country, he had an Egyptian friend who had my name. He'd never heard it before and really liked it. So when I was born, he used it for me. Funny thing is, he doesn't say it right. Or at least not how he heard it said by his friend . . ."

"How are you supposed to say it?"

I joked my way through the various pronunciations of my name — the original Arabic, which sounded nothing like how my

162

parents said it and which was different still from the way my kindergarten teacher had coined the American pronunciation, which had stuck ever since.

"So why couldn't your parents say it right?"

"They don't speak Arabic."

"They're not Arabs?"

"Well, no, they're from Pakistan, so — actually, they were born in India. But that's a long story."

"And you all moved here from Pakistan when you were in kindergarten?"

"I was born here."

He paused for a moment, picking lint off the stiff felt dome of his wide-brimmed trooper hat. From somewhere upwind of us, the sweet smell of burning apple wood was pouring into the air. "So where were you born?" he asked, suddenly tentative.

It was clear I'd made a mistake.

"Wisconsin," I said. It was another lie. Though I spent almost the entirety of my childhood and adolescence in Wisconsin, I was born on Staten Island. "Wisconsin," though, felt like a stronger move in this negotiation around the impression forming inside him.

"Never been," he said. "I just read this book, *The Looming Tower.* You heard of it?"

163

"It won the Pulitzer last year, didn't it?"

"It's pretty incredible."

"I know the writer. Lawrence Wright. Great guy."

I'd recently met Lawrence — or Larry, as he'd introduced himself — at a reading of a play he'd written about the Italian journalist Oriana Fallaci. We'd spoken afterward, an encounter I doubt he would recall and during which I would wonder if, in fact, his sympathies with Fallaci's troubling views on Islam were deeper than he was letting on in the play he'd written. In short, I was misrepresenting both my affection for — and proximity to — this famous writer in an obvious attempt to signal status and amiability, to get Trooper Matthew off whatever suspicions I worried he was now harboring.

He continued: "You know, I never knew that the guy who ran the whole crew of hijackers was from Egypt. For some reason, I thought they were all from Iraq. I thought that's why we went to Iraq. See, but the truth is, none of them was Iraqi. Not a one. They were mostly from Saudi. And Atta, Mohammed Atta, the guy in charge, he was from Egypt. Cairo, actually." So quickly had we arrived, via my father's best friend, on the subject of Atta. "My grandfather was stationed in Cairo during the world war. We

had a picture of him in front of the pyra-
mids. I used to dream about visiting when I
grew up, standing there where Grandpa did.
I had no idea the kind of hate they've got
for us." I bit my lip — literally — and nodded, hoping my silence would appear respectful. "I gotta say, for guys who're pure
evil," Trooper Matthew added, "the book
almost made me understand them. Don't
get me wrong. It's not like I felt for them or
anything like that. I mean, they're monsters.
But . . . you know, when you see what happens in their countries, and how messed up
everything is for them, how hard it is for
folks who live there, well, you start to get
how they're seeing the world. You can
understand how they start thinking Disneyland's really the problem with everything."

"Disneyland?"

"Yeah. Atta. He hated Disneyland.
Thought America was turning the world
into a theme park." Moments earlier, I
hadn't known better than to speak; now I
was certain silence was necessary. He was
fishing, his tone no longer declarative but
slipping — at the ends of phrases — into
the ostensible friendliness of the interrogative. "I mean, you can almost understand a
guy like that. You know what I mean?"

"You think? I don't know."

"*I* do. I really do." He paused again and glanced at me — I thought — with a look that drew out more distinctly the tapering almond shape of his eyes. "D'you know that when he returned his rental car on September ninth, he called the rental agency to tell them the oil light was on? Can you believe that? He didn't care about the three thousand people they killed, but he cared about the next person driving the car. You believe that? I wouldn't if I saw it in a movie."

"The book sounds amazing," I said after a short pause.

"Right," he said distantly. "I should probably get on the horn. Make sure those guys are on their way." The hat found his head again as he walked back to the driver's side to make his call.

He was still on the phone — running a check on me, I assumed — when the flatbed truck from Marek Auto Repair pulled up. The tow driver was a short, stocky man in denim overalls whose face was covered with blistering acne. He huddled over the engine to inspect. "Yep," he said. "Busted head gasket."

"You guys can fix that, right?"

"Shouldn't be a problem."

I looked over at the cruiser, where Trooper

Matthew's face was lowered, phone still to his ear.

The tow driver backed up the truck and lowered the flatbed. Once the cables were attached, the truck's squealing winch pulled my car up into place. It wasn't until the car was mounted and level — and until we'd gotten into the cab and were readying to go — that Trooper Matthew finally emerged and made his way to the tow truck's driver's-side window. He and the driver spoke about someone they both knew; I could tell he was ignoring me. I looked forward and did the same. As their conversation came to an end, the trooper put his hand on the door frame and leaned in:

"Staten Island, right?"

It took me a moment to realize he was addressing me. "What's that?"

"Staten Island, that's where you were born, not Wisconsin. Isn't that right?" He was staring at me now, his blank look less a provocation than an acknowledgment of betrayal — whether his or mine, I couldn't tell. What to say? How to explain that I'd been worried he had the wrong idea about me and I lied to let him know I was not the enemy he worried I might be? Was there really no way to convey this simple truth through the thicket of mistrust that had so

167

quickly grown between us? If there was I didn't see it. So I lied again.

"Oh, no. That's wrong. It's a long story."

My response didn't seem to surprise him: "You know you can always get that taken care of. All you have to do is take your birth certificate in."

"Was never a problem for me before, sir. But thank you."

I heard my combative tone; I hadn't intended it. He looked away, his tongue lodged against the inside of his cheek, fighting — I thought — the urge to allow, even encourage, an escalation. "Okay," he said finally, patting the door frame with his palm. "Hope everything works out with the car. Have a good day."

It was a Sunday. Though the tow service was running, the repair shop was closed. The driver told me someone would look at it in the morning and call with an estimate. If it was just the gasket, it would be fixed by Monday afternoon — assuming, of course, I hadn't driven the car for very long with a blown gasket. "Because if not, and if you've been letting the fuel mix in with the coolant or the oil for any length of time" — he paused and studied me, as if trying to divine whether I was the sort of person who might do a thing that stupid — "well, in that case, all bets'd be off."

The shop was in North Scranton, too far from the downtown hotel where the tow driver suggested I might want to get a room. I called a taxi. The route into the center of town took me through an outlying region of industrial lots, empty warehouses, acres of bare fenced-in asphalt; past curbs crumbling into the streets and roadside grass left to grow to knee height. The roads themselves were worn, pitted with holes, the fading yellow lanes and crosswalks barely insinuated by the disappearing paint. Signs of municipal neglect were everywhere, and an unusually abundant profusion of utility poles and sagging black lines defined all manner of helter-skelter perspectives through which to see the widespread disrepair. We drove past a series of impossibly long buildings, three tall stories of brick covered with rows and rows of broken windows. The cabbie noticed my interest and explained what I was looking at was once the great Scranton Lace Company. He was an older man with a pear-shaped face, thick along the bottom. He wore a faded cabbie cap, and the name on the taxi tag affixed to the back of his headrest read: MARK. "See, we didn't live too far from here when I was growing up," he said, sliding open the plastic window on the barrier between us so he could be heard better. "There was lots of Italians in these parts, on the other side of the river we just passed."

"You're Italian?"

"My grandparents all came over from the old country." He slowed and pointed at a street to our right: "When I was a kid, we'd ride our bikes over this way. You'd hit this road, and it was so busy back then. Like its own city over here. Three shifts going in and out every day 'cept Sunday. Hundred times as much traffic as there is now. That factory was running twenty-four hours, six days a week, making tablecloths, curtains, napkins, anything with lace. They had a bowling alley in there, if you can believe it."

"Really?"

"Oh, yeah. Sure. My uncle Jimmy had a girl he was seeing who worked there. One time she snuck me and my cousin in, and we went bowling! Four lanes, if you can believe it! I remember those long looms, the rollers turning. Ladies spinning, twisting yarn, their fingers moving on those machines like they were playing the piano. They didn't just make lace there. In the war, they made parachutes, tarps for the troops. That was before my time. I don't know how many people they had working in there. Must have been ten thousand. I mean, look how big it is. In the morning, they'd pour out into the bars along this way here." He was pointing at a row of boarded-up two-story buildings on his left. "One shift's drinking Jameson, the new one's finishing their eggs and bacon on their way in to start the day. Hard to imagine it, with everything looking so dead around here now. But trust me, it wasn't always like this, if you can believe it."

"How long ago was this?"

"You know — sixties, seventies."

With what was left of Scranton Lace behind us, we turned onto a road lined with businesses — a deli, a copy shop, a storefront fitness center — still solvent, though perhaps not by much. "Don't get me wrong. It's not like it was all some walk in the park back then. You know, being Italian in these parts wasn't easy. Wasn't easy anywhere, but especially not here. Germans, Scotch-Irish — they hated us. Called us cockroaches. When you think about it, weird thing is we were here before a lot of them even showed up. Working the mills, mines, but see, we didn't know how to get ahead. It wasn't our system. Unions, city councils, whatnot. All we knew about getting our needs taken care of was Cosa Nostra. For some folks, that was enough."

"Mafia strong around here?"

"Not anymore. But when I was growing up? For sure."

We turned again and drove past columned multistory homes from the early part of the last century. They were falling apart. "A made guy. That was a thing to want to be. With stacks of cash like stones in their pockets. I mean, I knew my share of them, 'cause my dad helped run the literary society over on Prospect."

"Literary society?"

"Dante Literary Society. It was a social club. I mean, it's still over there, but it's pretty dead now, like everything else around here. They started it in the Depression to help teach folks from the old country how to speak English, though by the time I was a kid it was mostly about teaching kids like us Italian. That and ballroom dancing, if you can believe it. Made guys hung out there pretty regularly. There was a room in back where they, you know — *played cards.*" His eyes — meeting mine in the rearview mirror — narrowed with a knowing smile. "Don't get me wrong; I thought about it. I had a moment when I thought that might be the life for me — nice suits, pretty girls. But it didn't take me long to figure out I wasn't cut out for that."

As we entered the downtown, further neglected splendors from the nineteenth century dotted the blocks, old Greek or Romanesque revival mansions, intermittent reminders of an era of great wealth long passed, crowded by the thoughtless array of the town's newer construction, the ad hoc styles and worn facades adorned with signs advertising empty space for rent. Mark pointed out the sturdy, unostentatious granite blocks and arches of the university; the dappled, rough-cut stone of the county courthouse; the creamy limestone of a building he called "the Electric." For a moment, here, in the center of town, against a garish late-afternoon sky that could have been colored by Hockney — heaps of silver-pink cloudy fluff against a cornflower blue — Scranton suddenly felt every bit the painted backdrop for the modern sitcom *The Office,* which was my only previous association with it.

"Here you go," Mark said as he pulled to a stop under the hotel awning. The fare was just under seven dollars. I fumbled through the bills in my wallet and handed him a ten. He put it in his mouth as he pulled a thick wad of singles from his shirt's breast pocket to make change.

"It's fine," I said. "Keep it."

He looked startled, his jaw slack with what I took for a disproportionate surprise. He thinks I have money, I thought as he thanked me with a deferential, distant nod.

MARY'S LATTICE, OR NIGHTWORK

Up in my room, I spent two hours on my daily writing practice of making detailed notes about the day, then I went out to Thai for dinner. The restaurant was the only occupied storefront on the block, and its luxuriant stone-and-bamboo interior belied the squalor outside. Through the window, I saw a cop standing over a homeless man across the street, trying to wake him. It turned out the man was actually dead. As I walked home after dinner, two EMT workers were loading the shrouded body into an ambulance emblazoned with the image of a crucifix on a mountain.

Back at the hotel, I made more notes as I watched the Patriots demolish the Redskins, then I went to bed. For many years — and still back then, but no longer — I used to sleep most nights with a notepad within easy reach on the bedside table and a tiny pencil tied to my index finger. It was a technique I'd learned from Mary Moroni, an aid to recalling my dreams, the presence of the pencil against my finger a sensate reminder — in those dimmest moments of faint arousal after a dream — not to fall back asleep but to reach for the bedside pad and make note of whatever I could recall. Mary had learned the trick from a follower of Lacan's Parisian seminars, a woman she'd studied with in the early '80s during a semester abroad at the Sorbonne. It was apparently a trick Lacan himself had used. Noting her dreams — Mary told me as we brought to a close an afternoon of prosodic analysis of *Leaves of Grass* — had helped her begin making sense of the unconscious, though using that term, she said, she believed was problematic: "I know it must sound silly to hear me say that sitting under the collected works of Freud." She glanced back at the block of beige volumes lined up in a lower corner of the mammoth bookshelf towering behind her. "Anyway, that's what Jenny" — Jenny was her girlfriend — "always says to me: 'If you hate Freud, why do you spend so much time reading him?' "

"Why do you?" I asked.

"I don't hate him, for starters. Do I think he was wrong about a lot of things? Yes. Women, especially, though not only. And what he was wrong about he was *really* wrong about. Was he power-hungry? Yes.

Was he a misogynist, a drug addict? Yes, and probably. But none of that changes the fact that he was a genius."

"Should I read him, too?"

"Absolutely." She turned in her chair and pulled out one of the beige volumes. "They'll probably be worth more when I die if I keep the dust jacket in good shape," she said as she slipped it off. "Like I said, it's not that everything he says is right. But he was the first one through the door. And despite his failings, he still went deeper than most ever will." She handed me the naked book across her desk: VOLUME IV (1900) *THE INTERPRETATION OF DREAMS.*

"I used to dream a lot as a kid," I said. "Intense stuff. But then it stopped. I haven't had a dream in years."

"You're still dreaming. You're just not remembering them."

That's when she showed me the trick with the pencil.

She suggested a short one, so that night, I snapped a new Dixon Ticonderoga number 2 in half and sharpened the jagged end before affixing it to my index finger with Scotch tape. It looked like the silliest of makeshift splints. (Luckily, my roommate at the time spent most nights with his girl-friend.) But Mary was right. Three times that first night, I woke with images in my head, the pencil proving enough of a prod to reach for the pad and start writing. As I scribbled in the dark — the scrawl would be hard to read the next morning, but it didn't matter; simply having written the dreams out had somehow fixed them in my mind — a spool of dream pictures poured forth, one recollected bit leading to another, then to a forgotten chunk, then to another dream I hadn't recalled even having until I was already in the process of noting it. It felt like there was more space inside me, I remarked to Mary the following week, more space than I ever realized.

Her smile seemed to say she knew exactly what I meant.

For the next month, our weekly study hour would be mostly taken up with talk about the unconscious. The reason she didn't like that word, she explained, was because it mystified rather than evoked. One had a sense of a thing that resisted meaning or formulation, something that wished to remain obscure, something often defined by Freud for his own purposes. She thought none of this productive. And while she wasn't advocating for any single way to reconceive the great Viennese thinker's concept, she had her preferred metaphors.

One was the dictionary. The latest edition of the OED — which had come out three years earlier, in 1989 — had 290,000 entries in it. Most people didn't know more than twenty thousand, she said. To know half that was to be considered fluent. Fluency was like the conscious mind, the array of possibilities contained in the words you knew. The unconscious, she suggested, was like the mass of words you didn't. Those unknown words and meanings — rhizomes of sound, radicles of signification — were like a body of forgotten roots still drawing sustenance from the dead matter of the lost languages buried in the living one we heard and spoke and wrote. She liked the metaphor of a dictionary, for it implied a task, that of learning the language richly and deeply — though what she didn't like about it was connected to this as well, the implication of something fixed, something that began and ended, that could be contained in a book you could hold in your hands. Her recent readings in mathematics had given her what she thought was an even richer way to reimagine the Freudian unconscious, she explained over coffee at the student union, where we'd ended up after one of our sessions in her office. She pulled a thick textbook from her bag and opened it to a page showing various diagonal and bulbous graphs; each diagram was labeled some form of mathematical "lattice." In these plots of interrelated lines, she spied visual corollaries of the human nervous system, the filigreed mesh of our perceptive apparatus. Each lattice graph emanated from and returned to a single point, which she likened to the prefrontal cortex — the seat of our conscious personality — which, she said, was informed by everything that teemed along the body's vast neural network but which barely registered most of it. "As an artist," she said, addressing me now as an aspiring writer, "the more you can dwell along the weave, feel the lattice at work, the closer you'll be to the vital, vivid stuff."

In noting my dreams those first few weeks, I was already making my own sense of what she might have meant by this, recognizing the way just remembering whose voice had last spoken in my head before I awoke could lead me back not only into the body of a dream but also, as I wrote it out, to the pieces and patches of the past — the threads of memory — from which it had been woven: a voice would lead to the insinuation of a room; recalling the room to the memory of a copper-colored rail alongside a hospital bed; to the nurse who tended to me for a month when I was sick with typhoid at the age of two; to a plate of ravioli tossed, at three, into a trash can when my mother went to answer the front door; to what were likely the first stirrings of my sexual desire at four, awakened by my aunt Khadija, an almost dead ringer for my mother, her sister — Freud was right! — sitting in a sunlit square as she read in our family room in Milwaukee.

The vivid stuff onto which I was stumbling was certainly vital, but only to me, I reported back to Mary. Who else would care about any of it? And if no one else cared, why should I? To what purpose all this self-absorption?

Mary responded as if she expected the skepticism. For the next few weeks, our literary hour would be filled with neurophilosophical speculation. Analysis of the Whitman phrase and Freudian code gave way to talk of Wittgenstein's language games and the phenomenology of perception à la Merleau-Ponty. The body's form and function shaped the mind's possibilities and ordered our grammar; our thinking could not be divorced from the bodies in which it took place. Dreams, she said, had been her best way into that simpler, more primal perception of being. What she saw and felt from that perspective felt more vivid, yes, and ended up being more enduring. I defied Mary to defend her assignment with facts — and statistics! I was a scientist's son, desperate, at the very least, for reasoned arguments to justify all this navel-gazing. She asked if the visionaries we'd studied — Whitman and Woolf, Black Elk — ever bothered to rationalize their surrender to the deeper currents of human experience. No, I said. They didn't seem to care in the least. "Then why do you?!" What a question to pose to a twenty-year-old!

I kept at it. I soon discovered that if I moved too much after I woke up, any memory of my dreams would vanish. Then it wouldn't matter if I picked up my pad, because there would be nothing to note. I told Mary this was happening, and she suggested that it was only the angle of my spine that mattered. If I didn't move my spine, she said, I wouldn't lose the dream. Then she added that even if I did end up changing the spinal angle, all I had to do was find it again. The dream would return. I didn't believe her.

"Just try it," she said. "See if it works."

Sometime around sunrise the next morning, I woke up, my head swirling with images. I rolled over to pick up my notebook.

All at once, the pictures were gone. I remembered what Mary told me to do. Rolling back to where I'd been, I restored the angle of my resting spine, and just as suddenly, thoughts and pictures and feelings flowed into me unbidden. The dreamscape was alive again. All of it. I reached for the pad and started to write.

The next week, when I told Mary her suggestion worked, she seemed amused by my incredulity. Then she went on to explain that, if what she believed was true — if, in some substantial way, a dream was actually the experience of language in the body — then the spine, or central axis of our neurologic lattice, was likely where much of our dreaming took place, a cognitive sap running from the roots of the body up into the branches of the brain. I didn't question her proposition or the metaphor she was using to paint it. The technique of retrieving a dream by re-creating the angle of my spine was proof enough to me that what she knew was real, whatever the reason.

I would stick with this form of nightwork for the quarter century to come. In time, I would come to concur with Mary's thoughts about language in the body, and I would spend years and days making my own sense of just how such a language could be apprehended. Like Mary, I would closely study Freud's early attempts to decode dreams — attempts glossed and argued over by the entire psychoanalytic tradition to follow — and marvel that his techniques still yielded worthy, enduring insights. I'm not prepared to make any grand claims here, though I will say this: living by the nocturnal glow of my dream life has proved rich, beguiling, instructive; it has given me ample occasion to question the nature of time, riddled as my dreams have been through the years with prognosticating encounters and apprehensions; but even these hints of the uncanny have not made up the most miraculous bounty of all this interrupted sleep. My dreams have taught me much about myself. I'm not sure I could sum up either the benefit or the challenge any better than Montaigne does in "Of Experience":

I take it for true that dreams are honest reflections of our inclinations; but there is art to making sense of them.

That night in Scranton, I dreamed about an upcoming wedding. My father and I were arguing over the invitations. He wanted to use postage stamps that bore the images of

183

various Christian saints. It made me angry. Then I was in the midst of a group of pilgrims on a stormy night. We made our way slowly along a narrow path on a steep hill. Many of us were clutching staffs to brace ourselves against the gusting wind. A few of the staffs had crossbars attached, but they were askew, not forming proper crucifixes. At the top of the hill, there was a grave, but everyone was surprised to see it was just an empty hole. The dead man had decided not to show. Someone complained this is what the dead often did in Kashmir. I awoke to a feeling of failure and threat.

At a coffee shop the next morning, I ordered a cup of tea and a Danish and sat down to work through the night's dream notes. In the decade and a half since Mary's assignment, I'd logged, annotated, and interpreted literally thousands of my dreams. The process I went through to make sense of them — as Montaigne puts it — still bore the influence of Mary and Freud. As Mary taught me to do with a poem, I started with the structure, then I worked through each of a dream's salient details by free association. With the dream I'd had the previous night, the structure wasn't obvious to me: a pairing of episodes without a clear thread to connect them — first the argument with my father about the wedding, then a procession up a hill path that led to an empty grave. No clear thread, I thought, though the sense of futility and failure I'd felt on waking — which lingered an hour into the morning — unified my experience of both parts. Perhaps working through the details, I thought, would prove more fruitful: the wedding seemed an obvious reference to one upcoming in my family. My parents had, themselves, been arguing about it just that weekend at Seneca Lake. My mother's older brother — my uncle Shafat — was remarrying. His first wife — Bilqis, a Pakistani — had discovered he was having an affair with a white American woman and left him. Now Shafat was marrying the mistress. Mother was disgusted by the whole thing and couldn't believe my father wanted to attend the ceremony; Father, for his part, thought my mother's reaction childish. Shafat and Bilqis had never been happy together. What was the problem? Wasn't it better for them to separate, especially now that one of them had found someone to be happy with? By invoking my father's support for Shafat's wedding and casting me in my mother's role in their argument, the dream seemed to be alerting me to some sympathy I shared with my mother on the matter that I was unaware of.

Then: the hill and narrow path. Something about the path reminded me of pictures I'd seen of the Great Wall of China. As I noted this, I suddenly remembered — as if the simple act of writing summoned the memory — a hill in the Punjabi village where my father grew up, at the top of which stood the small mosque that my grandfather led when he was still alive. Was this the holy ground toward which we pilgrims were making our way? At the summit was an empty grave. I'd seen a dead body loaded onto an ambulance just the night before, an ambulance painted with the image of another holy hill, Calvary. The dream's makeshift crucifixes and the empty grave suddenly seemed to cohere, summoning the tale of the abandoned tomb of Christ.

As I scribbled, I remembered something else: my father always said he wanted to be buried back in his village when he died. But Father's village was in Punjab, not in Kashmir, as this grave was in the dream. I lingered for a while on the mention of Kashmir, the dream's closing detail. I wrote around it. About how little we had talked of Kashmir in my Punjabi home, aside from the usual Indo-Pak chatter about the rightful owners of that disputed land, whether Pakistan or India, and how devious had been the British strategy to leave the matter unresolved, a site of perpetual conflict at the heart of their sometime colony. I wrote about the odd pink Kashmiri chai — served with salt, not sugar — that my father sometimes prepared when guests called. Neither association yielded any insight. I persisted, freely associating to the place, the word, the name, its constitutive phonemes. It wasn't until I gave up, closed and stowed my notebook, and was sitting on a toilet seat reading latrinalia on the stall door that I recalled: Shafat — my remarrying uncle — had come to America after a stint in the Pakistani army. His sister, my mother, sponsored his green card. I remembered her worries about how long the process seemed to be taking, which especially concerned her given that there was new trouble brewing with India and that Shafat was then stationed where the fighting was likely — in Kashmir. All at once, the dream's deeper structural logic was clear to me: it began with a hidden reference to Shafat, and it ended with one, too!

Shafat's complicated saga in this country deserves a treatment all its own, but here's the piece of it I must share now to convey why, as I sat on that toilet in a Scranton coffee-shop bathroom, my dream made sudden poignant sense to me: three years after 9/11, Shafat, a handsome, fair-skinned Pakistani man of above-average height, with a head of wavy hair he doused with tonic and combed flat against his skull; a military man by disposition and an engineer by training who was then working for a construction-crane manufacturing outfit in northern Virginia, where he was liked and his work was valued (as evidenced by the fast track of his multiple promotions and his $200,000-a-year salary); an amateur handyman who watched *This Old House* and spent whole weekends fixing up his two-story saltbox colonial; a reader of the classics who'd gone to the finest boarding school a lower-middle-class family in Pakistan could have afforded, where he'd read Baltasar Gracián's *The Art of Worldly Wisdom,* whose timeless and canny moral guidance he claimed to live by; a champion bowler on his school cricket team; a father to three sons who loved him enough not to abandon him after he married his mistress, despite the anguish this would cause their equally beloved mother; this Shafat, a criminal to his wife, perhaps, but in no way to the state, would end up in a Norfolk,

Virginia, jail one night, where he was beaten purple by a fellow inmate egged on, he alleged, by two cops who sat and watched as they drank beers. Earlier that night, after a beer of his own, Shafat had made the mistake of talking politics at a local bar where he liked to go, not far from the naval base. Perhaps it was his own army background that made him feel more at ease in this military town than he ever should have allowed himself to feel. I certainly doubt he'd had only one beer, as he's always claimed, and I can't help but wonder what Gracián would have made of his decision to share a tale about being assigned to a detail that picked up a covert American shipment at an airfield in Quetta in the late 1980s: two crates of new, mint-crisp $100 bills he said they'd been ordered to deliver to US allies in Afghanistan. They drove the crates to the border, where they were met by the man who would later be known to the world as the evil one-eyed Taliban cleric Mullah Omar but who, back then, was just another member of the mujahideen fighters battling the Soviet enemy. Omar had already lost his eye to a piece of shrapnel, which, legend had it, he cut out of its socket with his own knife. After the victory over the Soviets, Omar returned home to Kandahar and rose to prominence as an opponent of the corrupt warlords now in charge of much of the country. Omar was particularly incensed by the pedophilia widespread among the tribal elites. He and his vigilantes staged a series of guerrilla campaigns, freeing children kidnapped and held as sex slaves by various militia leaders, and word of these righteous exploits sent his popularity soaring. Such was the beginning of the movement that would come to be known as the Taliban. Or so Shafat explained to the bargoers around him, adding that, as much as we hated the Taliban in this country — and we had good reason; he wasn't denying that — we might do well to remember that those same people had once been on our payroll. They weren't always the monsters folks now made them out to be.

Or something to that effect.

What was he thinking? Is it really surprising that, just as he exited the premises, two officers greeted him in the parking lot with the news that someone had called to report he was making threats against America? It may not be obvious from this tale, but Shafat is not a stupid man, so I find it difficult to account for the infelicitous response he gave to this admittedly absurd question: "If, Officer, you consider a basic history lesson a threat against America . . ." — which was all those cops needed to hear to hurl him to the ground, put a boot to his face, and twist his left arm so far behind his back that he's since had to have the glenohumeral joint in his left shoulder replaced. Cuffed, taken in, thrown into a jail cell with a veteran who'd gone off his antipsychotics, Shafat had only just begun his journey into pain that night. For when that veteran heard the officers referring to Shafat as a member of the American Taliban, he started whaling on Shafat's face. As he cowered in the corner of the cell, being kicked and punched, Shafat spied the officers popping open their cans of Coors Light and settling into their chairs. The troubled vet ended up breaking two of Shafat's ribs and landed him in the hospital with internal bleeding. For a time, it looked like Shafat would be charged — not only with drunk and disorderly conduct and resisting arrest but also with the attempted assault of a police officer. All the charges were dropped when it became clear that Shafat wouldn't be filing a complaint.

Shafat's eventual divorce and remarriage are, I believe, inextricably linked to what happened that night. For it wasn't long after that when he began his unlikely affair with a churchgoing Virginian woman named

Christine. There'd been rumors he was going to church with her on Sundays and was thinking of converting to Christianity, rumors that would later be confirmed by the official change of his name to Luke. At that point, he and my mother were no longer speaking, but one of his sons would confide to me that "Luke" had tried to get him to convert as well and that one of his arguments for conversion — to his own son — was that he, "Luke," finally felt safe in this country because he finally felt like he belonged. Much of this I learned long after the dream I had that night in Scranton — the marriage was still pending; the conversion and name change still not official — but the underlying conditions shaping my uncle's life were part of a social logic that long predated it and that shaped my life, too. I believe my run-in with Trooper Matthew the previous afternoon activated the pertinent semantic nodes along my own associative lattice, to borrow Mary's metaphor again, yielding a dream that drew on the abuse of my uncle as an echo of my own bodily fears of the law in a post-9/11 America. But the dream was more than just an echo. For in it, I saw suddenly revealed a wider perspective on the failure and threat of our lives as Muslims here in America, a failure and threat my uncle Shafat would eventually believe he could solve by adopting the Christian faith. You see, we — Muslims — lived in a Christian land. That's how we saw it, at least in the families I knew. We lived in a Christian land, but we didn't understand Christianity. We didn't understand it; we didn't respect it. We thought it a makeshift, misbegotten offspring of the Judaic creed, an aggrandized misinterpretation founded on an ontological absurdity: that God would need a son, and that that son — supposedly divine — could perish in the flesh at human hands. All this and its attendant obfuscations — the Holy Trinity, the Immaculate Conception, the shell game of transubstantiation — we took for silliness. But here was the paradox: in order to flourish in this new land, we had to adopt its Christian ways, ways that befuddled us and that we disdained, ways we saw reflected in almost every aspect of American life. It might be hard for a non-Muslim American — an agnostic or atheist, or a secular humanist — to understand the perspective I'm describing, in which a sole signifier ("Christian") is used to stand in for the totality of American life. For indeed, where some might see modernity or individualism or mercantile democracy or the heritage of the Enlightenment or an irreducibly complex and endlessly heterogeneous nation, we saw Christianity. To us, it was all Christian. Not just the churches and their ice cream socials and Friday fish fries; or the bacon at breakfast; or the wine with wafers on Sundays and with everything else all week long. Not just the place names and first names drawn from the Gospels and the roll of Catholic saints; or the painted eggs in April and pine wreaths and winter sleds in December. No, I mean also the department-store sales in January and the interest-charging credit cards used at them; and the vacations spent at the beach driven by the bizarre urge to darken one's skin; and the shrill perfect fifths of a violin; and the notion that running a piece of toilet paper along your anus is enough to keep you clean; and the discomfort of working with a blade of cloth tied to your neck so tightly you can barely breathe; and the bikinis and knee-high skirts; and, of course, the needlessly happy ending to every story. I don't think we were exactly wrong to see things as we did. After all, it was even in the language we spoke here, its plain, unadorned beauty, its range of short, percussive verbs, its oracular strength, a language of the sermon and of world making, in tone and lexicon not just borrowed from the King James Bible but also shot through and through — even today — with the simple, active robustness of the Anglo-Saxon Christian Lord. And yes, the founding fathers had sued for religious freedom, a value much vaunted and advertised — which should have put us at ease — but of course we would learn (at school, at citizenship training) that those white-wigged Protestant fathers had mostly been making room in a new republic for competing factions of their various protesting Christian persuasions. Even the Enlightenment itself, the alleged origin of this national experiment, even this could not be divorced from the European Christian culture to which it was a response. And the secular humanism that resulted? The evolved-to-some, mutated-to-others fruit picked from long-tended orchards of Christian learning. In my dream, I saw an encapsulating mise-en-scène of our kind's failure to understand — let alone flourish in — this Christian land, an unwilling participation in its symbols, its rituals, and, as ever, our resulting disappointment. And though Father was depicted in my dream's first part as open to the Christian experiment — supportive of the mixed marriage, if you will, happy to see it "stamped" with the faces of the Christian saints — I was angered by his willingness to play along. Like my mother, I was resistant. Then: we make our way along a hilltop path, gripping poorly built crosses, our ragtag pilgrimage ending on high ground bearing the trace of my father's father's Islam but where, now, there's a Christian miracle we don't understand. The empty grave is no proof to us of new life, only a reason to complain that one of ours has been lost to us. Like my uncle Shafat, the dead man has forgotten his native land.

The dream appeared to sum up a dilemma not only of my childhood but also of my life even as I sat scribbling in that coffee shop in Scranton, no longer a practicing — let alone *believing* — Muslim and yet still entirely shaped by the Islam that had socially defined me since 9/11. But putting it like this only points to the partial truth. In my dream I saw a more integral one: that as much as I worried about my place in America as a Muslim — and, yes, I had good reason to; all American Muslims did; that terrible day in September foreclosed our futures in this country for at least another generation — as much as it bothered me, as much as I felt a victim of what this nation had become for us, I, too, had participated

196

in my own exclusion, willingly, still choosing, half a lifetime into my American life, to see myself as other. I'd woken that morning into a lingering mood of failure that mirrored a sense of defeat I never didn't feel, however subtly, and once I unlocked the connection between my uncle Shafat's saga and the dream's final mention of Kashmir — another land divided and at war with itself — this frame of failure made mournful sense. Wasn't it the inheritance of my own unwillingness to find my place, my spiritual defiance repaid in rejection, in the rootless, haunted sense of having foundered in my life as an American? I don't think it was just self-pity that caused me to shed a tear on that coffee-shop toilet seat. I was finally face-to-face with the deepest dimension not only of my own American dilemma but also that of all my kind.

LARCENY

The repair shop called with an estimate. Replacing the gasket would cost $900. I didn't have the money, but I had a card with just enough left on the credit line to cover it. For at least a half decade, I'd been transferring balances, applying for new lines of credit, cashing low-interest-loan checks I got in the mail to pay off higher-interest balances. I had a calendar on which all the payment due dates were listed, as some of the cards I carried didn't offer an auto-pay function. Missing a single payment could mean an interest rate of 25 percent, which, on a balance of $10,000, meant another $200 a month of accumulating debt. In total, the debt I was carrying at that point was close to $50,000.

I showed up at Marek Auto Repair in the late afternoon. A tall, skinny man in a tie with thin eyes and thinning hair — in his mid-fifties, I would have guessed — stood in the driveway, a cigar between his lips. He was staring at the trio of young white women in pajamas across the street, languidly pushing strollers along before them. "Fucking drug addicts," he murmured as I approached. "Neighborhood's crawling with them, like cockroaches." He pulled the cigar out. "Can I help you?"

"I'm here to pick up the Saab 900?"

"Head gasket. Right. You're the one my nephew called about. They're finishing up."

"Your nephew?"

"The state trooper who found you on the side of the road?"

"Right, of course. Sorry, I didn't know that."

That he'd had to explain this to me — I

could tell — irked him. So had my apology. His reaction, in turn, irritated me. With a last angry look at the young women across the street, he shoved the cigar back into the corner of his mouth. "I'm John, the owner," he said through his teeth. "I hear you're from Egypt," he said as he walked me up the driveway now toward the offices. I was perplexed. If anything had been made clear in my conversation with his nephew, it was that I *wasn't* Egyptian.

"No, I'm not. I'm from Milwaukee. Though my parents are from India."

"That right?"

"The name's Egyptian. But I've actually never been there in my life. And neither have my folks."

"So you're a mutt," he said with a snigger, "like the rest of us." Inside, the woman behind the reception desk — she looked Latina — was busy on the phone; John pointed at an open folder under her elbow. She moved, leaning to make room for him to reach in. "Got it," he said, catching me notice his stolen glance at her cleavage.

He led me back to his desk in a small office whose walls were almost entirely covered: ribbons from high school competitions; team pennants; newspaper clippings; a Biden '08 poster; a centerfold of a woman's sex, glistening labia parted, vagina exposed; and finally, a large reproduction of the World Trade Center as it had appeared from the ferry coming into the port before its destruction. At the heart of the still-standing towers, another image had been affixed, a portrait of a man with a narrow face and slim, slanted eyes. Floating above this picture was a crucifix, and, in the spot where Pilate's nailed notice INRI usually figured, the words NEVER FORGET floated in a yellow banner.

"So the gasket blew. We're lucky — we've got a great parts store around the corner. They had the part for the 900 engine, which isn't always the case. Sometimes a model like that can take a while. But anyway, good news is the engine didn't need rebuilding. Bad news is the coolant got into the catalytic converter. We had to replace that, too." He placed the bill before me. The price at the bottom read $2,500.

My heart was suddenly racing.

"The estimate was for nine hundred dollars. Nobody called me about a catalytic converter."

"No, we called. We must have called you."

"I'm sorry — uh, John. I got a call this morning about a blown gasket and that it would cost me nine hundred dollars."

"Do you remember who called you?"

"It was a man. I don't remember his name."

"I spoke to Jasmine about this. About following up to let you know."

"Well, she didn't. And if she had, I would have told her: Don't do the repair. I don't have twenty-five hundred dollars."

"We'll get to the bottom of this," he said as he turned to the door and shouted: "Jasmine! Jasmine!"

"Well, the bottom of this is that I don't have the money to pay you for this repair. So maybe just put the old converter back in, and —"

"Oh, we're not doing that. You're not driving that baby out of here without a new converter. It's not even legal with the emissions that'll be putting out."

"It's not due for inspection, so I don't think that's an issue —"

"Doesn't matter. That's not how we do things around here," he said smugly.

"Yes, Mr. Marek?" The woman from the front desk was standing in the doorway now, one arm akimbo, the other leaned on the jamb. She was wearing a yellow miniskirt and white high-heeled clogs.

"Jasmine, did we call this gentleman about his catalytic converter? You remember we talked about it just before lunchtime. We were supposed to call him back with the new estimate." Hearing this, she let out a squeal, her hand finding her open mouth, her eyes suddenly wide with what looked to me like phony shame.

"Oh, no . . . I'm so sorry, Mr. Marek, I forgot," she pleaded.

"Jasmine," he said firmly.

"So many things happening at lunchtime, Mr. Marek. We have that delivery and Martin go to the parts store —"

"Jasmine, that's not an excuse."

The exchange sounded canned, like a routine they both knew a little too well. She turned to me. "I'm so sorry, mister . . . I'm sorry I didn't call you," she said with the same pleading tone.

I didn't respond.

"So I don't know what we're going to do about this," John said as Jasmine walked out.

"I don't know what to tell you, Mr. Marek. You charged me sixteen hundred dollars I don't have. And you didn't ask me —"

"That was Jasmine's mistake."

"Be that as it may. It wasn't mine."

"You don't need to get rude."

"Rude? Maybe what's rude is that I still haven't even gotten an apology from you."

John laid his cigar in an ashtray and sat back in his chair. He'd registered the thrust, and his parry was delivered with admirable aplomb. It made me think he was actually enjoying this: "I'm sorry Jasmine forgot to call you. That's on us. But the truth is, if I'd known you weren't going to want to have that converter replaced, we would have asked you to come pick up the vehicle. There wasn't a snowball's chance in hell I was letting my guys put a new gasket onto an engine with *that* converter. No, sir." I didn't know what to say. He had turned his evident racket into a story about the morality of driving with a defective catalytic converter — something my father had been doing for years. "Yes, sir. What's right is right. I'm happy to hold on to the vehicle at this point while you figure out what you want us to do with it —"

"What I want you to do is take out the new converter. I want you to give me my car back. I will pay you for the line item that I approved. Here," I said pointing to the invoice. "That's what I want."

He was entirely unperturbed. "Well, I already told you. We're not doing that. I don't even think we have that old converter. I usually have those sent to another shop where they strip them for the metals. Those can be valuable."

"You didn't have my consent, John. You did the repair anyway. Now you've pilfered my converter and sent it off to be stripped. Maybe we should call somebody to help us figure out the legality of what you've really got going on here."

"And who would that be?"

"Maybe we have the authorities come by and sort this out. How does that sound?"

"You mean the *police*? Sure. Sounds great." He leaned forward and pushed the phone toward me. "The local precinct's on speed dial. Second button. I use it a fair bit. My wife works there," he said as he sat back again. Was he lying? Did he even have a wife? He wasn't wearing a ring. His fingers were covered in grease, so maybe, I thought, he takes it off when he comes to work. I wondered what his wife thought of that lurid, fading snapshot of a woman's wet sex hovering just behind him. Or the reception-ist and self-styled resident piece of ass man-ning his phone — and likely more — all too happy to play accomplice in his larcenous repair racket. And who was that fellow lost in the towers? He had John's eyes and, come to think of it, those of John's nephew as well. Was that his brother? Had the state trooper lost his father in the attacks? Is that why he was reading Larry Wright's book? What did any of it matter, anyway? The man had my car. I was a Muslim with a funny name. Whether he had a wife who was a cop or not, his nephew certainly was, and I'd lied to him the day before. Oh . . . and did I mention he had the local precinct on speed dial?

John watched me hesitate. Instead of reaching for the receiver, I got up. "I need to make a call," I said abruptly. As I passed Jasmine at reception, she flashed me a smile, a shoulder lifted, her head turned and tilted toward it. The seductive gesture made no sense to me.

Once outside, I didn't call a lawyer. I didn't know a lawyer. I called Wells Fargo. I had two cards with the bank, both maxed out. I'd recently torn up a letter offering to increase the credit limit on one of those cards. The letter had infuriated me, with its uplifting clichés about having the means to do the things that mattered most, the letterhead showing a gorgeous young interracial couple holding hands against the backdrop of a sun setting over Monument Valley. I had needed the money then — I always needed the money — and was tempted enough to find myself combing the fine print for the catch. I finally found what

I was looking for: the clause explaining that by accepting the credit increase, I was agreeing to have any outstanding balance refinanced at the new APR of 22 percent. I tore the letter in half. Then tore it again. And again. And again. Until the pieces were so small my fingers could find no purchase from which to tear them any smaller. I still have no idea why this particular invitation to self-electing predation got further under my skin than usual, but it did. And yet here I was, barely a month later, waiting to have my call monitored or recorded for training purposes.

"Hello, Mr. — Akh-a-pana?" It was a woman's voice, a slight delay and a practiced tone making her sound more like a robot than a human.

"Acquapanna? Is that what you said?"

"Oh, I'm sorry. How do you say it?"

What was I doing? How was insulting her going to help me? I forced a laugh and pivoted to humor: "Akhtar, actually. But it was close enough. You'd be surprised. I get called everything from Iran to Yoda."

"Yoda? That's a good one, Mr. — Akh-tar — is that right?"

The hint of warmth in her voice encouraged me. "Yes," I said, telegraphing warmth back.

"So how can I help you today?"

I explained the situation I was in, stranded in Scranton with an unexpected repair, the dispute, the need to get my car back. I told her about the letter I'd received with the offer of a credit increase on my card. I was hoping, I said, the offer was still valid.

I heard her punching keys on the other end. Then a pause. "Can I put you on hold?" she asked.

"Of course," I said.

When she returned, it was with good news. Her supervisor had approved a $2,500 increase on the card. The increase would take effect immediately to cover the repair. I listened as she hurried, flatly, through the terms of the new agreement. It informed me of what I already knew: that the balance my card was carrying — something north of $15,000 — would now accrue 22 percent interest. I could have taken a cab to the local loan shark and saved money. When she was done with the boilerplate, I thanked her profusely and hung up.

AN EPIPHANY (OF SORTS)

Back on I-81 heading south, I'd just crossed into New York State when my cell phone rang. It was my mother. She was worried. Why hadn't I called yesterday? I apologized, told her about the problem with the car. I hadn't wanted to concern her. My father overheard the mention of trouble with the car and picked up another receiver:

"What happened to the car?"

"Blew a head gasket."

"It's a lemon. I told you it was a waste of money."

"I know, Dad."

"How much did they charge you?"

"Don't worry about it."

"No. How much?"

"Just tell him, honey," my mother said.

"Guys, it's fine."

"Gasket can cost you," he said.

"It did. But don't worry about it."

He insisted: "*Beta* — just tell me how much it cost you. We can help."

"It's fine. Please. Guys, I know you want to help. You already help so much. I need to deal with this on my own."

"Okay," my mother said, quietly. My father was quiet, too.

Despite my protestations, I knew they were hearing the need, the distress in my voice. I knew they wanted me to say more. But what to tell them? That I was lost and broke and felt persistently humiliated and under attack in the only country I'd ever known, a place that the more I understood,

208

the less I felt I belonged? What was the point? My father would see an opening, quote Tony Robbins or Robert Kiyosaki, lecture me about the only obstacles worth taking seriously being the ones I put in my own way. My mother would stay silent through it all; this silence would irritate my father, make him strident and, eventually, accusatory. Later, when she was alone again, she would call and concur, complain, commiserate, promise the extra nightly prayers on my behalf, and, of course, remind me that my bedroom was always free if I needed some time away from the city. Deluded admonitions, however true; futile tenderness, however comforting. There was no point.

After hanging up, I drove in silence. The wheels grumbled along on the blacktop. The wind wheezed at the cracked window. Inside, too, I heard something — distilled and dour, the quiet rumble of a gathering truth. It would be another hour before I got to the city limits, but by then my mind would be made up: I was going to stop pretending that I felt like an American.

V.
RIAZ; OR,
THE MERCHANT OF DEBT

I left Scranton owing more money than I would make for the next two years, but the decision I came to during that drive home would be conclusive: I would soon begin a series of works founded on my new unwillingness to pretend I was not conflicted about my country or my place in it. Paradoxically, these were the works that would lead to me finally finding my way as a writer in my American homeland and to the success that would earn me enough money to settle my debts and start making the monthly ends meet.

But Scranton wasn't done with me:

Nine years later, this grim corner of the Keystone State would play a role in making me wealthier than I had any right to be — and through no effort of my own. I set no hit play or book there, inherited no parcel of coal-rich land, purchased no winning Powerball ticket from a local gas station on another fugitive trip through the Lackawanna Valley. No, it was Riaz who made me rich, and Riaz was from Scranton. From what I gathered, he had no better a time growing up there than I had passing through, though the depth of his enmity for the place would shock me. I know I'm getting ahead of myself here, but Riaz's tale would make me wonder if what William Gaddis once said about a writer needing a sufficient store of rage to sustain the will to write also held true for anyone chasing down his (or her) first billion. Maybe so. Maybe there's no way to get anything significant done in the world without anger. All the same, I still find it hard to fathom how anyone could nurse a grudge for so long, sustain for so many years the kind of focused rage required to execute as meticulous a plan for revenge as Riaz did against his native soil.

Before I say more, I should make one thing clear:

Yes, what Riaz did made me rich, but I knew nothing about it — nothing, that is, until well after there wasn't a thing I, or anybody else, could do to stop it.

1.

In the fall of 2012, I was introduced to one Riaz Rind, founder of a Wall Street hedge fund called Avasina — named for the medieval Muslim polymath Ibn Sina, whose original manuscripts he's collected for years. (Riaz is also one of the world's foremost collectors of rare Kentucky bourbons and Japanese whiskeys.) If his name sounds vaguely familiar, you've probably heard it at the end of some segment of public broadcasting "made possible" by the foundation that bears his name, the Riaz Rind Philanthropic Trust, committed to "changing conversations and improving lives." The conversations he wants to change are about Islam, and the lives he wants to improve are Muslim. Considering the scope of what he's admitted to me about his ultimate ambitions, the formulation is humble indeed: Riaz is not reserved in his praise of Sheldon Adelson — Zionist casino mogul and Republican kingmaker — or at least of Adelson's unapologetic advocacy for Jewish causes. Like Adelson, Riaz wants to shape not only the nation's policy but also its governing personnel, which is the only way he thinks we, Muslims, will ever truly be welcome here. The brass ring, that's what he's after. If anyone I know has a shot at it, it's Riaz.

We were introduced that fall because I had a play up in New York, the same work I mentioned earlier, containing dialogue adapted from the phone call with my mother in the wake of Latif's death. It was the second of the works to result from my so-called Scranton epiphany. Cast in the leading role was an American comedian of Muslim origin, one of the first to break through into renown, a man who owed a national following to regular stints on one of the popular nightly talk shows. (I will call him Ashraf.) Ashraf's many fans were surprised to discover he was a wonderful dramatic actor, and I attribute the frenzy for tickets during the final weeks of the play's run — with scalpers getting more than $1,200 a seat — to his performance in the role of a Pakistani-American corporate attorney whose warring inner loyalties tear his life apart. The show made Page Six not once but twice, and that's when the celebrities started showing up: Salman Rushdie, Tyra Banks, Cherry Jones, Jon Stewart, Connie Britton, William Hurt. Members of the Saudi royal family came. So did Chelsea Clinton and Huma Abedin. In the men's room, I waited at the sink for Steven Spielberg to finish washing his hands; at concessions, I spilled seltzer on Tim Geithner's cross-trainers. I recall one surreal afternoon two weeks before the end of the run, when — first on a bus, then on the street, and finally at a Starbucks in the East Village — I overheard three separate, unrelated conversations about "that new play with the Muslim comic," which, it turned out, none of the conversers had actually seen; all were wondering how they could get tickets.

Riaz heard about the show from one of the employees at his hedge fund, an analyst of Pakistani origin named Imran, who loved it and had gone to the considerable trouble of procuring a bootleg copy of the script. That copy made the rounds at the office — where there were two dozen other South Asians working — finally ending up in Riaz's hands. He sat down at his desk with the script one morning and, he would later tell me, on turning the final page some seventy minutes later reached for his phone not to place a call to a scalper he knew — what he was after a scalper couldn't provide — but to ring up the theater's development office. That was how I ended up with an email asking me to meet with a prospective donor who had offered $20,000 for house seats and a visit backstage.

It was a rainy night in late November. I

was in the greenroom drinking tea with some of the actors after the show when a thick bald man in a beige gabardine coat and olive Wellingtons stepped through the double doors, held open by a member of the theater's staff. The maple-wood handle at the end of his umbrella gleamed oriole in his grip. I recognized him immediately as Pakistani — not Indian — from the pallid fallow-brown of his skin, the sharp nose, the wide humid eyes lined with impossibly long lashes. There was something almost animal about his self-assuredness as he made his way toward us, an ample, undivided alertness in his movements that seemed to radiate from some unseen middle. Plump confidence was the impression conveyed by the secure grip of his green eyes and the knowing press of his thick fingers as he shook my hand and introduced himself. "Riaz Rind," he said warmly. As he turned to offer congratulations to the actors, I was struck by something gnomelike about him despite both his relative youth and adequate height and despite the teeming stubble along the bottom half of his face, which hardly qualified as a beard. I couldn't tell if his coat was hiding a disproportionate girth that would have accounted for the striking impression he gave of abundant solidity. "I worked at Skadden, Arps for two years," he said, turning to me. This was the New York law firm where my lead character worked, though naturally I had given it another name. "I know all about what your character was going through. And what a performance. I had no idea Ashraf was such a good actor." He turned to address the rest of us: "Is he here? I'd love to share my congratulations."

"Still in his dressing room," groused Emily, the actress playing Ashraf's well-meaning white American wife in the play. "Getting the lotion off his legs."

I explained to Riaz that Ashraf had a pre-show routine of applying moisturizer — he wore boxers through much of the first scene and was always concerned that his umber legs not appear too ashen — which had delayed the opening curtain more than once.

"Well, his legs looked great," Riaz said.

Emily looked at him, head cocked to one side, the thick jumble of her postshow hair like an auburn mop about her face. I thought I saw her clock the same curious midmost appeal that had no obvious source. "I interrupted you — what was your name again?"

"Riaz. Riaz Rind."

"I'm Emily."

"Nice to meet you, Emily. Again. Such wonderful work. Really."

"You have to say that, but thanks."

"How did you peg it as Skadden?" I asked.

"I'm sure it could have been a half dozen other law firms in the city," he said. "But the partner bullying an associate about Israel . . . I was there. I've seen that scene. I left five years before 9/11, so it wasn't as bad for me. But the writing was on the wall. I did the math and got out."

"The math?" Emily asked.

He scanned the room quickly, as if gauging how we might react to what he was about to say: "Support for Israel was the unspoken rule. I mean, it's what's in your play. I'm guessing either you worked there yourself — or you know someone who did."

"I have a friend," I replied, "who's Jewish, actually."

He nodded. "It was clear. No one was getting ahead with anything resembling a nuanced view on Israel. And by 'nuanced' I mean critical in any way — if you *weren't* Jewish, that is. And even if you were."

"Tell me about it," Emily said with a chortle, tilting her glass of whiskey toward him in a mock toast. No one laughed.

"But . . . I mean — we all have views that

217

aren't open to debate. Right? I know I do."

"That I hate men?" Emily said, drinking.

Riaz smiled. "That's hard."

"Hmm. I wish I could say that more often." Her gaze lingered on him, interested.

"All men? Really, Emily?" asked an irritated voice. It was lanky, long-suffering Andrew, one of the other male actors in the cast, British-born, with crooked teeth and thinning hair. He'd become infatuated with Emily in the early weeks of rehearsal, and, after a rumored hookup between them during a break in rehearsal one day, he'd proceeded to pen her a stream of increasingly unwelcome poems. (I'd seen them; they were awful.) She asked him to stop, but he wouldn't. That's when the director intervened and threatened to fire him.

"Even your dad, hmm?"

"Especially my dad, Andrew. You should know that."

"And why should I know that?"

"Because I told you; you're a lot like him." She looked away and drank.

Andrew glared at the side of her face, his cheeks flushed. Then he got up and walked out of the room.

I looked over at Riaz and saw an expression on his face I would see more than once as I would get to know him better in the

218

coming few years: his chin ever so slightly lifted, lips shut, a blank scrutinizing stare that expressed satisfaction without contentment. I didn't understand the look then but would later: he trusted discord; he thrived on it. Sowing conflict and observing the fallout was his modus vivendi. To him, everything was a negotiation — that was something else I would discover — and not only because he had spent so much of his time making deals. I believe he'd found his way to the work he did in part because of the bracing simplicity with which he saw life itself. It was all very basic: get what you want, by whatever means necessary. That was all well and good in the pursuit of objects, I once said to him over lunchtime burgers at Shake Shack. But what kind of path was it to good relations?

"Relations like what?" he asked.

"Like friendship," I replied.

It took a moment for the smile on his face to reveal its full, flattered nature. That's when I realized there was a tactic at work even then: he'd found a way to push me to say what he was hoping to hear, namely, that I valued his friendship. And yet his reply wasn't in the least friendly: "Friendship's great. But it never made anyone a billionaire."

2.

My encounter at the theater with Riaz was brief. Ashraf emerged from his dressing room not long after Andrew's outburst, and by then, it was already time for the stage manager to lock up. Emily suggested we all repair to a bar on the corner. I offered my apologies. For three weeks now, every morning at five thirty, I'd been waking up with dialogue running through my head, ready to write. I didn't want a late evening of drinking to interfere with the flow.

Two days later, I would hear from Emily that the night had ended at Riaz's place. I'd stopped in at the theater between shows that day and found her in her dressing-room doorway. Seeing me, she waved me inside with an impish grin. Her friend Julia — whom I'd met before, a raven-haired, lupine beauty — sat at the mirror, holding up a tumbler full of amber liquid to the light. "It even looks like it's got gold in it," Julia said as she brought the rim to her lips for a sip. Emily slipped back into her seat and watched as Julia savored the taste, her expressions shifting with unfolding wonder. She shook her head in disbelief as she handed the tumbler back to her friend. Emily took it now and sipped, licking her lips, tittering with delight and disbelief of her own. Then Emily handed the glass to me.

Some fifteen years earlier, in the mid-'90s, I'd somehow found myself at a dinner on the Upper East Side where a magnum of 1959 Château Margaux was opened for coupling with a main course of leg of lamb and where, once I'd tasted from the glass poured for me, I finally understood the logic behind spending thousands of dollars on a bottle of something to drink. I was no connoisseur. I couldn't tell a berry note from a chocolate nose or discern the hint of spring flowers the dining guest beside me picked up, she said, developing as it sat in the glass. What I experienced was, perhaps, all the more remarkable for my having so virgin a palate. On my tongue, the wine disappeared almost magically into pure sensation, an absorbing congeries of rich and dusky hints — insinuations of bitterness tempered by the faintest echoes of something once sweet, now round and gathering — a developing flavor that revealed some ideal to which my every previous encounter with red wine appeared to have been pointing all along. And even more remarkable than this almost disincarnate sensation was the disincarnation itself, the effortless sublimation of liquid into pure savor, conveying me to the threshold of some essential idea of wine itself, a frictionless passage into the immaterial that felt, quite frankly, like something metaphysical. My encounter with that '59 Margaux was the only thing to which I could compare the taste of what Emily handed me, a liquid drink — bright and burry, nested in a honeycomb-and-oak envelope — exploding with disarming immediacy into something beyond sensation: a shard of lightning caught in loamy water. Julia was right. It looked like there was gold in it, and it tasted like it, too.

"I mean, is that incredible?" Emily said, watching me.

"You're not kidding. What is it?"

She held up the bottle. "Twenty-three-year Pappy Van Winkle. The holy grail of bourbons. I've heard about it, of course — but I've never had any."

"How much do you think that costs?" Julia asked.

"If you can even get it. They make, like, seven hundred bottles of it every ten years. I have no idea what they charge at the distillery for it, but there's someone on eBay selling an unopened bottle for fifteen thousand dollars." Emily turned to me. "We ended up at Riaz's the other night. I mean, his place — it's unbelievable."

"Where is it?"

"East End Avenue. He's got the top four floors. You take an elevator to the first floor, and then he's got his own elevator for the floors inside the apartment. There's an indoor pool. And I don't mean a Jacuzzi. A pool. It's not small. Moroccan tile, foil arches. He took us into this room he's got full of Sufi manuscripts. Another room, just for bourbon, bigger than my living room. The walls on two sides are covered, floor to ceiling, with bottles — a butcher-block bar in the middle. I saw the Van Winkle on the shelf and flipped out. I mean, I just wanted to hold it, but he brings it down and breaks the seal, then pours me a snifter. I almost fainted. He watched me drink it. I must have looked like I was having an orgasm. He told me to keep it."

"He just gave it to you?" I asked.

She nodded. " 'I have more good bourbon than I'll ever be able to drink,' he said. 'Seeing the pleasure it's giving you is worth it.' "

"*That's* what he said?" Julia asked.

"Yep."

"Who is this guy?"

"He runs a hedge fund," I answered. "He came to the show the other night and came backstage."

"Is he hot?"

Emily considered the question: "I mean,

that's not the word I'd use for him, but he's got something. Definitely."

"Money," Julia said, her wolflike features sharpening with a thought.

Emily went on to confess that she'd seen Riaz the next night, too. He called before the matinee, and she went down to meet him and a group of friends after the show for Champagne and Venetian calf's liver at Cipriani, then for dinner a few blocks north at Carbone. After that, a smaller group of them gathered to get high at a loft on Church Street, where (she guessed) there was a quarter of a billion dollars' worth of art hanging on the living-room walls. Around midnight, the two of them left to get a drink at the Rose Bar, in the Gramercy Park Hotel, where Johnny Depp was sitting in the booth beside them and Kate Upton was making out with someone she didn't recognize in another booth across the room. Finally, they met another bevy of Riaz's finance buddies for bottle service at a private burlesque club on the Lower East Side called The Box. Emily estimated the evening had probably set him back fifteen thousand dollars. With wine — a Montrachet — the dinner bill alone had come to three and a half grand. "I've been in the city a long time. You see things. You hear about the kind of money people have. But it's a whole other thing to experience it."

We plied her for details and watched her enjoy an almost erotic relish in supplying them: the solicitude of waiters and waitresses accustomed to Riaz's habits and his tips; the fresh truffle shavings — boy, were they thick! — on their family-size portion of linguine Alfredo at dinner; the Francis Bacon triptych she'd written about in college and under which she had found herself getting high in that Church Street loft; the silky leather of the Mercedes limousine driving them about town all night long. As Emily talked, I kept being drawn to Julia's face. There was something about her eyes as she listened — something pointed and glistening — that magnified her radiance. She noticed my glances, and at one point, our eyes locked. I lengthened, shifting in my seat as she held my gaze. Her quick glance at my crotch quickened my pulse. As Emily went on, the looks between us flashed like arrows beneath the conversation. What was I seeing on Julia's face that so drew me? And what was she seeing on my own that kept leading her eyes back to mine? I remembered what Jacques Lacan once said about desire . . .

. . . and thought: Was Emily's narration of the previous night's splendors arousing a desire in Julia that I, perceiving it, desired? And was it my desire for her desire that she saw on my face — and seeing it, desired in return? Sounds like nonsense, I know. Yet what came to pass next was nothing like nonsense:

Emily got up to go to the restroom. Julia stared at me as I shifted in my seat again, a subtle smile on her lips. Behind us, the lock on the bathroom door snapped shut. Then Julia whispered: "Take me somewhere."

It was after six. The next show wasn't for two hours. I took her by the hand and led her through the double doors that opened onto the back of the stage. As we crossed behind the set's flats, I felt her want to stop me.

"Not here," I said. "I know a place."

The rehearsal room upstairs was dark and furnished as we'd left it when we'd moved to the stage — the dinner table at one end, the living-room ensemble at the other. Julia led me to the couch, where every day for weeks I'd watched Ashraf rehearse hitting Emily across the face. I would watch her tumble to the floor and cower, looking for

226

cover — all the while her hand furtively seeking a blood packet she would stick between her teeth. Seething, heaving, anguished, Ashraf would find her here, cornered against the cushions, and he would hit her again. And again. When he finally stopped, we would see the blood pouring from her mouth.

Against the backrest, Julia kissed me now, her breath moist and hot, her thin, strong tongue seeking mine. All at once, she was naked below the waist and I was on my knees, my head between her legs. She was soaked. I kissed at her knob and pressed past to lick inside. Her moans were tight and short; her grip against the back of my head was strong. She thrust herself against me — against my nose, my teeth, my tongue — grinding now as she swelled, her sex dripping with my saliva. My fingers disappeared inside her, searching for her spot. She clucked as I ate, and my fingertip found her barely raised rough patch. I pressed. She moaned. I played and pushed and slobbered, my nose wet with her pleasure. I felt her nails in my head, and her body grew still against my mouth. Her noises were different now, quiet sobs, like muted cries for help. And then her pleasure seemed to change again, her grip on my head loosening now as the order of her sounds coalesced into a high-pitched squeal, an alarm of disbelief. She pulled me up. "I want you inside," she whispered into my ear, her hands already searching for me.

"I don't have a condom."

"I'm on the Pill."

"But —"

"Why? Do you have something I don't want?"

"No, no," I said.

No sooner had I said that than her lips were on mine. She unbuckled and released me. I pushed her back, and she fell onto the ocher cushions, stained with stage blood. Her legs were parted; she was doused and gleaming.

I wanted to eat her again, but she wouldn't let me.

"Fuck me. Hard. Now."

I saw myself in the rehearsal mirror across the room. I thought I looked scared. I looked away and poked at her, rubbing myself along her wetness. She pulled her shirt over her head, then grabbed me from behind and pushed me in. Her heat was electric. I started gently, but this was clearly not what she wanted. She pushed herself against me. "Harder," she said.

I tried.

"Harder," she said again.

"I don't want to come."

"Then don't come."

Her forbidding tone freed me. I started to move now more like I thought she wanted me to. "Fuck me like you hate me," she hissed quietly. "Fuck me like I'm garbage." I held her against the couch, my face inches from hers, and started to drive against her harder than I thought I should. "Like I'm garbage," she said again and again.

I looked up and saw us in the mirror. I didn't recognize myself. My face was flush, my eyes wide with anger and need. I saw my dark body and, beneath it, the heap of her glimmering whiteness. I watched myself drive into her over and over. "Yes, yes, yes . . ." I heard her chant as I played at rage. I stared down at her body. It glowed and mocked me. I suddenly needed more of it. I pawed and groped. I gripped her ribs and shoved and knocked and pushed. No purchase on her white flesh was enough to satisfy me. I wanted to own it. I wanted to destroy it.

She stared up into my eyes now, her head tilted, her upper lip curled, a searching, helpless look on her face. I fucked her with a fury I didn't know I could muster, and as I did, whatever she was seeing on my face appeared to be what she wanted to see. The refrain of her unruly sounds now began, words dissolving into the host of almost animal sounds she started to make, the croak and blare of a climax breaking forth from somewhere much deeper inside her than before. She came, and I came, too, but my orgasm didn't end with my release. Impossibly, I stiffened further, long with lust as I kept at her. The more I did, the more I wanted, the more she came, the harder I got, the harder I gave. I lost track of time. I don't know if we were at it four minutes or forty. All I know is I never experienced anything like it before. Or since.

3.
I wouldn't hear from Riaz until six months later, in the spring of 2013, when the play he'd come to see was awarded a Pulitzer. His congratulatory note to me was warm. I responded in kind. He replied with what seemed a halfhearted invitation to meet up for a drink: he was busy; never the master of his schedule; could we look to a night week after next or sometime before Memorial Day? As the appointed evening approached, an inevitable excuse was made, another date proposed, followed by another excuse and request — now sent from his

secretary's email account — to reschedule. Fine, I replied. I didn't expect a follow-up.

Two weeks later, on the eve of Ramadan, I was surprised to see his name come up in my in-box. He wanted to wish me well, whether I was planning to fast or not. (I wasn't.) For him, our holy month was a time to reflect, he wrote, to indulge his gratitude for what he had rather than his desire for what he didn't. Even on the days he didn't fast — which was most of them, some years — he tended to moderation and appreciation amid the striving. It was a sane-making time of the year. The email contained no changes of font style or size, which might have signaled formulaic copy interpolated into the body, and it was specific enough in places for me to conclude he'd actually taken the time to write this note to me alone. Another note arrived two days later, just after a series of suicide bombings in Rawalpindi, where much of his extended family still lived and where — I'd mentioned in an earlier email to him — he knew some of mine did, too. The tragedy initiated an intimacy, and our correspondence now took a self-revealing turn. I would learn that his parents, like my own, had immigrated to America after the quotas for people from the subcontinent were lifted in 1965; they'd settled first in Philadelphia, then moved to Pittston, a town along the Lackawanna River just south of Scranton, where his father found a job managing the furnaces at an industrial glass manufacturer called Lackawanna Glass Works. I learned, too, he was not only the firstborn son on either side of an enormous family but also the first of the extended brood to be born in America. This fact alone, he wrote, he thought largely responsible for his success; it had meant expectations of existential magnitude; he guessed his name was likely uttered in the prayers of no less than a hundred members of his family each and every day — after all, he financially supported more than twice as many.

I didn't know much about his business back then. He would never walk me through the details of what he actually did (and I wouldn't do my writer's due diligence until much later, when I decided to tell his story here). I remember him describing himself to a group of my friends — the evening of my forty-second birthday — as a merchant of debt, riffing off the birthday gift a group of my theater mates had pooled their resources to buy and frame for me that year: a single page of *The Merchant of Venice* from the Second Folio. Riaz's quip drew a flurry of questions about the apparent absurdity of selling debt, all of which he fielded graciously, answering in simpler terms than I would have thought possible:

Debt had value?

Yes. Like any loan, debt generated a regular payment, and that payment, the simple fact of it — depending on how reliably it was expected to be made — could be sold.

But who would want to buy it?

Big money. And the bigger the money, the more urgent the need to find a lucrative parking place, a spot you could put all that cash and watch it grow.

How did it work?

Managers in control of the world's various mountains of money bought loans from original lenders in order to have the scheduled loan payments appear on their books; cash flowing in like that — month in, month out — was enough to put those managers' restless minds at ease, and for good reason. It was usually easy money.

But how did it work, exactly? How did you make money holding debt?

Holding a good loan — whether for a car or credit card, home or university tuition — meant you could expect it to be paid in full, pocketing not only the profit from the interest paid but also the entirety of the underlying principal as well. As long as you'd done your homework right and bought the right loans to the right loanees, he explained, debt was the best investment out there.

Assessing the viability of loans of all sorts — according to Google — was the expertise of Riaz's firm, Avasina Associates. Their website was sleek and unrevealing, like a willfully spare downtown storefront, advertising exclusivity by signaling its lack of interest in your business. The clutter of press on the first page of the search results revealed that he'd made a fortune in the aftermath of the mortgage crisis, loading up on home loans nobody wanted anymore, renegotiating the terms to help homeowners avoid foreclosure, later selling those renegotiated loans to municipalities across the country. He was much lauded in the pieces I read and had even ended up on a *CBS Sunday Morning* segment about compassionate finance. How had he kept people in their homes *and* made a killing? "There's no substitute for good old hard work," he replied coyly against the backdrop of the East River as seen through the mural-size windows of his kitchen. In 2011, *Forbes* magazine had lauded the "monster trade" that returned to its municipal investors an "eye-popping" 30 percent and went on to wonder if — with a little luck! — Riaz might soon end up on its list of the four hundred richest Americans. Cheekily, I sent him a link to the article with a note asking if he might have some good news in the coming year. He sent back one that read: "Fake it 'til you make it" — punctuated by a winking-face-with-tongue emoji.

I've skipped around a bit . . .

It would take another half year of appointments scheduled and rescheduled over email before we were to meet again in person. It was the fall of 2013, and the occasion was an invitation to join him at a gala in honor of the New Khalwati Order, a modern Sufi *dergah* on Duane Street across from Duane Park in Tribeca, led, since the death of its founder, by a white convert, the wayward scion of a famous Austrian mining family who called herself Mariam Meriha. I was already acquainted with Sheikha Maria — as she was known to her followers — having met her on two occasions, once at the *dergah* itself, where I'd gone one Ramadan Thursday in the mid-aughts to participate in their weekly service. I found her kind and clueless in her tall white *sikke* and abundant shawls. After a sermon in which she exhorted us all to care for ourselves, she led us through a disheveled hourlong *dhikr* — or Sufi ceremonial chanting of the divine name — that culminated, comically, in a welter of whirling urban professionals tumbling into each other and over themselves, a scene that I could only have imagined, before seeing it with my own eyes, as a scene in some satiric novel about Muslims in America.

Riaz and I arranged to meet up before the gala for a drink. When I arrived, he was leaning against the thick zinc counter at the end of the bar, already halfway through a Manhattan and chewing on the Maraschino. Almost at once I found myself struck by the same thick charisma I'd discerned the first night we met. I'd remembered him as stout, but looking at him in his two-piece suit, I could tell he wasn't. Not really. As we chatted, some part of me was only watching him, trying to make sense of — what was it, exactly? Charm? Confidence? Magnetism? There was not a whit of will or self-manipulation about it, but something muter and more elemental at work, like the balanced girth of a standing stone on Salisbury Plain. I observed him as we spoke, wondering: Is it the money?

By the time my martini was served — up,

wet, dirty — I was unloading my skepticism about a Sufi order throwing a New York City gala to raise money, which, I joked, made only slightly more sense to me than a group of Carmelite nuns manning fairground booths at a carnival for the same purpose. "The gala was my idea," he confessed with a chuckle. "The *dergah* needs renovations. I've known the sheikha for years from *dhikr* on Thursdays. I try not to miss it when I don't have to."

"Thursday *dhikr* at the Khalwati Order," I offered wryly.

"You've been?"

"I have."

"It took some work to overcome her resistance to the idea," he said, noting my reserve. "They really do need the money. And this way, I figured it would be good for the foundation, too. Any chance to get a different image of Islam out there."

"One that looks more like Lauren Hutton."

"If it gets us onto the society pages? Absolutely." It was my turn to chuckle. At least he was aware how shallow it seemed.

"A few years ago," he went on with words — I thought — he'd used many times, his assertive baritone now sounding somehow labored, "we funded a study, focus groups,

237

interviews with people around the country, all walks of life. 'What do you think of Islam?' Not just the obvious. We wanted to dig past the conscious stuff into the unconscious stuff, too. What we discovered? Top five words people associate on an unconscious level with Islam? *Anger. Separate. Suicide. Bad. Death.*"

"In that order?"

"Well, *death* was first, actually."

"Pretty bleak."

"Isn't it? Because, see, usually when you dig down into the unconscious stuff, which is harder to get to — takes more time, costs more money — and I've done it before, with municipalities around debt initiatives. Even with the really scary stuff that people don't get, like mortgage bonds after the crisis, deep down, even there you can usually find a silver lining, something they heard when they were kids, an association to some word or concept you can build on. Not here. Not with Islam. Group after group. The same story. Like cancer. Nothing positive."

"Even Cat Stevens?" I joked. " 'Wild World'? 'Peace Train'?"

"Believe it or not, that actually came up. They felt betrayed. Like Islam made him stop singing."

"Right."

"So like I was saying . . . the company that did the study, when they wrote about the findings, they put a quote at the beginning of the report, their way of summing up the problem as well as the challenge. I have it here." He pulled out his phone and tapped at the screen, then handed it to me:

The established majority takes its we-image from a minority of its best, and shapes a they-image of the despised outsiders from the minority of their worst.

"Whose quote is it?"

"A sociologist named Norbert Elias. German Jew who left in thirty-three, when the Nazis took over. Saw what was coming before most did. Which isn't a surprise, for someone who can have a thought like that."

"Remarkable," I said, handing the phone back to him.

"Isn't it? I mean, when I first read this, I thought, 'This is it. This is what we're up against.' In this country, the white majority is basically blind to the worst in themselves. They see themselves in the image of their best, and they see us in the image of our worst."

"I get it —"

"— Muslims, blacks, whatever. To me, this

wasn't just an analysis of the problem, it pointed at a solution."

"How so?"

"Do what they do. They push the minority of their best in our faces and then pretend that's the whole picture. We need to do the same. Shove the best of our minority down their throats."

"Seduction at the hands of Sheikha Maria . . ."

"Precisely." He grinned, lifting his glass to finish his drink. "I mean, in a way, you're doing your own version of the same thing, aren't you?"

"Am I?"

"Laying claim? Owning what they think they see in us, then turning it right back at them. 'You think this is us? It's actually you.'"

It was an incisive articulation of my artistic procedure, but something about it felt askew. It took me a moment to find words to adjust the imbalance I thought I heard. "You could put it that way. Or you could say I'm just trying to show people as they are, no better, no worse. Which means I'm trying to show *us* as we are, no better, no worse."

"And how are we?" The charming diffidence with which he posed the question only partly hid the dismissive sarcasm at its root. I sensed the temperature in me rise.

"Do we really want to get into this?"

"Why not? It's just a conversation, right?" He looked over at the bartender, then back at me: "Another round?" he asked.

"Sure," I said.

"We'll do this again," he told the bartender, pointing to the drinks, then turned back to me with a shy, prepossessing smile. "C'mon. It really is just a conversation, right?"

"I mean . . ."

"So tell me: How are we?"

The thought of going into it pained me. I didn't want the argument. I didn't feel invested anymore in the ideas I had about our kind, however accurate I believed them to be. My critiques were taken for attacks — and I understood why. We, Muslims, were constantly besieged by a culture that didn't understand us, that didn't want us. It was why I only ever voiced my thoughts indirectly, through that particular prevarication called art. I didn't see the point of harping on "our" issues in public when it was evident "their" mishaps and blind spots were so much more pressing. The existential threats to our species were not coming from us but from the proliferation of their "enlightened" way of life to every corner of the planet. Wasn't *that* the necessary critique now?

And yet, as Riaz waited for me to respond, I could feel myself being drawn out. I could feel I wanted something from him, though I wasn't sure what it was. I took a moment and another sip, and when I finally replied, it was with words I, too, had used before, but only with myself: "We are more obsessed with what *they* think of us than what we think of ourselves. We spend way too much time trying to correct the impression the West has of who we are. We've turned this defensiveness into a way of life. Edward Said writes a book about how wrong they've been about us, and it becomes our bible, a high road to self-knowledge. But that's not what it is. Not remotely. Constantly defining yourself in opposition to what others say about you is not self-knowledge. It's confusion. That much I'd figured out by the time I was in high school." He was quiet. Whatever he'd expected me to say, this didn't seem to be it. On some level, I must have known I was attacking what he saw as his purpose in the world.

"We've had good reason to be obsessed with how wrong they've been," he finally said, visibly irritated. "I mean, even this

242

conversation we're having right now: You were born here. I was, too. But we're referring to ourselves as coming from somewhere else. How did *that* happen?"

"I don't know how it happened for you — but in my house, it didn't happen because of *them*. They didn't make us feel like outsiders. We *were* outsiders. At least my parents were, because you know what? They came from somewhere else. *That's* what outsiders are. And it didn't bother them. There was a culture here they had to learn — and they never really did. Not the way those who are born into it do. Don't get me wrong. My father loves America. Loves it more than makes sense to me sometimes, frankly. He thinks he's American, but what that really means is that he still *wants* to be American. He still doesn't really feel like one. It's been forty-five years, and he still doesn't really understand what it means. Because being American is not about what they tell you — freedom and opportunity and all that horseshit. Not really. There *is* a culture here, for sure, and it has nothing to do with all the well-meaning nonsense. It's about racism and money worship — and when you're on the correct side of both those things? *That's* when you really belong. Because *that's* when you start to represent

243

the best of what they think they are, to come back to your quote."

"Your point?" His tone was sharp.

"My point is just that *we're* not really all that different. We do the same thing they do: we make ourselves out to be better than we are. And what really doesn't help is how we end up using their contempt as an excuse to avoid our own failings."

He was leaning at the bar, staring into his new drink. "So what are they?"

"What?"

"Our failings?"

"Riaz."

"Just one. Humor me." The crowd at the bar had been growing. And though we were not the only ones with raised voices, we were the ones being noticed — two brown men arguing was apparently a thing to make sure one kept an eye on. Riaz pulled out a handkerchief and wiped his face. For a moment, he looked tired, as tired — I thought — as I felt.

"Fine," I said. "Here's one: When are we going to stop talking about the Golden Age? About how we kept Aristotle alive. How we invented algebra. How we laid the foundations for the scientific method. How we —"

He cut me off: "What should we do? Let them forget? Pretend it's not true? How is that better?"

"Do it all you want, just don't pretend it means anything. It doesn't. The winners write history. I shouldn't have to explain that to you. So they take credit they don't deserve. So what? It's never been any different. Back then, when we were winning, we did the same thing. Now they are. Writing history the way they see it. The real mistake is to expect that anybody would do otherwise."

"What would you have us do?"

"For starters? Spend less time dreaming about the Golden Age and more trying to understand how we fell so far behind. Because *that's* the problem. We're caught in this awful cycle of belatedness and inferiority. It's made us feel weak. For generation after generation. And being weak has made us angry —"

"And how is what you're saying any different from Bernard Lewis?"

"Bringing up Bernard Lewis is not an argument."

"He did a lot of damage to the world with that 'clash of civilizations' stuff."

"He called us angry and made us look bad. So what? So now we're supposed to say, 'We're not angry'? Even if we are? Are blacks supposed to go around pretending not to be enraged about the shit they go through in this country every day? Just because it makes them look bad to white people? They're angry, and they've got damn good reasons to be. And maybe we do, too. So maybe if we spent a little more time trying to understand what we're carrying — instead of complaining about Bernard Lewis — maybe if we did *that,* we wouldn't be dealing with this death cult that calls itself a religion and that's eating us alive."

He stared at me now with the strangest look. It was a mute gaze, consumed and inhuman, the way a river boulder might have stared back at you if it had eyes. And then, all at once, the expression was gone, and in its place was a childlike smile. We're back on the same side again, I thought, watching him take another sip, clearly pleased. In denouncing ISIS — I surmised — I'd pronounced a reassuring shibboleth. He could be sure now I was not the worst of what he feared: an intellectual apologist for Muslim violence. He signaled to the bartender that he wanted to settle up.

"I can tell you why we fell behind," he said with an almost cheery tone. I wondered if he was starting to feel the liquor.

"What?"

"I said: I can tell you why we fell behind. I've actually thought a lot about this."

"That wasn't what I was getting at —"

"Didn't you just say we should be spending more time trying to understand why it happened?"

". . . I mean, sure."

"That *isn't* what you said?"

"No, it is."

"And I'm saying: I can tell you why."

Just then, the bartender dropped the check into an empty glass before us. I reached for my wallet. Riaz stopped me, placing his black Amex card on the bar. "Thank you," I said, certain, now, there was no way to avoid the rest of this conversation: "So tell me. Why'd we fall behind?"

"The corporation. Plain and simple."

"The corporation?"

"The Romans created the corporation. It enabled them to protect assets from being redistributed after an owner's death. Which meant money could have the time to really grow, take on its own center of gravity. We had no way to do that. Muslim inheritance laws are very clear. After death, the estate has to be divided among the wives and heirs. Because there was no loophole to get around it, businesses didn't outlive their founders. Everyone wrote short-term contracts with each other, because you were always afraid parties in a deal would die, and you'd have to go to the wives and kids to be made whole. One-off deals were the rule, as there was no good way to shelter long-term ventures. Which meant no path to long-term material investments."

"We didn't have any correlate for the corporation? I didn't know that."

He shook his head: "Complete liquidation of assets in every generation until the late eighteen hundreds. Do you have any idea what that meant for private enterprise? And it only changed once we finally took a page from the Europeans and built a corporate concept of our own. But at that point, their money'd been growing for six hundred years! That's banks and industries with a *half millennium* of accrued capital. *That's* why we're behind. Because Muslim laws were trying to take care of wives and children! We're behind because we cared more about what happened to people than money! What about getting *that* message out there!"

I laughed. "That's a good one."

"And the best part? It's all true. Even though almost nobody knows it."

"I'm surprised you haven't already hired a writer to script the film."

"Why do you think I'm paying for your

drink?" he said, laughing, as he signed the check.

On our way to Gotham Hall, I noticed the tension between us had given way to something light and playful, our banter lubricated, no doubt, by the liquor and — at least in me — relief, a sense that the conversation I'd dreaded had been worth risking after all. Whether we'd agreed or not, the exchange felt enlivening. I felt myself hoping our time together wouldn't — like one of those medieval Muslim business deals he mentioned — end up being a one-off encounter.

At the corner of 36th Street, I spied the sheikha emerging from around the corner. She was tough to miss. Poised on the sidewalk, regal in her marigold robe and a dark conical *sikke,* her chin nobly tilted to the towering facades around us, she looked every bit the European-gone-native in some unwritten Bellow novel of Eastern Anatolia. Then, all at once, like a rarely sighted bird easily spooked, she turned and hurried for the entrance. As she scurried away, I pointed her out and commented about the opulence of her robes. "I mean, it is hard to make a case for giving her money when we all know how much she's already got."

Riaz shot me a curious sidelong grin. "You

don't even know the half of it," he said, stopping on the corner to tell me the story: It wasn't until her father died, two years earlier, that she discovered he had written her out of his will. Her shock wasn't just emotional. Her plans for the order — proliferating along both American coasts, each of its half dozen *dergahs* led by a female sheikha, the only Sufi organization whose every branch was run entirely by women anywhere in the world, as far as Riaz knew — depended on the money she'd expected to inherit. Yes, she was still wealthy enough to never have to worry about her personal expenses, yet now, worry was all she did. Signs of emotional chaos were growing, and Riaz was concerned that her mental state was jeopardizing the order. She showed up one day at his office with estimates in hand for work on the Duane Street building that couldn't be put off any longer — the least of which totaled more than $400,000 — and proceeded to have a panic attack on his couch. He told her he would help her raise the money, which was how the whole idea for the gala came about.

All this Riaz shared with me matter-of-factly, without any of the hushed and huddled complicity of rumor, indeed, as if nothing untoward, or even that remarkable, was being divulged. But the evident breach of the sheikha's confidence was not lost on me. As we made our way up the building steps, removed our wallets and phones, and marched through the metal detector flanked by the Gotham Hall security officers on high alert — no doubt alarmed by the preponderance of Muslims coming through the doors — I remember feeling flattered. I knew already how deeply Riaz had drawn me in. I was pleased to think that perhaps I, too, had done the same.

4.

I saw more of Riaz than I would have expected to in the coming months. As a regular invitee to his foundation's events, I found myself in the presence of one remarkable American after another, each Muslim, each involved in some work that made my self-absorbed preoccupation with drama and contradiction start to seem not only trivial but also shameless. These people were changing the world — one grant, one prison inmate, one neighborhood block, one translation, one voting drive, and, yes, one PR campaign at a time. There was Sami Sleiman, the Syrian-born, Los Angeles–raised founder of Haqq, a community network that provided the safety net he believed local

251

government should offer (but rarely did) to those in need — a food pantry, a walk-in clinic, a community arts center and café, a career-counseling service for former felons and at-risk youth; Hafsa Hossein, a Chicago-born, Harvard Law–educated attorney who — when she wasn't filing briefs on behalf of accused Muslims deprived of their legal rights — ran a multilingual website committed to gender equity in Islam; George Iqbal Shawn, a white convert to the faith, a former journalist sickened by what he saw as a media industry fatally beholden to sowing anxiety and fear, who now spent most of his time in Turkey, toiling in refugee camps and extricating Western youths from the clutches of ISIS across the border; Janan Gul, a French-born cartoonist of Persian origin at work on a graphic retelling of Rumi's relationship with his Sufi master, Shams, the first volume of which had already made the bestseller lists in a half dozen European countries; Kamal Morse, an all-star linebacker for the Oakland Raiders who left the NFL after a religious experience in Mecca that inspired him to start a mosque and, when he ran afoul of the local authorities, to run for city council in his native Kansas City. Riaz was particularly affected by Morse's tale. He got choked up while introducing Morse at the event in his honor, outlining the moving saga of how the former football player had not only prevailed in bringing a house of Muslim worship to his community but also transformed his local government in the process.

The foundation raised money, generated press, and, maybe most important, provided an excuse to ask the wealthy and influential for help. If sufficiently moved, they might do more than just open up their pocketbooks. Organizations like these, I would learn, depended on relationships with those who had access to money and power, depended on populating their boards with people who not only understood the stated mission but also made it their own. I would learn all this when I joined Riaz's board myself, an invitation extended to me despite the fact that I had access to neither power nor money. But I did have a Pulitzer, Riaz joked, and more important, he felt my "somewhat contrarian" views would help keep the foundation on its toes. Most of the board agreed; I was elected with only one dissenting vote. That vote came from an avuncular sometime professor of Islamic studies, now a college dean, who'd tried to teach my works only to discover — filled as they were with extremists of various sorts; teeming with buried, toxic postcolonial resentments; compromised by concessions to dominant narrative structures — that his students could make no productive sense of them. To assign my writings — he'd contended at the vote and would later explain to me during a coffee break at my first board meeting, his genteel, Cambridge-inflected reserve tested by the fierce emotion he felt about the matter — was to discover how effective they were in galvanizing every negative impression of Islam one could imagine. I was not writing literature, in his view, but rather emotionally charged rhetorical delivery devices passing for art; it was anti-Muslim muckraking, offering deceptively compelling illusions of reasoned argument in service of the destructive tropes Riaz's foundation was working hard to undo in the first place. Admitting me to this board was, in a word, a disgrace — though apparently not disgraceful enough to merit his leaving it. I took his animadversions in stride. What else was there to do but thank him for his thoughts and pretend I didn't care?

Joining Riaz's board exposed me to aspects of the world I'd only read about. He fast-tracked me onto the executive committee, then turned me into a trusted sidekick. I met Hillary at the State Department. I sat next to Elon Musk at a donor dinner prepared by Alice Waters herself at Chez Panisse. I went backstage at *Hamilton* with a group that included Mos Def. I went fly-fishing in Idaho with Fareed Zakaria, golfing at Pebble Beach with Neel Kashkari. I flew first class to Venice, where Riaz and I spent three days on the Lido at meetings with Muslim artists there for the Biennale, then we spent three days in Abu Dhabi at a conference devoted to Islamic microfinance. A week later, we were in Frankfurt to host a gala where we raised more than a half million euros to support gay Muslims being persecuted in Chechnya. In Chicago, we dined at Alinea with Jeanne Gang and John Malkovich. In London, I shared a samosa with an MP at Chutney Mary. At the American Academy in Rome, Don DeLillo spilled Chianti into my soup.

As I made the rounds of these exclusive haunts, I came to be seen (and to see myself) as an honorary member of the privileged class. Invitations poured in. To artist residencies in Wyoming and Marfa. To the juries of the film festival in Rotterdam and a drama award in Oslo. I was asked to oversee the dispensation of funding to young writers in the "Middle East." At Sundance, they comped me in a multifloor suite; in Munich, I was put up in a villa built for the Fairy Tale King himself. One night, at a fund-raising dinner at Blue Hill at Stone Barns, an Italian industrialist and his wife overheard me complaining about getting work done in my apartment in New York — the construction on my block was deafening. They approached me after dessert with an offer to take up residence at their exquisitely quiet summer house on Lake Como. They would be traveling through the steppes of Asia in July and wouldn't be using it. My neighbors next door, the wife informed me, would be George and Amal Clooney — if they were there.

I went. I didn't finish the play I was writing. I was too busy playing basketball and drinking Aperol spritzes with the Clooneys' houseguests.

I was getting used to asparagus season in the Marchfeld and Sauternes with my fois gras. It hadn't taken me long — a mere eight months of playing Riaz's show pony — to start taking myself for a latter-day Saint-Simon or Samuel Pepys. I noted details of meals eaten and hotel rooms booked. My Moleskines were replete with thumbnail portraits of the wealthy and powerful, their crepe de chine dresses and Italian wool blazers, their obsession with faience and face-lifts, their drunk, lazy tongues, the putrid odors of their scented aging, the hors d'oeuvres (and cocktail waitresses) chased across the room, the private jets, the summer homes, the winter homes, and absolutely everywhere — or so it seemed — the yammering about works of art they neither understood nor liked but on which they regularly spent more money than I expected to make in my lifetime. I imagined I was penning a coruscating catalog of the new aristocracy, an outline of their outlandishness, an indictment of the enduring, indelible stain of human status seeking. In fact, my journal was no such thing. It was fatuous and self-regarding, full of obvious critique and sloppy language. Worst of all — and I do hope it will not compromise too much the reader's view of me, though I would understand if it did — I was a pig with women. The episode with Julia at the theater in the wake of Riaz's first visit still haunted me — an object lesson in proximity to wealth as an aphrodisiac and the seemingly endless depth of my own racially charged sexual hunger — but oddly, not in the way it had been most remarkable, for the capacious, self-revealing pleasure that had subsumed us both. That elemental reciprocity appeared to have been lost on me. Instead I feigned interest and intimacy and offered mediocre, absent-hearted sex to more lovers than I'd like to admit. I didn't seem to care. After all, there was so much fucking to be had and with so little effort.

In the words of George Monbiot, I'd become a neoliberal courtier, a subaltern aspirant to the ruling class, bearing the foundation's not-for-profit coat of arms expressly for that purpose, an eclectic and exemplary defender not only of inalienable human rights and enlightened rage but also of freedom itself, both sexual and monetary, an eager frontline recruit for the purported progressive ideological battles of our time. My awakening from this stupor of self-congratulatory entitlement would be swift and brutal. An accumulation of private and public misfortunes — a copper penny rash on my palms, my mother's death, the election of Donald Trump — would disabuse me of my will to benevolent privilege. I'm ashamed it took me so long to wake up to the bankruptcy of this purported moral vision. Until then, I was susceptible; I was culpable; I was a willing and enthusiastic advocate; this vision of the good life felt good indeed; I was a believer in the politically enlightened late-stage capitalist individualist creed; I loved Obama; I was tongue-tied with awe when I met Sergey Brin. Who could blame me? What more, what better, for me, for anyone else, did the world have to offer?

Before my tumble from this worldview, I spent more time thinking about money than ever before. I knew the life I was leading was predicated on capital. I knew I didn't have any. How much longer would Riaz let me float along on the swollen river of his seemingly endless lucre? I didn't know. Money was no object to him, of course, but I could see the writing on the wall. Whatever luster I possessed for those he used me to impress would eventually fade. They would tire of my ten-cent words and my canny political provocations. I would fall out of favor, and when I did, it would mean returning to life in my dim, tiny Harlem one-bedroom with only my imagination — and my iPhone! — as sustaining distractions. No more fancy scenery to oppose to my fear, to the constant worry that I mattered not a whit to anyone beyond myself. Put crassly, I didn't want a life in which the 2 train was how I did most of my traveling. Indeed, I now despised the subway — its screeching, the press of its surly, smelly throngs, the predicate of predetermined stops that shaped my daily itinerary. With Riaz, I rode about in that sleek black Mercedes limousine that had so enchanted Emily on their night out. I felt the same about that quiet enclave on wheels as it slipped through the city's hustle-bustle, parting the crowds, fetching us from one door, dropping us at another. If we walked, it was because we wanted to! I knew I would never have money like that but also knew — had always known — the usual pittance that foundered in my checking account was not enough. I needed more. Much more. The example of my friend Danyal Ramin had haunted me for years. Danyal was likely the most extravagantly talented of my college classmates, a theater artist who'd studied in Vermont with the Bread and Puppet troupe before starting his own group in Brooklyn; a visionary designer and director whose arresting shows went up at the Public and were invited to Avignon and Salzburg; a singular voice hailed by critics as a New World heir to Tadeusz Kantor; and a man who'd gone for much of his adult life without health insurance. He got married. Had a child. The pregnancy was covered by Medicaid, and so was the new family, until they weren't. When Danyal was diagnosed with a rare blood disorder, well, you can probably guess the rest of the story, its entropic denouement by now as much a staple of American life as apple pie: a well-meaning crowdsourced appeal online raised enough money to keep the wolf from the door, but only for so long. Treatment was expensive — the medications alone ran into the hundreds of thousands — but his parents found the money. He survived. His theater company didn't. Neither did his marriage. Last I heard, he'd moved back home to North Carolina, where he was working at a Starbucks. At least the job gave him benefits. A once-in-a-generation talent, mind you. Making double-shot extra-wet lattes for real estate agents on bathroom breaks between appointments.

Danyal was but one of many I'd seen fall prey to the gap between the logic of their talents and the treachery of an American society that abandoned the weak and monetized the unlucky. You had to be brain-dead not to know you couldn't really flourish in this country without inordinate amounts of cash or extraordinary luck. I'd been the beneficiary of the latter and had always worried how long I would make it without more of the former. In the wake of my experience with Riaz — my initiation (if you will) into the reality of the only *good life* in our great land — my concerns about money were no longer just prophylactic, various forms of worry about rainy days. No. Now I realized what I'd been missing all along. Here was true *freedom*. Serious money was the only path to liberation from the indentured servitude of twenty-first-century lower- and middle-class American life.

An artist? Really? Are you kidding me? And you expected *what*, exactly?

Indentured servitude. It was a formulation I took from Riaz. We spoke often and at length about what it took to flourish in what he called the System. Riaz was not alone in diagnosing social ills, bandying about the latest statistics, conceiving of paths to better futures for his fellow man, woman, and dog — these favorite pastimes of the moneyed class, though Riaz went deeper than most. To him, the System was fully evolved, by which he meant optimally effective and efficient. It specialized in the manufacture of debt, which was the great enabler of capital, the surest means to, yes, *indenture* the vast hordes of the lower and middle class (and the nation's youth) to the process of money's growth. For what grew now were not communities or economies but capital itself — and debt was the means, which meant it was also, now, the dominant cultural logic. Debt prescribed social realities, guarding and guiding the choices that made up most contemporary human lives — domicile, health, education, the prospects of one's progeny, and now (and most centrally) access to the devices that did the lion's share of one's cognition. Of course, Riaz explained, debt had always been a way to entrammel the masses — it was from him I first heard that famous John Adams quotation: "There are two ways to conquer and enslave a nation: one is by the sword, the other by debt" — but something was different now. With the advent of Reagan and the innovations of Milken, this predation on the populace was now the very basis of our increasingly global economy. The current of anger growing across the world had nothing to do with immigration, he believed, but was all about the System that debt had created, an inescapable, asymmetrical, transnational force. The people paid into this regime with their catalogs of monthly debt payments and subscription fees, all to support what was now the only true political order of our time, a corporate regime that offered no representation, no vote, no participation in either the velocity of its appetites or the bearing of its destructive course. If you weren't part of the System, you were just grist for its gullet; your life and the lives of those like you were mixed and milled into portfolios of fixed monthly payments — for everything from cars and college tuition to streaming services and same-day delivery — payments that accrued only to the benefit of the ever-increasing mountains of money that were our real masters. People felt all this without knowing it, Riaz would say, and the effectiveness with which the truth was kept from them was a sign not only of the System's genius but also of its maturity. (Even the System's own crises, like the near-collapse of the financial system in 2008, ultimately served — Riaz would explain — only to expand the reach of its ever-more-encompassing power.)

If he seemed to speak in moral terms, it wasn't because he believed things needed to change. He felt certain no such change was possible. But to "make a real mark" — he would say — you needed to understand what everyone was up against; there was no excuse for anything less than all the clarity you could muster about the world as it truly was. Back then, I thought I understood what mark he wanted to make and imagined I was helping him to do it, however modestly. In truth, I thought I understood it better than he did: that the charity was cover — psychological and otherwise — for his race to a billion dollars. Once he had that, I thought, he would finally feel redeemed, finally feel that he was the best of what Americans thought they could be, finally know that he belonged.

It turns out I was projecting. I had no clue what he was really up to.

And it wasn't until I saw my own money grow that I would find out.

5.

When my mother died, in May of 2015, she left me $300,000. I did the usual thing someone in my shoes did: succumbed to the advice of a financial planner, who offered to invest it in the stock market for a fee. The concerns I owned went down and up and down again, and after months of fretting — for, in the circles in which I now traveled, all the talk was about another looming financial crisis — my holdings showed a net gain of $14. Riaz offered to invest the money for me. We were enjoying a drink in his kitchen, a superlative Japanese whiskey for which he'd paid some astronomical amount of money. Chilled with granite stones, it was yet another invigorating march of contradictions — rich, crisp, mellow, bright — so common to my time with him.*

* If I've been drawn to fill more space in these pages detailing the various luxurious appurtenances of my time with Riaz than describing the man himself, there is a logic to it. I'm not sure my time with him ever really encompassed much more than my avid delight at the sundry rare benefits I enjoyed because of him. A flat, abstracted portrayal — punctuated by moments of ecstatic material wonder — is perhaps closer to the truth of so much of my actual experience of him, less a person to me than an idea, an object, a protector, a purveyor of fulfillments, a means to some ever-elusive end, and I suspect this was mutual, at least the means-to-some-end part of it. Of course, I'm leaving out the many episodes of human warmth that would have conveyed a fundamental tenderness beneath his otherwise almost mineral mien. I'm ignoring the moments of touching vulnerability, such as when, the morning after an all-night blowout at his palatial digs — replete with drugs and costumed dwarfs and a protracted donnybrook between two New York titans of debt over Benghazi and the Clinton emails — I walked into his bedroom and found him on all fours with a penis in each end. I'd long since concluded Riaz was gay — he never dated

women, and I found his gaze often lingering on strapping young men like the two he was sandwiched between that morning — and I suspected, despite his fabulous wealth and forward thinking, that he still harbored a profound and crippling Muslim shame about it. In the days that followed, I saw a more fragile man than I ever had seen and ever would see again, his resolute core softened, his need for a real friend finally revealed — or so it seemed. It was during the first week of the US Open that year, and we spent two days wandering the grounds, eating hot dogs, drinking beer, dipping in and out of luxury boxes. He told me of his first crush, a boy in the fourth grade he still dreamed about; he told me he suspected his sister, too, had been gay, which he thought was why she'd killed herself. For those two days, he seemed like a different person to me, light, pliant, able to convey with little more than a sidelong smile that he appreciated — even needed — me. And then, just as suddenly, it all vanished. Had it taken two full days to sound me out? To be sure that I, a fellow Muslim, was more than happy to accept him as he was? Or was he fishing for something else? I would come to wonder if perhaps I'd been an object of sexual interest to him all along, if perhaps he thought I was gay, too, locked even deeper in that closet than he was. Whatever the

I sipped and marveled; I marveled and sipped. Riaz seemed vaguely distracted as he stared out his wall-size view of the day fading above the East River and, beyond it, the low-slung, dimly lit industrial thorp of waterfront Astoria. He mentioned rents in the South Bronx rising. I mentioned I had money I needed to invest.

"How much?" he asked.

I was embarrassed to say, but I did. To my surprise, he was impressed. He knew my mother, though trained as a doctor in Pakistan, had only briefly worked as one here in America. That she'd been able to put aside that much money to leave me when she died was no insignificant feat. "She left another three hundred to our local mosque in Milwaukee," I added.

His eyes lit up at the mention of the mosque; he wanted to know who'd started it and when. I told him I wasn't exactly sure who, but it opened in the late '70s. I recounted the troubles I remembered between the various ethnic groups — Albanians, Arabs, Hindustani Muslims — who had

reason for the brief window of his appealing availability, by Labor Day weekend, it was gone, and that dazzling, ceramic impenetrability was back . . .

raised the necessary funds together but then couldn't agree who was in charge.

"What was the process with the municipality?"

"What do you mean?"

"The city paperwork. Was there any trouble with that? I mean, because it was a mosque?" His interest was uncharacteristically pointed.

"I don't know. I never heard anything about it. This was so long before 9/11. I don't think folks in Wisconsin had the first clue what Muslims even were back then."

"Where I grew up, they knew, all right," he said with a sudden, vivid anger. "And they were vicious about it." He paused and got up, then went to the kitchen counter, where he stood beside a thick bouquet of large round purple-pink burrs in a crystal vase. He loved these flowers — if you could call them that — and always had them in vases around the house. I didn't see the appeal. They had no scent, they weren't particularly pretty, and if you weren't careful, the thorny stems and bulbs could draw blood. He set down his glass and reached in carefully to arrange the bouquet.

"What is that stuff, by the way? I always see it when I'm here."

"Tartar thistle," he said. "There was a field

of it behind my mother's backyard when she was growing up in Rawalpindi. She found some in the Poconos one summer, and you would have thought she'd struck gold. She clipped a bagful and planted it in our backyard in Pennsylvania. That first summer it took over the garden like wild mint. Tough as hell."

"Looks it."

"Full of life. Whenever it spilled out into the yard, it was impossible to kill. There's only one store in the city that carries it. And the only reason they do is because I have ten dozen delivered to me every week. One of the great things about having money."

"Unlimited thistle delivered to your East End Avenue doorstep anytime."

He smiled, but thinly, as if battling a disturbing thought. Back at his seat, he poured himself — then me — more whiskey and, setting the bottle down on the floor alongside his chair, began to tell me a story in which I would eventually descry the outline of all his essential choices. It was about his father's attempt to start a mosque, first in Wilkes-Barre, Pennsylvania, and later up the road in Scranton. His father's name was Aftab, and he'd never been particularly religious back in Pakistan — or so Riaz had been told by people who'd known his father back then. In America that all changed. Homesick, Aftab substituted faith for his homeland, Riaz believed, and became the sort of Muslim who always fasts and never misses a prayer.

Back then, there was nowhere to pray with the community on Fridays, nowhere to take your kids to learn their Quran, nowhere to practice your Islam with others like you. As the Muslim population in the Lackawanna Valley grew — and it grew quickly — Aftab became fixated on the idea of opening a mosque. He was no imam, so he didn't feel he could do it on his own, but he knew a grocer in town from Egypt, Alaa Ali, who'd studied at Al-Azhar University, in Cairo. Aftab approached Alaa Ali, and the two of them plotted to get something going.

On Main Street in Wilkes-Barre, not far from the barbershop where they both got their hair cut, there was an empty storefront. Both had the thought it would make a perfect little mosque. They walked by it together one Saturday morning and noted the phone number in the window. Aftab called it when he got home. By week's end, they'd put a deposit down on a lease.

Word got out through the chamber of commerce that a mosque was going into the empty storefront, and neighboring businesses went to the city council to stop it. But Aftab and Alaa Ali prevailed; in less than two months, after a modest build-out, their new mosque was open — and there was trouble from the start. It was early fall, 1979. There was no longer a shah in Tehran, and Khomeini was saying lots of very nasty things about what America had done to the Iranian nation. Then, of course, came the hostage crisis. That first week in November, the front door of the mosque was spray-painted with silver crosses; not too long after that, someone smashed a window and tossed a pig's head into the foyer. Riaz remembered helping his father scrub at the bloodstained grout between the tiles. It wouldn't come out, and they would end up retiling the entry.

Police reports were filed, but nothing was done. The local sheriff looked like Mr. Clean and knew what he thought of Muslims, namely, that they needed to go back to wherever they came from, which is what he told Aftab to his face when he tried to follow up about the complaints. On the last day of Ramadan that year, the congregation at the new mosque was so large there wasn't room inside for everyone to pray. Worshippers spilled out onto the sidewalk and front lawn, prostrating themselves in unison, muttering Arabic verses — to the abject horror of many a Main Street onlooker that day. Sheriff Clean showed up with his men in the middle of prayer, barking orders and manhandling the prostrated Muslims to their feet. Riaz was twelve and saw his father thrown against a squad car and cuffed.

A year of harassments followed, culminating with his father being accosted by the aforementioned sheriff when Riaz's younger sister — then fourteen — attempted suicide and ended up in the ICU. It seems the sheriff had seen some *Nightline* piece about a Muslim honor killing in Germany, which convinced him there was more to the girl's attempt on her life than adolescent angst. He stopped Aftab in the hospital corridor and demanded to know how often he beat his children. The episode would turn out to be one humiliation too many. Aftab resigned his position at the Wilkes-Barre mosque, which shuttered its doors.

At that point, Aftab was working in Scranton. Interest rates were falling, and the junk-bond craze had begun. Young financiers were flush with easy money and using it to take over companies, chop them up, sell them off, and pocket the proceeds. The glass manufacturer where Aftab supervised operations was just one of countless companies to succumb to this, the era's poisoned fate. For months Aftab worried about what would happen to his job until he realized his managers would keep him if he helped them figure out how to cut costs. Aftab worked up a solution to increase the plant's efficiencies that resulted in eighty-five pink slips, and now the Rinds became local pariahs for a reason other than their Islam.

As all this was transpiring, Aftab was hatching plans for a new mosque in Scranton. He found a small building on the city's north side he expected would draw less attention. He collected funds from the community for a deposit and was waiting now for approval of the land-use permit allowing a mosque on the premises. All the trouble down the road in Wilkes-Barre meant that the Scranton city council was treating the issue with extra attention. At the council hearing, a group of locals from the glass plant who'd lost their jobs thanks to Aftab's memo showed up and caused a ruckus. They jeered and chanted against Iran, though of course Iran had nothing to do with any of it. Aftab wasn't even from Iran, he tried to explain when it was his turn to speak. But one of the city council members had a sister who'd also lost her job at the glass plant and moved for a vote to adjourn the hearing. For months to come, Aftab's permit would languish, neither approved nor denied.

It was early 1983, and the season of the Rinds' misfortunes had only just begun: Though the nation's economy was finally recovering from the oil shock, the new owners of Lackawanna Glass Works were flirting with insolvency from all the debt they'd taken on to buy the company. It was time to sell it piecemeal. The complex was shut down, and everyone lost their jobs — including Aftab. A few weeks later, Riaz's sister attempted suicide again and, this time, succeeded. Aftab fell to pieces. He and his wife sold their house and moved to Arizona to be close to relatives who'd settled there. It helped his parents to be near family, Riaz said, but neither of them would ever truly recover.

And neither would he, I thought.

Night had fully fallen over the East River, and the lights along Astoria's waterfront twinkled, sparse, serene. Riaz stood and emptied what was left of that sublime whiskey into our tumblers. Throughout his telling, I'd watched the flashing anger in his eyes grow stronger, steadier, watched the incandescence of his rage brighten and consume some essential kindling that, now spent, left him looking enfeebled next to that vibrant magenta thistle. "You can probably understand why I wanted a life for myself where I was never at anyone's mercy," he said. "And I mean *never.*"

I certainly could. That and more.

He proposed we go out for dinner; I accepted. Over a dry-aged rib eye and a Duckhorn Merlot our conversation wound its way back to the money my mother had left me. He was spinning off a division of his fund, he said. The new company would do exactly what his fund already did, but now for itself rather than for client investors. When you ran a fund, he explained, you saw fees, which were great, but no one went supernova on fees. But that — going supernova, that is — was exactly what was about to happen to him. "We're going public in two months. We're oversold. I've been turning money away from people I owe big." He paused and smiled at me before completing the thought: "But if you want to give me the three hundred K, I'll wedge you in from my end."

6.

My $300,000 bought me 125,000 shares of Riaz's new outfit, Timur Capital, at the pre-public-offering share price of $2.40 a share.

On the first day of trading, the price jumped to just north of five dollars. Riaz warned me this might happen, that I would be tempted to double my money, but he didn't advise it. If I could, he said, I should resign myself to holding on through the inevitable ups and downs for twelve to eighteen months. The company was putting together something big, which, once announced, would change everyone's perception of what could be done in the space. At that point, he thought a share price closer to $20 was likely.

The following year I saw less of him. I had plays going up all over the world, and what time I didn't spend traveling I spent trying to write. I was in Finland when the announcement finally came, the one that Riaz had promised. Timur Capital had been buying apartment buildings in advantageously priced urban upmarkets: Chicago, Austin, Charlotte, Minneapolis, Orlando, among others; they bought the buildings outright, lowered rents modestly for tenants who never missed payments, then bundled the accumulated rent payments into bonds they sold on the open market. The demand was startling. Renting was the new long-term housing paradigm; fewer and fewer could afford to buy. Figuring out how to transform rent payments into liquid bonds was a lucrative — and news-stealing — alternative to the much-maligned bundled mortgage bond. Within a week, Timur was trading at $16, and then, after making the front page of the *Wall Street Journal* two months later, the price would jump to $22. That's where I sold, in January of 2017.

I was in Medina on the afternoon I officially became a multimillionaire. As I stepped out into the blue dazzle, a chorus of muezzin calls filled the air. I felt a pleasure as subtle and complete as any I've ever known; I felt bright and safe and whole. What an extraordinary irony, I thought, to receive this news in the Prophet's own city, of a fortune made through the purchase and sale of interest, so forbidden, so reviled in our faith. So perhaps it was fitting that when I got back to the hotel, the first thing I did was search online for a Manhattan liquor store that had Pappy Van Winkle twenty-three-year in stock and could have it delivered to Riaz before close of business that day. There were two. I put the $12,000 bill on my Amex as a token of the gratitude that — I wrote — I had no words to convey. The next morning I awoke to an email from him. It read: "As long as you keep writing, it'll be thanks enough. And now you've got no excuse!"

7.

By that time, though I had no way of knowing it, Timur Capital was under investigation by the Securities and Exchange Commission. A handful of small municipalities had invested in the company's rent-backed securities and lost their proverbial shirts. The communities in question alleged they were steered toward higher-yield, higher-risk assets without a full disclosure of just how high-risk those assets actually were. This part of the complaint was hearsay, as the complainants had all signed on various dotted lines, and it was just as likely that the fine print warning them about the risks had gone willfully unread, busy as all these small-town big shots were being wined and dined by a big-city company sales staff Where the SEC got involved was in how Timur managed its own relationship to these particular sales. They apparently took out insurance against the riskiest of their bonds — but not for the buyers' sake. In market lingo, they "shorted" their own securities, which meant, in layman's terms, they peddled wares they knew were worthless, bet against them, and when the wares in question lost their value, as expected — or so it was alleged — Timur Capital made a killing. "Betting against your clients" is what it's also called, and it got regulators interested. Some of this I would learn when a rangy agent from the SEC showed up on my Harlem stoop one afternoon the summer after I sold my shares. She flashed a badge and a perfunctory smile. "Mr. Akhtar?" she asked.

"I'm sorry . . . Can I help you?"

"Agent Watkins, SEC." I must have looked as confused as I felt. She clarified: "The Securities and Exchange Commission."

"Okay, right . . ."

"I was hoping you would have some time to talk to me about Riaz Rind. Maybe tell me a little bit about your involvement with his foundation and Timur Capital, LLC. As I understand it, you sold a very large block of stock in Timur Capital just this past March."

"So, um, is there a problem? Do I . . . need a lawyer?" On my lips, my questions sounded like lines badly delivered in a turgid potboiler.

Her reply was no less hackneyed: "Not unless you've done something you don't want me to know about." She shot me a reassuring smile. "Honestly? I'm just here to talk to you about Mr. Rind, and any time you can spare'd be appreciated. I mean, you *can* call a lawyer if you want, of course. I can't stop you from doing that." Tossing her cigarette to the step, she crushed it underfoot, then looked up at me with sudden worry: "I'm not supposed to do this — but do you mind if I use your restroom?"

"No, no, sure — Agent Watkins, is that right?"

"Zakeeya Watkins," she said, showing her badge, grateful. "New York office." How to process the flurry of mixed signals, now threatening, now conspiratorial, now solicitous, now vulnerable? I stepped aside and let her pass. Inside, she followed me up three flights and stopped, visibly winded, as we got to my apartment door. "Gotta quit those damn things," she said, rubbing her palm across her forehead. Once we were inside, she disappeared into the bathroom. I waited nervously for the flush to sound, realizing her ruse of needing the toilet — rudimentary as it was — had worked. When she emerged, she sat down on one of the two folding chairs at the folding table that passed for my dining table. I asked if she wanted coffee. "Sure, if you're making it — This it?" she said, looking around. "This is where you live?"

"As you can see . . ."

"There another room?"

"Well, just the bedroom," I said, pointing at the room's only door. "It used to be a studio. They put up a wall, but it still doesn't feel like a one-bedroom. It's big enough for me, though."

"Not the place I expected for a person like you."

"What kind of person is that?"

"The kind that sells one hundred and twenty-five thousand shares of a stock he got before the IPO."

"It was a friends-and-family thing."

"But you're not family."

"No, ma'am, I'm not" — I found myself "ma'am"-ing her — "but I've known him a few years now."

"How'd you meet?"

As I made her coffee, I shared the outline of the story. The meeting at the theater; the gala events that led to a board appointment; my involvement with the foundation as an advocate and executive committee member; the money my mother left me; Riaz's offer to invest it; the ups and downs of Timur stock; and finally, and most important, Riaz's early prognostication of a $20 share price, which he said was likely, but not certain, and which had predated my sale by fourteen months. There was no way any of it could have been construed as insider trading, which was the only thing I thought she was wondering about.

"You know where it's trading today, right?" she asked.

I told her I hadn't kept track since the sale.

"Forty-five dollars as of an hour ago," she said, watching for my reaction. "Kinda makes you wish you hadn't sold, huh?"

"I don't know. Not really," I said with a shrug. "I barely know what to do with the two and a half million I made. I'd have no idea what to do with five. It might actually make me want to start spending it."

She shrugged and pulled out her notepad. That's when I realized she was only now getting to the real reason for her visit: "Did Mr. Rind ever mention anything about Wilkes-Barre or Scranton, Pennsylvania?"

"Well, I mean, sure. I mean, that's where he's from."

"But anything about selling product to those municipalities?"

"Not that I remember."

"Not that you remember?" She didn't believe me.

"No. I mean, no. Not about selling product."

283

"So what did he say?"

"Is there a reason you're asking?"

She paused and, instead of answering, asked another question: "He ever talk to you specifically about Temecula, California?"

"No."

"Murfreesboro, Tennessee?" I shook my head. "Sheboygan?"

"Sheboygan, Wisconsin?"

"Mmm-hmm."

"What's this about?"

"You really don't know?"

"No," I said emphatically. "I really don't."

She'd pulled out another cigarette and tapped it against her thumbnail as she studied me, still waiting — it seemed — for some sign that would indicate, once and for all, whether I could be trusted. "Did you ever discuss Timur Capital business in your capacity as a board member at the foundation?"

"Never did. I didn't even know about it until Riaz offered to invest the money I got from my mother."

"But you did purchase shares while still on the board?"

"Yes, but like I said, there was just that one conversation before I invested. He told me he was happy to look after my money. I gave him the cash. I got a notice I was a shareholder. After that, from time to time I would get an email update. That was the extent of it."

"You never asked him any questions about the business, or . . ."

"I probably did. But nothing specific. 'How's it going?' 'I really hope you don't lose my money.' I mean, I had a Google alert on the company, so when something came out in the press, I'd shoot him a message to congratulate him if the news was good. I thought I understood the business pretty well, but not well enough to pester him about it."

She nodded, slipping the cigarette behind her ear. "So there was never any discussion of these municipalities I mentioned, no discussion that you were a party to — or that you overheard during your tenure at the foundation?"

"Well, no, that's not true. I did hear about each of those places. Just not from him."

"Because . . ."

"Because those towns blocked mosques from being built in their communities." She nodded, clearly aware of the fact, making notes as I spoke. "We'd hired a PR firm at the foundation to work on placing a story about what was going on in those places."

"And?"

"That story got placed. Got a fair bit of traction, actually."

"And that's all you heard?" she asked, looking up from her pad; her tone was skeptical.

"That was it. Honestly."

She checked her notes again, then took another look around the apartment.

"So this is really your place?"

"I have a toothbrush in the bathroom and a rental lease to prove it."

She smiled. "I spent a good chunk of my childhood three blocks over. On One Forty-Seventh." She got up from the table.

"On Malcolm's block?"

Her eyes brightened. "My grandmother knew him. Used to see him going out with those crazy zoot suits — before he met Elijah." She'd made her way to the window now, where I'd taped a faded snapshot of my mother to the jamb. The photo showed her as a young woman in a red-and-white *shalwar kameez,* with a white *dupatta* draped around her shoulders. "Who's this?"

"My mom. When she was twenty-three."

"Beautiful lady. Might want to find a nicer place for the photo."

"I — uh — she died a year ago, and . . . I put it there — I mean, I know it's going to

286

sound strange, but — I've been dreaming about her a lot . . . That she doesn't want to leave. So I put it there by the window so she knows . . . I mean, if she's still here, somewhere . . ." I stopped. I wasn't sure why I'd told her this — and now I was getting emotional.

"You're letting her know it's okay to go," Zakeeya added kindly. "I get it."

"We've all got our magical thinking, right?"

"Wouldn't get through a day without it," she said as she made her way back to the table. "Look. You're probably going to hear about this in the next day or so. But those cities are filing a class-action suit. Your friend sold them a lot of junk debt, debt they're convinced he knew was going to default. They think he did it to retaliate."

"Retaliate?"

"For the mosque thing."

When she said it, I realized: Of course. Of course he did.

I don't know what warmed her to me — whether it was Harlem, or my humble surroundings, or my mother's photo, or what I would come to suspect: that she was Muslim, too — whatever the case, Zakeeya sat down at the table again, and instead of asking me more questions now, laid out the class-action complaint as she understood it. The SEC was looking into it, too, she said, because Timur had taken out short positions against the debt they'd sold the municipalities. When that debt defaulted, Timur made a killing. All that said, she added, it still wasn't clear if any laws had been broken.

By now, I felt comfortable enough to hazard a comment I don't expect many SEC agents would have appreciated: "I mean, honestly, what you're describing doesn't really sound any worse than what Goldman was doing in 2010," I said.

"Your friend's no Goldman Sachs."

"That he's not."

"Wrong color," she said as she stood, buttoning her blazer. "And praying to the wrong God. But you didn't hear it from me."

The suit never made it past discovery. I sought out one of the court reporters who took and transcribed the depositions. She agreed to sell me copies for a hefty fee — $9,700 — on the condition that I mask any details that pointed back to her if I ended up writing about the case. As I read through the transcripts, it was clear the decision makers on the various city councils in question had been duped, but more or less willingly. They'd taken gifts, had their "road show" trips paid for by the company, gone to the drunken parties, slept with the prostitutes. A city comptroller took her family on vacation for a week in Cabo San Lucas, most expenses paid; an alderman ended up with season tickets to the local NFL team, despite a ten-year waiting list. In almost every case, it wasn't just that the fine print hadn't been properly read: it was that the people doing the reading didn't even seem to understand the very nature of the underlying security that they were about to purchase. What's more, many of the "honorable" city officials implicated had already demonstrated less-than-honorable judgment in the allocation of city money; the rent-backed-bond buying spree was just the first time they'd all been burned so badly. As for Timur Capital, Riaz's sales staff was covered. The fine print in the contracts was certainly convoluted, but unequivocal. The undersigned were duly warned about possible short positions that might be taken out against any or all of the securities being sold.

In other words, there wasn't a case.

I was startled at the incompetence — even malfeasance — so abundantly on display at the municipal level. It was startling to see in this picture of America a nation so much like the one my parents described in Pakistan, where cutting corners, taking bribes, selling perks — all this was just business as usual. There was no honest way to make a good living back home, my father used to say. Corruption in Pakistan was endemic; escaping it was a good part of the reason he'd wanted to come to America in the first place. If those court transcripts are any indication of the larger state of affairs in American towns and cities, let's just say my father may have been somewhat too rosy in his take on corruption in this country.

Of course, there's no excuse for Riaz's swindle. The resulting deficits in those places hurt the people who live there — hurt their children, their elderly. In one of the cities, the situation was so bad that budgets were cut, a hundred public employees lost their jobs, and bankruptcy was averted only by raising property taxes 30 percent and lowering city salaries — including the mayor's — to the equivalent of minimum wage, $7.25 an hour at the time. In another, the sewer and parking authorities were sold off to the highest private bidder; so were the water supply and the public parks.

It may sound as if my outrage over all this is muted by the benefit I've reaped. It's not. But it is the first time I've been forced to dwell so deeply in a fundamental contradiction of what's become of our much-vaunted American way. Mark Twain doubted there was a writer yet born who could tell the truth about himself. You'll have to make up your own mind about me — but I don't believe I'm offering a defense of either myself or Riaz in stating what I take for the obvious: holding stock in Timur Capital isn't any different from owning a stake in Nike, or Apple, or Exxon, or Goldman, or VW, or Boeing, or Merck, or any of the storied firms whose shares make up retirement nest eggs and college funds across our divided land, companies known not only for their progressive giving and canny political stances but also for cheating and abusing their workers, duping their customers, destroying the environment, selling goods that don't work, manufacturing cars and drugs and planes that kill, profiting in ever newer, ever more ingenious ways off the bait and switch of the permanent corporate lie, namely, that the customer — rather than profit at any and all human cost — is king. In this era of capital's unquestioned amoral supremacy, the only course-correcting moments of clarity — what passes for moral comeuppance, that is — are drops in stock price. Last I checked, Timur was still rising. Nothing unusual, then, about my unscrupulous gains except that I can't ignore them. Still, I'm surprised Riaz got away with it. Milken did something similar in his own era — brilliant scion of a generation of Jewish fathers shut out by the white-shoe world, avenger of his tribe who found new ways to use debt, dodged the laws, pulled the wool over the nation's eyes in his quest to torch the WASP establishment. But Milken paid for his rage. He paid dearly. Riaz is just getting richer.

POX AMERICANA

VI.
OF LOVE AND DEATH

It is joy to be hidden but disaster not to be found.

— D. W. Winnicott

Of the women I slept with during my season of sexual fecklessness, I least expected Asha would have been the one to give me syphilis. Incidences of the so-called Great Pretender were surging in this era of transactional sex, and it was much reported that parts of Brooklyn were showing rates of the disease not seen since the nineteenth century. That year, I'd had quite a bit of sex in Williamsburg, where the numbers preponderated, and thus assumed — wrongly — that I'd contracted the malady somewhere between Bedford and Graham Avenues. After the diagnosis, I strained to recall even the most peripheral apprehension of an incipient chancre — a discoloration, say, on any of the various vulvic folds at which I'd slobbered, into which I'd pushed — but my recollections were vague at best, for by the time the panties were off I wasn't usually much given to the inspecting mood. The shaved pubus was legion then, and I would end up suspecting I'd simply missed the lesion, mistaking it for yet another ingrown hair on the verge of releasing its pus.

Asha was well and smoothly groomed, without so much as a bump or razor scratch from her mons pubis down to below her introitus. Every three weeks, she would pop two Advil and drive the mile and a half from the fourplex she owned in the Montrose section of Houston to the wax salon closer to downtown, where her aesthetician poured and spread scorching wax onto her labia, waited a half minute, then ripped the seal, which plucked every nascent hair from its follicle. Asha was long accustomed to keeping her genitals hair-free, though not as a capitulation — unwitting or not — to the pornographic ideal engulfing us all. No. Her bald sex was a Muslim thing. The trips to Apple and Eve Brazilian Wax were a holdover from her childhood years as a believer.*

* Removing pubic and armpit hair is a unisex Muslim custom that dates back to the Prophet's supposed enjoinder about necessary hygienic

There were others: the hodgepodge Ramadan fasting, the avoidance of pork, the use of her right hand when she ate and of her left whenever she reached for toilet paper, and of course, lingering guilt over the more than occasional indulgences in Cab Franc and Syrah. My point is she wasn't exactly a believer, and she wasn't exactly not. She'd grown up with these things (as had I), and they clearly still held some meaning for her (as they did not for me), even if that meaning had almost nothing to do anymore with a yearning for heaven or a fear about ending up in hell.

I say "almost" only because Asha was never really clear about what she actually thought when it came to the end of life or the end of times. Both her parents are religious, though Asha used to joke that her mother's faith had as much Oprah and Jeane Dixon in it as it had of the Prophet Muhammad. As a teen, she ran into some

---

practices. According to one tradition, the practices are five: shaved pubic hair, circumcision, trimmed mustaches, clipped nails, depilated armpits; according to another, the practices are ten, and the five more added to the previous include brushing one's teeth and using water to clean oneself after both urination and defecation.

fairly baroque trouble with them over normal teenage things that only ever got her "American" friends yelled at or, at worst, grounded. There was more corporal punishment in her family than most in this country would be comfortable with (usually by her mother's hand), and several times she found herself locked in her room for days at a time and occasionally starved (as her father had been as a child). Typical of Asha's generous embrace of things as they are was that she never seemed bitter about any of it. She didn't hold it against her parents that, as she put it, they couldn't make their peace with the consequences of having had children in a culture that wasn't their own. She saw their dilemma with compassion. At root, she believed, they never really understood how American they *weren't.*

In the four months Asha and I spent not quite dating and not quite not dating, I would meet her folks three times: twice at the ranch-style house in Spring, Texas, where she (and her two sisters) grew up; once when they all came through New York and we spent an afternoon wandering the halls at the Museum of Natural History. By that point, her parents knew I was more than just a "friend of a friend" who happened to be in Houston on the weekend of the Prophet's birthday, which her family always celebrated by having friends and family to the house for dinner. I think they liked me, though mostly — I suspect — because I was nothing like the man they'd spent seven years desperately hoping their daughter would leave.

More on that shortly.

Her father, Haris, is not entirely dissimilar to mine. Though physically they look nothing alike — Haris is short and built like a barrel; he'd played rugby as a young man and then "put on the pounds," he joked, patting his gut as we passed beneath the Blue Whale — he and my father share a fundamental optimism about this country that shaped their saucer-eyed, New World wonder as well as a blunt brashness encouraged by their adopted culture: sunny and sure to some, naive and cocky to others. Central to their ideas of themselves as American is that they "get" this country, "get" how the system here works, and, above all, that they "made it." For Haris, "making it" meant growing that initial gas station–convenience store, for which he'd barely been able to gather a down payment in 1975, into a chain of a dozen such across the Houston area; acquiring more real estate

— the reason why Asha owns a fourplex, living in one apartment, renting out the others; and, finally, what he was most proud of, the board positions at the local chapter of the Lions Club and the chamber of commerce. When he became a citizen, in '86, Haris promptly raised an American flag in the front yard and began an epistolary second life that, when Asha told me about it, conjured up a middle-class Muslim analogue to Bellow's maniacal, missive-writing Moses Herzog. Inspired, Asha said, by the judge's stirring paean to America's democratic ideals at his swearing-in ceremony, Haris started to pen fawning admonishments — and later, provocations — to famous now-fellow Americans: Lee Iacocca, Armand Hammer, Ann Richards, Muhammad Ali, John Wayne, Tip O'Neill, Lee Meriwether, James Michener, Ross Perot . . . just to name a few. Enshrined on the fridge door were two of his prized possessions: a signed reply from George H. W. Bush himself — with a blue smudge of ink the color of the autograph proving it was real — affixed by a magnet next to a snapshot of Haris posing with then vice president Bush at a Fourth of July parade in downtown Houston.

Despite the accumulation of outward

markers denoting his American belonging, Asha thought her father was still at heart an Old World man. The light of a Texas sun may have poured through their windows, but in those rooms, her father's beloved Urdu *ghazals* drenched the family's ears with loss, lamentation, lush and endless regret. His self-styled American extroversion, too, she thought was fundamentally Punjabi in origin, loud and warm and overly familiar, disarming to the stoic locals who came by to do house repairs or meter readings, an amusing eccentricity to his employees and customers alike. Even those letters to the powerful and famous that he spent so much of his time on — and collected into a self-published book that Asha kept on her nightstand — even these were quintessentially Pakistani in their themes, containing as they did: exhortations to recognize the border threat; warnings about corruption in politics both local and national; reminders of the myriad forms of succor America had enjoyed from Muslims during its long battle with the Soviets; and, most amusingly, abundant references to a rumor still current in much of the Muslim world, namely, that Neil Armstrong had converted to Islam.*

* Details differed depending on who you heard
the story from, but, in broad strokes, it went
something like this: When Armstrong stepped out
onto the lunar surface he heard a voice crying out
a sublime, otherworldly song. He didn't know
what he was hearing, but he never forgot it. Years
later, during a trip to Egypt, he heard the Muslim
call to prayer for the first time and realized that
was the song he'd heard on the moon. Praise of
the Muslim God. One variant of the tale depicted
him as hearing the call to prayer not just on land-
ing but also in the rocket ship on the way to and
from the moon; still another cast Buzz Aldrin in
the role of resident Judas, who heard what Armstrong did but denied it for the sake of his dis-
sembling Christian tribe. Every version of the tale
ended the same way, with Armstrong adopting the
faith. I'd been hearing the story — now in one
form, now in another — since I was a boy, and
Asha's father had been writing to famous Americans about it for almost as long. She said she
wouldn't have been entirely surprised if his obsession had played some part in the State Department's decision to issue an official response in
1983: "While stressing his strong desire not to of-
fend anyone or show disrespect for any religion,
Armstrong has advised the Department that
reports of his conversion to Islam are inaccurate."

As she did in her father, Asha saw signs of a less-than-easy Pak-American alloy in her mother. There were the obvious, amusing juxtapositions — a PTA president who wore *shalwar kameez* and *dupattas* to meetings populated with mostly white suburban Texas housewives; the horoscopes she brought to her weekly Quranic study group; the Iftar dinners that took place at Burger King — but the more telling contradictions were subtler, darker, and most encompassed, for Asha, by her mother's inability to imagine that women had any other place than behind their men — and that those

---

The State Department letter wouldn't do much to stanch the rumor. When Armstrong died, in 2012, I heard more than a few complaints from family members (and others) that none of his Western obituaries referred to his conversion. I understand the stubborn attachment to this silly tale. It makes sense of the moral conundrum presented by those images of American boot prints pressed on the face of our holiest of holy symbols, the moon, which orders our years and toward which we lift our hands in supplication whenever the curved sliver of its renewed light appears again in the darkening sky. Yes, the West may have been sophisticated enough to get there, but what it heard once it did was still all about us . . .

men must be Muslim. Indeed, trouble over the white boys who filled Asha's girlhood dreams would be long, protracted, decisive, and violent.

Asha's parents didn't let her leave town for college, so she went to the University of Houston, graduating summa cum laude. She aced her LSATs and got into law school at the University of Chicago, which made it hard for her father to stop her from leaving home, though before she left he wanted her to arrange her marriage to a first cousin in Pakistan. She refused. Unbeknownst to him or her mother, she was already in love with someone. His name was Blake. He was from Kansas and was playing basketball for Houston on scholarship. They met at a frat party her sophomore year. She got so drunk she passed out, and Blake took her back to his room, where he tucked her into his bed. She found him snoring on the floor on the other side of the room the following morning. So began a tumultuous on-again, off-again romance that would last through college and lure her back home once she took her law degree.

While she was away in Chicago, Blake, passed up in the NBA draft, signed a two-year offer to play professionally in the Baltic States, and the consequences of his itinerant life in the arena towns of Latvia and Lithuania would affect not only Asha but also, eventually, me. Baltic life offered few consolations: the hotel rooms were frigid and small; the food was revolting; worst of all, almost no one spoke English. Longing for comfort and distraction, Blake found it the only place he could, in the arms of local girls bewitched by the spindly, red-headed young American grimacing through the pork-and-herring salads and sipping lager in their town squares in his down winter coat. This was where Blake developed the sexual habits that Asha would complain to me about — the choking, the wanting to be choked, the video cameras through which they watched themselves in the act, the prostitutes. In Minsk, he tore his ACL at a playoff match, extinguishing his hoop dreams for good. Back in Houston, he took a job at a Honda dealership, where he was still working when Asha accepted a position at the Houston-based Saudi-American oil services conglomerate Aramco so she could move back home to be near him. It was through her job at Aramco that I met her.

I've given you a picture of at least part of Asha's birthday suit but no proper sense of what she looks like: an abundant head of dark brown hair with honey highlights to match the sparkling hazel of her wide-set eyes (which are her mother's); an upturned snub nose that almost looks like it was broken once and never correctly reset; a short mouth with a pouting lower lip much fuller than the upper; and something wild and welcome about the way these all come together that lends a hardscrabble grace to her beauty. Like her face, her body brims with defiant life: she has her father's build, athletic, almost stocky, a short torso with wide hips — like those fertility figurines excavated from the Indus Valley ruins at Harappa, not far from the plains that were her father's ancestral home. The night I met her at the Harvard Club, in late November of 2014 — where Riaz had sent me to mix and mingle at an oil industry event on the foundation's behalf — she was wearing a form-fitting gingham dress, and her striking figure was very much on display. I noticed her immediately in that dreary bay of navy blazers; I noticed her and thought I noticed her notice me. I tarried, palavering with a Saudi executive whom Riaz and I had met in Dubai. Later, as she headed to the bar for a refill, I sidled up alongside her. She was getting a mojito; I asked for the same. She complimented me on my jacket — a

Nehru in a calico print. I told her I loved her dress, and she smiled. There was, then, that inevitable lull when a mutual yearning for intimacy has clearly announced itself but when even the earliest rudiments of a shared language to enable it have yet to be found. She lingered in the pause, sipping. There'd been much chatter in the room that night about the price of oil, and so I leaped into the breach by asking where she thought it was headed next:

"Oh, God. I have no idea," she said with a self-deprecating laugh. "What is it now?"

"I think it's lower than people like. They seem pretty upset about it."

"So you don't know, either?"

"I was just trying to impress you."

That seemed to bring a twinkle to her eye: "Now, why would you try to do that?"

"I think the question is why *wouldn't* I?"

"Well . . . that's very flattering. But you might want to slow down."

"Seventy in a fifty-mile-an-hour zone?"

"More like eighty in a twenty-five."

"Ouch. Okay. Got it."

"Good," she said. " 'Cause I do think you're cute."

Across the room, I noticed a white-haired man staring at us. He was wearing a pinstriped suit somewhat too small for his portly frame, and his face was covered with the splotchy bloom of a hardy Scotch habit.

"So what is it you do?" she asked.

"I'm a playwright," I said.

"A playwright? I didn't even know that was a thing."

"It's definitely a thing. It means I write plays."

"I just meant I didn't know someone could, you know . . ."

"Make a living at it?"

"Yeah, exactly."

"Hard to believe, but true."

"I'm sorry, I didn't mean to imply —"

"No, no. You're right. It's not really on the radar here. In this country, I mean. If you mention Broadway, people usually think you're talking about musicals. Most of us actually make our living in television."

"Is that what you do, too?"

"Last few years I've been lucky. Haven't had to."

She lifted her glass. "Here's to continued good luck, then." She touched her glass to mine, and the gesture appeared to stoke the ire of Ruddy Face, who was still glaring and making no attempt to hide it.

"That guy keeps looking over here —"

"That's my boss," she said, shooting him a short, inattentive smile.

308

"He doesn't look too happy about something."

"About the fact I'm talking to you, probably."

"Me? Really? Why?"

"Why do you think?" she responded, with a weary look.

"He have a thing for you?"

"I mean . . . not really . . . but yeah. Inappropriately possessive. Constantly needing credit for not acting out. You know, the usual."

"I'm sorry to hear that."

She shrugged. "Let me go do the rounds. There's some people I'm supposed to connect with. Unfortunately, you're not one of them — at least as far as he's concerned."

"Do your thing."

But instead of leaving, she lingered: "Can you stick around? Maybe a drink when we're done? I know a great place in Chinatown."

"I'd love nothing more."

And with that, she smiled and marched off, stopping — I assumed — to placate her boss before heading off into another room. He shot me a look once she was gone, then turned and walked off, too.

I meandered, mingling, took cigarette breaks, came back, circulated some more. It was two hours before she was done. By that point we'd both had more to drink than I think either of us realized. She took my hand as we stepped out onto 44th Street, her fingers electric in my grip. We found a cab on Fifth Avenue and ended up on a narrow side street in Chinatown in front of an unmarked door guarded by a bouncer in a bow tie. He recognized her and let us in. At a covered booth in back, we sat side by side — shoulders touching, arms grazing — and had more drinks. We talked about our families and our apartments. She told me about her shih tzu, Tucker, and how much she hated leaving home because she knew how much he missed her. I confessed the only pets I'd ever had were fish. At one point, she asked when my birthday was. I deflected; I'd never liked birthdays, I told her, even as a child. The day's preordained centrality always struck me as coercive; at best, I sensed people were happy about a thing they knew they had, too; I felt them celebrating themselves. Seeming amused by what she would later describe to me as my "fetching pretension," she didn't relent. She wanted to know the date.

"End of October," I offered.

"*After* the twenty-second?" she asked playfully. I nodded, finally sharing the date, and

I saw her eyes soften with a thought. She blinked twice now as she looked at me, then blinked again. I noticed her lips barely part, and the tip of her tongue dart in and out between her teeth.

Feeling her hand on my knee, I leaned in for a kiss.

Back in her room at what was then still called the Trump SoHo, we fucked twice that night on a bed that was bigger than my bathroom, then fucked again on the couch as the sun came up over her staggering view of lower Manhattan. I loved how she tasted — sweet and clean, like mountain water — and I ate her out as we waited for the eggs and pancakes we'd ordered from room service. We kissed as we chewed. I confessed that I couldn't remember ever feeling so knocked out by someone. She smiled coyly and complained about her all-day meetings and a late-afternoon flight back to Houston she couldn't change.

"It's fine," I said. "I'll come see you this weekend in Texas."

She looked surprised to hear it. Pleasantly, I thought. "Really?"

"I mean, if it's okay . . ."

"Of course it's okay. I mean, I'd love it. I just —"

"What?"

Her pause lasted long enough for me to register a doubt. "If you change your mind, I want you to know I'll understand."

"I won't change my mind."

"But if you do, it's okay. This was great. Really great. And if you walk out of here and realize you got caught up in a moment and didn't really mean it —"

"I do mean it," I said forcefully. I was being sincere and wanted her to know it. I didn't want her to think I was going to disappoint her. But I wasn't reading her right. She wasn't actually afraid that I'd lose interest. If anything, she was afraid I wouldn't.

Our night together had been unusual for her, I would discover. I was only the fourth man she'd ever slept with and the only one she'd ever slept with on a first date. Why me? Because, she said, she was completing her Saturn returns. And: with Venus dominating her chart and now in transit through her fifth house, she was entering a period of unusual upheaval and singular encounters. A psychic she consulted at least once a month predicted that, on an upcoming trip, she would meet a "dashing Scorpio" who would "sweep her off her feet." The personal theme for the period ahead was embodiment; if life was a school, it was time to take the curriculum. She should allow herself to enjoy her time with this man fully, the psychic (named Nancy) said, for though the connection would present as uncommonly strong, it would likely be fleeting. He might fall for you, Nancy said, but don't worry about breaking his heart — he can take it. Besides, he's nowhere near ready to settle down . . .

"Duly noted," I quipped, not without some irritation, when Asha told me all this that following weekend at a resort built to resemble a Renaissance palazzo in the Central Texas town of — I am not making this up — Florence. Initially, she'd told me she was going to be in Austin, an hour away, on business and wanted us to have time together without any distraction. Once I'd gotten there and settled, and once we were both sore from an afternoon and night of sex, she confessed the real reason for the remote location: she hadn't wanted us crossing paths with anyone she knew back in her hometown. It was then that she also told me about Nancy, about our predicted encounter, and — mostly crucially — about Blake, who, it turns out, she was still very much seeing.

She'd been with him for the better part of

nine years. They'd broken things off for the umpteenth time in the weeks before the trip to New York, where she'd met me, but gotten back together two days before I'd landed in Texas. She knew it wasn't fair not to have let me know before I left — she said — but she didn't regret it. She'd wanted to see me again, and now that she had, she was certain she wanted to keep seeing me. She knew it would sound strange and probably more than a little fucked-up. She'd never cheated before in her life, she said, adding in a hushed tone that she would understand completely if all this turned me off.

It didn't. It gave me a hard-on, actually.

After we had sex again, we talked more about it: she told me Nancy didn't see things being over with Blake, not even close; they were meant to be together, though it wasn't clear from their astrological charts they would weather the considerable planetary impediments in their way. "I know I probably sound bat-shit crazy," Asha said as I nibbled her shoulder, "and maybe I am; I mean, Blake thinks so, and so does pretty much anybody else I ever tell about Nancy, at least when they realize I'm actually making real relationship decisions based on the advice I get from her — but whatever, I'm used to it at this point. I don't know why people think I haven't gone through this myself — I mean, really *looked* at it. I have. I'm a lawyer. And it's not like I don't know that Nancy *knows* how I feel about him. I know she knows. And of course, it's occurred to me maybe she's feeding me that line because she knows it's part of what keeps me coming back at sixty dollars a session. I know all that. But I listen to what resonates and what feels true. And there's a lot of that in what she says. That's a fact. It just is. I mean, it's hard to argue with results like her predicting I'd meet you. Right? I mean, okay — so let's pull that one apart. Maybe I just needed to be encouraged to step out of my comfort zone. Maybe that's all Nancy did, open me up to the possibility of meeting someone — which she knows I'm generally not. Maybe she just gave me permission, and that put me at ease, and that's what led to me doing something I never do. I mean, *never.* When I hear about my girlfriends' one-night hookups? They sound like nightmares! So if that's part of it, I mean, my *suggestibility,* fine. But it doesn't account for the part that's you. Right? A Scorpio? Okay, so sure, there was a one-in-twelve chance of that; so maybe the numbers came out in Nancy's favor — like they pretty much do *all the time.* Fine.

But what about Venus transiting *your* fifth house, too? I checked your chart this week. I mean, *that's* weird. And it starts to make you feel like you have to do more work to explain it all away than just accepting it for what it is. So whatever. If that's all it is, some combination of suggestibility and coincidence, so be it. I'd rather live this way than the alternative."

One of the reasons Asha could go on without so much as a hesitating pause had — I suspect — something to do with what she was reading on my face as she spoke: interest, encouragement, assent. I, too, had long harbored a secret penchant for this sort of thing. Though never tempted by psychics or tea leaves or tarot cards, I had always gone about my days with the assumption of some unseen but dimly legible order beneath the bright clatter of Creation. In leaving the theism of my Muslim childhood behind, I never did entirely abandon its deepest underlying logic. I didn't know if there was anything like a God. I didn't care. But it was mostly clear to me we were not just castaways in some tohubohu bearing an ensign of meaning only for those desperate enough to concoct one: I felt mostly certain more was going on than met the eye — despite not having a real clue just *what* that "more" might entail. My assuredness on these matters owed less to faith than it did to experience, for I'd been hearing echoes of the uncanny since early childhood. Indeed, coeval with the birth of memory itself is the steady, reassuring recollection of my dead older brother, Imtiaz, already deceased when I was born; a recollection not as a figment of family lore — my parents rarely spoke of him; had no pictures of him up on our walls or shelves — or as chimeric companion; rather, as a presence: soothing, inquiring, somehow noble. I knew he was mine before I ever thought he might be my brother. I called him Joe. My parents called him my imaginary friend. When I was four, I asked my mother if we could have the fish tank back. She looked at me, horrified. Joe said we had orange fish in the room, I said, and he wants to watch them again. She asked me to repeat it. I did. Then she slapped me and started to cry. Apparently, before I was born, there actually had been an aquarium in the room beside the bed in which I slept, and Imtiaz would gaze into it endlessly. Father and he would go to the fish store to pick goldfish for that tank, and when Imtiaz died, it bubbled softly away in that now empty room, too painful a reminder for both of them. Father released all the fish into a local pond and hid the tank in the garage.

I'd never known any of this.

When I say I felt him as a presence, I don't mean to imply that I ever spied his form or heard him speak in any other voice than my own. Even so, his tenor and texture were not of me. To become aware he was present felt like a kind of play initiated by something only different from myself because it felt like him. He's with me still, an aegis, a daemon, a mood of particular calm, a name I give to the great-hearted goad — not heeded often enough — to hold my tongue, to wait my turn, to stop and inquire. As I grew older, I would learn more about my brother from my mother's sisters, from my father — and, once my mother died, from her journal. I was told he was thoughtful, affectionate, graceful beyond his years, that he loved to draw and would spend hours a day absorbed in the pictures he incessantly made — mostly of fish. No doubt there was much idealization in all their recollections of him, bereaved as they were by his death at the shocking age of five, but notwithstanding, so much of what they said to me I felt I somehow already knew. As an adult, I would wonder if I'd picked up on some still palpable emotional residue,

318

still carried, still felt by my parents — the raw data of their grief, if you will — that I made my own. This vaguely conceived notion was certainly infinitely less objectionable than the entirely indefensible conclusion that I might be actually communing with the gracious spirit of my fish-adoring dead brother.

When I was eight:

I dreamed that my mother's mother's mother was being chased by God. In the dream, God was a large, angry cloud, so large, in fact, I couldn't see Him. I saw her running and saw that everywhere she ran, she couldn't escape Him. The next morning, I came into the kitchen to find my father consoling my mother. Her sister, my aunt Nazneen, had just called from Rawalpindi. Their grandmother — my great-grandmother — had died that night.

There's more:

The following winter we were in Pakistan for Christmas break and staying in my father's northern Punjabi village. I remember a meal in the courtyard with the village imam. He was a slight middle-aged man with a long bister face framed by a henna-red beard. His teeth were square and orderly and flashed in his mouth as he spoke. I wondered if they were real. At some point during dinner, my legs got sore. And then the soreness spread through my body. That night I came down with a fever that lasted two days. On the second night, my temperature spiked to 104. As I lay sweating in a wicker bed in my grandmother's room, I started to hallucinate that the sky was coming apart into chunks of bread and bone. I was scared one of these would crush me. My father climbed in beside me, caressed my forehead, sang quietly into my ear to calm me. I fell asleep and dreamed of the same village imam with the curtain beard and square teeth, accompanied by a throng of elders — men and women — in shawls and beards. They had all come to see me, forming a line so long it led out of the bedroom, through the courtyard, and into the village square. They were all holding water from Zamzam* in their cupped palms, and one by one, they dripped the holy water on my forehead. Finally, my bed was taken

---

* Zamzam — a holy well in Mecca allegedly revealed to Hajar, Abraham's wife and Ishmael's mother, brought forth by her thirsty infant's restless foot. It is a common Muslim belief that the water confers health and blessings; a 2011 BBC investigation revealed it contained dangerous levels of arsenic.

out into the courtyard, where they all gathered in a circle that turned quietly around me.

For months after that illness, I would dream of grandparents and grandparents of grandparents coming to visit; I dreamed of a desert vista filled with my ancestors praying in unison; I dreamed of the dejected Prophet wandering through the empty streets of my suburban subdivision at night. He had a green scarf on his head and looked like Tafi — the man I'd seen at the well as a child — but I knew in the dream it was Muhammad. This dream I relayed to my mother the following morning as she cracked eggs into a skillet for my breakfast before school. As she cooked, she asked me to repeat the dream again, and I wouldn't understand the intent, furrowed look on her face as she listened until I heard her repeat on the phone — to what must have been a dozen friends and family over the next few days — almost word for word what I said. She was bragging: seeing the Prophet in a dream was a badge of honor in our Muslim faith, and especially so in her family. The most outwardly religious of my mother's sisters, Khadija, had famously had her own dream about him and had this to say about mine: it was well known that the Prophet slept and rose early; for him to be wandering at night signaled turmoil; he was dejected, she believed, by the plight of Muslims in America; that I had seen him on our local streets meant that I would become a great American imam someday, perhaps great enough finally to make this nation of unbelievers see the truth. Of course, Father thought it was all nonsense, and not just of the usual unthinking Muslim grade; this "great imam" stuff was a particularly noxious form of nonsense he didn't want repeated — he told Mother — as it threatened to "swell up" my head. She didn't abide the warning, though I think my father was probably onto something.

By the time I hit puberty, the dreams stopped — or at least I stopped remembering them, which is what Mary Moroni would suggest my sophomore year in college when she taught me the trick with the pencil. I alluded before to encounters and apprehensions prognosticated by my collegiate nightwork, but these were mostly visions of trifles: a classmate in the same blue sweater and orange pants she walked into the auditorium wearing the next day; the final score of an upcoming varsity football game dreamed about three days before it took place; a bazaar stand in an African country where I was haggling with a vendor over melons, this on the eve of an economics exam on which the final question involved the particulars of the East African melon trade (which we'd never discussed — either East Africa or melons). The only such college premonition to touch me in any personal way was of a violently pink room glimpsed during a wet dream and suddenly recalled by the offensively pink tiles of a bathroom on the third floor of the ladies' dorm across campus where — later that semester — I was losing my virginity in a shower. Over the years, I stopped paying much attention to these inexplicable ruptures of the time-space continuum — stopped paying attention, that is, until attention was demanded. As a boy, I'd dreamed of my great-grandmother's death, and thirty years later, I would dream of her daughter's death. I saw her picking fruit in a pomegranate grove. She fell, and I awoke. The next day, my grandmother died of a heart attack. Two days before 9/11, I dreamed of an attack on Manhattan.

I trust I've made my point, namely, that there was history behind my inclination to take Asha's kooky confessions at face value. Perhaps our shared proclivity for omens was nothing more than self-involvement mas-

323

querading as communion with the numinous; perhaps it was a New World outcropping of our forebears' superstitions. I've stopped trying to understand it all, and though I offer my account here with self-restraint (for, reader, I could go on), I can't renounce this bizarre tendency simply for the sake of preserving what little reliability I may still possess as narrator of these songs and stories. I have to own it; this brand of crazy is fully baked into me.

Much of the foregoing I've shared in hopes of offering a bare minimum of context for a startling conclusion I would come to nine weeks into my relationship with Asha — if a *relationship* is what you could call it, considering that Asha was still very much *with* Blake the entire time we were together — namely, that she was my match, the person meant for me, and, against my better judgment (for I knew she didn't feel the same way), that she was the woman I would and must marry. Our sexual connection, the quirky familial and orphic concordances, all these certainly fed my conviction, but the decisive piece was infinitely more banal, or at least less outwardly remarkable. And it crept up on me.

We were in a Starbucks on the Upper East

Side. We'd been walking for hours, and I was tired. We went inside, and I took a seat at an empty table. I watched her order herself a cup of tea and select a packet of chocolate-covered cookies for us to share. At the condiment counter, standing next to a hunched elderly Jewish woman, Asha tore open a packet of sweetener and mixed it into her cup. As she reached to toss the stirrer, the older woman stopped her and made a comment. Asha then handed her the stirrer, which the older woman now used to stir her own drink. When she was done, she and Asha shared a smile, and the older woman tossed the stirrer away. As Asha watched the older woman trudge to the open door, the expression I saw on Asha's face was one of tenderness to which, I dare say, even the great Raphael could not have done justice. After the older woman was gone, Asha came to join me, offering her cup for a sip. As I drank, she ran her smooth, tea-warm palm along the side of my face. I felt simple, small, calm; without worry or complication; I felt at home.

Back at my place, I chopped onions and garlic for the murgh karahi and dal tarka she made us for dinner. We ate with our fingers as we watched a true-crime special on TV. Yet another husband had killed his spouse to be with a new lover. Our sex that night was different. It was the first time I cried in her arms, and when I woke beside her the next morning, the light in the room — bleeding through the blinds — was a brisk, bright gray. It was a clear, quiet light I didn't recognize. There was not a thought in my mind as I lay there listening to my heart thrum softly in my chest. I turned to face Asha's sleeping profile, and a shard of a dream suddenly gleamed inside me: Asha and I are both in traditional Pakistani dress; I'm applying kohl to my eyes; she lifts her pink kurta to shave her underarms; I see her belly; she's pregnant.

I studied her face as she slept. By that morning's unusually pristine semilight, her skin was the color of pekoe and turmeric. My own skin — darker, a shade of murky copper — had long been the source of a central confusion: since childhood, I'd felt a visceral disgust for the sickly tints of the white skin I saw everywhere around me, the blanched arms and legs, faces the color of paste, flesh devoid of warmth or human glow, a wan affliction incomprehensible to me except as something to be hidden; I'd felt all this since childhood, and yet, para-doxically, the fact that my own skin was *not* white had only ever seemed surpassingly strange. Indeed, later, through my adolescence and early adulthood, the experience of seeing myself in a mirror took me aback. It was nothing about my eyes or nose or lips — nothing about my face except for its tarnished-penny hue. In my complexion alone I saw a person I didn't recognize, someone who, had I seen him in the school hallways or at the mall or municipal swimming pool, I would have thought did not belong here. I knew that about myself because I knew that was how I saw others who looked like me. My likeness in the mirror was a reminder of something about myself I always chose to forget, something never available to me except when confronted by my appearance: that though I didn't *feel* "other" in any meaningful way, I clearly appeared *only* that way — at least to myself.

Being confounded by one's own appearance must count as among the most commonplace of human experiences, but the feeling has a special strangeness when coupled to the matter of race. Having grown up in the western suburbs of Milwaukee, endlessly encircled by whiteness, it stood to reason my darker skin would come to define me, but what still mostly eludes me is how exactly this came to pass. There were no traumatic episodes with cohorts in school; no well-intentioned teachers and mentors ennobling my difference; I had no problem fitting in or finding girlfriends; at home, my parents never complained about anything even remotely resembling bigotry. The Wisconsin of my youth was still proud of its homegrown progressivism. It was the birthplace of workers' comp and Bob La Follette's Wisconsin Idea, that academic and scientific research should be placed in the service of the public good, a place — so unlike the eastern Pennsylvania of Riaz's youth — where the only tribalism I ever witnessed growing up concerned the local football team. And yet as my darkish body ripened, my disgust for white bodies was now squared by desire. My wet dreams were only white; I longed for white faces brightened by the sight of my darker one, imagined white breasts and thighs, white fingers on my thickened brown-red penis — all of which, of course, reveals a socialization into the politics of race touching the very core of my being. And yet that morning, as I lay beside Asha, our dark hands side by side against the snowy covers, I felt — for the first time I could remember — no confusion at all, felt that our brown hues looked unerringly correct, a conclusion that felt all

the more convincing and forceful for proceeding not by a process of thought but
from an afflux of feeling, a trickle of sudden
wonder that had her as its miraculous
source. Of course, it was love I was feeling,
though I'm no longer clear what sort,
exactly — whether it was love for what I'd
never been able to accept about myself (my
color), which I *mistook* for love of her, or
whether (as I believed that morning) I'd
fallen more deeply for another person than
I'd known was possible.

Asha wasn't in a cuddling mood. She
woke and turned away from me, pleading
her bad breath. She grabbed her phone as
she got out of bed and went into the bathroom. I heard the faucet, then the shower.

I got up and started coffee, then chopped
some of our leftover karahi into a bowl of
eggs with chilies and coriander. I buttered
two chappatis and heated them on a skillet
as the omelet cooked. When Asha emerged
in a towel, her wet hair slicked back, texting
on her phone, she looked delighted to find
breakfast ready. My heart leaped as she
wrapped her arms around my neck and
nuzzled her still-moist cheek against my ear.
Her phone buzzed with a text. As she sat
and tore a piece of bread for her eggs, her
phone buzzed with another. She glanced at

the screen, then turned it facedown on the table, annoyed.

"Who is it?" I asked.

She shrugged and shook her head, by which she meant to convey, I think, both that her response would not have surprised me *and* that it was nothing worth talking about — which could only have meant it was Blake.

"What does he want?"

"I don't want to talk about it."

"Fair enough."

I was feeling hopeful and defenseless — hopeful with my longing to speak even just a hint of what I was feeling for her that morning; defenseless from a growing sense that, in fact, she'd already picked up on something new in me, something needy and pleading, and was now plotting her escape from it.

"So whose cross is that in the bathroom?" she asked.

"Huh?"

"On top of the vanity. I needed a Q-tip. I knocked the jar of coconut oil. There's that silver necklace with a cross on it . . ."

"Oh, right. That."

She misread my embarrassed smile: "What was she like?"

"Oh, no. It's not that . . . It's mine."

"Really? Why do you have a cross?" she asked.

On any other morning, I would've lied. But not on this one. Even if I couldn't tell her I'd fallen in love with her, she deserved the best of me — even if only for my own sake. "It's from 9/11," I said. "It's kind of a long story, I mean —"

"It's okay," she said as she chewed. "We have time."

I took a breath. I began again: "Back then, I had a TV in my bedroom, and the first thing I would do when I got up was turn it on for the weather. That morning, though, I remember they were showing a live feed of a fire in the upper floors of the first tower. The announcers kept saying a small plane had hit the tower, and I remember thinking — as I went into the bathroom — of JFK junior's plane going down in the Atlantic Ocean. I was putting toothpaste on my toothbrush when I heard someone cry out on the TV. I went back into the bedroom and saw there'd been a new explosion. Another plane had hit the second tower. I knew right then. I don't know how I knew, but I did."

"Knew what?" she asked.

"That it was us. That we did this."

She was quiet, but her guarded look

wasn't hard for me to read. If I was cannier, dear reader, I would recast that expression on her face, offer an airbrushed look of offense as prelude to a vociferous objection on her part, then follow it all with a concocted back-and-forth that made clear her Muslim horror over the attacks, no different in kind from that of any non-Muslim. If I cared less about it all, I would write it like that to save myself the likely grief ahead. But I won't write it that way, because that's not what happened. She didn't speak because, like me, she was used to the sermons and family dinners replete with complaint about murderous American meddling; worry over Muslim land and lives lost; praise of Hitler and rage against Israel; self-reproach about the pathetic state of our own imperial destiny. Like me, she'd heard many times that a figure would rise among us to overthrow the illegitimate rule of these Europeans and neo-Europeans, that we were destined to take the world back from these spiritual ghosts one day. They'd turned their back on God for money, and we knew that could only end badly. They were a category of human with no measure beyond themselves. They honored nothing. It was no surprise the very planet itself was dying under the watch of their shortsighted empire. The day would come when we would take it all back and restore to it a rightful holiness. She'd heard it all so many times — though we would both hear it less and less after the attacks. She looked away now with the subtlest of discouraged nods, the expression on her face — I thought — charged with chagrin.

I went on: "My phone rang. I only had a landline back then. It was my parents. They were scared. I mean, they were relieved I was fine. There wasn't any reason I wouldn't be. I mean, in all my years here, I'd only ever been that far downtown twice. But then again, you never know. They made me promise I wouldn't leave the house. I didn't tell them I was supposed to go to my friend Stewart's place to print out a play I'd just finished. He was a graphic designer and had a fancy laser printer he was letting me use to print copies to send to theaters and festivals.

"It was such a gorgeous day outside. Everybody remembers that. How clear and blue it was. Uptown, there was a gentle breeze coming off the river. It still felt like summer. People out in the streets — but nobody was going anywhere. I remember thinking that it didn't seem like a Tuesday morning.

"Stewart's door was open. I found him standing in the hallway outside the kitchen, crying. He just kept repeating over and over that the tower was gone. I didn't understand what he meant. I went into the living room, where his roommate — who was white; Stewart is black — was watching it all on their huge plasma screen, a thrill in his eyes. He turned to us: 'It's all happening now,' he said. 'The shit show's finally started.' Then he started laughing. Stewart screamed at him to stop. Apparently the guy had been saying that all morning. Stewart started crying again, and his roommate jumped up from the couch and stormed out.

"I stood there and watched. Soon enough, the second tower just disintegrated. Right there. Right before my eyes. A column of smoke and powder tumbling down, like some terrible black flower collapsing in on itself. Stewart lost his shit. He howled and keened. I held him while I watched the footage of the second tower collapsing over and over.

"I called my parents from his kitchen. I knew they would be trying to reach me. My mother was beside herself. 'Where are you? Why aren't you picking up?' I told them I'd gone to a friend's house to not be alone, and then *she* started crying. My father told

me she was worried about my cousin Ibrahim, who lived downtown. He was at NYU,
in his second or third year, living in a dorm
down in the financial district, which I
remember thinking was weird when he first
told me — but NYU had started buying so
much real estate in the city, and they had
these empty buildings down there they were
putting students into. My father'd been trying Ibrahim, but it was almost impossible to
get through to anybody's cell phone that
morning.

"Once Stewart's boyfriend showed up, I
left his place and went out into the street.
From where I was, you could see the smoke
and smell the faintest traces of it on the
wind, though that far north — I was in
Morningside Heights — the wind was blow-
ing in the other direction. It felt safer to be
uptown, but something was pulling at me to
head south. I don't know why I wasn't more
scared about what was happening than I
was. The only thing that kept going through
my mind was how shocked I was not to feel
even a trace of surprise. Some part of me, I
realized, had been expecting something like
this for most of my life.

"The subways weren't running. The
streets felt strange. There were people in
them, and cars, and buses. They all seemed

to be moving at the same speed. I'd had a dream about there being an attack in the city a few nights before —"

"You did?" she asked.

"Yeah. That there was an attack and that people were buzzing in the streets like insects. It looked the way ants do after their colony's been destroyed. That's actually the thing that sticks with me the most, that animal sense of fear.

"I started walking. I walked down Broadway, through the Upper West Side, through midtown — people were pouring out into the streets, stopping to talk, people who clearly didn't know one another huddled in groups, corner after corner. In Times Square, the scene was eerie. Traffic was at a standstill. Thousands of people were standing and staring up at the huge screens everywhere, watching it all like it was a scene in a movie.

"In the electronics stores farther down Broadway, the walls of TVs were showing the same thing, over and over — the fires, the smoke, the second plane flying into the side of the building, the falling bodies, the collapsing columns of steel and powder, the shell-shocked survivors covered in that white, ghoulish dust.

"There was a blockade at Twenty-Third

Street. I told the officer guarding the gate I was trying to get to my cousin at NYU, and he let me through. At Fourteenth Street, the policeman told me they weren't letting many people below Houston, and nobody below Canal. No exceptions. Here, the smell was so much stronger, like sugar and wood on fire with bitter smoke that stuck like grit to your teeth. Above us, a mountain of rising smoke towered over the buildings. It was so vivid it almost seemed alive. Angry. I remember suddenly understanding why the Hawaiians thought of volcanoes as gods. I was coughing now, and the air was getting worse. It didn't seem to make much sense going any farther.

"I should've gone back. I should've gone home, or to someone's place, like so many of my friends would end up doing. But I didn't want to. I felt like I needed to be close to what was happening. So I walked west along Thirteenth Street to see if there was a better view from that side. On Seventh Avenue, people were coming uptown, some of them covered in that white dust. Everybody was worried there would be more attacks, and I heard people say there were boats at the pier taking groups off the island. Another person said she saw on some TV that Palestinians were cheering in the streets. She looked at me. 'Can you believe that?' she asked, seething. 'I mean, can you believe that?'

"There used to be a hospital on Twelfth Street and Seventh Avenue called Saint Vincent's. Believe it or not, my dad actually worked there for a few months when he first came to this country. I saw a line in front of it, twisting around the block. I asked an older woman what the line was for. 'To give blood,' she said. Someone else asked what my type was. I told her O negative, and I heard a few people say I should get in line. I'd been told before my blood was good for transfusions. If I couldn't get farther downtown, at least giving blood was something I could do.

"The guy in front of me was, I don't know, maybe late fifties. With a blue shirt and thick lips, muttonchops down his cheeks. He kept staring at me. I finally asked him if everything was all right. 'Well, I think the answer to that's pretty fucking obvious.' 'Yeah, well, I was just wondering why you keep looking at me.' 'Where are you from?' he asked, making no effort to hide his aggression. 'Uptown?' I said. I knew what he was asking. By that point, I knew word was spreading that Muslims were behind the mayhem. I'd felt it from the woman back

338

on Fourteenth Street, and I could feel it in the way some people were looking at me now. The guy in muttonchops asked me again where I was from, and I told him again I was from uptown. 'You a Moslem?' he asked. Whatever he saw on my face as I hesitated was the answer he needed. 'You are, aren't you?' 'Is there a problem, sir?' 'Fucking Arab Einstein over here wondering if we got a problem,' he said now for the others. Someone told him to leave me alone. 'I don't know what you're doing here. We don't want your Arab blood.' I laughed without intending to, and that made him angrier. 'You think that's funny? You think that's funny, you fucking Arab?' 'Would you please shut up, sir?!' I shouted suddenly. I could hear I sounded weak, which only made things worse. 'Don't you tell me what to do, you fucking terrorist.' And then he said something I still don't understand: 'We should have killed you all when we had a chance.'

"There were a lot of people watching us now. Some of them were pressing in. It seemed like some of them felt the way he did, though I could hear the ones who were trying to get him to leave me alone. The guy kept shouting: 'We don't need your Arab blood! Nobody wants your fucking

339

Arab blood!'

"I remember him making a movement toward me and a large black man in an army cap stopping him. That's when I felt the warm wetness along the inside of my leg and looked down to see a dark stain creeping down the inside of my jeans. Everyone watching saw me notice I'd urinated on myself. Suddenly, I was shaking. 'Leave him alone,' a woman said. The guy in muttonchops was doubled over, his laugh like a witch's cackle. 'Look at the fucking Arab tough guy,' he shouted, pointing. 'Fucking peed himself!'

"I didn't say anything. Some feeling was caught in my throat — I couldn't tell you if it was anger or fear — and it mixed with the odor of smoke and dust. I couldn't have made a sound if I tried. I wanted to cough, but instead I turned and walked away. I heard the guy behind me still yelling. I walked as fast as I could. I wanted to run, but my knees were too weak, and I was worried I would fall and look even weaker. At the first corner I got to, I went left so none of them could see me anymore.

"I walked and walked. My leg itched along the damp inside seam with a terrible bristle. Tears were coming up now, suffocating like snot. I heaved and coughed. My breath went in and out of me, and I couldn't control it. I started to sob, so I stopped and covered my face even though I saw no one watching.

"When I finally looked up from my palms, I noticed I was in front of a Salvation Army thrift shop. Standing in the doorway was a balding man in a pastor's collar. He had a double chin and circular glasses frames, and he approached me with a tender look. I started crying again. He handed me a handkerchief — one of those old hemmed pocket squares. I wiped my eyes. I blew my nose. He put his hand on my shoulder and asked me if I wanted some water.

"Once we were inside, he disappeared in the back. I could hear people listening to a radio. The narrow entry of the storefront was filled with racks of clothes pressed too tightly together, I thought, for anyone to browse — the rows and rows of fading dresses and blouses, the sweaters and suit jackets and winter coats, and strewn everywhere below them, the heaps of worn shoes. I remember thinking that no one in those towers would ever be wearing clothes now, these or others, a thought that made some sort of poignant sense to me then but never would again. I'd been overhearing from people in the street that more than fifty thousand had probably died that day.

"On a wire rack next to the cash register, I saw dozens of necklaces for sale. There was a whole row of them with crucifix pendants. Without thinking, I reached out and took one. I heard the pastor coming back, and I slipped it into my pocket.

"I drank his water and thanked him. I pulled out my wallet to give him money, but he wouldn't take it. I tried to insist, but he stopped me. I wanted to tell him about the necklace, but I was embarrassed. I didn't want him to think I needed Christ. 'God be with you. God be with us all,' he said as I walked out.

"I started to walk back uptown. Somewhere around Thirty-Fourth Street, I stopped and put the necklace on, and I didn't take it off again for three months."

I'd thought about it all countless times since that day, about how I would write it, what form it would take, how to shape the details of my peregrinations on 9/11 into a dramatic speech someone could someday speak on a stage. But I never did write it. I'd never even spoken of it to another person before that morning.

Asha had watched me silently as I spoke, a gravity and stillness in her eyes, but when she realized I was done, something changed.

She seemed to force a laugh: "So you stole it?"

"I tried to give him the money. I wasn't trying to steal it."

"I could never do that."

"Take a cross?"

"Wear one," she said shortly. I understood. We — like all Muslims — had grown up on tales of the first believers valiantly persecuted for not denying their faith. "Did it help?" she asked.

"Let's just say I didn't have any trouble until I took it off. That's when the dirty looks started, more stuff like what happened at the hospital."

"Like what?"

"Look, it's not that big a deal. I don't want to —"

"No, what?"

"I mean . . . the usual. The tense looks, the double takes, the old ladies worried when they see me on the bus or the subway. The shit people say under their breath. The Mets game where some drunk guy starts calling me Osama. And then I get thrown out of the park for the argument we get into . . . I mean, none of it was anything like what you all were dealing with in Texas, guys walking into gas stations and shooting clerks, the rest of it . . . but we had stuff up

343

here, too. Cabdrivers pulled from their cars. People jumped in the streets. People losing their jobs, even on Wall Street. I wasn't wearing a turban, so that helped. So did the cross. I'm pretty sure of that . . ."

"But then you stopped wearing it?"

"After a while, I just couldn't see myself in the mirror with it anymore. Once the fear died down just enough."

"Why'd you save it?"

"I didn't. I mean, I didn't intend to. Where you found it's where I put it when I took it off. I forgot I even had it."

She bit down on a piece of buttered chappati. "We bought flags," she said as she chewed. "Big ones, small ones. The Pakistanis in Houston went crazy with the flags. A friend of my dad's would walk around with the pole stuck into his lapel buttonhole, with the flag waving around under his chin."

"We did the same —"

She cut me off: "But I never heard about anybody wearing a cross." I didn't know what to say. "So what ever happened to your cousin?" she asked.

I was the one to force a laugh now, aware I was appearing weak, wanting to find some way back to seeming strong. "He'd gotten homesick for Pakistani food and went to

stay at his aunt's in Tarrytown. He was supposed to be back in the city that morning,
but he didn't get on the train. I was wandering a war zone while he was happily eating
his *nashta* of parathas and sooji halwa."

"Probably not happily, right?"

"I mean, no. Of course not. I just
meant . . . if you knew him . . ."

She wasn't amused. "Did you ever go back
and pay for the cross?"

"No." I lit up with a sudden idea. "Maybe
that's something we can do together . . ."

Her ensuing silence completed her retreat.
I can't say I didn't understand it. I, too, had
long avoided revisiting the terrible isolated
sadness of it all, avoided any reminder of
our repulsive condition, at once suspects
and victims when it came to this, among
the great American tragedies. There were so
many awful reasons we'd spent much of our
lives desiring whites — and here I was il-
lustrating the worst of them. She picked up
her phone and went to the couch to read
what had come in — presumably from
Blake — as I'd spoken. I got up and went
to the window to sit on the sill for a smoke.
The morning's light was unchanged, clean
and gray, but there was no longer any
comfort in it. I lit up and drew troubled
relief into my lungs; behind me, Asha's

fingers clicked away at her phone's screen. As I listened to her text, I knew I'd made a mistake from which we were unlikely to recover.

I doubt there was any point at which Asha seriously considered a future with me, but if she did, if she had ever wondered dreamily, the way I did, what it might be like for us to marry and have children, I don't think she wondered any longer. We lasted two more months, during which time my attachment to her grew stronger and hers to me weakened in perfectly indirect proportion. I will spare you the portrait of my mounting romantic insecurities, the episodes of jealousy over Blake, the humiliating erectile challenges, the torrents of needy nighttime tears. I bought a slightly included carat-and-a-half engagement diamond and asked her to marry me. Twice. Some of this apparent desperation, I must have known even then, was the result of my mother's decline. She was dying slowly, surely, yet I rarely cried at her bedside. There, my days of vigil were limned with unruly hope, for as I stared at my mother's morphine-slack face, I dreamed of another, and every reprieve from my mother's slow demise led back to Houston, despite Asha's reluctance to have me. Her place was off-limits, so I would take a room at a hotel I knew she loved across town, a converted antebellum mansion, still well beyond my means. I would book a suite for two nights and hope she could be persuaded to stay in for room service on at least one of them.

The end finally came over the phone.

She'd told Blake about me, which had the effect — I would later conclude — she'd been hoping for all along: he, too, confessed his infidelities, and after a teary reconciliation, they decided to give up their extracurricular involvements and double down on the relationship. She wished me only the best ahead, she said. I was an amazing person, and I deserved more than what she could give me. Asha sounded like she meant these kind words — or at least like she was trying to — but beneath the patient, saccharine tone, I picked up a dispassion it was hard for me to accept. Could it really be I was simply an errand to be completed, a loose end in her life that needed tying up?

Barely a month after our breakup, I awoke in my childhood bed, the same bed where I'd masturbated for the first time at the age of twelve, and watched in horror as milky fluid pumped forth from my penis, unexpected, and I, convinced that I'd irrevocably spilled something essential from inside me, pulled off the pillowcase and tried to gather up as much of the sticky mess as possible, in case I might need it for the doctor. I awoke and rose, and as I made my way to the bathroom, I recalled a dim piece of a dream in which my hands had been on fire. At the sink, I turned the faucet knobs and felt an uneven, chalky thickness along my fingers. I turned my hands over to find a stippling of copper lumps across my palms. I was certain I knew what I was looking at. In college, I'd written a paper about Shakespeare's late obsession with syphilis — "limekilns i' the palm" — and had spent a long afternoon at the campus medical library, transfixed by the color plates showing pages of variations of the dusky-red palmar rash common to the disease.

Downstairs, my father was bent over a small saucepan in the kitchen, stirring the medley of breakfast tea leaves, cardamom pods, and skim milk that, once strained, had forever been his daily morning brew.

"Hey, Dad."

"You want some tea?" he asked. He sounded exhausted. He'd been sleeping on the couch beside her for weeks now, up every few hours to feed her pills or porridge.

348

The circles under his eyes were dark and deep.

"No, thanks. How's she doing?"

"Same old. About time for the new dose."

"Can I talk to you?"

"Isn't that what we're doing now?"

"No, I mean — can I talk to you in the garage . . ."

"You want to talk *in the garage?*"

"Yes."

I bypassed the pantry for the mudroom and looked back. "Please?" He stared at me for a moment, then shook his head and switched off the stove fire. As he came up behind me, I reached for the door handle, but then stopped myself. I wasn't sure if I should touch it.

"What's going on?" he asked.

"Could you, uh, open it?"

"You're standing right there . . ."

"Could you please just open it? I'll explain in a second." I moved to make room for him. With another irritated look, he reached across me and pulled the door open.

The garage had no cars in it — Father'd gotten rid of Mother's car some time ago and left his own in the driveway out front. Piles of domestic debris lined the oil-stained bay, a cargo of never-quite-discarded things: the first television (small, black-and-white) my parents had bought in this country; an old microwave without a door whose inside walls were thick with years of curry splatter; dismantled table and box fans; suitcases filled with the saris and shawls and *shalwars* my mother would buy on her trips to Pakistan and never wear when she came home; the Apple IIe on which I wrote my first short story and the printer into which I'd fed the ream of perforated paper it was printed on; my dead brother's tricycle; his shattered fish tank; a quartet of torn bike wheels taken from as many ten-speed and twelve-speed family bikes; an enormous '50s-era Texaco sign saved from the gas station in Baraboo my father once owned; yard tools, toolboxes, a rusting rotary saw no one had used in years; an Atari video-game console and two plastic bags filled with game cartridges; crates upon crates of expired coolant and motor oil and Snapple iced tea and Listerine my parents bought in bulk during a brief membership at Sam's Club in the late '90s before canceling their membership after an altercation with a store manager; the mounds of fishing gear — rods and nets and reels — from my father's middle-age obsession with freshly caught panfish, deep-fried Lahori style, which delight my mother had enjoyed perhaps

even more than my father did; and everywhere below and between this ad hoc history of our family's life, the rolled-up
Persian rugs, wrapped in moth crystals and
plastic, the relic of my father's bizarre passion for purchasing and smuggling into this
country the contraband carpets for which
he never found any use. I nudged the light
switch on with my elbow and led him into
the lurid pool of light beneath the single
yellow bulb, showing him my hands.

"Huh," was all he said as he held my
wrists, turning them back and forth gently
as he studied my palms.

"Looks like syphilis, doesn't it?"

"Syphilis?" he said, astonished. "Are you
sleeping with prostitutes?"

"I mean, no . . ."

"So why do you think it's syphilis?"

"That's what it looks like. I mean, doesn't
it?"

"What do you know what it looks like?"

"I don't know, Dad — I wrote a paper
about it in college. I'm just saying . . ."

"Paper? About syphilis?"

"And Shakespeare."

"He had syphilis?"

"Some people think he did. Yeah."

"Is that right?" I'd never seen him so
fascinated by anything I'd ever said about

351

Shakespeare before.

"Anyway, I'm just saying — doesn't it look like a syphilis rash?"

"Could be. Haven't seen a case since medical school. And the only time I ever see this kind of thing now is with bacterial endocarditis."

"What's that?"

"Infection in the heart."

"And what are the symptoms of that?"

"Fatigue, fever —"

"Haven't had those."

"Trust me, you would know you had a problem by the time there's a rash like this. And that one usually looks smaller anyway," he said, pondering my palms anew. "Toxic shock sometimes, arthritic complications . . ."

"I don't think it's arthritis. My joints have been fine."

"Did you write a play about that, too?"

"A play? No. I said a paper, Dad. Like a report . . ."

He shrugged at the evident irrelevance of my clarification: "What you think is fine and not fine doesn't matter. You need to get to the emergency room."

"Can I take the car?"

He shrugged. "I would drive you, but someone has to stay with her —"

"No, of course. It's fine. I feel fine. I can get myself there."

"I'll get you the key." He stopped on his way back to the door inside: "Just wipe everything off, okay? The steering wheel? If you touch anything else? You know what? On that shelf with the garden tools" — he was pointing now at the sagging plywood shelf on the far wall — "take those gloves. You can wear those."

"You want me to wear gardening gloves?" I asked, but he was already disappearing inside.

I pulled the gloves he was talking about from under a pile of trowels. The notion of wearing mud-caked gardening gloves over the lesions didn't strike me as particularly hygienic, but when Father returned with the car key, he assured me — with a dismissive Indo-Pak bob of the head from side to side — that any incidental contact with dirt now dry for years was nothing to worry about. "Just put them on, you know, in case you're right. So you don't, you know, get it all over the car."

The local emergency room was empty, and I was seen right away. It was a small hospital perched on a wooded hill, one of the first to go up that far west of the city, where professionals didn't start settling among the farmers until the early '70s. The attending ER physician was, like so many locals around whom I'd grown up, a particular breed of Wisconsin paradox: tender and Teutonic. Seeing my hands, she suspected at once — as I had — syphilis and asked about my sexual history. Yes, I'd had multiple partners in the last six months — though only one for the last four. Yes, some of that sex was unprotected. Her pitched features sagged with what seemed a disapproving thought as she tore the nitrile gloves from her hands. She explained that though she'd yet to encounter an active case of secondary syphilis in that idyllic suburban enclave where my parents lived, she was aware of the unusual rise in rates of the disease across the country; a good portion of the most recent issue of the *Annals of Emergency Medicine* was devoted to the subject. The latest clinical thinking suggested administering the penicillin treatment for the illness if it was suspected — barring allergy to the medication, of course — even before the test results came. The good news, she said with a sudden smile, as if announcing an attraction she thought I might enjoy at the upcoming state fair, was that if it *was* syphilis, and only syphilis — unfortunately,

HIV was often a companion ailment, but we would know about that very shortly because a strip test would tell us within minutes — the cure was simple and the prognosis great.

After the phlebotomist took my blood, the attending returned to the exam room with a polyglot trio of young visiting foreign medical graduates in tow: Chinese, Colombian, Ghanaian. They crowded in to introduce themselves and stare at my palms. Only one of them — the Colombian resident — had ever actually seen a secondary syphilitic rash. Here I was, a teachable moment. The attending warned that a test result would be needed to confirm the diagnosis but then addressed the residents with a certainty about the distinctive lesions that belied her note of caution, using a pencil to point out the breaking skin along the largest of them; if it was indeed syphilis, she explained, any of the broken sores they were seeing were actually contagious. I saw the Chinese resident visibly cringe. The attending went on to explain that the palmar rash was often accompanied by another on the soles of the feet and, in some cases, even the torso and back. "Fortunately for this patient," she said with a smile, "not in his case." Even so, they pored over every inch of my skin, then watched their instructor stick a needle into my ass and pump me full of penicillin. If I didn't need to be out and about, the attending said as she stuck a small adhesive bandage to my butt, it was probably best I rest — with minimal contact with others (and none of a sexual nature) — for the next few days.

Something strange happened when I got home.

As I walked into the house, I heard my mother was awake. Her lucid moments were rare now — and not particularly lucid — mostly coinciding with the short windows between her doses. I pulled off the blue nitrile gloves I'd been given in the emergency room to replace the filthy gardening gloves I'd shown up there with — I didn't want to alarm her — and rummaged in the mudroom bins for something else I could use to cover up my hands. All I could find were two thick rabbit-fur mittens. I recalled Father bringing them home as a gift from a trip to Iceland and Mother laughing at how they looked when she slipped them on. I didn't remember her ever wearing them again.

In the family room, she was lying propped up on the couch. Father sat beside her; he was feeding her from a bowl. "My hooonnneeeyy," she slurred sweetly. Her smile was weak, but the brightness in her eyes — above the mass of mostly unmoving gray flesh on her face — matched the delight in her voice.

"Hi, Mom."

"Yoguuu, yoguuu," she cooed over Father's extended spoon.

"You having some yogurt? Is it good?"

"Gooo . . . Gooo . . ."

"Can you put her music on?" Father asked, gesturing at the portable CD player on the fireplace mantel. He inserted another spoonful of yogurt into her mouth and watched sternly as I pulled the mitten from my hand to press Play on the console with my index-finger knuckle. The buoyant notes of a polka waltz began, the cheery, syncopated beat filling the room with anodyne joy. Mother discovered the music in the '80s on local radio stations that played it late in the afternoons and early on the weekends. As she got older, polka became a bona fide obsession. While she was still well enough, packages from Amazon filled with CDs of her latest obscure discoveries would arrive weekly. She abhorred what passed for mainstream in the form, the slick, soulless schlock of Jimmy Sturr, say, and her command of the various schools was truly remarkable. She could untangle the advent of trumpets into the Cleveland-based Slovenian style from the Wisconsin-based strains that leaned Czech in their embrace of a smaller brass sound. Particularly enamored of Bavarian polka, she would call the local DJs to champion tiny bands from backwater towns like Kiel and New Holstein, where German was still a language spoken in the streets. Father never got her love of this music, but I thought I did. It was fun, simple, orderly; it pointed back to an Old World, not her own but old and native all the same, a homespun Wisconsin reminder she was not the only one who'd come here from somewhere else, not the only one still working to keep alive the memory of another place.

Father patted at her lips with a washcloth and stood up. "I luuu youuu, I luuu youuuu," she burbled.

"I love you, too, Ammi. I love you so much."

She tilted her face and closed her eyes, offering her barely puckered lips. I hesitated. Of course I wanted to kiss her, and yes, she was dying already, and no doubt it was unlikelier than unlikely she might get sick from the simple peck she wanted, but all the same, even the remotest possibility of

358

giving your dying mother syphilis is an occasion for legitimate pause. I leaned in and felt the tip of her mouth — still wet from feeding — against my cheek. I turned and kissed hers, too. Contact made, she relaxed back into the cushions and closed her eyes.

I looked up and saw Father glaring at me from the kitchen.

"Outside," he said curtly. Back in the garage, I told him the attending suspected syphilis; she'd given me the intramuscular dose of antibiotics; test results would take three days; until then, I should lay low. "And don't kiss your mother," he added with a grunt as he marched back into the house.

It was then that a discomfort I'd been feeling between my legs for some time finally drew my notice. I had a hard-on, and not of the usual wayward form: mostly firm, somewhat not, amenable to digital adjustment, a cupful of blood lost en route back to the heart. No. This was as fully distended an erection as I could recall, but with not a whit of pleasure or sexual sensation to it. No throbbing need, no promise willed or sought — just a rigid ache.

I went back into the family room and slipped quietly into the armchair by my dozing mother's side. I watched and listened, her quiet snore belying the evident strain of her breath, the light crease on her forehead, a signal, I thought, of her reabsorption into the narrow black sack of her pain. The image was Tolstoy's from the late tale about the unremarkable death of a vain government bureaucrat. *The Death of Ivan Ilyich* was among my mother's favorite books. She'd given it to me when I was in high school, and I'd read it many times since. As she died, I'd taken it up again, a way to feel closer to her, no doubt, but also to populate her mute suffering with speakable meanings. Reading by her side, I would look up from the pages and wonder if the glorious end of Tolstoy's tale — when death envelops Ilyich with its simple light — was in sight for her yet. I wondered if her pity had yet turned from her own predicament and to us, still caught up in all the self-deception of the living. On his deathbed, Ilyich came to regret all the time he'd wasted on appearances, on needing to seem worthwhile in the eyes of others. I knew she had other regrets of her own. I knew she felt her life had passed her by. I'd always suspected that she regretted her marriage to my father, though I didn't yet know about her feelings for Latif. She would sometimes say her cancer kept coming back because it was trying to tell her something. It wasn't until she died and I read her diaries that I had any idea what she thought the message might have been.

When the tumor was initially discovered, it was already fully interlaced with her spine; no surgery could be performed to remove it. She'd been through chemotherapy three times in thirty years and was resolved not to put herself through that again — which meant she was reconciled to dying of the illness this time around. Sure enough, without the aggressive chemical treatment, her tumor slowly spread into every part of her. By now, as she neared the very end, if the timing of her successive doses of Vicodin or Demerol or oxycodone or morphine — or whatever combination my father chose to give her — were not lined up exactly right, the resulting pain would rage through her entire body. The veins in her neck bulged, her fingers and toes crimped, her face pushed steadily farther and farther into the couch's cushions, the usual, steady moans now replaced by something that looked like it required so much more from her than she could possibly have to give. Mostly, though, she slept, her pain bearable through a pill-induced haze.

I would sit beside her as she dozed and wonder what, if anything, was haunting her beyond the body's torment, beyond the pain and the fear of more pain. I wondered what unresolved questions about her life dangled in that narcotic darkness. I read into the subtlest shifts of her expression and sought to redeem her inner life as if it were that of a character in a book. Such was my habit, imagining the inner landscapes of others and drawing their portraits — ultimately — from the model I knew best: myself. I knew I was mostly staring in a mirror as I watched my mother die. I knew it was mostly futile. I did it anyway.

Mostly futile, but not entirely. For all the literary speculation about her secret summations brought me to see how little I really knew her and confronted me with the deepest resentment of my life — that despite the daily demonstrations of love, the doting, the sacrifices, the unceasing maternal care, I never truly felt loved by her. I'd never felt loved because I'd never known who was loving me and never felt certain she knew whom or what she was loving. She complained so often of my remoteness over the years, my difficulty showing affection or speaking about my life and feelings with her — her diaries were filled with observations about how bottled up and laconic I was, how endlessly it frustrated her. I never felt she saw me; or, rather, never felt certain the person looking out at me was really and truly her and was really and truly looking out at me. I saw now that the source of my life's work — reading, literature, theater — was in part the pursuit of something as simple as my mother's gaze, a gaze she gave happily to books. Was it a coincidence I, too, had sought the comfort of books as a child? Wasn't I seeking her attention? Isn't that what I really wanted as I would sidle up to her warm body on the couch as she read, a book of my own in hand? So many times, I didn't even read, I just pretended to, wanting to be close to her. I vividly recall one snowy afternoon, the bright winter glare reflected in my mother's eyes as they scanned page after page, and me, watching her sidelong, jealous of the object that so commanded her being, wishing I, too, could find some way into the rapture of that avid gaze. Is it really a surprise that even words on the page would end up not being enough? That even these I needed to impose on the countenances of countless others by means of the stage? This was not about neglect or disregard. It was about access. I never felt like I had access.

Except when we were in Pakistan.

One of the final proper conversations I

had with her while she was still mostly in possession of all her wits — and with her habitual reserve softened by the approaching end — was about Pakistan, or our respective relationships to it. She was sitting up, nibbling on a piece of freshly made laddoo from the sizable new Indo-Pak grocery that had opened a couple of miles west of us, in a strip mall behind the new casino that now sat where, when I was a child, there'd been a middle school. (It was astonishing to me that there were enough of us now in the area to justify the new grocery store's generous square footage, its aisles and aisles of packaged naans and dals and sacks of basmati, the masalas, the pakora mixes, the biryani mixes, the dazzling mounds of cayenne and turmeric and ground cardamom, the tins of ghee and bottles of bitter pickle, the rows of fresh mint, coriander, methi, of our native fruits — mangoes, guavas, lychees, Punjabi kinu — and, as one approached the registers, the prolonged counter of Desi sweets of every known form, the barfi and laddoo in particular, Mother thought, as tasty as she'd ever had them, even "back home," and which Father would dutifully fetch a few times every week, the last of her edible pleasures.) She was munching on that piece of besan laddoo, its beige crumble adhering to her lips, when suddenly, she stopped chewing. Her mouth sagged; her eyes welled; her voice quivered with sudden regret:

"I'm so sorry, *meeri jaan*."

"For what, Mom? You don't have anything to be sorry about —"

"You were so happy there."

"Where?"

"Back home. You were always so happy back home."

I paused, moved. With her end in view, her emotions had never been so clear, her face never as radiant; in moments like these, her beauty was heartbreaking.

"Why are you apologizing?"

"I never saw you like that here."

"I don't know, Mom."

"No, no," she said with an endearing firmness. "I never did." And then, all at once, shifting. "You didn't know that?"

"What?"

"That you were happier, when you were there?"

I smiled to hold her attention as I considered. The most vibrant of my childhood memories were those of life in my father's village and of the interlocking rooms in my mother's family's sprawling Rawalpindi bungalow. I loved being there, but I never pined for it when we returned. Not like she did. As a young boy, I often remarked how much happier she was when we were in Pakistan. I used to pray to God for her to be happy like that in America, too. "I was happy you were happy, Mom. It was nice to be with family."

"It was, wasn't it?"

"And it was nice not to be in school."

"You didn't like school," she said, frowning playfully.

"No, I didn't."

"I'm sorry."

"That you made me go to school?"

"No," she moaned, her face collapsing with sudden despair.

"What is it, Mom?"

"I'm sorry we brought you *here.*"

"Mom. I've had a good life here."

She stared at me for a long moment, as if confused. "You have?"

"I'm happy."

Her forehead creased with sudden concern. "I don't think so."

"I am. I've always been a little serious, right? Isn't that what you say?"

"Too serious."

"But it doesn't mean I'm not happy."

"Strange happiness."

"I get to do what I love. I'm a writer. Can

you believe it?" I smiled. "I'm happy."

She studied me for a moment, her head cocked cutely, a loving tenderness pouring into her eyes. "That makes me happy," she said finally. Then, almost as an afterthought, she added: "I never really liked it here."

"I know, Mom."

"You do?" She seemed both surprised and pleased to hear it.

I nodded. Then her expression changed again abruptly, narrow with a troubled thought.

"What is it?" I asked.

"Don't be mad."

"About what?"

"You're one of *them* now. Write about *them*. Don't write about us."

"But I don't choose my subjects, Mom. They choose me."

"You can change that."

The laddoo finished, she closed her eyes and leaned back to rest . . .

Perhaps it was the growing distraction of my aching crotch, perhaps it was just the proper order of things finally being restored, but as I sat beside her now, my painful distension only worsening, I could no longer make sense of my long resentment toward her. To have held on to it for so long, to have shaped so much of myself around it, seemed so unreasonable. A sudden, simple question loomed: In expecting what she couldn't give me, hadn't I rejected what she could?

I got up and turned away from her, and from my father, who was still in the kitchen. I reached inside my pants to adjust. As I touched myself, the pain was sharp and startling, like the snap of a charley horse.

I swallowed a yelp and headed upstairs.

In my bedroom, I undressed with difficulty to my boxers, sat on my bed, pulled off my mittens, and pulled out my phone. The spasm slowly released, but the erection didn't soften. I peeked inside; I'd never looked so large. Priapism is what some websites were calling it, a condition in which the veins of the penis abnormally constrict and the blood that flows in can't flow back out. It was a side effect of some drugs, though there was no reference to penicillin being one of them. An ice pack and aspirin were suggested, and if the erection didn't subside after two hours, the sites recommended a trip to the emergency room, where I could be injected with a drug that would regulate the blood flow. I dreaded the prospect of returning to the ER to have my penis shot up by the very attending who had shortly done the exact same thing to my rear end. There had to be another way.

Just then I heard a soft knock at my bedroom door. It was Father. "What are you doing in there?"

"Nothing, Dad. Just checking something on the internet." The door yawned open just enough to show his face behind the crack.

"That day nurse is coming for a few hours. I need to get out."

"I can watch her, Dad."

"You know, if she has to use the bathroom . . ."

"What time's her next dose?"

"I'll be back before then."

"Where you going?"

"I don't know. Maybe walk around the casino."

"Okay. I'll be here."

"I'm not leaving yet. Nurse has to get here," he said as his face faded from view. I heard him quietly disappear down the stairs.

On internet forums, victims of extended painful erections traded home remedies and extolled the benefits of Benadryl, jogging, cold showers, warm showers, and, of course, ejaculation, even though it was contraindicated on more official medical websites. I had trouble imagining how I could make that work considering the discomfort. I took one of the mittens and slipped it over myself. The rabbit fur felt soft against the pain. As I moved it gently, I closed my eyes and summoned Asha's body, the slope of her thin neck, the muscled ridges of her thick back. I recalled my lips on her lips, the clean, sweet taste between her legs. I imagined she'd come back to me, wet with love and longing. I kept the glove moving up and down, up and down. More than anything sexual, it was the memory of her eyes — wide and hazel and fierce — that sustained me through my physical distress, until at last they broke through the ailing and dissolved both pain and pleasure into a brief, bright blankness, a tiny shudder, and a release I barely registered into the sagging gray Icelandic mitten my mother had barely worn and would never wear again.

By week's end, the diagnosis of syphilis confirmed, I'd left messages for all seven of the women I'd had sex with in the past half year, apologizing for the risk to their health, offering to pay for their tests. After ten days, Asha was the only one who still hadn't called; as it turned out, she was the one who had it. Blake had it, too — or, rather, had had it just two months prior. She'd known and never told me because at the time her own test had come back negative. No longer. When she finally called to explain all this, it wasn't long before she was fighting back tears:

"I'm sorry."

"It's okay, Asha."

"No it's not."

"This stuff happens. It's okay. I got the shot. I'll be fine. Did you get one, too?"

"Why are you being so understanding?" she asked sharply. "I mean, if you'd given me something, I'd be pissed."

"I just think it's okay. I don't think you should beat yourself up about it." I heard myself say the words and knew they weren't exactly true. I was trying to make the best impression.

"Well, I *am* sorry."

"I appreciate that, but I'm just saying —"

"No, I mean about us. I'm sorry about what happened between us." I felt my pulse quicken with an abrupt, unreasonable joy. "I was using you. To get back at him. And I got you sick. And he got Maryanne sick."

"Maryanne?"

"My tenant downstairs. With the beagle. He's a fucking son of a bitch. My mother's right. He's never going to understand what he has. He treats me like shit, and I keep going back for more. He treats *me* like shit. He treats my *parents* like shit. He fucks my friends. I mean, even Tucker hates him. And that's saying a lot. There's something wrong with me."

"Tucker hates him?"

"Can't stand him. Barks at him whenever he's around. Always has. Won't go near him. I always thought it's because he's so tall."

"Maybe it is."

"Maybe it's not."

There was a silence. I wasn't sure what to say. It hadn't been a surprise to hear her say she'd been using me, but that didn't make it hurt any less.

"You in Milwaukee?" she asked.

"Yes."

"How's your mom?"

"Hospice nurse seems to think she's got at least three weeks left. She's sedated most of the time, so . . ."

"I'm so sorry."

"I'm just glad they've finally got her on a morphine drip."

"I'll say a prayer for her," she said. I didn't respond. I heard her breathing on the other end, and then: "I should go. I'm sorry I got you involved in all this. I really am. I wish you only the best."

"Funny. That's what you said to me last time we talked."

"I meant it then, too."

372

"Mmm-hmm — well, anyway. I still love you. I know you don't want to hear it, but I do. And probably always will."

"I don't think it's me you love. I think it's some idea you have —"

"Idea?"

"Yeah."

"What kind of idea?"

"I don't know. I'm not you."

"But you must have thought about it. If that's what you felt, right?"

"I don't know, that, like, I was a solution or something . . ."

"A solution?"

"Please don't yell."

"Are you kidding me? This is nowhere close to yelling."

"I should go."

"So go, Asha. Just fucking go," I snapped. She didn't hang up just yet, but my outburst poisoned that final silence between us. This wasn't how I wanted us to end. But I didn't say anything. She murmured goodbye, and the line went dead.

Three months after that call, once my mother was dead and buried, I saw photos on Facebook Asha posted from an engagement party in Pakistan: her own. Done up in a gorgeous gold-and-azalea-pink *shalwar kameez* and *dupatta,* her eyes rimmed with blue kohl, her hands and wrists covered with interlacing floral *mehndi,* she beamed along-side her glowing parents amid the delighted throngs I assumed were her various relatives, present and future. One picture showed her on a white couch, a Pakistani man in his early thirties kneeling before her, slipping a ring onto her finger. He was broad, with an imposing aquiline profile that gave him an air of potency only partly mitigated by his Coke-bottle glasses. The groom was tagged in all the posts as Rifaat Chaudury, but all I could gather from the attenuated public profile on offer was that he'd gone to the same medical school in Lahore where my parents met. My subsequent Google searches yielded pages of Rifaat Chaudurys in East Punjab — there were literally hundreds — more than a few of them doctors. Nothing more about the Rifaat in question, which meant nary a clue about how they might have met beyond Asha's tersely captioned photos. I'd been seeing something among my various younger cousins here and abroad: dating sites like Shaadi and Ideal Rishta, where the proposals often came within weeks of first contact — a twenty-first-century version of the traditional Pakistani arranged marriage.

My best guess was that Asha's imminent nuptials were similarly self-concluded, though I would never know for certain.

In the months that followed, I would pull up her Facebook profile and scroll through the dozens of uploaded photos of her life back home in Houston after the betrothal. She was wearing that ring in every one, smiling against backdrops I knew: the park around the corner from her place, where we'd once walked Tucker together; the sushi place she loved in Montrose; even a snap-shot of her hair-removal specialist at the Brazilian spa holding her ring finger, mouth agape with campy awe. Later, I would find photos of her husband-to-be's first visit to Houston; the family trip to the Galleria and the Menil Collection; another set showing her father deep in conversation with his future son-in-law as both huddled over bowls of what looked like ramen. The album was captioned: "Our men."

Then one day, as I struggled to make headway at my writing desk, I clicked on her name to find her profile again. What popped up on-screen was only her small square photo and, beside it, a thin box I could click to send a friend request. It had taken months, but she'd finally gotten around to unfriending me.

VII.
ON POTTERSVILLE

Just remember this, Mr. Potter: that this rabble you're talking about — they do most of the working and paying and living and dying in this community. Well, is it too much to have them work and pay and live and die in a couple of decent rooms and a bath?

— George Bailey,
It's a Wonderful Life

I've known Mike Jacobs — a Hollywood agent of some renown — for almost fifteen years, and his politics have always baffled me. Mike is black, but he didn't vote for Obama in either 2008 or 2012. As he put it: he only ever saw in then candidate Obama (and later President Obama) a man of color whose personality was riven with concessions to the white majority — of which, of course, Obama's mother was one — concessions Mike believed impaired his ability to know who he was as a black man in America. When Obama won the first election, Mike predicted that he would be an ineffective president and, more important — at least to Mike — a terrible advocate for blacks in this country.* (For the first six years of Obama's presidency, it was hard to argue that Mike had been wrong about either thing.) In 2008, Mike would have voted for McCain but for the presence of Sarah Palin on the ticket; he left his ballot's vote for president blank that year. In 2012, he voted for Romney. I have not been able to make good sense of how Mike squares his predilection for Republican politics with the fierceness of his advocacy for black life in America — he donates more money than most people I know earn each year to black causes in our country — though he explains it with recourse to some variation of the usual Republican talk about taxes, self-reliance, and learning to fend for yourself.

I'll get to that part later.

Mike grew up among the poor in Alabama. (His father was a lawyer, and while they were not better off until Mike was in his late adolescence, they were never as poor

---

* I am following Mike's practice in not using "African American" here and throughout.

as their neighbors.) As a child, Mike saw firsthand a cycle of dependence and frustration fostered by handouts. The most significant issue facing black Americans, he believes, is that ours is a country designed through and through to keep them down. In order to change it, black Americans don't have to just recognize that fact — most do — they also have to change the way they think about themselves and their lives because of it. And now I quote him, because there's too much at stake if I get the paraphrase wrong:

I hate that quality about us, always waiting for someone to save us, make things right, cut us some slack because we deserve it. Sure, we've been through a lot, and it's hard to be "us." I'm not denying that. But they're not gonna change this country for our sake. We have to do that ourselves.

He said this to me over a poached-egg-and-smashed-avocado toast at the Standard hotel in downtown Los Angeles. I was in Hollywood for "meetings" a few months after winning the Pulitzer, in 2013; I'd been inundated with offers from studios to write some version of the same story, each pitched to me as the next necessary pop-culture corrective in which a "good" Muslim works with (or in) law enforcement to uncover and eradicate a "bad" Muslim. Some of these projects already had scripts and were looking for a writer to come in for what they called an "authentic polish" — others needed a writer to give first flesh to these plastic bones. I'd known Mike from the time when he'd been my neighbor in New York, a young tax lawyer at a firm that also practiced entertainment law. It hadn't taken him long back then to figure out he wanted to be an agent, and it was not much longer still before he became one. We'd stayed in touch over the years, so I'd come to ask his advice: I didn't want to write any of these silly stories I was being offered; but was there some way to reroute the new attention along more fruitful lines?

Mike showed up at the restaurant a few minutes late in a gleaming maroon Maserati, his just-shaved head catching the sun as he emerged from the driver's seat. I was seated at a window booth above the parking lot and had a clear view of him as he pressed a tip into the young black valet's palm. As Mike walked off, I noted the valet's surprise at what I assumed was the generous tip.

Mike entered the dining room with a boisterous greeting to the women at the hostess station; the bright clip-clop of his leather-soled oxfords announced his lively gambol. We hugged, and he sat, pulling out his gum and pressing it into a square napkin. He warned me he didn't have long. One of his most important clients — an erstwhile child star who'd finally broken through into adult stardom — learned that his costar (a woman) had been given a larger gun in a pivotal scene, and he walked off the film. Said client had been AWOL for three days, and Mike just learned that morning of his whereabouts: a palatial Airbnb in the Hollywood Hills, replete with a crew of hookers, coke, and more Viagra than he could ever use. Mike would be picking him up in a couple of hours to take him back to the set.

I won't indulge in a protracted summary of our meeting that morning, for it's not the story I want to tell here — which is neither Mike's story nor my own but the tale of a certain rarely remarked-upon shift in our nation's economic politics that I was unaware of until Mike explained it to me some three years *after* that breakfast in Los Angeles, during the spring of 2016, as Donald Trump was criss-crossing the nation and sowing chaos in the Republican primary ranks and when Mike correctly predicted that Trump would be our next president.

Before I get to that, though, there's a little work left to do here first:

That morning in 2013, he told me something about Hollywood that would help me make sense of the place and its products: the movie industry was founded by families from New York's garment district and still bore every essential mark of the fashion business — the fixation on surface over substance; the terror of missing out on the latest fad; the fawning and listlessness and social desperation; and, above all, the endless turnover. Careers were like the latest fabrics, bought in bulk or by the yard, on which preformed narrative templates could be traced, cut, and quickly discarded when the public tired of them. Novelty, ephemerality, single use, mass production — these were the town's innate, enduring values, and Mike's advice to me that morning was to see the studio's new interest in me through this lens: all anyone in Hollywood would care about was my Islam, no matter what any of them might say. I was the latest print of a rough fabric everyone seemed to think would sell like hotcakes if only someone could figure out how to shape it into something folks might at least want to try on. "If you give them what they want," Mike advised, "you can be *that guy* out here. They're all looking for him. But if you don't want to play along — and I'm guessing you don't — then you're probably just wasting your time."

There was one other thing he said to me that morning: the town was Jewish. Even those who weren't had formed themselves to the habits of a business that had been started by Jews and where Jews were still smarter and more experienced than the rest. It was something he actually liked about Hollywood, he said. "It's not like with WASPs. Here, you know where you stand with people. They tell you." But he cautioned me to be mindful that, as a Muslim, I might be seen as an enemy. "Get out in front of it," he suggested. "Find ways to let them know up front that you're not coming for them."

"Coming for them?"

"You know — that you're not against what they stand for."

"Meaning . . ."

"Israel, the rest of it."

"Mike —"

"Don't get defensive, bro. I'm just looking out for you."

"I'm not against what they stand for. My favorite writers are all Jewish. I've been going to school on Philip Roth and Arthur

Miller since I was in my teens."

"All good," he said, only partly smiling. "Make sure they know it. You'll be fine."

It was all typical Mike Jacobs, the caustic, well-intentioned directness, the charged racial views offered without judgment or apology. He owed what he sometimes called his "cheery pessimism" to his father, Jerry, also a lawyer, whose shadow loomed large in Mike's life. Jerry Jacobs gave up a career in Washington, DC, to move the family back to Opelika, Alabama, where generations of Jacobses had lived for over a century. It was a remarkable choice considering the start he'd made: right out of law school, Jerry landed a clerkship under Spottswood Robinson at the US Court of Appeals for the District of Columbia Circuit, the highest appeals court in the land. Stately, mild-mannered "Spotts" Robinson was a legend at that point, the first lawyer to argue *Brown v. Board of Education,* later the first black judge to be appointed to the DC Circuit. Clerking for Robinson back then — this was during the 1980s — was a stepping-stone without equal for a young black lawyer like Mike's father. But the professional prospects, however bright, didn't ultimately blind Jerry to what was taking shape in DC, the rise of the ideological framework he foresaw would hurt American blacks more than anyone realized. So Jerry decamped from the nation's capital for Opelika, where he joined a local law practice, served on the city council, and eventually got elected to the Alabama House of Representatives. I met Jerry once, when he and Mike's mother were visiting New York in the late '90s, a sinewy, balding man with a high-pitched voice and a spectacular mustache. It was immediately obvious just how much Mike owed to the man — the preemptive exuberance, the jaunty physical rhythms. Even the faint traces of deeper, world-weary fatigue I'd divined in Mike's distracted pauses and half smiles. Years later, Mike mentioned in passing that his father's favorite movie star was Jimmy Stewart — and that his favorite film was *It's a Wonderful Life* — and I would imagine I'd stumbled onto the source of that high-strung, high-octane charm innate in father and son, the peculiar, willfully boyish strain that only partly masked a deeper battle against disillusionment. It was an emotional alloy familiar to anyone who knew Stewart's heroes, all characters whose infelicitous confrontations with America's darker truths left them, in one way or another, spiritually crippled.

Cheery pessimism. Or weary idealism. Take your pick.

It's hard from the perspective of more than two years now — as I write these words in the summer of 2018 — to recall just how unlikely Trump's rise felt while it was happening. Before he secured the nomination, in July of 2016, and even as late as early March of that year, Trump's outlandishness, his flagrant disregard for any of the accepted rules of engagement, his ignorance of the issues, his willful mendacity and vulgarity, the constant stream of his demeaning offensiveness, all this seemed to bode ill for his ultimate chances. It was a much-repeated platitude that Trump was one inevitable faux pas from flaming out. But by April it was clear Trump's mishaps were only swelling the ranks of his supporters. Trump would crush his opponents in the weeks ahead, first in New York, then in Pennsylvania, at which point his path to the general election — and a catastrophic loss to Hillary Clinton — appeared all but certain.

Mike was in New York on business in early May of 2016, a week after the Pennsylvania returns. We met for a drink at Red Rooster in Harlem, a popular spot for high-end soul food along Lenox Avenue, owned and operated by Marcus Samuelsson, a Swedish chef of Ethiopian extraction. Bill Clinton had apparently been for dinner the night before, hosted by a gaggle of hedge-fund managers, and the restaurant staff was still aflutter from the visit. Clinton had gone back into the kitchen to hang out with the busboys and line cooks, the bartender bragged to us as he poured our martinis, marveling at the man's political skills and bemoaning Hillary's charmlessness. Once the bartender was out of earshot, Mike announced to me that Trump would be our next president.

I laughed. "You're kidding, right?"

"Not at all."

"You actually think he's going to win?"

"I do."

"Why?"

He took a moment to consider: clearly this was not just small talk to him. "Let's get a table," he said. "I'm hungry. And this is going to take a while."

I'm ashamed to admit how little I knew about Robert Bork before that night at Red Rooster. During Mike's father's clerkship under Spotts Robinson, Bork was one of the judges also seated at the DC Circuit. This was three years before Reagan nominated him to the Supreme Court in 1987, the same year of the infamous senate hearings that would deny the judge's nomination, hearings so rancorous that in the popular vernacular Bork's name would become synonymous with any concerted political attack on a career or nomination. I vaguely remember the fuss at the time but don't recall having any sense of what it was all about. (I was fifteen.) In college, I would be taught that Bork's America was one

in which women would be forced into back-alley abortions, blacks would sit at segregated lunch counters, rogue police could break down citizens' doors in midnight raids, school-children could not be taught about evolution, writers and artists could be censored at the whim of the government, and the doors of the federal courts would be shut on the fingers of millions of citizens.

The quotation is from Ted Kennedy's attack on the man during those '87 hearings, an address that would end up shaping the image of Bork for a generation to come: that of a conservative ideologue who sniffed decadence in Dixieland music and detective fiction, whose vision of a healthy society

387

resembled a reactionary fever dream, and whose defeat in those confirmation hearings was seen to signal a decisive victory for America's progressive ideals.

All this was an unfortunate and misleading simplification.

Bork's real influence on American life would have little to do with his reactionary cultural and political views. It was as an antitrust ideologue — who believed that the only meaningful check on corporate power should be the competitive threat of other corporations and that the consumer's benefit should be the only metric to gauge whether the government had cause to intervene — that Bork and his ideas would fundamentally reshape our country. His notion that the collective good was determined solely by benefit to the consumer would prove to be the necessary lubricant in the world-historical shift to the form of free-market capitalism that has engulfed the planet. To call him a conservative is to miss the point. There was nothing conservative about his antitrust views, at least not in any traditional sense of the word *conservative*. Bork, along with economists like F. A. Hayek, Milton Friedman, and James Buchanan — figures whose work I had never studied or even read until after that night in Harlem — advocated not the conservation of traditional structures but the abolition of them; they wished to eliminate all real checks on private enterprise; and they believed, in contradiction not only to all common sense but also to Gödel's theorem, that the Market could be depended on to regulate its own aberrations and idiosyncrasies. In other words, however much Bork and others like him may have inveighed against personal liberties in the public sphere, they were positively gaga over individualism's most wanton, unfettered forms in the private sector. Indeed, I've come to think that the central political paradox of our time is that the so-called conservatives of the past half century have sought to conserve almost nothing of the societies they inherited but instead have worked to remake them with a vigor reminiscent of the leftist revolutionaries they despise.

Over Hot Honey Yardbird and the Obama Short Rib, Mike explained to me what his father had come to understand about America during his clerkship on the DC Circuit in such close proximity to Bork at the height of the Reagan years. Even back in the mid-'80s, the city's political culture was still one of gentlemanly exchange; partisan arguments before the bench or on the Senate floor were put aside when it was time for martinis and oysters at Occidental or Old Ebbitt Grill. It was at a similarly collegial evening in Georgetown that Bork found himself seated next to the young black lawyer he recognized from Justice Robinson's team. The two men launched into a lively conversation. Mike said that his father discovered in Bork that night someone far more personable than he'd expected given the man's haughty demeanor on the bench. Bork, too, was impressed, and that evening initiated a friendly intimacy between the men, which, as it grew over the following weeks and months, made Jerry's boss, Spotts Robinson, more than a little uncomfortable.

For their part, Spotts and Bork had been on terrible terms ever since issuing differing opinions in the case of *Dronenburg v. Zech.* In the spring of 1981, James Dronenburg, a twenty-seven-year-old petty officer in the navy, was caught engaged in "homosexual acts" in the naval barracks and honorably discharged. He filed suit, claiming the discharge violated his constitutional rights. The case wound its way to the DC Circuit, where Bork voted with the majority to uphold the navy's decision to punish the young gay man. Robinson wrote an angry dissent, which provoked a dismissive personal rejoinder in the majority opinion penned by Bork. The relationship between the two judges had never been great, but after *Dronenburg* they barely spoke any longer. Irked by Bork's interest in his clerk, Spotts advised Jerry to be careful: Bork's imperiousness toward black appellants and solicitors was a sure sign of racism; there had to be some ulterior motive at work.

Meanwhile, Bork had introduced Jerry to someone at the White House; a pair of subsequent lunches led to a brief audience with the Gipper himself. Though it was never made explicit, Jerry gathered there was a need for black faces to support the administration's deregulatory initiatives. In particular, black businesses across the country were starting to organize against Reagan's new antitrust policies. It was an era of easy money; mergers and takeovers were all the rage. Ever-larger companies were swallowing up market share, putting smaller businesses out to pasture, offering the promise of lower prices to compensate for the havoc wreaked on American Main Streets. At an earlier time in the nation's history, the federal government would never have allowed the naked corporate grab then under way; in the late '60s, even a potential 8 percent market share was cause for the courts to block the merger of two grocery store chains in Los Angeles. The judges explicitly sided with those who stood to lose their jobs and their businesses — even if the grocery merger might mean lower prices for consumers. Bork destroyed this way of thinking. In 1978, he would publish *The Antitrust Paradox,* a book responsible for entirely reframing our ideas about corporate competition and the benefit to the consumer, a book described as the most cited work on its subject in American history. In his years before sitting on the DC Circuit — teaching at Yale Law School and working in the Justice Department under Nixon — Bork had educated and promoted a generation of disciples who shaped opinion from the bench, on the nation's business pages, and in America's boardrooms. Increasingly, the benefit to the consumer would become the dominant metric of the common good, and that benefit would be solely defined by the lowest price. A company's scale no longer signified a potential abuse of power, only opportunity, for the bigger you were, the more power you had over your suppliers and employees; greater latitude to cut costs with impunity meant passing on savings to the consumer. The consolidation began in grocery stores* and other retail establishments and would later expand to banks and insurers, railroads, trucking, airlines. (Decades later, of course, this process would culminate in the rise of companies of almost God-like proportions, merchants of human attention and data whose digital technologies and algorithms would come to command our very cognitive activity itself.)

Concussive scale, market share, shirked responsibility to communities and workers: all this has been permitted — no, *encouraged* — because of a so-called benefit to the consumer. But to hear Mike tell it, in the mid-'80s black intellectuals and businessmen were already wondering whether

* A company like Walmart was only possible in this new regime, coming to control more than 50 percent of grocery sales in more than forty metropolitan areas by 2015, in contrast to the measly 8 percent market share that was seen as anticompetitive by the courts of the late 1960s; or Amazon, which, in selling books for less than it costs to manufacture them, would first drop its wrecking ball into the publishing world and, later, use the same scorched-earth business model to attempt the wholesale dismantling of brick-and-mortar retail itself.

the nation could really thrive through buying alone. Is that all we were as Americans? Consumers? Certainly we were also laborers and owners and perhaps even *citizens* as well. Was there really no need to protect these aspects of our social being, too? Did the nation's welfare truly amount to little more than saving money at the cash register?

If you were black in the '80s, Mike said, you couldn't ignore what the new laws really meant. Black banks, black insurers were getting bought up by white-owned holding companies and turning their backs on their new black customers; these growing conglomerates were not locally owned, had no local stakes, and had no incentive to attend to the needs of communities they didn't live in, didn't understand, and, frankly, didn't like. And connected to all this not very thinly veiled commercial racism was something people like Justice Spottswood Robinson couldn't forget: that their civil rights battles had owed more to black-owned businesses than most would ever understand. Economic independence was essential to the battle for full rights; the money to sustain the struggle had to come from somewhere; most often, it came from local black businesses. Black grocery store owners bankrolled bus boycotts; black drugstore owners financed "wade-ins" at segregated beaches; black funeral owners pulled their money from white banks until whites only signs were removed from water fountains and bathrooms.

In the series of meetings that young Jerry Jacobs took with members of various federal agencies and lobbying firms, he started to get a better picture of why they wanted him. Scarred by their defeats in the civil rights era, convinced beyond any doubt of the transformative force of organized black protest, Reagan Republicans were taking no chances. They were worried about a critique already current in the black community, one that gave the lie to all this talk about efficiency and the consumer good, a critique articulated even before the Great Depression by none other than W. E. B. Du Bois:

To ask the individual colored man to go into the grocery store business or to open a drygoods shop or to sell meat, shoes, candy, books, cigars, clothes or fruit in competition with the chain store, is to ask him to commit slow but almost inevitable economic suicide.

Recruiting black lawyers to serve in the cause of deregulation had become a top priority, and Bork, according to Mike, had identified Mike's father as a perfect candidate. Jerry Jacobs would be offered a job at the Federal Trade Commission in 1986, but by then, after having flirted with Reaganites for more than a year, he'd figured out what they were up to. The way Jerry saw it, they had no illusions about the future; they saw the rising tide of racial diversity and its economic and political consequences; they were plotting their response — a reassertion of white property rights, an accumulation of power in corporate hands to ensure that whites remained in charge.

Spotts Robinson patiently watched as his young clerk was slowly disabused of his illusions around these modern heirs to the party of Lincoln. Honest Abe was probably rolling over in his grave, Spotts would say; he'd risked so much to free American blacks from slavery, and here, folks like Baker and Bork and Atwater were using his party's great name to slip them right back into chains, albeit financial ones. When I first knew Mike, he had tried his hand at a screenplay, and that night in Harlem I finally understood where the inspiration for it came from. The screenplay told the story of a young black lawyer lured by the promise of influence and wealth, tempted into a self-enriching cause that leads to his betrayal of a beloved paternal mentor — a thin, stately, self-effacing attorney from the Old South in the mold of Spottswood Robinson. Far more than its plotting — which, I thought, owed too much to any number of John Grisham thrillers — the moral of the story was complicated and appeared indebted to what Mike's father learned about himself during his DC years, perhaps to what Mike felt his father still hadn't fully learned as well: point of view is always shaped by desire; if some part of you doesn't trust your desire, then you better not trust the picture of the world it's giving you.

Eventually, Mike came to see his father's decision to leave the nation's capital and come home to Alabama as marred by sentimentality. It was all well and good to want to do right by those you loved. But as Mike saw it, you better have a real idea of what that might actually entail. His father had certainly seen what was starting to happen in America, but Mike wasn't sure he'd understood just how little a person could do about it from a law office on Main Street in Opelika or even from the statehouse in Montgomery. The new political order was mercantile at its root, shaped and paid for by the cash accumulated in the coffers of bigger and bigger business — and what it was doing to black businesses it was doing to everyone. Chains and conglomerates weren't shuttering more black concerns than they were white ones. The mistake his father made, Mike started to understand, was to see all this solely through the lens of race. Locality itself was in decline, as dollars were drained from the American heartlands and allocated to points of prosperity along the urban coasts. In the South, it was in farming that you saw the worst of it. People — black, white, or brown — couldn't live off their land anymore. Corporate consolidation led to larger and larger tracts and the increasingly automated systems required to water and harvest them. Prices for produce dropped, yes — but so did the tax base. There'd never been more jobs that paid so little, most of which went to migrants who didn't object to making a pittance. Towns were poorer, which meant schools were poorer, too. Public education started to crumble. So did the roads and bridges. There were fewer landowners giving less money to an ever-dwindling number of churches and charities. Everywhere you went, people poured into big-box stores to spend less on things they had less money to buy. The twenty-year downward slope of opportunity and morale in places like Opelika and Wichita and Grand Rapids and Scranton — and just about everywhere else across middle America — defined a descent from which, increasingly, there appeared to be no recourse. Suicide was on the rise, and so were drugs, depression, anger.

And all this was *before* the financial crisis.

What Mike said to me that night in Harlem six months before Trump's election was that he had started to see what was happening not just to the black community but also to the very notion of American community itself. His father's ideas, his own life in Opelika — these had prepared him to understand the implications of what he was learning in courses such as Corporate Tax Theory and Topics on American Property Law. Like Riaz, Mike started to see that there was no way to turn back the tide of what had begun in the '80s. Our ideas had changed. Yes, money had always been central to notions of American vitality, but now it reigned as our supreme defining value. It was no longer just the purpose of our toil but also our sport and our pastime. We discussed a movie's weekend gross before its plotline, an outfielder's signing bonus before his batting average. The market had seeped into our language; we sought *upside* and minimized our *exposure* and worried about the best *investment* of our *sweat equity*. Even suffrage was monetized, true political power lying not in the ballot box but in one's capacity to write a check. We were now customers first and foremost, not citizens, and to *buy* was our privileged act. No longer ruled by a personified abstraction, Zeus or Yahweh, we now appeased a material one: the Economy. We feared its humors; we were grateful for its dispensations; we tended to its imagined well-being with our ritual purchases. When the Economy was well, we were a happy people; when the Economy faltered, premonitions of doom were never far.

Unlike his father, Mike would leave Alabama for good. He would go first to New York, where I met him, then to the West Coast. He'd met and married a woman from Michigan, which, he said, gave him a Yankee perspective on the looting of American life he'd seen back home: his wife, Morgan, had grown up in Flint.* That night at

* I suspect, if you're still reading this book, you're the sort of person who's already aware of the mind-boggling municipal boondoggle that, in 2012, corroded the city's pipes and had the children of Flint drinking water from what one of-

400

Red Rooster, Mike said something that reminded me of Mary Moroni's lecture remarks almost a quarter century earlier, about American self-pillage and plunder, but in a more despairing key:

It's like nobody even sees it like a country anymore. I don't know if they ever did, but they sure don't now. My dad used to say it's 'cause they've had to accept us coming into their part of the picture. We ruined it for them. Everything was fine when we were picking their cotton, but now that they might have to be picking ours? That's enough to say: "Fuck it. This ain't my place anymore. I'm gonna change the rules, take what I can, hide behind some gate, and fuck the rest."

Mike didn't see a political solution. To him the Democrats had betrayed not only blacks but also the country itself. Liberalism, as it was practiced today, was no less a route to self-enrichment than its opposite

ficial would call a lead-coated straw — a tale that, if it wasn't real, would read like the kind of tragic farce I used to associate with Gogol's Russia or some Third World banana republic concocted by Naipaul.

was. One needed look no further than the ever-rising post-presidency net worth of the Clintons — the blockbuster book deals, the $750,000 speaking fees — to recognize there was no longer a competing ideology in America. Everything was about getting rich. At least Republicans were honest about it. Mike saw a country where people were poorer, where they were lied to, where their lives felt meaner, where they had no idea how to change any of it. They'd taken the unprecedented step of putting a black intellectual into the highest office in the land, a man who promised change but offered little, whose admittedly genuine concern was marred by his superciliousness, who gloried in his pop-culture celebrity while bemoaning a system whose political dysfunctions prevented him from leading. Obama's victory had turned out to be little more than symbolic, only hastening our nation's long collapse into corporate autocracy, and his failures had raised the stakes immeasurably. Most Americans couldn't cobble together a week's expenses in case of an emergency. They had good reason to be scared and angry. They felt betrayed and wanted to destroy something. The national mood was Hobbesian: nasty, brutish, nihilistic — and no one embodied all this better than Donald Trump. Trump was no aberration or idiosyncrasy, as Mike saw it, but a reflection, a human mirror in which to see all we'd allowed ourselves to become. Sure, you could read the man for metaphors — an unapologetically racist real estate magnate embodying the rise of white property rights; a self-absorbed idiot epitomizing the rampant social self-obsession and narcissism that was making us all stupider by the day; greed and corruption so naked and endemic it could only be made sense of as the outsize expression of our own deepest desires — yes, you could read the man as if he were a symbol to be deciphered, but Mike thought it was much simpler than all that. Trump had just felt the national mood, and his particular genius was a need for attention so craven, so unrelenting, he was willing to don any and every shade of our moment's ugliness, consequences be damned.

As I walked home after our dinner at Red Rooster — up Lenox and then west, across 141st, the night was brisk and the street uncharacteristically quiet. I made my way past the empty basketball courts abutting the perimeter of the public housing projects. Mixing along the sidewalk were the scents of wood fires and marijuana smoke. As I approached Frederick Douglass Boulevard, I saw an orange couch in the middle of street and ahead, on opposite corners, two groups of young black men who paid me no mind as I passed. One of the groups was huddled around a box, picking at a frosted cake with their fingers.

My building was at the top of the hill off Convent Avenue. I marched up four flights of steps and, once inside, made a beeline for my notebook. For the next hour, I sat at the folding table in my kitchen, writing out an account of the evening, some twenty pages, front and back, shorter on details than it was on my disorientation. Despite my affection for Mike, despite my respect for the unusual granular purchase of his intellect, I couldn't pretend to myself I didn't think he was full of shit. His criticisms of Obama sounded petty. I suspected envy. I thought his prognostication about Trump's victory was wrong. My father had "thoughts" about Trump, too, and those were silly. I concluded that my front-row seat to all *that* nonsense was no worse a perspective than Mike's wide-ranging abstractions — probably better. If anything, I saw in my father's silly infatuation with Trump a human component at work —

weak, irrational — that didn't fit tidily into the clean shapes Mike was drawing around the national spirit. Ever the artist, I trusted the mess.

I noted the fiery turn our talk took at the end of dinner, when he brought up just how much he hated paying taxes. At root, he said as he picked at a piece of sweet potato pie, a government built by whites could only be expected to do harm to black people. I knew my Baldwin; I'd read Ta-Nehisi Coates; I didn't doubt what he was saying was probably right, but hearing it still shocked me. I glanced over my shoulder at the table behind us to see if our neighbors had heard him. Then I remembered where we were.

As he inveighed against the evils of government and being forced to pay into them, I will admit I thought I heard him reframing talking points already familiar to me from the GOP. The fierce glimmer in his eyes as he spoke made less and less sense to me as I mulled the staggering paradox at the heart of his politics: he believed the American government didn't deserve his dollars because they would be used against him, a black man, forever the American enemy; so he voted for candidates who promised to lower his taxes, which meant he was ever more inclined to vote Republican, fully cognizant that Republicans were only more and more open about their intent to further ruin the lives of American blacks.

What was I missing?

"You're missing the forest for the trees."

"Mike. I don't understand —"

"What they built, they built for themselves. The system they've got, we ain't gonna change that."

"But you're not even trying."

"That's not true. I am."

"How? Not paying taxes? Really?"

"The more you have, the more you can do. That's the only way to change anything here. Money." He paused. "You ever hear that thing about the Taino Indians praying to the pile of gold?"

"No."

"It's a crazy story, bro. But it kind of says it all. You know who the Taino were, right? They were the natives on a lot of the Caribbean islands before the Spanish showed up. When they got here — the Spanish, that is — it turned out all they were looking for was gold, and the Taino were happy to lead them to it. It didn't mean much to them. Soon enough, the Spanish put them to work digging up that gold, though. Turned them into slaves. Word got out. So now, when the Spanish showed up on some new Taino island, the natives would just flee. They'd take their boats and head to a different island. They got pushed around the Caribbean, island after island — until they decided to make a last stand. But not by fighting. Instead, they gathered all the gold they could find and put it in a big pile. Then they prayed to that pile to let the white man leave them alone. To let them have this final island. They had their own gods, but they prayed to the gold. As they saw it, that was the white man's god."

"Your point?"

"Gold ain't got no mercy. Those Indians were right. For white people, it's all about the cash. Always has been. And we're living in a world *they* made. See, maybe if we play *our own* game by their rules, maybe then we got a shot. But that means we gotta be keeping our money. We can't give it to them. And we have to use it, because it all boils down to the spend. How much you are willing to spend to make what you want happen out there in the world . . ."

That night at my folding table, I transcribed the conversation as I recalled it and found myself only more dumbfounded in reading it back. Mike had spent the better part of two hours vilifying the white corporate property grab, and here he was advocating the conditions for an eventual corollary black one. Hadn't he been making a case for a larger vision of the nation than one riven by race? Hadn't that been the whole point of what he was saying about Trump? That the nation *as a whole* had been suffering? That it behooved us finally to see it *that* way? I started to doubt there was any cogent way to square his so-called concern for dwindling community with his support for Republicans who — per his own analysis! — had done so much damage to the foundations of American community in the first place. Wasn't he just a hypocrite, like the rest of them? And what in God's name did the *Taino* have to do with any of this!?

I wrote and wrote, but nothing I wrote moderated my frustration. I sensed there was something here beyond my ken, but I wasn't convinced understanding it would make any difference. At some point, I shut my notebook and went to bed, but my aggravation lingered and led me back to my laptop, where I bounced about for an hour between websites about antitrust law and posts on Facebook about Trump's latest antics. I tried to sleep again, but still couldn't. Around 3:00 a.m., I got out of bed again, turned on the TV. On some barely known cable network pages way down on the on-screen guide, I noticed an airing of *It's a Wonderful Life* under way.

The movie's charcoal shades were both brisker and more somber than I recalled, like a chiaroscuro in some American Caravaggio. It was at that point in the story where Jimmy Stewart's suicidal George Bailey is being led by his guardian angel through what would have become of his beloved town of Bedford Falls if he'd never been born. Now the town is called Pottersville, renamed for the avaricious banker Henry Potter, who has basically taken it over. Without Bailey's building and loan association, there's no longer a bank in town lending money at a fair rate to the local working class. Potter has been able to buy all the real estate and establish a monopoly that has its residents paying him rents they can't afford. What was once a quaint, lovely, idyllic town is now a dreary, debt-ridden slum. Capra's vision of municipal nightmare in Pottersville had been terrifying to me as a child, its sleazy, neon-lit enticements — the gambling, the drinking, the prostitution — without a scintilla of human allure, a foreboding police state where every relationship we've come to love in the film has succumbed to death, despair, or the bleak grip of Potter's greed. I couldn't then imagine a place like Pottersville being real, growing up as I did in an affluent westerly suburb of Milwaukee not unlike Bedford Falls. But now, as I watched the film for the first time in twenty years, my thoughts still addled by Mike's vision of our country, Capra's evocation of America's darker side seemed nothing if not prescient.

I'd never realized just how much the movie was about money. George Bailey is a banker. The plot is set in motion by the loss of a client's deposit. The antagonist is another banker, a predatory lender, who refuses to loan George the money to cover the lost deposit. An upcoming audit is what drives George to attempt suicide: his life insurance policy can cover the shortfall, keep the building and loan solvent, and ensure that his customers won't be thrown out of their homes. In his guardian angel's tour through a world without him, Bailey comes to see that the good of his having lived on earth was that he was able to keep his fellow citizens in homes of their own, sheltered from Potter's exploitive rentals. Even the film's extraordinarily moving finale — through which I cried that night, as ever — showed the townspeople of Bedford Falls gathered around their beloved loan officer, George Bailey, all with cash donations in hand to cover the missing deposit, a joyous celebration of fiscal surplus, as George realizes that he has even more money now than what's needed to save his bank from collapse.

I run the risk of drawing too strong a conclusion here, but only because I'm trying to balance what I would come to understand with what I still couldn't see: that this most enduring of American Christmas tales, among the most popular of all American works of art, had already envisioned the nation we would become — impoverished, indebted, a place where our softer stewards had succumbed to the hard pinch of profit for its own sake, where our fates had been subsumed by the owners of property, where the American dream was suffering literal foreclosure, where even our most affective dilemmas could only find true resolution through the accumulation of cash. Not to see this picture of the country was, in fact, to choose not to see it. In a year's time, my shares in Timur Capital would make me rich enough finally to understand what I hadn't with Mike that night: money comes with its own point of view; what you own, when you own enough of it, starts making you see the world from *its* perspective.

That night at Red Rooster I had wanted

to hear something else. I'd wanted Mike to affirm — despite the encompassing cynicism of his worldview — that he still believed the arc of history bent, however slowly, toward justice. But he was saying: he didn't believe that. He was saying: property has its own interests, and those interests will always be served above others. And he was saying: justice is the will of the strong borne by the weak — and those who *own* are the strong. In giving up the liberal humanist illusion, he was also making the only honest case he felt he could to preserve the hope this illusion fed. Back then, I couldn't hear these nuances, for I still believed — as George Bailey puts it in the quotation that begins this chapter — that the living, dying *rabble* matter more, *must* matter more, than what their accumulated rents are worth to an owner on a spreadsheet; back then, I was still hopeful that history would eventually favor the meek and righteous; back then, I couldn't assemble the various pieces in a way that would account for the darker truths I was resisting.

The movie ended just before dawn. Something was stirring inside me. I got up from the couch and went to the window, where the earliest light of day was appearing beneath the clouds over East Harlem.

Through the single-pane glass, I heard the faint screech and churning of a distant toiling sanitation truck. I remember standing there, sensing the swell of something new inside me, something hard and vivid, chilly, for which I had no good words. My favored music was too tender, marred by private yearning and compulsive need. I would have to find new words. A new language. Colder notes and meanings. Jangled chords for shriller songs — hymns to the esoteric din, to decline, to the dollar, to our ailing nation and its foundering myths. But all that — like President-elect Trump — was yet to be. What I sensed that morning at my window in Harlem was only this: the time had come to start listening beyond my hopeful heart.

VIII.

LANGFORD V. RELIANT; OR,
HOW MY FATHER'S
AMERICAN STORY ENDS

1.

In October of 2012, my father saw a patient by the name of Christine Langford, a fair-haired, newly pregnant twenty-six-year-old woman with a long-standing heart problem known as long QT syndrome. Christine had been diagnosed in childhood with the condition, which, triggered by exercise, emotional excitement, or sleep, can lead to a particularly serious form of irregular heartbeat. Specifically — and crucially to this story — "long QT" refers to a longer-than-normal interval between two beats of the heart, an elongation that can provoke a chaotic heart flutter that, if it goes on for any extended period of time, often results in sudden death.

Long QT syndrome appeared to run in Christine's family. Her mother, Corinne, had it, and long QT caused the death of Christine's sister, Kayleigh, when Kayleigh was nine. The girl's heart stopped beating as she napped one Sunday afternoon after helping her grandfather tend to the cows on the family farm in Kendall, Wisconsin, a small community in the far western reaches of the state. After Kayleigh's death, extensive tests on the girl's tissues and on the rest of the family would reveal that Kayleigh, Christine, and her mother were all carriers of the gene for long QT syndrome.

For years, Christine and her mother took beta-blockers, medications that slowed and regulated the heart's beating, and neither of them experienced any significant heart symptoms from that point forward. But then Christine got pregnant. While surfing the internet one night, she came across an article that warned of potential prenatal risks to the fetus from some beta-blockers. The medication she'd been on since she was a young girl was at the top of the list. She called her doctor the next morning. He referred her to my father — then considered to be the state's leading specialist in all manner of arcane heart-rhythm problems.

By 2012, Father was nearing the end of his career. He'd been through two and a half boom-and-bust cycles: his first cardiology practice — as you'll recall — going fully out of business in the early '90s, his second practice only barely averting collapse in the aftermath of the World Trade Center attacks. Across the country, brown doctors saw their patient load decline after 9/11, and my father's cardiology group — staffed almost entirely with South Asian physicians — was no exception. He lost 40 percent of his business within three months; most of those patients never came back.

To compensate for lost capacity, Father came up with a counterintuitive strategy: expand into the farther rural reaches of the state. People out there had heart problems, too, of course, and they usually traveled hours to be seen, often needing to stay overnight in big-city hotels when they were scheduled for tests. Father believed — and convinced the doctors in his group — that shorter drives and the prospect of sleeping at home the night before a procedure would outweigh any conscious or unconscious bias a patient might have.

As my father tells it, it was a full five years before his group saw results, but by 2007 they were seeing more patients than any other cardiology practice in the state. It wasn't long before their startling growth drew the notice of a corporate health-care network I will call Reliant Health for the purposes of this narrative. In 2010, my father's cardiology group would get bought out by Reliant, and the resulting clash of administrative cultures — one driven by doctors, the other by MBAs — forms an important backdrop to the story I'll be telling here.

Christine saw my father at a clinic in La Crosse, a small city along Wisconsin's western border with Minnesota, a place known to most, now, for having lent an archaic Old French version of its name to America's most popular brand of flavored sparkling water, La Croix, a drink concocted there in the early '80s and eventually sold to a publicly traded holding company based, for the tax purposes of its owner, in Fort Lauderdale, Florida. Christine lived an hour southeast of La Crosse, in a small town called Westby, where she worked as an elementary school music teacher and taught private piano lessons to pupils on Saturdays. Father remembered this detail about her in particular, as it came up during her examination, how she gave piano lessons and how his son — I — used to take them. Something else Father recalled about that exam was the argument it provoked with Thom Powell, the administrator at Reliant overseeing the group's business. Ever on the lookout for new ways to increase revenues, Powell had recently ordered his doctors to shorten their visits and delegate more of their duties to the group's nurse practitioners; this was cheaper and created more room in the schedule for the lucrative billable appointments with MDs. When Powell discovered from an end-of-week report that Father had spent forty-two minutes with Christine — the average was ten minutes per patient — he went ballistic.

The reason for Christine's considerably longer-than-usual exam was a series of EKG scans in her case file that Father worried had never been read properly. They showed the expected elongated QT intervals, but not only that. Father thought he saw further irregularities in the scripts, irregularities that suggested another potential problem: Brugada syndrome, the ailment that brought Father and Trump into contact in the mid-'90s. Father was particularly concerned by the hints of Brugada he was seeing on Christine's EKGs, as the beta-blocker she was taking, propranolol, was dangerous for Brugada patients, quite apart from its prenatal risks. After spending the extra time to take Christine's complete medical history, Father told her that nothing he'd heard convinced him she *didn't* have Brugada, and the only way to know for certain was a gene test that typically took six weeks, even when expedited. Considering that propranolol was potentially harmful to her fetus, he advised her to think seriously about discontinuing it until they were able to run the necessary test, and perhaps for the full term of her pregnancy, no matter the result. His advice was offered with the usual disquieting medical equivocations: as a specialist only just familiar with the details of her case, he could give her the information; the decision was for her to make with her cardiologist. Father recalled that she pressed him for a more definitive answer. "Do you mind, Doctor, if I ask — do you have a daughter?" she asked.

"I don't," he said after a moment's hesitation.

"If you did, and if she had my medical history — what would you tell her to do?"

As I've imagined the moment — with Christine on the examining table, looking over her shoulder at him; Father already at the door, his hand on the knob — I see Father register something that moves him to stop. Against his better judgment, he entertains the thought experiment. Then he finally says: "I would tell her to stop taking the propranolol."

Christine took his advice.

Two weeks later, she and her unborn child were dead.

2.

The first I heard about any of this was on the morning after the night I drove up from Chicago to fish my father out of jail. It was late October in 2017, and I was in the final week of rehearsals for the opening of my newest play. I'd been in the rehearsal room with my phone on silent until late that evening, which is why I initially missed his call from the police station. He'd left a slurred, reluctant message in a pebbly bass that sounded nothing like his usual voice: "*Beta.* I'm in the Elm Brook jail. You can call Benji. He said you can come and get me if you can."

Benji was not his lawyer but the deputy police chief of the village of Elm Brook, the small, mostly affluent suburban community where I'd grown up and where my father still lived in 2017. Benji and I had been in school together since the third grade; part of the same summer swimming-lesson cohort and Dungeons & Dragons group; we'd been backfield defenders on the JV soccer team together and served as members of the student council our senior year in high school. I knew his parents; he knew mine. He was the only one of my high school friends to personally pay his respects after my mother's obituary was printed in the local paper. His own mother's long terminal illness is what had brought him home after college upstate; when she died, he ended up staying in Elm Brook, marrying a fellow high school classmate of ours named Jess, and joining the local police department.

Outside the theater, it was a nippy, overcast night. The sounds of traffic and the passing El echoed against the brick-and-glass facades rising everywhere in this corner of the Loop. From a nearby kitchen, the smell of seared meat wafted along the sidewalk on which I paced, phone to my face, waiting for someone at the Elm Brook police station to pick up.

"Police department," a woman's voice finally answered. "Can I help you?"

"Deputy Fitzsimmons, please."

"What's your business?"

"I got a call from my father. Who I think is being held there . . ."

"Right," she said, clearly apprised.

"He left a message for me to call Benji."

"Hold, please," she said as she left the line and dropped me into the middle of a Viennese waltz. In the storefront windows across the street, I saw the reflection of the theater's marquee directly above me. The title of my new play had just gone up. MERCHANT OF DEBT, it read in bloodred block letters. Underneath it was a harmless but irritating indignity: my name was misspelled, a wayward letter misplaced from my last name into my first. The receptionist's voice interrupted the music. "Hold, please, sir," she said. After a long silence, I heard his voice, that distinctive nasal growl that — along with so much else about him: the broad freckled face, the strawberry curls, the patient, unassuming solidity — had remained mostly unchanged since high school.

"Hey, buddy."

"Benji, hi. How are you?"

"Can't complain, can't complain. I mean, all things considered — you're down in Chicago right now, right? If I've got that straight? Got something going up?"

"I am. Opens Monday."

"Yeah. Saw it on Facebook. I keep up with you."

"That's nice to hear."

"Yeah, no. It's amazing."

His enthusiasm was touching, but I wasn't sure how to respond to it. "Benji, what's going on with my dad?"

422

"Right," he said, not quite dropping the bright tone. "You know there's that new casino just past where that middle school used to be . . ."

"Sure."

"So Jess has been working as a dealer there. Last few months, our shifts have been matching up. I've been picking her up after work. Don't know if you're aware, but your dad spends a lot of time there —"

"I have some idea."

"Anyway, he was pretty lit tonight, making a stink. Security showed up, and he just sorta walked out in a huff. I followed him out into the parking lot, and I see him getting into his car. I mean, he's tripping over himself, I doubt he can see straight, but he's gonna drive? I stopped him before he got out on the road. It was messy, but I got the cuffs on him and brought him back here."

"Wait: So did you arrest him?"

"I was off duty. So I just kinda brought him in. Didn't book him. He's sleeping now."

"In the cell?"

"Yeah. I just, I don't know — I thought it might send a message. It's not the first time we've seen him like that at the casino. Jess was saying it's been getting worse. Your dad's a good guy. What he did for my dad

423

when he was sick I'll never forget. So I figured maybe a little wake-up couldn't hurt. I'll admit, I knew you were in Chicago. I know it's an inconvenience, but if you could come get him yourself — I don't know, it would make things a lot easier . . ."

"Of course. I'll come up right now. I can probably be there by eleven thirty?"

"Cool. I'm gonna get home and get the kids to bed. I'll text you my cell. Give me a shout when you get close, and I'll come back to meet you."

"Thanks, Benji. This is all very thoughtful of you."

"Like I said, buddy. Your dad's a good guy."

The drive home was a straight shot up the interstate, ninety-four minutes without traffic, according to my iPhone — on which I also spent most of that drive on a conference call with the production's creative team. We were three days out from our first performance, and the lead actor still didn't know his lines. The evening run had been mostly a disaster, and the director was convinced the issue was psychological. She thought the actor in question had yet to get over his initial misgivings about playing the role. Before taking it on, he'd expressed his worries that the character — more than partly inspired by Riaz — was too ambiguously drawn when it came to the central moral matter. He wasn't sure, he complained, if he was being asked to play a hero or a villain. "How about neither?" I'd responded when our agents arranged for us to meet for dinner in New York.

"How about both?" he countered coyly, biting on a bread stick. I'd been there before, glad-handing a star over a drink or meal, trading compliments as we sniffed out each other's vanities. I'd done it before and never well. *What's the harm in playing along this time?* I wondered. I conceded the counter — and did so by way of needlessly flattering his intelligence — but I would regret it. He would take my encouragement for permission to create a version of the character entirely too buoyant and one-dimensional, too indifferent to the murkier tonal range that was the essence of the play's dramatic plight. His cloying take hadn't worked in the rehearsal room and was working even less now that we'd moved onto the set. The director wanted me to give in and let him keep some stage business I'd hated since he introduced it early in rehearsal — in which he needlessly gave out money to a character who worked for him in the opening scene. The gesture was gratuitous and unjustified dramatically, but he'd gone to great lengths to build it into the physical action. When I asked him to explain why he was doing it, he lectured us on the importance of a save-the-cat moment — his name for any early story point where the hero does something the audience will find appealing (like Sigourney Weaver — he explained — saving Jonesy the cat in that first scene where we meet her in *Alien*). "Your play doesn't have a save-the-cat moment; I'm doing you a favor," he said. I responded by laughing out loud. From that point forward, things only got worse between us. Every time I saw him do his save-the-cat nonsense, I told him to stop. He wouldn't. And then he told the director he didn't want the writer talking to him anymore. The day before, on set, he'd done it again, and I stormed out. We were at a standstill, and the director believed the tension between us was the real reason he couldn't remember his lines. She counseled me over the phone to give in: "Just let him have it. It doesn't hurt the play. If he sees you soften on this, he'll feel like he's won something. It'll be the boost he needs. I won't be shocked if he shows up the next day line-perfect."

I was skeptical this was all it would take, but I told her I was game to try.

Our call ended as the exit for Elm Brook approached. A steady light rain had been falling since I'd crossed the border into Wisconsin, and here, where the off-ramp and road into town were paved with a speckled beige-gray concrete, the wet surface sparkled beneath the streetlamps. The town center was two miles down a sloping road, and the police station sat just past a raised set of train tracks in the building that also housed the local library. I pulled up into an empty spot alongside the only squad car parked in front and got out just as an approaching freight train sounded its horn.

Inside, the passing rattle of train wheels on rail joints sounded surprisingly close, floating in through the open barred window in the cell where my father snored on his side, a Green Bay Packers blanket covering much of his torso. The cell was large and clean, with a single bench of dark varnished wood on which my father slept. Benji unlocked the jail door, pulled it open, and stepped inside. He got to his knees and gently prodded Father awake. Father roused, grumbling, then turned and lifted his head. His sleepy eyes narrowed with suspicion as he registered Benji, then widened with sudden alarm as they found me standing beyond the bars. He looked like a frightened child, I thought, a forlorn runaway. "Hi, Dad," I said gently, hoping to soothe him, but he only sighed, his head dropping back against the bench.

"Can I go now?" he demanded with a petulant bray. Benji didn't reply. Father sat up, glowering. "Hmm? Can I go?"

"You're free to go. You always were — as long as there was someone to drive you home."

"Where's my car?"

"At the casino."

"You separated me from my *veeehicle?*" I would have laughed at the question if I hadn't heard the earnest outrage in it. He was clearly still drunk and confused.

"Just trying to make sure you don't hurt yourself or someone else, Doctor."

"Good Samaritan. Yeah, yeah," Father groused.

"Dad. You might want to thank Benji for helping you. It could have been a bad situation if —"

"What do you know? Hmm? Were you there? I didn't see you. I never see you anymore."

"Doc —" Benji interjected gently.

"Okay, look. Fine. Thank you, Benji.

Thank you for humiliating me in front of my boy. Who thinks he's better than everyone now that he's *famous*. But you know I was not nobody, either."

"— Dad."

Benji shot me a quick dissuading glance.

"I used to treat famous people, too. I was a doctor to kings! Did you know that, Benji?"

"That's what you were saying, Doc."

"Kings!"

"So I'm gonna go get your things," Benji said. "And let you gentlemen be on your way."

"My car?" Father asked again, confused.

"I'll take care of it, Dad. Don't worry."

Benji headed up the stairs as Father tottered to the cell door, still finding his feet. I reached out for his arm, which he snatched away angrily, banging his hand against the bars. He yelped, cursing in Punjabi, *"Bhenchod,"* then trundling off up the stairs to the front door.

I met Benji at reception, where he handed me Father's wallet and keys. "I'm sorry about that," I said. "He's obviously embarrassed —"

"Please. It's nothing. Compared to stuff I've seen? He's a kitten."

"Pretty oversize kitten."

429

"Aren't we all?" Benji said with a smile. "Is it true he was really Trump's doctor?"

"Did he tell you that?"

"Said he treated him for a heart problem years ago. They were friends."

"I don't know about the friends part, but yes, he was his doctor for a while."

"Wow. What a trip — maybe have a real talk with him tomorrow . . ."

"Absolutely. And thank you, Benji. This was incredibly kind of you."

"Good luck next week. With your opening."

"Thanks," I said, heading for the exit. I stopped in the doorway: "You want to come?"

"To what? Your opening?"

"Be my guests. Monday. You and Jess."

"You sure about that?"

"One hundred percent."

"I'd love that. Let me check my schedule and get back to you."

Out in the parking lot, I found Father already nestled in the passenger seat. I drove us home in silence, not realizing — until we were in the driveway — that he'd fallen asleep and was now drooling against the glass. After waking him, I took him inside into the living room, where I helped him onto the couch on which my mother had died and where he'd slept every night since. As I unlaced his shoes, he started to drift off to sleep again, mumbling my name and something else I couldn't make out.

"What was that, Dad?"

"I saaaid . . . if she waaaas my own daaaughter, I would have dooone the saaame."

I was confused. "If *who* was your own daughter?"

"Christiiine," he blared. He turned away from me again as I pulled off his socks. He kept muttering into the cushions. It wasn't long before he was snoring.

Who Christine was and what she might have had to do with being his daughter I wouldn't understand until the next morning, when he told me about his case. The reference to his daughter had confused me only because I knew he had one, a daughter, my half sister, whom I'd discovered two years earlier in an episode at once absurd and improbable, which surely merits extended treatment of its own. And yet though I've clearly shown neither shame nor compunction about exposing my loved ones — and myself — to the ridicule likely headed our way upon publication of this book, I've decided (mostly) to leave my half sister, Melissa (not

her real name), out of it. She's young. She's
had no proper father (she and my dad
haven't spoken for years). She's still trying
to find her way and herself and certainly
doesn't need this headache. Oh, and let's
be clear about one thing before I offer this
briefest of ex parte accounts:

We did not. Sleep with each other.

It was in February of 2016 that I found
myself ensconced deep in the toe of a scarlet
tufted horseshoe booth on the main floor of
a Manhattan strip club. Trump had just won
the New Hampshire primary. I was there
with a group of young husbands and bache-
lors celebrating the impending nuptials of
our friend Ashraf, the actor and comedian
who'd starred in two of my plays. Ashraf
and the other celebrants had all repaired to
the private rooms for Champagne and
dances (and likely more). A barely clad
shapely young woman found me sitting
there with only my drink to keep me company. Her skin was not quite as dark as
mine; she wore a nose stud, and her eyes
were lined with a thin rim of kohl. She went
by the name Noor. I wouldn't buy a dance
from her, but she planted herself beside me
anyway. I found her lively and acerbic,
mature beyond her years. (She said she was
twenty-four.) My interest in her choice for

an Arab stage name got her on the topic of sexual fetishes. She told me a story about a friend — like her, part Muslim — who turned tricks advertising herself in a face-covering niqab on erotic websites. I was startled to hear, even anecdotally, of the demand among US war vets to act out sexual fantasies on a female Muslim cipher. Most of them, Noor said, wanted to fuck her friend with her veil on. I caught the inkling of a story and gave her my card. Three days later she called me, and we met at a Korean restaurant in midtown. I sat across from her and took notes for an hour as she alternated between tales of her life in the sex trade and a bi bim bop without beef. We saw each other twice more before the evening when I ended up in her living room in Woodside and, on a bookshelf just outside the bathroom, I noticed a picture of my father.

I'll leave the rest for you to imagine.

I confronted my father that night, in a conversation that had him in shock, and ended with him hanging up on me. The next day, he called, sniffling, humbled, contrite in a way I'd never heard him. He had always planned to tell me someday, he said, and was glad I finally knew. He'd tried to do the best he could given the situation, he explained. He loved his wife; he loved his mistress; he loved both his children. He'd been too weak to make a choice, and Melissa's mother — bless her heart — hadn't pushed him. He always assumed my mother suspected something, but — bless *her* heart — she never asked. To hear him tugging at me for sympathy made me livid, but I kept my anger to myself. I told him Melissa was stripping, which surprised him. She needed money to get back into school, I said. He promised to send her what he could; I would eventually give her more. That summer, she returned to community college, studying to be a stenographer. She's almost done and, yes, still works in a strip club a few nights a week. Even if she didn't need the money as much as she did, she says, she wouldn't give it up; she's too used to what she calls a "certain intensity of attention" she just can't get anywhere else.

The morning after my father's trip to jail, I found him downstairs at the kitchen table, perusing the sports page, a pair of cracked readers perched at the edge of his nose. "You want me to make you a cup of tea?" he asked in a basement baritone as he sipped from a cup of his own. "Just warning you, though: there's no sugar."

"It's fine. I'll make coffee."

"We're out of that, too."

I went to the cabinet and pulled out a glass, filled it with water at the sink, then sat down across from him. "What happened last night?" I asked.

He shrugged without looking up from the paper. "I got bad news. I needed to take the edge off. I just — I let it go too far."

"You seem maybe to be doing that more and more —"

"— I'm a grown man," he snapped. "If I want to drink, I'll drink." I watched him turn the page and pretend to read.

"So what was the bad news?"

He looked up now, but not at me. Through the view out our sliding kitchen doors, a pair of deer were moving along the tree line at the yard's back edge. They stopped, one of them lowering its black nose to the grass, the other seemingly distracted by something in the woods. Just then, a third deer appeared: a buck with an imposing tangle of antlers on its head. "They're like rats," Father said blankly. "Can't get rid of them. Got into the garden this year and ate everything down to the roots. Even after I put all that rhubarb in to keep them away. What am I going to do with rhubarb?"

"You could make pie."

435

"What?"

"Rhubarb pie?"

He looked at me, completely dumbfounded. "What is *that*?"

"Forget it, Dad . . . What's the bad news?"

"I'm being sued. For malpractice."

"By *who*?"

He brushed off my concern as he pulled his readers from his face. "It's nothing new. This has been happening since 2014. The attorneys kept telling me it would get settled. It was the deadline yesterday. No settlement, so now we have to go to trial next week."

"Who's suing you?"

"Family of the patient. She was young, but she was the breadwinner. Her husband is on disability. Injured in Afghanistan, I think." He stopped again. "The science is on my side. I already know that, but it's what everyone else is telling me, too."

"So why did your lawyers want to settle?"

"Legal fees. Press. Headache." He stopped. "The company's lost two malpractice suits in the last two years. They're worried about losing a third one now."

"But the science is on your side?" I asked. He nodded, proceeding to tell me the story of Christine. As he spoke of her, something vivid and mournful came into his eyes. His description of her was spare — a pleasant young woman, two months pregnant with her first child, who reminded him, he said, of some of the girls he'd seen me grow up with in the area — but the emotion in his voice as he recalled her case sent me searching for an image of her online later that day. I found a picture of her standing alongside the pupils in one of her music classes, a woman with a face more round than oval, framed by two waves of parted shoulder-length hair; her nose was large and Roman, and its faintly rounded bridge connected two unusually wide-set eyes. I also found a photo of her gravestone, where not only her name and dates were etched into the granite but an image as well: that of an antlered buck towering over a lounging doe.

3.
Langford v. Reliant went to trial the following Monday at the La Crosse County Courthouse with Judge Elise Darius presiding. I missed jury selection and opening arguments because of my show in Chicago. Opening night went fine. Benji came with his wife. "Pretty neat stuff," he said to me on the way out, "though I'm not so sure about what you wanted me to think about that guy." The reviews the next day indicated

a similar ambivalence. Compelling but marred by reliance on stereotype is how I would characterize the general critical sentiment. Exactly what the stereotype was in this case, no one made very clear. To a critic, they yearned for a Muslim character driven to valiant ends by unimpeachable motives, not the tortured, vindictive antihero on display center stage for so much of the evening. In our era, one increasingly without political nuance, Muslims were just the minor premise of the social syllogism that formed our American nation's outraged theory of the downtrodden: you were either for the victim or against her. Muslims were victims. Therefore you could only be for a Muslim or against her. It didn't matter if you *were* one already. Art, like everything else, was drowning in the tidal wash of ubiquitous and ascendant anger. Authenticity was measured now in decibels. Every utterance, every expressive gesture, was read as a pledge of allegiance to some discernible creed. The politics of representation were in ascendance, increasingly mistaken for the poetics of narrative craft. One reviewer commented that she was giving up what little hope she'd ever harbored that I might move on from this "constant parade of Grand Guignolesque Muslim caricatures ranting, raving, refusing the promise of America." She had Muslim friends, she wrote, and they *loved* this country as much as she did. It had never occurred to me that jingoism — however nuanced — was part of my job description.

On Tuesday, my commuter flight from Chicago into La Crosse was delayed, and I didn't get in until after 11:00 p.m. As I checked in at the front desk, I heard my father's voice coming from the hotel bar. I stopped in before going up to my room and found him leaning into the counter, watching as the bartender poured him a double Bushmills, neat. He turned and saw me in the doorway. His face lit up. "That is my *son*," he announced, stumbling from his stool to gather me in his arms. He reeked of whiskey. "My wonderful, wonderful son," he chimed sloppily as he presented me to the bartender, a thickset bearded man pushing thirty, maybe. "A famous man now. More famous than his father."

"Dad —"

"Killed the father. Isn't that what they say? You did it, *beta*. You killed me."

I made a show of ignoring him. "I'm sorry, sir. He's under a lot of stress —"

The bartender shook his head, not seeming bothered in the least. "I was getting a

439

kick out of your dad here telling me about your success. Working with the stars in Hollywood now, he told me. That's gotta be neat."

"I mean, I'm not really working in Hollywood, but . . ."

Father's sudden angry frown was clownish. "Yes, you are!" he shouted. "You *are* working in Hollywood! Writing your own TV show. Why are you lying to him?!"

He needed a splash of cold water.

"Dad. I *was* working there. Then I got fired. Did you forget that part?"*

His cheeks dropped, and his smile vanished, the sudden, crestfallen look on his face revealing the nasty mood I knew was rumbling underneath this carelessness.

He retreated to his bar stool, dejected.

I signed for his bill and cajoled him into

* After three years of passing on offers from Tinseltown, I'd finally capitulated. The project was an adaptation of a French detective novel in which one of the protagonists was a Muslim. The producer who'd persuaded me to come aboard was, like me, the child of Pakistani immigrants. She didn't last six months on the job. After she was fired, I started to get notes from the studio about adding a terrorist subplot. I refused. And then I was fired.

440

the hall and elevator. Upstairs I took him to my room, filled a cup with water, and made him drink it before heading into the bathroom. When I came back out, I found him watching CNN. The day before marked the thirtieth anniversary of the Senate vote rejecting Bork's Supreme Court confirmation, and the channel was still running its segment about the man's legacy. "I don't care about this bullshit," Father said, pointing the remote to change the channel.

"No, Dad. Leave it. I want to see this."

"Ancient history," he said. I sat down on the bed and watched, surprised by a report that didn't once mention what I now understood to be the man's real American impact — as the Robespierre of the consumerist antitrust movement. Father poured himself another whiskey from the minibar and got back into bed. When the segment ended, he muted the commercials, muttering to me about the day's humiliations: the blatant lies in the plaintiff's opening statement, his fellow physicians not bothering to phone him, the insulting message someone he called Quaker Oats had left on his voice mail. He was being treated like a common criminal, he complained, when all he'd tried to do was help that girl. "I would have done the same thing if she was my own daughter," was the refrain he repeated as he dozed off to sleep.

The following morning: water, greasy eggs from room service, Advil. I walked him down the hall to his room and waited as he showered. He was gruff and complained as I got him into a blue shirt and black suit. Hannah, his lead lawyer, had picked his attire. Black for all her physician defendants, he told me, contrary to received courtroom wisdom. Black signaled status and authority and tended to alienate juries, but in the case of malpractice, authority was precisely what the plaintiff's team would work to undermine, so black was best. It was a performance, and the costume had to be right, she'd said. He handed me the tie she'd brought with her, a simple midnight-blue pattern. "She's a good lawyer. Nice person. I told her you were coming. She wants to have dinner with us tonight. If you can."

"Of course."

He nodded distantly. I could tell he was feeling fragile. "Not too tight," he said softly, as I nudged the knot to his bulging Adam's apple. I noticed his bottom lip start to quiver.

"Dad," I said, and tried to hold him, but he wouldn't let me.

The courthouse was a ten-minute walk

away. By the time we got there, he'd mostly put his vulnerable state behind him, though when Hannah found us on the third floor — just outside the courtroom — she wasn't fooled. She was an intense woman with intelligent eyes that scanned him now, mercilessly. He introduced us, and she shook my hand warmly. Then he shuffled off to use the restroom. When he was gone, Hannah dropped her gregarious front.

"He looks terrible," she said bluntly. "Was he drinking last night?"

I nodded. "I found him at the bar when I got in. Close to midnight. He'd been at it for a while, from what I could tell."

"Jesus fucking Christ," she said as she bit into her lower lip.

I felt the need to make an excuse for him: "It's really only been like this since my mom died."

"I've been doing this twenty-five years, and I'm telling you: he needs to stop. When we're done, he can go back to it — whatever the reason. But until then, not a drop. I've already told him: if the insurance company finds out he's drinking like that — and we lose? There *will be* consequences. And he won't like those."

"I'll talk to him."

"He needs to get it under control," she

said again, her nostrils flaring as she marched into the courtroom.

The chamber had nothing even vaguely ennobling about it — no vaulted ceiling, no Greek columns to remind us of the birth of democracy. There was no mahogany finish or railed balcony for onlookers. Not an echo of Maycomb or a hint of that soundstage replica of the New York court where three decades of rightful justice were meted out by the hour on *Law & Order.* The wood on the walls didn't look real, though it was — broad maple planks finished with a sickly yellow varnish. No one sat upright. Not the jury, not the plaintiff or their lawyers, not my father or those few of us, like me, looking on. We were all sinking into our scooped-out seat bottoms, our buckling spines chilled by the steady whisper of cold air trickling down through the vents above us. At one point, I started to wonder if this was what it would feel like to be trapped in the crisper drawer of a fridge — by any measure, hardly a place to battle for one's reputation.

Father was the only person of color at either of the tables before us; I was the only person of color in the audience. There were two jurors of color, one black, the other Asian. In total, I counted thirty-six whites around us. Christine's family was there. Her mother was going to be testifying; her widowed husband, Nick, was officially listed as the plaintiff. Nick Langford was a pale, depleted figure — unshaven, dour, with a full head of unwashed sandy brown hair. He'd come into the courtroom that morning in a bright orange hunting cap and camouflage vest. The brim of that orange hat peeked forth from one of the vest's front pockets, and the vest was dangled over the armrest of his chair in full view of the jury. No black suit for him, I thought. He looked every bit the part of a husband broken — a half decade on — by grief. Beside him sat his lawyer, an imposing brown-haired man in a visibly threadbare suit that seemed to match, at least in spirit, his client's attire, a plaid wool jacket pilled in places, the edge of its collar frayed from years of rubbing up against home-starched shirts. A bushy goatee encircled his lips, and he was shuffling papers before him with the disregard of a man more used to holding a Pabst Blue Ribbon — or a .45 — than a manila folder. Even his name seemed to fit the role: Chip Slaughter.

The bailiff announced Judge Darius's arrival. We stood; she made her entrance; we sat. A short woman with a sallow face

445

behind thick lenses, she beckoned both counselors to the bench, where she addressed them in a measured tone. The court's atmosphere, silent with expectation, was so much like that moment backstage before every show when actors are called to their places and the stage manager makes the final rounds to ensure all are ready to begin.

Quiet envelops the audience.

The lights dim.

The curtain rises:

(As the attorneys return now to their seats, the Judge looks over to the Bailiff. He rises.)

BAILIFF

The court calls the plaintiff's first witness, Corinne Hollander.

(On the other side of the aisle in the audience, a portly, plodding lady stands and slowly makes her way down the aisle. She has a washed-out mien: her silvering hair, her skin covered with chalky powder. Against this mask of white, her thin lips are drawn in crimson. The effect is almost ghoulish — also by design, I assume. She sits just as the soughing sound coming through the ceiling vents stops. The Bailiff steps forward.)

BAILIFF

Please raise your right hand. Do you swear to tell the truth, the whole truth, and nothing but the truth?

CORINNE

I do.

(The Bailiff returns to his seat as Slaughter rises from his place at the plaintiff's table and takes hold of a walking cane I only now notice has been dangling from the end of the table.)

SLAUGHTER

Hi, Corinne. How are you doing today?

CORINNE

I mean . . . fine. Fine.

SLAUGHTER

(approaching, his gait assured despite the limp) *A little nervous, maybe? It would make sense if you were, right?*

(He's standing before her now, the palm of his free hand flat against the corner of the witness box. She nods.)

SLAUGHTER

So we spoke about this last night. And last week, too, when we went through what to expect. All you have to do is answer the questions to the best of your ability.

(Slaughter's voice is louder, clearer than it needs to be. A robust tenor whose primary audience is not Corinne but the room. Again she nods. Her eyes glance across the faces of the jury. I see her steal the briefest of worried looks in the direction of Father's table.)

SLAUGHTER

And if you don't understand a question either I or anyone else asks you, ask to have it repeated or clarified. Don't be shy.

JUDGE

(interrupting) *Counselor.*

SLAUGHTER

Your Honor?

JUDGE

If the witness needs guidance, I'll be the one to provide it.

SLAUGHTER

Of course. My apologies.

JUDGE

(curt) *Go ahead and get started.*

(He nods in a show of respect, shoots the jury a sheepish look — and a rakish smile. His appeal is undeniable.)

SLAUGHTER

Just so everyone's clear, Corinne. You were Christine Langford's mother?

449

CORINNE

Am. *I am her mother. That's how I still think of it.*

SLAUGHTER

Of course. I'm sorry. — She was the eldest, am I right? Of your three children?

CORINNE

That's right.

SLAUGHTER

When did you and your husband realize Christine had a heart issue?

CORINNE

After the death of our other daughter.

SLAUGHTER

Kayleigh?

(She nods. When she speaks now, we hear her reedy, nasal voice properly for the first time.)

CORINNE

When she died is when me and Christine started having trouble. That was when we got ourselves tested.

SLAUGHTER

Trouble with your hearts.

CORINNE

Yes. Problems with our heart rhythm.

SLAUGHTER

How old was Kayleigh when she died, if I can ask?

CORINNE

Nine.

SLAUGHTER

And she died in her sleep — isn't that right?

(She seems as if she's about to speak, but she doesn't. Her silence answers the question. Slaughter waits before prodding anew, now more gently — though still with enough volume to be heard by all.)

SLAUGHTER

Do you mind telling us what happened?

CORINNE

She'd spent the day with her grandfather on the farm.

SLAUGHTER

Kendall Dairy, is that right?

CORINNE

Yes, that's right.

SLAUGHTER

They make their own buttermilk, don't they?

(A titter of recognition ripples through the jury.)

CORINNE

It's true. Folks tend to love it. They make it a different way. Something about the enzymes. A lot of stuff I don't know anything about.

SLAUGHTER

Best buttermilk around these parts, in my opinion.

HANNAH

(from the defendant's table) *Objection, Your Honor. Relevance?*

JUDGE

Sustained. Chip, please spare us the scenic route.

(Slaughter looks entirely unconcerned by the instruction. He leans into his cane, turning away from the jury and back to his witness.)

SLAUGHTER

So your daughter Kayleigh had been on the farm that day . . .

CORINNE

Helping her Nano with chores. She loved being outside with the animals. My dad used to say she was going to keep the farm going when she grew up. Anyway, when she got home, she said she wanted to take a nap.

SLAUGHTER

Was it a normal thing for her to be taking a nap in the afternoon?

CORINNE

Napping in the afternoon on weekends is something everyone in the family tends to do. When they were kids, it was usually because we made them do it. Not because they wanted to.

SLAUGHTER

But on this afternoon, it was her idea.

CORINNE

It didn't seem like there was anything wrong with her. Just a long afternoon. — *She was sleeping on the couch in the family room, and I was in the kitchen. It had just started raining* — *and I heard the strangest sound I've ever heard in my life. Some kind of gurgling. I thought maybe the window in the family room was open, that there was something going on in the gutter from the rain. When I went in to check what was happening, I saw the saliva coming out the side of her mouth. She looked . . . limp. Like she just wasn't there anymore.* (after a long pause) *She never came back.*

(The jury is rapt. The emotion on her face — and in the room — is undeniable. This is when I realize that the mise-en-scène has worked: the lifeless makeup, the offhand accumulation of details about things like naps and buttermilk, even the Judge's reprimands — all have built to this moment of startling emotional purity: before us, a mother remembers the death of her child. I hear a sniffle from the jury box. I can feel the pity and sorrow in my own throat, too.)

SLAUGHTER

I know this is hard.

CORINNE

— It's okay. It's for a good reason.

HANNAH

Objection. Leading.

JUDGE

Sustained. (gently) *Please, Mrs. Hollander, stick to answering questions.*

SLAUGHTER

How long after Kayleigh dying did you all start developing heart problems of your own?

CORINNE

It's hard to know if one thing started the other. I've always been a little short of breath, shorter than normal, even as a kid. Doctors looked into it, but no one found anything.

SLAUGHTER

You were tested for cardiac problems?

CORINNE

Not the way I was after Kayleigh's autopsy
— and the episode Christine had.

SLAUGHTER

Could you tell us about that?

CORINNE

It was a few weeks after Kayleigh died.
We were out in the front yard. It was Christine and her brother, the cousins, me. We
were expecting the in-laws, and when they
pulled into the driveway, we saw the front
grille of the car was covered in blood and
fur. They'd hit a deer on the way over.
When Christine heard them say that, when
she realized she was looking at parts of a
dead deer, she just went down.

SLAUGHTER

She fell down?

CORINNE

Like a sack of potatoes. I couldn't find a pulse on her. She had that limp look like Kayleigh did. I was in shock. I mean, I'd just lost one kid. Here I got the other on the ground. I started screaming, and, I don't know — it seemed like maybe she heard me. She came back.

SLAUGHTER

That's when you all had tests run?

CORINNE

On Kayleigh's tissues, too. Turned out me and her had the gene for this thing. Long QT. I mean, I was already in my midthirties, and nothing'd ever happened to me. But I'd had it all along.

(She pauses, briefly glancing in the direction of Father's table again.)

CORINNE

I mean, I know whatever happened to Christine in the driveway isn't usual for the long QT we've all got — which I guess is

458

supposed to happen when you're sleeping. At least I know that's what the doctor from the city thought.

SLAUGHTER

Dr. Akhtar? Sitting over there?

CORINNE

He kept mentioning that Brugada. I guess he's some specialist of it.

SLAUGHTER

When did you see Dr. Akhtar?

CORINNE

After Christine saw him. She got pregnant and was worried about the beta-blockers. So she went in to get an opinion. He told her to get off it. She came over that night after the appointment and told me I should do the same.

SLAUGHTER

Get off the beta-blockers?

CORINNE

Yes.

SLAUGHTER

Why would she think you should be going off of them, too?

CORINNE

I mean, that's what didn't make sense to me, neither. But this new doctor was saying it was worse to be on them with our long QT. And even worse if we had this Brugada thing. I'd never heard of it. And anyway, we didn't have any problems while we were taking the beta-blockers. For years we didn't. Not her, not me. That's what I told him.

SLAUGHTER

Do you remember what else you may have told him?

CORINNE

When he told me I should get off the beta-blockers, I told him what happened when another doctor tried to get me off them before. It was scary. My heart racing and whatnot. I ended up in the emergency room. I wasn't going to do that again.

SLAUGHTER

What'd he have to say to that?

CORINNE

Frankly, not much . . .

(Her dry delivery draws an audible laugh in the jury box. I see Hannah shoot Father a sidelong look at the defendant's table.)

CORINNE

Anyway, it was a short visit. He took a look at my chart. Made some diagnosis about maybe there being this Brugada problem. Told me I should get off the beta-blockers. I told him what happened that one time when I did. Then he was out the door. That's what I remember.

SLAUGHTER

And you didn't go off the medication like your daughter?

CORINNE

Hell, no. Anyway, I wasn't pregnant, so there was that, too.

SLAUGHTER

Did you advise your daughter to stay on it?

CORINNE

She was a grown woman. Wasn't my place to tell her what to do. That's not the sort of parents we've ever been.

SLAUGHTER

Was that the last time you saw Dr. Akhtar?

CORINNE

We saw him again maybe a week after Christine died. Nick, her husband. My husband, Hal. The family doctor.

SLAUGHTER

What was the purpose of this second visit?

CORINNE

To figure out what to do about me. Now I had two kids dead from this thing. We wanted to make sure I wasn't next. Though the way I was feeling then, I wasn't sure I much cared if I did end up next.

(Pause. For the first time, the emotion Corinne has been fighting the entire time breaks through. Slaughter pulls out a pocket handkerchief and offers it to her. She considers the cloth square for a moment, then shakes her head. She's not going to let herself cry. She dabs at the corners of her eyes with her closed fist. Slaughter folds the handkerchief and returns it to his inside jacket pocket. He steals a glimpse at the jury, and I realize his job with this witness is finished. Her portrait is complete, the various images of her now richly fused into the vivid personage seated before the jury: a devoted and still-suffering mother; stoic; humble; the scion of a beloved local dairy family; an appealing witness and reliable narrator of

463

her own travails — and because of all the foregoing, a trustworthy guardian of her dead daughter's continued interests among the living.)

SLAUGHTER

What do you remember about that appointment?

CORINNE

My husband asking him point-blank why he took her off that medication cold turkey. "Why didn't you taper her off it?" I remember Hal using that word. *Taper.* It's what we saw on the internet. You're never supposed to just stop with the beta-blockers.

SLAUGHTER

Did you tell him that?

CORINNE

I don't remember what I told him. I'd just buried my second child. I was in no state.

SLAUGHTER

What did he say to your husband?

CORINNE

He didn't answer. I remember him being pretty nervous.

SLAUGHTER

Can you say more about that?

CORINNE

I remember him coming in and saying he was sorry, saying he'd just gotten in from Milwaukee. But then he looked away from me the whole time. Away from all of us. Looking at the walls, the floor when he talked. He looked guilty to me.

HANNAH

Objection, Your Honor. Inflammatory.

JUDGE

Sustained. Mrs. Hollander, please refrain from that sort of . . .

CORINNE

I just meant he looked like he was feeling guilty.

HANNAH

Your Honor? Please?

JUDGE

Mrs. Hollander. Find a different word for it, please.

CORINNE

Okay. I didn't mean anything. Just that he felt bad about what happened. Like that was the reason he couldn't look any of us in the eye.

(Slaughter's gaze dances across the jury, settling briefly back on his witness. Then he turns to the Judge with a half smile . . .

466

Nothing further, Your Honor.

. . . and heads back to his seat.)

In her cross-examination, Hannah, Father's lawyer, would establish two important things: (1) Father wasn't the first doctor to worry about the Hollander family using beta-blockers to treat their long QT syndrome; Corinne had attested to that fact herself. (2) He was certainly not a *disengaged* caregiver. On the latter point, Hannah was able to interpolate into the session an anecdote about Father's troubles with the state years prior for insurance-only billing. Back in the '90s, if one of his patients didn't have coverage and couldn't afford to pay, he didn't even send them an invoice. The state found out and reprimanded him. Chip Slaughter objected vociferously to her clearly instrumental digression. The judge sustained his objections, and the jury was instructed to ignore what they'd just heard. Little matter. The point was made. Father was the sort of doctor in it for the right reasons. He cared . . . *by definition.*

In the wake of Corinne's powerful testimony on behalf of her daughter, these were the necessary rebuttals, and Hannah made them effectively, even forcefully. But as I watched her work, skillfully building her argument, pacing in her dark Mephisto wedges and long navy jacket, eyeing witness and jury through light, clear eyeglass frames that matched her pearls as well as the white highlights in her salt-and-pepper A-line bob — and in an accent that stood out for barely sounding like one; she was from Maryland — I couldn't help but feel uneasy. There was no gentle, rippling laughter in the jury, no sounds of recognition — just silence. I'd never been in a courtroom before, and I was surprised at how similar it felt to sitting with an audience as it watched a play. Years of putting up plays in front of audiences left me with little mystery when it came to their shifts in collective mood. I was rarely unclear about an audience's moment-to-moment interest — avid or riven; when its sympathies shifted; when the plot was lost. The jury's mood seemed no less obvious. In this case, with Hannah, it was one of suspicion. To them, she was going after someone whom they now saw as one of their own. Hannah was another outsider who just didn't get it.

Some of this Hannah was aware of — or so she claimed over dinner that night. I met her alone; Father didn't want to go out. The restaurant she suggested was a defunct paper mill now converted into a gourmet restaurant that served locally sourced food. Paper had once been *the* thing in these parts, until the early aughts, when it became cheaper to cut down local trees and pile them into containers to be sent to China, pulped into paper *there,* then packaged, shipped *back* across the ocean, and loaded onto American trucks for domestic delivery. It wasn't just paper. This was the model for all the long-standing local industries: furniture, stamping, tool and die. Even lumber was having trouble keeping up with forests halfway across the planet, where gene-edited trees produced stronger, softer wood in larger quantities than the natural forests in Wisconsin ever would. And in so many of these erstwhile factories, mills, lofts, and warehouses — buildings that were often the very reason these towns even existed — antiques were now sold, candles made, Pilates taught, incense burned, and cavatelli served with venison *ragù.* The last was described on this La Crosse eatery's menu as the chef's homespun homage to his father, a hunter who loved few things more than his freshly hunted deer meat. I wasn't tempted. I ordered a burger with Gruyère from Monroe. Hannah had a frisée Cobb salad with pork-belly bits from local pigs. She'd ordered Merlot, which sat idly in a stemless glass alongside her smartphone. She seemed to be making a show of not drinking it.

"I've told your father this is not about winning the case on the merits," she said after we'd spent some time trading details of our respective biographies — she'd gone to school at Yale, worked as a tall-ship captain on Lake Erie for three years, then as a chef in New Orleans for a half decade before going to law school in Madison, where she'd ended up marrying and raising a family — "it's about making sure we don't lose it on the optics. To them, your dad's an outsider, a city doctor, an immigrant —"

"Yeah, I was surprised how she kept mentioning that. Doctor from the city. Doctor from Milwaukee. I don't even think she said his name."

"She didn't. That was by design. There's a lot of animosity out here for folks from the cities. Milwaukee. Madison. Minneapolis. The anger is real. And it's not even as bad in a place like this as it is in some of the outlying counties. When we try a case in Jackson or Trempealeau, we don't take our own cars anymore. We rent. Compact, economy. I've had colleagues get tires on a Lexus or Audi slashed in a court parking lot."

"In a *court* parking lot?"

"People are really angry." Her phone lit up with a text. She looked down and noted the message with irritation, then swiped and turned the phone over. "Look, you drive around the back roads through most of this state — and trust me, I've done a fair bit of that, meeting with clients and spending so much time at these small-town hospitals — the poverty out there is real. Houses are falling apart. Roads. Towns. People aren't taking care of their things, their yards. Not taking care of themselves. Nothing's cared for anymore. And it's not just that folks don't have the money to do it. They haven't had that for thirty years, but now they don't even have the will to make a show of it. When you lose *that*? We're talking about a different order of despair. And when you've spent six or eight hours out here just driving past the broken-down farms and homes, the empty towns, the dying Main Streets — and then you drive into Madison or Milwaukee? It's like something out of science fiction. I mean, the wealth is screaming out at you. Even just the fact of there being people out and about, with somewhere to go.

471

Storefronts that actually have businesses inside. People going to buy stuff. These folks get to the cities once or twice a year. They see that. They see the difference. They don't like it."

"Probably hard to blame them."

"I've got my own thoughts about it all. I feel like sometimes people are using the situation as an excuse not to do anything about their own lives. But who am I to judge? The point is, that gap between the cities and the rest of the state is a big part of what we're up against with your dad. Especially now that a lot of that anger's being directed not just at city folk but also at immigrants."

"I can imagine."

"He's brown. They can't say his name. It's just a matter of time before they find out he's a Muslim . . ."

"How would they find that out?"

"Chip Slaughter is not going to lose a chance to make that an issue. Trust me. I tried a case against him not three years ago. Indian doctor. Pediatric oncologist. Wasn't able to save the kid. Anyway, same as your dad. Tricky situation, but the science was behind him. On the merits, there was no real question. Went well in court. Then the day before closing arguments, San Bernardino."

"The attack?"

She nodded. "This was not some high-profile case with sequestered jurors and whatnot. They come in that morning; they've been watching the news. You could see it in the way they were looking at him. And this defendant wasn't Muslim. He's a Hindu. Guy probably hates Muslims more than they do."

"So what ended up happening?"

"Chip didn't let them forget it. Hobbling around on that cane, mispronouncing the doctor's name in his closing argument. Then apologizing. Then doing it again. Bringing up stuff that had nothing to do with the case. That the defendant had a foreign medical degree, how he'd worked in Dubai. It was a masterpiece of innuendo."

"I meant to ask, what's up with his leg?"

"Car accident when he was younger. High school or college, from what I gather. It was apparently pretty bad . . . Anyway, the innuendo worked. The case ended in a mistrial. Two jurors just couldn't get over the trust hump. Two elderly ladies."

"White, I'm assuming."

"You know what? One of them was Hmong. When you're dealing with some-

473

thing like terrorism, a juror's race won't tell you much. That stuff scares the shit out of *everyone*. Whatever their color." She finally reached for her wine and sipped. "What happens in the news, we can't control. But what *is* in our control is how your father handles himself in court. Today? Was not acceptable. Not a good look for him or our cause. If he's not willing to help himself, there's only so much the rest of us can do."

"I'm talking to him."

"I can't tell you what to do. But if he was my father? I wouldn't just talk. I wouldn't let him out of my sight. Not until we're done with this thing."

4.

After dinner, we walked back to the hotel together. I left her at the elevator to peek in at the bar. The stools along the countertop were empty. The only patrons inside were a young couple nestling on a love seat before the fireplace. Upstairs, as I passed his room on the way to my own, I stopped to listen at the door. I didn't hear anything. I knocked lightly, but there was no answer. I checked my pocket for his key and remembered I'd left it on my dresser before going out to meet Hannah.

Back in my room, I sat down at the desk

and pulled out my computer. After my habitual twenty-minute distraction on Twitter and Facebook, I spent the next two hours making notes about the day. The technique I used for this sort of recall owed much to my years of noting dreams. I dispensed with chronology and stuck to detail. The more vivid the fragment, the sound, the image — and the more exhaustively elaborated through language — the richer the associated cluster of recollections it spawned. The process was counterintuitive, akin to restoring the incidental sedimentary layers on a piece of extracted ore. The mind recalled the essence and discarded the dross, but the dross was what swarmed with generative life. That night, as I wrote, wherever recollection alighted led me back to the teeming soil of Corinne Hollander on the witness stand.

It was almost midnight when I stopped. I turned on the TV. Colbert was talking about Trump. So was Fallon. Trump was on *Nightline,* Fox, CNN, CNBC. We were a nation in thrall to our own stupidity. What passed for politics now was just dramaturgy. Sow conflict, promise consequence. Perhaps Plato wasn't wrong to warn us about a city overrun with storytellers.

I did what everyone else did. I watched.

And kept watching.

At some point, I decided to check in on my father. I found his key where I'd left it, on the dresser. Down the hall, I slipped it into the lock. As I nudged the door open, I saw that his lights were on. Both beds were empty. The bathroom door was ajar — empty, too. I tried calling his cell phone.

It went straight to voice mail.

Downstairs, he still wasn't in the hotel bar. I described him to the bartender, a woman with two platinum pigtails and a rash of blue-green tattoos along her neck and arm. "Doesn't ring a bell," she said as she chopped at a block of congealed ice cubes. At the front desk, neither of the attendants had seen him.

I wandered the halls downstairs that led to the meeting rooms. I checked the bathrooms. I checked the bar again, then loitered in the lobby and stared out the front window into the parking lot. Above a row of factory lofts lining the river was a billboard with an array of silly characters dressed up as a deck of cards.

My heart sank with a dispiriting thought.

I marched back to the front desk and asked one of the attendants how far it was to the casino on the billboard outside. "Oh, it's only twenty-five minutes on the inter-

476

state," she offered happily. "We have a shuttle, but . . . Brynne?" She turned to her coworker, who was already tapping at a keyboard.

"Looks like it's not back this way for another hour or so," the other attendant said.

"How late does it stay open?" I asked.

"Twenty-four hours."

"Jesus," I muttered, provoking an offended look from the one called Brynne. "Sorry," I said. She looked away, leaving me to her colleague. "Would you mind calling me a cab?" I asked.

"Sure. Usually takes around three minutes," the first attendant said, reaching for the phone. "You can wait out front," she added blankly.

The cab took longer than three minutes to show up (and would take longer than twenty-five to get to the casino). It was a mud-spattered orange minivan with a graying and surly driver. I got in; he tilted his head toward me to wait for my destination. "The casino," I said. In the rearview mirror, I could barely make out his face; the brim of his dark cap was lowered, and a thick, yellowing walrus mustache covered much of his lower face. As we merged onto the highway along the Mississippi — whose

477

wide, winding surface glimmered a calm, glassy black in the moonlight — he finally spoke: "What's your game? Slots, cards, dice?"

"I'm not a gambler, actually," I said.

After that, he didn't say another word to me.

It was 1:15 a.m. by the time we pulled into the parking lot of a warehouse-size prefab take on a timbered hunting lodge, and just beyond it, a four-story concrete hotel tower. HEADWATERS RESORT AND GAMES was the name on the flashing marquee. A staggering footprint, I thought, for a casino in these parts. I paid the driver and offered him an extra twenty to stick around and wait. "No need. Tons of rides out here," he said.

I gave him the twenty anyway.

"Good luck!" he shouted through the open window as he drove off. Inside, slot machines blinked and chimed, beckoning with soft, cheery sounds. They lined the entry, defined a path through the main room, formed an enclosure around the gaming pit; the slots were everywhere, though most of the stools before them were empty at this late hour. I passed an elderly couple with two canes and a bucket of coins between them, their inert faces aglow with neon blue as they inserted and depressed, watched the whirring wheels. Farther on, a man in a hunting jacket was slouched at a machine with a slot handle in his grip, snoring.

Down in the pit, the roulette and baccarat games were closed, but there were a handful of blackjack players at two tables; none was Father. Farther on, behind a worn velvet rope, four white men and a brown lady sat around a poker table, assessing the handful of flopped cards before them. Father wasn't there, either. I checked the restrooms, then found another, smaller room filled with slots. No luck. I tried his cell phone again. Straight to voice mail.

As I emerged back into the main room, I found a striking older man with sun-worn skin standing in the hallway, staring at me. His hair was long and black, gathered into a tail down his back; his hands — covered in clear plastic gloves — clutched the handles of a trash can on wheels. "You looking for someone?" he asked.

"Actually, I am."

"Older guy? Brown, like you?"

"Yes."

"On the couch under the mural," he said, pointing at the part of the room opposite the poker nook. "He slipped me a few bucks

479

not to tell anyone he was back there," the man said. "But I think he needs you to take him home."

"Thank you, sir. Thank you very much." I pulled out my wallet to fish for a bill, but he waved it away. "I don't have that coming, but thanks anyway."

He sauntered off pulling the trash can along behind him as he went.

The mural in question was a Northwoods landscape in silhouette against a garish sunset. Sure enough, there was Father, lying on a leather couch under the outline of an eagle soaring into the disappearing sun.

"Dad," I said, reaching down to nudge him. "Dad. You have to get up. Dad. Dad . . ."

"I'm not sleeping," he groaned; he didn't sound particularly surprised that I'd found him.

"Then what are you doing?"

His eyelids crept open now to reveal a leering, suspicious gaze. "*Think*ing?" He was clearly drunk.

"Well, you can do that back at the hotel."

"Don't. Tell me. What to do."

"You have to be in court tomorrow."

"I said: *You* don't tell *me*! You're not the parent!" Across the way, one of the poker players looked up at us from her cards. I sat

480

on the couch's armrest and lowered my voice.

"Dad. I don't know what you're doing, but you have to be in court at eight thirty tomorrow morning. Can we please get back to La Crosse?"

"Or else?"

"Or *else*? You were hungover in court today. It didn't look good. Keep that up and you *will* lose this thing."

"What do I care?"

"You don't mean that."

"Serve that Quaker bastard right."

"Who?"

"*Quaaker Ooats . . .*" he blared. The irritation seemed to rouse him; he sat up.

"Dad. I don't know who that is."

"You want to know why I was nervous?" he asked suddenly. I had no idea what he was talking about and said as much. "Christine's mother. What's her name?"

"Corinne."

"Right. Corinne. She said I looked nervous when they all came to see me. She was right. I *was*. That bastard Powell made me sit down with a lawyer before I went in to see them. Warned me not to say anything. Liability."

"Who's Powell?"

"Thom Powell. The *big boss*," he said

481

mockingly. "We call him Quaker Oats — he looks like that guy on the box. Like his evil twin." I laughed. He smiled. After a moment, he said quietly: "Don't judge me."

"For what?"

Then not so quietly: "I said, Don't. Judge me. For *anything.*"

"I'm not."

"You *are.*"

"I'm just trying to help. I love you, and I'm worried. That's all this is. Love." As I spoke, I thought I saw something fall from his eyes. He looked at me now, pure and helpless, hopeful.

"Okay," he said. "Get me some coffee. Then we'll go."

I leaned in, my hand to his face, and kissed him on the forehead. "I'll be right back," I said.

That night, I slept in his room. Sometime before 7:00 a.m., I heard him get up and start brewing coffee in the bathroom. The machine's sputtering fully woke me. The shades were lifted; the room was filling with morning light. He emerged from the bathroom, two mugs in hand. I was surprised to see him looking as fresh as he did. "The coffee's not very good," he said handing me one of the mugs. "I'm sorry about last night," he added after a moment.

"Let's just try to stay the course, Dad. Get through this." He nodded. "I was thinking maybe we call Sultan and ask if he could come and spend next week here?" Sultan was one of my father's oldest friends, a member of the same medical school class cohort — like Latif Awan — that came to America in the late '60s. When his wife died, in 2010, he quit medicine to start a restaurant in Omaha, where they'd settled. He and my father spoke almost daily.

"I don't need Sultan," he said gruffly.

"I have to be in New York on Monday. If Sultan can be here until I get back on Thursday, you'll have someone here to support you."

"I'll be fine."

"Dad, you need support. I would, too, if I was in your shoes. It stands to reason."

He scowled, pulling the mug from his mouth: "Why do you always talk like that?"

"Like what?"

"Stands to reason."

"I just meant — it makes sense that you would need support. Anyone would. It's normal."

"Then just say *that.*"

"I thought I did."

"Simpler is better. Someday you'll learn that."

He looked away and drank. "Do you think I was a good father?"

"What?"

"I said, do you think I was a good father?

"What's the connection?"

"I'm just asking. I want to know."

"I mean . . . yes."

"That's what you tell your friends? When you talk about me? That I was a good father?"

"My friends?"

"Your friends — or when you write about me."

"I haven't written about you, Dad."

"Not yet. — So, what? Do you say good things?"

"I mean, sure."

"Sure?"

"Mostly. I mean, who says only good things about anything? What are you worried about?"

"I'm not worried. I want to know what you really think. About me. As a father." His directness was disarming. "Was I *okay,* at least?"

"You were better than okay. I don't wish you were any different."

"But . . ."

"Sometimes I think you could have been happier."

"I'm fine."

"You and Mom."

"What about us? We were fine. You don't know everything about us."

"I'm just saying."

"What? What are you saying?"

"Dad. You asked me. I'm telling you —"

"Telling me what? That I wasn't happy? Who's *happy?*"

"Why are you getting mad?"

"I'm not."

"You sound mad."

"Well, I'm not."

"I'm just saying, maybe you could have let yourself be happier. Then maybe you and Mom could have . . . enjoyed each other more. And maybe that would have been nice. That's all I'm saying."

"Mr. Head Shrinker," he quipped sarcastically as he got up. He walked into the bathroom and turned on the shower. Then I saw him appear in the doorway again. He said something I couldn't hear over the rushing water.

"I can't hear you, Dad."

He pulled the door shut behind him and repeated himself: "I don't know if you realize. You have land in Pakistan."

485

"Okay . . ."

"I'm just telling you. I want you to know. After partition with India. They gave my grandfather one hundred acres."

"In Jhelum. Yeah, I know."

"No, that's the family house. Two acres, *maybe,*" he said dismissively. "I'm talking about a *hundred* in Bahawalpur. Beautiful land. Mango groves."

"Okay."

"That hundred was split between three sons when he died. One of those sons was your grandfather. When *he* died, I got sixteen acres, my sisters got the other sixteen."

"Why are you telling me this?"

"So you don't care about your land in Pakistan?"

"It's not my land."

"Not yet."

"You're starting to freak me out."

"Why?"

"Land back home? Are you a good father? Is there something you're not telling me?"

"I'm telling you about your land in Bahawalpur."

"Sixteen acres. Mango groves. Got it."

He grunted in response, lingering a little longer at the door, his hand on the knob.

"Is there something else?" I asked. He shook his head and disappeared inside.

5.

Father was on his best behavior for the rest of the week, and his case seemed to follow suit. Three specialists took to the witness stand on Thursday, two to endorse the medical logic behind his guidance to Christine and her mother and a third who tried but was unable to effectively deny it. I sensed the jury's disappointment at the turn things were taking, as they heard testimony that clearly challenged a bias against Father they'd already formed. On Friday morning, as Hannah predicted, Chip Slaughter announced to the court he planned to call only one witness — because Friday's afternoon prayer was scheduled at the local mosque for shortly after twelve o'clock, and Slaughter didn't want to be the reason the defendant missed his "Muslim worship." The interjection caused a flurry of objections and concern, with both counselors ending up in a private conference in the judge's chambers. But when they returned, the only consequence was a short speech from the judge about the irrelevance of the defendant's religious views, and even the correction seemed to serve Slaughter's ends.

Both days, a man with a huge, ruddy face and chin-length shocks of steel-gray hair kept coming in and going out of the court-room. This was Thom Powell. To me, he didn't bring to mind the Quaker on the box so much as some wastrel mascot of the Constitutional Convention — which is to say that Father's whole "evil twin" thing actually did make sense. In the sickly light of the courtroom, his broad, bony face was pitted, with blotches of magenta. Father would explain to me later that Powell had been on high alert since learning of Corinne Hollander's testimony. He'd driven up from Madison to assess whether it might not be better to pull the plug and settle, even at this point — the number would be painful — rather than risk another malpractice loss. From what I could gather of his demeanor — and the affirming, encouraging looks he traded with Hannah throughout the session — it certainly appeared to me like he wanted to keep fighting it.

After we adjourned on Friday, neither Father nor I availed ourselves of the chance to offer our Muslim prayers. After lunch, as we were checking out at the front desk, Father asked if I would pay for his room. He was a month behind on his Amex payments, he explained when Brynne stepped away from her computer. He didn't want to risk having the charge declined. It didn't occur to me to be concerned; I told him I was fine to pay.

The route back to Elm Brook took us through Wonewoc and Spring Green, small towns with libraries I wanted to visit on the way. Republicans in Madison — where they controlled both houses as well as the governor's mansion — were more than a decade into a sustained attack on the state's intellectual infrastructure: school funding was dwindling; history and philosophy and literature and music and sociology departments were being shuttered; libraries found themselves each year with less money for fewer books and programs. It was the damage being done to libraries that I took personally, and I was resolved to do something, however humbly, about it. I'm not sure it's worth telling here the story of exactly how it was I came to the idea of visiting municipal libraries in my travels around the country and giving away money. Suffice it to say it's what I'd started doing a few months after Riaz made me rich. Five hundred dollars meant a library wouldn't have to stop buying the best new novels coming out after July; as little as a thousand could keep a book club going for another year. I knew almost nothing about most of the communities I visited; usually, I was there to speak at a college or support a small production of one of my plays. But the towns of Wonewoc and Spring Green were different. The former is home to an author, David Rhodes, who has written what I consider some of the finest fiction about rural American life since Sherwood Anderson; as for the latter, I'd been there already a half dozen times. Spring Green was the unlikely site of one of the nation's finest outdoor classical theater companies. Tiny as these towns were — with populations of 816 and 1,637 respectively — each mattered disproportionately to the cultural life of my home state.

It was over an hour to Wonewoc, part of it on the interstate, the rest by way of a county road carved through the heart of the Driftless Area, a rugged, stream-rich region named for its escape from the flattening glacial drift of the last Ice Age. Father wanted me to drive and offered to navigate. He held the phone, which directed us along a narrow, undulating road, past fields of soybeans, alfalfa, cornstalks, mud. Cows tottered on pitched pastures through which — as in some early Dutch landscape — a teeming brook tumbled or a knotted, solitary trunk stood watchful guard over acres and acres of empty rolling space. The land seemed to have been shaped for effect, the bluffs and ridges releasing views of a sky that looked bigger, bluer, filled with vivid, rippling clouds. There was majesty here, and it imbued even the endless parade of dilapidated barns and neglected homes — all as Hannah had described over dinner — with natural dignity.

Father wasn't paying much attention to the scenery. He'd been on the subject of Reliant and Thom Powell for much of the ride, and as we turned onto a sloping dirt road — which our handheld navigator promised would save us ten minutes — he started in with a story about Powell I found hard to believe at first. And this despite having heard so many anecdotes from my father over the years about unethical medical practices: the overbilling, the phony drug trials, the aggressive diagnoses, the unnecessary procedures. Nothing could have prepared me for the tale he would tell me now:

Before joining Reliant, Powell had worked for Chiroh Health, a similar health-care company just across the state line. In the early '90s, Chiroh purchased a cardiology practice not dissimilar to Father's, run by a doctor named Rex Dumachas. Tall, blond, dashing, Dumachas had played college baseball at a Big Ten school — All-American — before going to medical school and ending up in interventional cardiology. Dumachas approached his job as an athlete would — driven by the competition, reveling in the physical demands — and his surgical output reflected it. Some weeks, upwards of eighty patients would come through his operating room to have their arteries widened and stents put in, an unheard-of number, Father explained.

Dumachas had been working at this prodigious pace for two decades, and by the point of his medical group's sale to Chiroh, Dumachas's handiwork was the stuff of local legend. But there were also murmurs of darker things. For years, Father had heard that Dumachas was more than a little too eager to cut you open and send you a bill. Some called him greedy. Having offered a number of second opinions for patients who weren't convinced they needed the procedures Dr. Dumachas was suggesting, Father concluded the same.

In fact, greed didn't even begin to cover it.

For fifteen years, Dumachas had not only performed unnecessary procedures on his patients, he had also used those unnecessary procedures to harm them. Gaining access to their coronary arteries, he would go in with his catheter and intentionally abrade an area along the healthy arterial lining. This created a future site of plaque buildup and eventual heart disease, each such abrasion worth at least a half million dollars in billable follow-up for a decade to come. It was criminal conduct, of course, but it didn't come to light until after Chiroh bought the practice — bought it in large part for the extraordinary cash flow produced by these criminal activities, which Chiroh was not aware of and which were discovered, Father said, only because of an affair with an OR nurse gone awry. A participating accessory in his scheme, Dumachas's jilted mistress took her revenge by alerting the administrative authorities; an internal review of patient records followed and found the recurrence of heart disease in precisely the same spot on the same coronary artery in over 2,500 patients. Statistically implausible at best.

Here's the Thom Powell part: Dumachas's patients were now Chiroh customers; Chiroh owned this problem. For a publicly traded company, disclosure of such an indefensible travesty would have wiped out the stock price, to say nothing of the potential billions in settlements the company would owe if it somehow survived that initial hit. It was of paramount importance to Chiroh that no word of Dumachas's crimes got out.

Powell was a corporate generalist — a tax lawyer who'd found his way to litigation and later into administration by way of business school. He'd managed operations and logistics for a cable company in Tennessee and helped steer a multistate food services operation through bankruptcy before going to Chiroh to work in risk management. Here was the strategy Powell developed to manage the crisis: An unexpected round of layoffs was announced, a position or two from every level of the organization, including doctors; this was the shot across the bow intended to sow fear and set the stage for later compliance. Separately, Rex Dumachas was quietly offered a generous severance, contingent on his leaving the profession for good. (The last thing Chiroh wanted was for him to start up with his shenanigans somewhere else, get discovered, and have the trail lead back to them.) As another condition of his severance, Dumachas furnished a list of everyone in the organization he knew to be aware of his conduct. Not only were these employees *not* fired; to a person, they were also offered signing bonuses on contract extensions — but only after signing ironclad NDAs. In short, Dumachas retired early in Arizona, and those aware of the harm he'd done to his patients were rewarded for their silence. The crisis was managed; the stock price continued to rise; Powell got a promotion. It was shortly after all this that Reliant Health poached Powell away, and it was during the Powell years that Reliant grew into the juggernaut that would purchase Father's group and eventually go public.

Father learned of the Dumachas crisis from an enemy Powell had at Reliant, a fellow administrator worried about — what else! — his job. At that point, there was no love lost between Father and Powell, and the tattling administrator was trying to shore up support for his own position with doctors in the group. In Father, he found a sympathetic ear, for though Father had been an early advocate of being bought out by Reliant, it hadn't taken him long to change his mind. Powell ran the company the way he'd handled the crisis at Chiroh: with ruthless focus on the twin corporate values of increasing share price and limiting liability. Medical care was almost an afterthought. And yes, Father had dealt with corporate, nonmedically trained administrators his whole career, but Powell and his crew were different. This was a new breed he saw coming into the profession: the in-house counsel elevated to decision maker, the bean counter ennobled by an MBA, the resident financial functionary whose contributions to staff meetings included advice on ways for employees to help the company avoid excessive tax depreciation on fixed assets. These were corporate zealots — "fanatics of the data" was Father's coinage — as fixated on spreadsheets as he thought they should have expected doctors to be on patients, but it was clear that patients, like stationery expenses, were just another line item. "Quality care" — like the company's name itself — was just copy, an advertising slogan to be plastered across the billboards and brochures that showed multicultural, multigenerational families smiling at sun-soaked kitchen tables.

Now, Father had been complaining about Powell and the corporate medical model for years, and I'd long since concluded — ungraciously — that his problems were mostly about his ego. After all, he'd been the group leader before the corporate buyout, and now he was just another employee. He had taken the money; what did he expect? But hearing him unload about Powell on the way to Wonewoc, I started to see a different picture, a bigger picture, one that showed him in a more generous light and began to make new sense of his plight in that La Crosse courtroom. He'd insisted on doing the job as he believed it should be done. If patients everywhere were more and more discontent, it was — he thought — because doctors like him had ceded autonomy to managers like Powell, who apparently didn't care, fundamentally, whether their patients lived or died — as long as the company wasn't sued.

As we rolled off the dirt road and onto the asphalt byway that led into town, I asked why he hadn't gone public with what he knew about Dumachas and Powell's cover-up. "It was leverage," he said with an evident hint of defensiveness. "I wanted to make things better for us, the doctors. So we could do our job."

"But what about all those patients?"

"It's terrible."

"But I'm guessing they still don't even know what happened to them."

"How could they?"

"Didn't you think they deserved to know?"

"You think *I* should've told them? How?"

"I don't know. Talk to a journalist. The

authorities. Somebody."

"With what evidence? Patient records are private. Everybody signed nondisclosures."

"There's ways around that stuff. Subpoenas, litigation. Whistleblowing."

"— Subpoena? From who?"

"I don't know, Dad. A grand jury, I suppose."

He glared at me with visible disgust: "I start creating *that* kind of trouble? Powell would have *buried* me. Buried. Who benefits from that?"

"Yeah, but still —"

"What *still*?"

"When nobody says anything, that's how people can keep doing stuff like this."

"What are you, a child?"

"What is that supposed to mean —"

"You think I didn't go over this in my own mind?"

"I'm not saying that."

"I *did*. I *thought* about it. And I did what I thought was best."

"And what was that?"

"I told you. To use it as leverage. To get things we needed. To do the job better."

"So did you?"

"What?"

"Use it as leverage?"

He looked down at the phone. "Make

your next left," he said. "That's Main Street. Library is farther up." Around us, the hardwood groves and muddy fields had given way to a baseball diamond and, beyond it, the rest of a municipal park. A row of brick buildings appeared now, apparently the town center. As we slowed into the intersection, I stopped for a pair of young mothers in coats and pajama bottoms pushing strollers across the walkway. "Thom knew," Father finally answered. "He knew I knew. That was the leverage. I got things for the doctors and nurses I could not have gotten otherwise. I got things for the patients."

"Left here, right?"

"Yeah," he said. Then: "It's why he's never been able to make nice with me. I mean, not that I wanted to make nice. I didn't. I don't. But it's a fine line between that and getting fired." He paused midthought.

"What?" I asked.

"No, no — it's nothing."

"What is it?"

"I see you *scribbling* all the time."

"Yeah? I'm a writer, Dad."

"Well, you might want to take your notes with you when you go to the bathroom next time."

"Did I leave them out at lunch?"

"You write it all down, don't you?"

"You looked at my notebook?"

"— Everything. Details and details. How do you not get bored?"

"It's my job. I have to make note of the details in case I need them later. There's a lot of labor involved."

"Well, I just hope you'll be fair. I hope you won't make me look like an *asshole*."

I never recalled him expressing concern about what I might write about him, and now he was mentioning it for the second time in as many days.

"If I write about the case . . . ."

"You will."

". . . *If* I do, I wouldn't be writing about *you*. But some doctor *like* you."

"Who everybody will think *is* me."

". . . And who will definitely *not* be an asshole."

I laughed; he didn't. "Okay, over there, on the left. The yellow one," he said, holding the phone up. He was pointing to a squat, square mustard-colored building with a sign over the front door announcing its purpose: PUBLIC LIBRARY

"I don't see parking," I said.

"It's probably in back. Use that Kwik Mart," he said, indicating the gas station convenience store adjacent to the library. "I'll go in and get a few things." I slowed and signaled, then turned in to the parking lot. If I wasn't particularly mindful about my parking angle, it was because I didn't have any reason to be.

Father pushed open his door. "You want something?"

"I'll come with you. I need to use the bathroom."

Behind the register inside was another heavyset young woman; she was staring down into her phone. The odors here were pungent, off-putting: the burned coffee and cleaning bleach, the desiccated wieners slowly turning on the roller grill. Father headed for the row of refrigerated cases displaying beer. I wove my way through the aisles to the bathroom in the back corner. When I came back, I found Father perusing a rack of potato chips, a six-pack of beer nestled into his armpit. I noticed a narrow, clean-cut man in the store now, maybe forty, with a furry head of white-blond hair shorn close to his skull. He was standing at the press rack by the register, magazine in hand — but he wasn't reading: he was watching Father and me. I heard him speaking, but I wasn't sure to whom. "Fucking rule of law. There's laws for a reason," I thought I heard him say.

"You want some chips or something?"

Father asked me sweetly.

"I'm fine. I've still got water in the car."

He nodded and headed for the register.

As we approached, the blond man held his ground, staring at us as Father laid out his merchandise before the clerk.

"Will that be all?" she asked without interest.

"That's it," Father said.

"— You know, there's rules for a reason," the blond man blurted, clearly addressing us.

Father looked over at him, confused. "I'm sorry. Were you in line?"

"I'm sorry. Were you in line?" the man repeated, mocking.

I saw Father bristle. "Is there a problem, sir?"

"— Dad."

"I don't know, *sir — is there?*" the man shot back with a smirk. His small teeth were gnawing on a piece of gum. To call the thin row of hair above his upper lip a mustache wouldn't exactly have made sense.

"We don't want any trouble," I said, stepping forward to pay. I dropped a twenty on the counter and indicated I didn't want change.

The blond man snickered loudly: "No trouble? So let me ask you, is that your car

502

out there?"

The clerk interjected wearily: "Chuck, these folks are just trying to buy some stuff. You want to leave it alone?"

"I leave it alone when they fucking learn how to drive in this country."

"What country? Hmm — ?" Father snapped. "What country is that?"

"Dad. Let's go —" I said, grabbing the beer from the counter with one hand and Father's elbow with the other.

"This fucking country, you *monkey*. This is not some *zoo*. We got rules here. Rules of fucking law. Learn how to park your fucking car in the United States of America."

"Monkey!? Monkey?!" Father shouted back as I snatched him to the door and pulled him through it.

Outside, I saw my offense: an admittedly blithe parking job that had the front end of our car pushing into an adjacent spot. Two spots over, a Ford pickup was gurgling, with no one in the front seat. Mounted to the grille was a cracked buck's skull and an uneven coil of bony antlers protruding from it. Behind us, Chuck emerged outside just in time to hear me urge Father to get in the car.

"Yeah, that's right, *Dad*. Get in the car. Monkey say, monkey do."

503

Father turned toward him, screaming. "Will you shut up!!!"

"Dad. Stop it. Get inside," I said, pushing him into the passenger's side, my blood racing.

"Can't wait 'til we build that wall to keep you fucking apes out."

"*You're* the *fucking* ape!" Father shouted. As ever, that most natural of American imprecations sounded decidedly unnatural on his lips: "*Fucking* ignorant! Don't want to work and don't want anyone else to!"

"Why don't you fuck..*ck..ck..*ing learn to *speak-a-Eng*lish —"

"— We speak it just fine," I spit back at him.

"Oh, nice. So the monkey boy's got some lip on him, too."

"Go fuck yourself," I added as I pulled at the driver's-side handle. My reflexive glance to note his reaction revealed something I'd missed until now: a strap led down one side of his torso to a leather bulge on his flank.

He saw me notice his gun, and he smiled: "Can't wait when we build that wall to keep you critters out." What I felt in that moment was brief, but I won't ever forget it. The sight of the gun, the visceral threat and primal fear it triggered, the elemental urge to protect myself, the asymmetry of our power in that moment — all of it combined to set something ablaze inside me I'd never experienced before. I wanted to kill him. But the immediate awareness of just how powerless I was to do so threw me back onto myself in a way that eats at me to this day, almost two years later.

Father was saying my name, trying to get my attention. I finally found his eyes. "Let's go." His measured tone was filled with alarm.

Chuck began to say something about the wall again, but I didn't hear most of it. He stepped forward as I started the engine. His hand found its way to his piece as I reversed. Behind him, in the doorway glass, I saw the clerk standing and watching as she munched on chips. I put the car into drive, accelerated onto Main Street, past the library, and out of town.

6.
For the better part of Trump's first year in office, Father and I mostly avoided the subject of our president. I didn't bring up the man, and if Father did — usually to complain that we weren't giving him a chance to succeed — it was never with much conviction. When he mentioned Trump, I didn't push back. I wouldn't soon

forget the dissension the 2016 election had caused between us. I didn't want to go back there again.

There was another reason I kept silent: I felt him coming around.

Early in May, *Time* magazine reported that the president served himself two scoops of ice cream at White House dinners while serving his guests only one; Father read that on the same day that Trump fired FBI director James Comey, an unlikely twinning that provoked a curt, uncharacteristically irritated comment about his sometime acquaintance, now leader of the free world.

"Why is he so petty?" he asked over the phone that night.

By mid-August, after the torchlit white supremacist rally in Charlottesville — and after the president refused to condemn the perpetrators three days later — Father's loyalty seemed to have been affected. The daily cascade of insults and untruths, silly grudges, ceaseless attention seeking — all this was no longer amusing. Before, Father had been inclined to read into this dysfunction an estimable defiance, a fighter's pluck. But now, as Trump defended the "good people on both sides" in Charlottesville, Father couldn't hide his disbelief. A week later, when Steve Bannon lost his job over the fracas, Father said simply, "That was a good thing. Maybe now, Donald can finally get to work."

But in September, during a trip home for the weekend, as I watched a news summary showing snippets of the president's address that day in Alabama — where he promised an unruly, cheering crowd he would build for them a "great big beautiful wall" — Father, marinating a steak in the kitchen within earshot, turned to me during the commercial break and said:

"I wish he would stop talking about that wall." I nodded, but I didn't say anything. He went on: "I mean, what's the point? A wall won't keep anybody out. You just dig under it. That's what we did when we were children."

"You dug under walls when you were a kid?"

"In the village. When my mother would lock me and my sisters in the room until we prayed. I dug a hole so we could come and go. She never even knew . . ."

"I don't think it's about keeping folks out, Dad."

"So what's it about?"

"Giving them a thing to fixate on. It's classic storytelling. A visible, tangible goal.

That's what gets an audience rooting for a hero."

"Tangible?"

"Every good story has the same shape. The beginning establishes a goal, the more tangible the better. In the middle we watch the fight toward that goal. The end is what happens when it's been reached, or when reaching it's finally failed. What I always say when I teach is: the longer the middle, the better the story. The middle is when we still don't know the outcome. That's when we care the most about what's happening. The longer you can keep the audience engaged in the pursuit without actually resolving that pursuit — that's real mastery."

"So maybe he doesn't want a wall."

"Wouldn't surprise me. As long as there *isn't* a wall, he's got an antagonist. The people stopping him from building it."

"It's like a game," he said.

"A game?"

"You know, a match. It's most exciting to watch when you don't know who's going to win."

"That would be the idea."

"What a joke," he said, heading back to his bowl of marinade.

But it wasn't until the night we got home from Wonewoc that Father finally admitted

508

his feelings about Trump had changed. He confessed that he didn't recognize the man he'd known a quarter century earlier. Perhaps the pressure and criticism that any president had good reason to expect had warped what was ill prepared and vulnerable in him. Maybe it was true that he wasn't cut out for the job after all, and now the country was suffering because of it. He twisted off the top of the last unopened bottle of beer we'd bought at the Kwik Mart, sipped, and paused. Then he finally came out and just said it: "Trump was a big mistake."

I hadn't seen Sultan in half a decade, maybe longer. Since then, he'd found religion, which made him the object of some considerable derision on Father's part, at least from what I gathered whenever I heard Father on the phone with him. They spoke so much, so regularly, I could only have imagined just how tiresome the constant ribbing must have been to Sultan. Apparently, he gave as good as he got on the other end, but still I wondered why he put up with it.

Father and I drove to the airport the next day — Saturday, which was also my birthday — and waited in the food court for Sultan's flight to land. At one point, Father left to make a phone call, or so he announced with somewhat more formality than was either usual or necessary. It all made sense when he returned after ten minutes bearing gifts: a Green Bay Packers sweatshirt and a chocolate croissant. "I was going to get you a book, too, but I couldn't figure what kinds of things you read anymore."

"The sweatshirt's great, Dad."

"You don't have one, right?"

"I do not."

"And I know you love chocolate croissants."

"Well, I mean, for breakfast."

"You can eat it tomorrow."

"Also nice to know what's for breakfast a day early."

Father shrugged. "There he is," he said, looking up at the bank of televisions above us.

"Did his plane land?"

"I meant *Dave* — but yeah. Looks like it just landed." Alongside the blue screens showing arrivals and departures, another showed David Letterman holding forth as a guest on some daytime set in Burbank. "I really don't know about that beard. I'm glad your mother never saw that."

"Yeah. I'm pretty sure she wouldn't have

been on board with the beard."

"She would have *hated* it." Father's chuckle gave way to pregnant silence. I could tell he was remembering her and thought I could almost see her image in his eyes. He smiled: "Like that time she called his doctor . . ."

"Called whose doctor?"

"Letterman's. She never told you? When he had quintuple bypass? This was maybe, I don't know, twenty years ago."

"I think I remember him having bypass, nothing about her calling . . ."

"She cold-called NewYork–Presbyterian intensive care. Pretended she was a physician on his team. She asked me exactly what I would say if I were calling from out of town to get an update on a patient."

"You're kidding."

"This is Dr. Akhtar looking to get an update about Mr. Letterman's condition," he said, mimicking her. "Your mother could be a very charming woman when she wanted to. She had the name of one of his doctors from the newspaper. Asked for him directly."

"And?"

" *'Oh, of course, Dr. Akhtar. We'll get him your message right away.'* Very deferential. Fifteen minutes later, the phone rings. There he is, on the phone. One of Letter-

511

man's specialists. Who then spends five minutes running her through the procedure in the operating room. Where they started, where they ended. What his condition is now. I'm listening on the kitchen phone. Trying not to laugh," he said, laughing now. "She really never told you?"

I shook my head. "David Letterman."

"Him and that polka. That's what kept her going at the end." He paused. His right hand had found his heart. He grimaced as he rubbed there, mindlessly. And then, all at once, he was on his feet: "We should get to the baggage claim. So we don't miss him."

Downstairs, it wasn't long before Sultan emerged from the gates in his billowing light-brown *shalwar kameez;* he had a shawl over his shoulder, and on his head was a flat off-white skullcap.

Father didn't miss a beat, gibing in Punjabi: "There he is, in his tortilla."

Sultan bit down on his grin: "Very funny, very funny." His accent wasn't nearly as strong as most I'd grown up hearing in my father's generation of South Asian immigrants.

"I like tacos, too, *yaar.* But who puts them on their head?"

"Dad —"

512

"What?"

"That's offensive."

Sultan stopped me. "This is nothing, *beta*. Compared to what I'm used to." He hugged Father. "It's so very nice to see you, too, Sikander." Then he brought me in for a hug as well. "I hear it's your birthday?"

"Well, we've all got one."

"I got you something. But it's in my bag. So I'll give it to you when we're at the house . . ."

He'd lost weight since I last saw him — close to eighty pounds, he would later tell me, the result of a stapled stomach — and it showed in the sagging skin under his chin and along his neck. I'd always thought he looked a little like a sea lion, his eyes lower on his face than was perhaps usual, his button nose and flat upper lip protruding almost like a snout. With thinner cheeks, his now narrower face no longer had the same benign appeal.

"You didn't need to get me anything, Uncle."

"But I wanted to."

Behind us, the belt was moving; bags dropped from the chute. "Which one's yours?" Father asked.

"Brown duffel," Sultan said.

"Not that silly Louis Vuitton."

"Yes, Sikander. That silly Vuitton." Sultan turned to me, winking. "I just love it so." He clapped Father on the back as they stepped to the carousel's edge. To either side of me, I felt the disbelieving white gazes — an older couple to my left; a younger family of four to my right — looks that conveyed not just the affront of our swart joy but also, even more keenly, its apparent implausibility: How was it possible? their faces seemed to say. How was it possible people who looked like us would not be eternally subdued by the fact of their unceasing suspicions?

I glared at them all until it was only the children not looking away.

Father grabbed Sultan's Vuitton duffel when it appeared, and we made our way out to the car. On the way home, Sultan told us about the passenger first seated next to him on the plane, an elderly woman with an emotional-support terrier who'd inquired if he was a "Moslem" — he told her he was — and then, assuming he would want to be reseated because of the dog, apologized to him for forcing him to move. The woman was surprised to learn that Sultan didn't have a problem with dogs and so wouldn't need to be moving, at which point *she* then requested to be moved. Sultan seemed amused by the episode as he relayed the apology offered by the fellow who took her place — also older, also white — which included a comment about the unfortunate direction the country had taken under our "orangutan in chief." As he repeated the insult, I noticed Sultan watching for Father's reaction. If Father had one, he wasn't showing it.

By the time we got home, it was time for late-afternoon prayers. Sultan asked if we had a prayer rug he could use. If not, a clean towel would do. I went searching through the house. In my parents' room, I found my mother's red-and-black rug — given to her by her parents on the eve of her departure for the New World — still laid out, its top left corner folded over, indicating a final interrupted prayer she intended to come back and finish but never did. Father hadn't picked up the rug since her death. We'd both avoided dealing with her things for more than two and a half years now — her closets were still full; so was her vanity counter in the master bathroom; even the glass tumbler she used was still perched on her nightstand. I muttered an apology to some imagined maternal ghost, folded the rug up, took it down to Sultan, and pointed him in the direction of Mecca. I lingered in

515

the hall just beyond the doorway and watched him lower his head and bow, then prostrate himself, his lips silently moving with ritual verses; the calm that came over me was hard to ignore. It had been two decades since I'd prayed in the Muslim way. Perhaps, I thought, it was time to try again.

Back in the kitchen, I found Father tinkering with a cocktail set, measuring out vermouth into a jigger, then dumping it into a shaker. "What are you doing?" I asked.

"Making martinis," he said with a puckish grin.

"Since when do you drink martinis?"

"I don't. But *he* loves them."

"Sultan-Uncle?"

"First time I ever had a martini — it was with him," he said as he screwed on the cap of the shaker. "Back then, he was a martini *junkie.* We'll see how serious he is about all this new holy baloney," he said as he started to shake the mixture.

To my surprise, Sultan didn't refuse the glass Father offered him when he showed up in the kitchen after his prayers — though it was just to taste. He brought the wide-rimmed glass to his lips and sipped. "Too much vermouth," he said with a frown.

"Just what's in the recipe," Father said.

"Maybe there's something wrong with the

vermouth."

Father took the glass and sipped. "I like it," he said. "But I'll make you another if you want . . ."

"Enjoy it, Sikander. Even in the unlikely instance you *can* get it right, which I doubt, I'm not interested." Sultan turned to me: "Come on, *beta*. Let's give you your present."

Upstairs in the guest room, he pulled a gift-wrapped book from his Vuitton duffel and handed it to me.

"Pretty big," I said, weighing it in my hands.

"I hope you don't have it already."

I tore off the wrapping. It was an old edition of Rumi's *Mathnawi*.

"I don't. I've always thought I needed to read it."

"That's what I thought when I saw your play. You know, they did it in Omaha."

"You thought I needed to read *Mathnawi*?"

"You're making fun of him at one moment in the play, and I just thought, 'He doesn't know Rumi, because if he did, he wouldn't *want* to make fun . . .'"

"I don't make fun of Rumi. I make fun of the guy who thinks he knows something about Islam because he's reading Rumi."

"But anyone who reads Rumi *does* know

something about Islam, *beta*. Something good, something important. For me, *that* book is my Quran." He'd started emptying his bag, removing socks and underwear, his shaving kit. "I mean, don't get me wrong, I liked your play. It was wonderful. Funny and sharp. But here and there, a little shrill. You know what I mean?"

"Shrill?"

"Everybody has flaws — we're no exception. But we're under attack in this country now. We have to stick together. It was clear to me that audience of Nebraskans had no idea what you're writing about. They were thinking, 'He's Muslim. He's saying Islam is bad. He must know. He's on the inside.' "

"— Which is, of course, not what I'm saying."

"And *I* know that. But *they* don't. In this time, you have to be careful. Don't get me wrong. It's a wonderful play. You're a wonderful writer. Just wonderful."

"Thanks, Uncle."

He stepped over to the dresser and pulled open a drawer to stow his things.

Of course, it hurt to hear him speak about my work this way. I didn't think he was right, but the kindness with which he offered his criticisms — which, I knew, were evidence of his having somehow been hurt by the work — left me feeling there was no point in arguing. "Uncle, thank you for coming. He needs the support. It's been complicated . . ."

"I know, *beta.* We talk." He turned back to his bag for more things: "You're a good son to be taking on this chaos he's putting himself through. I mean, to lose all that money. He's so lucky to have you. I could never expect the same from my kids — but then again, they're not you."

"What money, Uncle?"

Sultan looked up at me. "He hasn't told you?"

"Told me what?"

"Hmm. I see . . . I know he was going to tell you. He told me that."

"Tell me what, Uncle?"

"I don't think it's my place."

"It sounds pretty serious. You've got me worried."

"I'll talk to him. I'll encourage him to tell you now."

"Uncle —"

"And if he doesn't, I will. I promise."

Father suggested tandoori for dinner, and I knew it was to get under Sultan's skin. Sultan was thinking of shutting down Trunk Road, the restaurant in Omaha he'd left his practice to open. Like Father, Sultan was a fanatic for the Lahori style of North Indian cuisine, and according to him, his restaurant was the only place in Nebraska (or neighboring Kansas, for that matter) where you could get a proper Lahori meal. Since the recent clampdown on immigrant visas, staffing the kitchen with a cook who really knew how to make the food properly — and part of the whole point for Sultan had been to have a place where he could get his beloved Lahori paaya and lamb chops! — was now increasingly complicated. The few such cooks still legally in the country had jobs in the bigger cities, and for around a year now, the food at Trunk Road had suffered. It wasn't just work visas for the cooks that were the problem; dealing with patrons was harder and harder, with everyone so quick to anger over the smallest things. Worst of all, no one seemed to have the money (or time) to be eating out anymore — at least not at the sort of place like Trunk Road, neither particularly cheap nor particularly expensive. Less and less place left in America, he said, for the middle class of things.

Predictably, Sultan complained about Trump over our seekh kebabs and sabzi masalas. We listened as he laid out just how unreasoned and self-defeating the administration's anti-immigrant logic was to him: "It's not just that they won't *let* anyone come here now. They're trying to make it so no one *wants* to come. Graduates like us? If we're young, coming out of medical school, why would we want the headache? We'll try somewhere else. And do they think that will be good for the country? At least fifty percent of the best doctors in America were not born in America. At least fifty percent. That's just a fact. I mean, correct me if you don't agree, Sikander."

"In research, probably higher."

"Right. And what could be more important than that? New cures, new vaccines — where are they coming from if not from the immigrants? He doesn't like Mexicans, he doesn't like Muslims, he doesn't like Africans — in the process, he's making it more and more unlikely that *any* good doctor, good scientist, will come here. No matter where they're from. And who will suffer the consequence? The American patient suffers. That's who."

"But Uncle, I mean . . . since when has the system cared about the American patient?"

"Okay, *beta*. But I'm not just talking about people from North Omaha. I'm talking about the ones with money, too. The ones who *can* get the best care. They'll suffer like everyone else. I mean, when that bastard in the White House had a heart problem, who did he call? Your father. First in his class at King Edward Medical College. That's who. You get rid of that pipeline, who benefits? No. One."

"Then they'll be stuck with the local boy who postpones a procedure so he can get an extra day on his ski trip in Aspen," Father said acerbically.

"I guess I'm just saying, patient care has never been a priority," I said.

"I'm not sure that's true, *beta*. Democrats have tried. They have. Obamacare —"

"What a disaster," Father interjected.

"Okay, Sikander. I get it. But at least he was trying. Right? At least it was an effort."

"You left medicine before that debacle started. Okay? You don't know the first thing about it. Don't lecture me about —"

"I'm not talking about your salary, Sikander. I'm talking about *the system.* They can put a man on the moon, but they can't solve health care in this country?" Father signaled his lack of interest by waving at the waiter and asking for another beer. Sultan continued: "Look, this country has been good to us. I had my children here. They're miserable — there's no secret there — but they would have been just as unhappy back home in some different way."

"What's your point?" Father was irritated.

"You know what my point is."

"Our lives are *here,* okay? Our kids are *here.*"

"No one's saying they're not."

"We don't like what's happening politically, so we jump ship? Is that it? After all this country gave us?"

The conversation between them had taken a sudden turn I wasn't following, as if they were picking up an argument they'd been having for some time.

"We paid our taxes, Sikander," Sultan said. "At least I paid mine. I took no money from the state. I cared for these people, their children. I don't feel I haven't given back. Maybe what I *didn't* do — and what you didn't, either — was give back to the country that really needed us." Father shrugged. Sultan turned to me: "The thing I never got used to here was not really understanding what people are thinking. Everybody coming from so many different places, so many different experiences, everybody looking at the same things in completely different ways. For years, people are telling me, 'You don't smile. You have to smile more.' I heard it so much I ended up taping a note card on my bathroom mirror to remind me. 'Glue a smile to your face before you leave the house.' If you smile like that in Pakistan all the time? They think you're a fool. But if you don't smile like that here, you have an attitude problem."

"You do have an attitude problem," Father said playfully.

Sultan ignored him. "They call it a melting pot, but it's not. In chemistry, they have what they call a *buffer solution* — which keeps things together but always separated. That's what this country is. A buffer solution."

"Are you taking notes?" Father asked, turning to me as his beer arrived.

"He doesn't need to," Sultan answered for me in a tone somewhat sterner than I thought made sense. "Your son knows these things already, Sikander. He's writing about it. We're the ones who didn't know."

Father sipped, sipped again, then placed his beer carefully on the napkin before him. He looked up at Sultan with a wooden stare. He didn't speak.

I finally asked the obvious question: "Are you thinking of going back to Pakistan, Uncle?"

Sultan's reply was careful, cagey, intending — I realize now — a meaning beyond its words. In retrospect, it's hard for me to believe that I didn't divine what he was trying to tell me, but I didn't: "So many of us are thinking about it, *beta*. We're all wondering in our own different ways about how to find our way back home."

7.

October was the cruelest month that year, with our country awash in violence. Back on the first of the month, in Las Vegas, a shooter had opened fire on an outdoor country music festival from the makeshift turret of his thirty-second-floor hotel suite. For ten minutes, bullets poured onto an unprotected crowd, injuring 441 and taking fifty-nine lives. The following twenty-eight days would see a further twenty-four mass shootings in fifteen states, bringing the month's toll of fatalities to eighty-two, with 532 injured.

On the last day of the month, Halloween, sometime after 3:00 p.m., as my father was likely returning from lunch for an afternoon session of his second week in court, I was waiting for a latte at a West Village coffee shop when I heard an onslaught of passing police sirens. I went to the window to see what was going on. Behind me, a patron announced there'd been an attack of some sort along the West Side Highway. The barista behind the counter — now staring down into her phone — read out a bystander's description on her Facebook profile of a pickup truck plowing into pedestrians along the Hudson River bike path. Within minutes, eyewitnesses on Twitter were being retweeted, their accounts already referring to a "terrorist attack." Some claimed they saw the perpetrator escape from the truck — dark-skinned, long-bearded — and heard him shouting "Allah-u-Akbar" just before being shot in the gut by the city police. I retreated from the ad hoc comity forming itself in that coffee shop; I didn't want to pick through the details with my fellow patrons. I'd learned my lesson on that day sixteen years earlier when my curiosity led to a downtown encounter from which my American self would likely never entirely recover. I went out into the street and flagged the first cab home.

Over the next few hours, I monitored the story's developments from back at my place in Harlem. Sure enough, the attacker was Muslim, an immigrant from Uzbekistan approaching the end of his Saturn returns. He'd rented a truck in Passaic, New Jersey, around an hour before driving it into Manhattan, where he killed eight and injured eleven. According to pundits, he was the second mass-murdering Muslim immigrant to come into this country on what was known as the Diversity Immigrant Visa lottery, the other being the Egyptian shooter who attacked an El Al counter at Los Angeles International Airport back in 2002. We were told our beloved Halloween parade was to proceed as scheduled that night, though not before the governor took a moment to sing the city's praises and remind us how truly exceptional we were, which, of course, was why we'd been attacked, a sentiment shared by the mayor, who added to the usual formula about the attack's cowardly nature only that it was "particularly" cowardly. Ever since Susan Sontag was pilloried for suggesting, in 2001, that *coward* surely wasn't the right word for men who fly themselves into buildings, I knew it was better not to be too bothered by this habitual misuse of a word whose *actual* meaning was never relevant to the situation at hand. When people are in pain, they don't always mean what they say.

I'd left a message for Father shortly after getting home earlier that afternoon, but it wasn't until much later that night that he rang me back. Or his phone did. When I picked up, Sultan was on the other end. He was calling from somewhere in public, and it wasn't easy to make out what he was saying over the surrounding din.

"Got your message, *beta*. Thank you. We were worried when we heard the news."

"Yeah, I'm fine. I mean, I wasn't that far from it this afternoon."

"Tragic. Just tragic."

"I know. — So how'd it go in court today?"

"That's actually the reason I'm calling." I thought I heard concern in his voice.

"What happened? Did it not go well?"

"No, no. It went fine. I mean — so what happened, after the session, they heard the news about this attack near you — your father's attorneys, well, the guy with the long hair, who's in charge . . ."

"Thom Powell . . ."

"I don't know his name. Your father calls him Quaker Oats —"

"Same guy."

"They made a new offer to settle with the patient's family. And the family accepted."

"You're kidding."

"No, I'm not. Your father's lawyer explained to me they were in a similar situation before because of an attack that happened in the middle of the trial."

"Yeah. It was San Bernardino. Hannah told me about it."

"Well, they didn't want to take a chance on a repeat." On my television screen, local news flashed once again through a montage of smartphone clips shot in the aftermath of the attack. Bike parts and other debris were strewn along the green path, as were the dead bodies.

"Is he there?" I asked. "Can I talk to him?"

"He's upset. I don't blame him. Now it's in the database for everyone to see. But the good thing is — it won't hurt him. He's at the end of his career. And maybe this is just the extra push he needs to finally get out."

"Are you with him? Can I talk to him?"

"Yes, I'm with him. I'm not sure it's the best time."

"Where are you guys?"

He hesitated before saying: "A casino not too far from the hotel . . ."

"Yeah, I know where it is," I said, disheartened by the reliability of my father's new dysfunctions. "Okay, well, I'm around. Whenever he wants to call."

"Don't worry. I'll keep an eye on him. And I'll make sure he calls you tomorrow."

The rest of what happened for my father transpired in rapid succession: barely a week

530

after the malpractice settlement, Sultan's ninety-two-year-old mother fell in her Lahore bathroom and broke her hip. Indebted, he said, to Sultan for his visit and seeing an opportunity to put some healthy daylight between himself and what had just happened in La Crosse, Father decided he was going to join his friend for his trip back to Pakistan to deal with his mother's situation. In order to do so, though, he would have to resign his position at Reliant effective immediately. Leaving when there was still time on his contract would mean losing his retirement bonus, but so be it. At seventy, he was already a year into the maximum Social Security retiree payout, roughly $3,600 a month. It was time to start a new chapter. Father explained all this on the phone in a tone that was now delighted, now defensive, as if he were hoping for my encouragement but expecting my censure. His tone and the jumble of ill-advised options all started to make more sense when he finally got to what I gathered was the real reason for his call:

"Sultan's flight is leaving day after tomorrow. I want to be on it with him. The only thing is . . ."

"What?"

"My credit cards."

"What about them?"

"Maxed out."

"Yeah? What's going on with you and your money, Dad? Everything okay?"

"Why?"

"You're the one calling to ask me to buy you a ticket."

"If you don't want to help, then just tell me."

"That's not what I'm saying."

"Well, then we need to book the tickets. On this kind of short notice, they're expensive."

"How expensive?"

"Um, you know, five thousand?"

It wasn't the number that fazed me; it was his blasé manner: "What do you mean 'maxed out,' Dad? You have an Amex platinum. They don't have a limit, right?"

"I don't have it anymore," he replied lightly.

"What happened?"

"I stopped paying. They canceled it."

"Why did you stop paying your Amex? What's going on?"

"It's a long story."

"Sultan mentioned you were having some trouble with money. He wouldn't tell me what it was. He said you were going to tell me." I waited; Father was silent on the other end. "Do you want to tell me what's going on?"

His reply was wan: "No."

"Maybe you should tell me."

"Another time."

"Dad —"

"I've done a lot for you. How much money I've given you over the years. No questions asked —"

"Dad —"

"Now I'm asking, and you're behaving like I owe *you* something? Forget it! Just forget it!"

"It's fine. I'll buy it for you."

"No questions asked!"

"Okay."

"I'm your father."

"I said okay."

"Good. Thank you. How do you want to do it? I mean, if you just send me your credit card information I can book?"

"Send me an email with the details, and I'll take care of it."

He hesitated, then said "Fine" and hung up.

Twenty minutes later, I got the promised email. He'd lied about the departure date, which wasn't for another three days; he'd also lied about the availability of cheaper tickets. A search online showed an ample supply on at least a half dozen flights for the date listed, most costing no more than $1,500. But Sultan was flying on Emirates into Lahore, he explained when I called him back; he needed to be on the same flight so they could travel together. I didn't want to argue with him. I read him my credit card information, and he bought the ticket himself — $5,700 with fees and taxes.

The following day he called with more disconcerting news. He changed the date of his flight into New York. He would be in the city tomorrow afternoon. He used my card for the $250 change fee; he hoped I didn't mind. And: Was I free for dinner? I was. Did he want to stay the night at my place? No, he replied gaily. He'd booked a room at the Plaza. They were having a special rate, and he couldn't resist. "Did you use my card for that, too?" I asked, irritated.

"I hope you don't mind."

I don't know how Father scored a reservation at Eleven Madison Park for a 7:00 p.m. dinner on a Thursday night. I'd only been for lunch — appropriately enough, with Riaz — at a table just a few feet from James Murdoch, his wife, and Google's Eric Schmidt; there hadn't been an empty table at that lunch hour, and I recalled Riaz telling me it could be even harder to get in for dinner. Somehow, Father got a table. The choice didn't surprise me. His hankering to mark his status was as innate to him as his Punjabi accent. And in theory, I didn't mind the notion that we were meeting for dinner at Eleven Madison Park, where a meal for two could easily set us back three bills. But why now? Why the needless luxury when he didn't have the money to spend on it anymore? For years, I'd been hearing tales of my friends' parents getting older, the bizarre moods, the night terrors, the disturbing lapses in memory, the peculiar new inclinations, the mottled new colors to their personalities. I assumed at least some of Father's behavior around money was related to his advancing age. As I walked over from the subway, crossing Madison Square Park, I resolved to force the conversation with him that night. I needed to know what was going on.

But he wasn't alone.

He was sitting in a corner at a table for four, and beside him was a woman in red. Across the room, I couldn't tell if her hair was white-blond or white-gray, but even from a distance, her face was striking — round eyes and a long face I recognized at once from her daughter: it was Melissa's mother, Caroline.

I could hear my heart inside my ears.

Father saw me and rose. There was something spry about his escape from the corner, something firm in his embrace that I didn't recognize. I smelled the alcohol on his breath, but he didn't seem drunk. "Ayad, there's someone I want you to meet," he said, holding my arm now, his voice quivering just enough for me to notice that he was nervous.

"Yeah, I think I got that already . . .."

He turned back to the table, still holding my arm. "Caroline," he said, presenting me, "this is my son." She stood, her small, veined fist closed tightly around her napkin, her striking face softened with a searching half smile. She reached her other hand out toward me. Her grip was warm and wet.

"It's so nice to meet you," she said quietly. As I began to take my place, Father lingered beside me with a vacant look. "Sikander," she said, again softly. "You can sit down now." The way she pronounced his name — with the proper emphasis on the second syllable and its gentle d, and all the correct proportions to the vowels, all the more striking for being spoken with an American accent — signaled an intimacy between them I couldn't deny. She encouraged him to sit again, but he didn't move.

"What's going on?" I asked.

"I'll be right back," he said.

Once he'd disappeared beyond the row of tree-tall bouquets dividing the dining room, I realized just how angry I was.

"I'm sorry," she said softly.

"For what?" I asked. I heard myself. I sounded like an asshole.

"I asked him to make sure you knew. I didn't want you to be blindsided. I wanted to be sure you knew. So you had a choice."

"A choice?"

"About whether you were okay meeting me or not." She paused. "You've been part of my life for so many years. I just . . . I feel like I know you. I know how much he loves you. How much you love him. I just want to . . ." She stopped, her lips holding in — it seemed — a feeling of sympathy she wasn't sure I would want to feel from her.

"It's fine," I said. "It's not you. It's him. He's been very unpredictable lately."

"I know," she said with finality.

And that was all we said. I sat there in silence and stared down at the table. I could still feel my heart in my ears. I realized I couldn't stay, but I knew I couldn't leave until he returned. And then, all at once, he was back, slipping into the corner place beside her. He still looked nervous, but I couldn't deny what I saw before me: he'd never looked so much himself — which is to say, that face I'd known my whole life seemed more clearly what it was, what I'd always known it to be, as if some intervening, disfiguring filter I'd never understood to comprise so much of his appearance had fallen away, and, for the first time, I was beholding him without it. "So," he began brightly. "The bathrooms are stunning. I highly recommend the trip." Neither of us replied. He pulled his readers from his breast pocket and picked up a menu just as the waiter appeared and asked me what I was drinking.

"Not sure yet."

The waiter nodded and turned to my father, indicating his almost finished drink: "Another vodka gimlet, sir?"

"Please," Father said politely, tossing back the rest and handing him the glass.

"Go ahead and bring the whole bottle," I blurted out to the waiter, who looked understandably startled.

"I'm sorry, sir?"

"I said, just bring him the whole bottle. He's probably gonna go through at least that much by the time he's done."

"Ayad."

"What, Dad?! Hmm?"

He looked up at the waiter. "Just the gimlet will be fine. Thank you."

Caroline was moving along the bench to the table's edge. "I'm just going to freshen up. I'll be right back," she said meekly as she got out and left us.

"Can you be civil, please? Can you stop behaving like a child?" Father glared, then took up the menu.

"Civil?!" I yelped. "*I'm* the one behaving like a child?! *Me?!* —"

"I said stop it —"

"I'm the one who needs *babysitting* through his court case? Drunk in casinos, in jail? I'm the one who's supposed to be civil?!" If I'd been paying attention, I might have noticed the silence growing around us.

"That's enough."

"You're right. It is enough. You mind telling me what's going on with you?"

"With what?"

"What happened to all your money?"

"None of your business."

"Isn't that exactly what it's become now that I'm paying for all this ridiculous stuff —"

"*Ridiculous?* You think I didn't pay for *you?* For *years?*"

"Don't change the subject."

" *'Just one more month, Daaad. I'll have rent next month, Daaad.'* " His high-pitched, open mockery of my American accent continued to draw the notice of those around us.

"You've been using that one on me now for ten years. I couldn't make it on my own. I needed your help. I know that. I'm sorry! I'm sorry it took me so long! How many times do I have to thank you before you'll leave me alone about it? I couldn't have done any of it without you! You're the only reason any of it happened! Okay!? Does *that* make you happy!?" I was shouting, and around us, the dining room had gone silent. I thought I felt Father's impulse to strike me — or maybe this was only the consciously admissible form of my own long-buried desire to hit him — and saw the scarlet bloom rushing up his neck. My heart lurched, stuffing my ears with its relentless throbbing. "You're an embarrassment," he said nastily as he lifted the menu again and hid himself from me. I saw the waiter heading for our table with the maître d' in tow. I wasn't about to be chastised in public any further.

"Fuck this," I said, then got up and walked out.

The night was brisker than I recalled. At the corner, whatever was coursing through

my veins pushed me into the oncoming traffic. Car horns blared as I wove my way
across Madison Avenue back into the park,
defiant. The rage felt like a heat that would
burn me if I didn't release it. But where?
How? On whom? On what? A young couple
passed me, arm in arm. I suddenly wondered if my fists could be used to shake the
feeling. To ask the question — I knew —
was already to avoid it. I wanted to scream;
I knew I wouldn't do that, either.

I staggered a little farther into the park
and fell onto an empty bench. My eyes
burned. I buried them in my palms and
rubbed, and kept rubbing. There, inside, I
saw him. He was large, and I was small. I
remembered watching him from a doorway
in our first house, standing by a window,
impossibly grand in the daylight, opening
and reading mail. I longed for him then, to
be lifted in his arms, in that light. It was a
yearning I'd felt my whole life. Hadn't he
done that? Hadn't he and Mother given all
they could? Why hadn't it been enough?
Why, despite all they'd given, all they'd
done — both of them, their whole lives —
why had it still never felt like enough?

The tears were coming up now from a
pain in my chest, from a longing fissure in a
heart I'd always known was broken.

I felt my phone vibrating in my pocket. I pulled it out to see two missed calls from him. I had to go back inside. I couldn't pretend I didn't want to. I couldn't pretend I didn't need him.

I headed back to the restaurant.

As I emerged from the park, I saw him on the other side of Madison Avenue. He was standing beside a cab and helping her into the back. It looked like he was going to follow her in. "Dad!" I cried out. And again: "Dad!" He heard me and looked up. I saw her long, worried face appear in the window. He leaned in and spoke to her, then shut the door and stepped away from the car, watching it pull off and disappear up the avenue.

I crossed the street and found him leaden, retreated.

"I'm sorry," I said, starting to cry again. I didn't know what I was apologizing for, but I knew I had to apologize.

"No, no," he said, shaking his head slowly. "No," he said again.

"Dad, I'm sorry. I'm so sorry," I said again, grabbing his coat and pulling him toward me. He resisted my embrace.

"No, *beta,* no."

But I pressed in and drew him closer, pressing myself to him, feeling him as tightly against my body as I could. I held him there until he stopped resisting. It wasn't until he tried to speak that I realized he was also crying now.

"I lost it all," he moaned into my shoulder. "All of it. I lost it all."

I didn't ask for an explanation. I didn't want one. I didn't need one. I was sure I would find it all out soon enough. Only the embrace between us mattered now. If only I could hold him closer, I thought, hold him longer, maybe what was broken in both of us would finally be mended.

I don't know if, when he boarded that plane for Pakistan the next morning, Father knew he wouldn't be coming back. Some part of me thinks he did. He left behind a Gordian knot of liabilities, unpaid bills, and loans — the second mortgage he'd taken out on the house was three months in arrears, and foreclosure proceedings were already in the preliminary stages — and his bank accounts were empty, even his IRA, to fund a gambling habit that had enriched the coffers of our local casino by almost $2 million. It was all so clear in hindsight, the disrepair into which his life had been falling for some time; I was angry at myself for not noticing the magnitude of the problem in time to do something.

I won't bore you with the details of how his legal and financial troubles were eventually untangled, but the fact that his attorneys in America had been fully empowered with the necessary authorities before he left indicated to me — despite his protestations to the contrary — he'd been thinking about an escape for some time. The process of discarding his and my mother's things — he didn't want anything saved except the family photographs — was undertaken on the weekend of April Fools' Day in 2018. By the second week of May, the house in which I'd grown up was sold and painted a bright new shade of gray.

As for Father's situation, his Social Security benefits were enough to ensure a secure, if modest, life on sixteen acres of mango groves in Bahawalpur. I missed him, of course. And he said he missed me, too. But in our Skype sessions and phone calls, I could tell he was doing better than he had done in years. He wasn't drinking nearly as much, though finding a drink when he wanted one wasn't as hard — he was happy to relate — as he worried it might be. He was also relieved there was no way to gamble away what little money he had left. Islam had at least that much going for it. "Better than a twelve-step program," he joked as the muezzin's call sounded from the village mosque in the background. Yes, the Pakistani homeland he'd hated for the entirety of his American life — or so he'd led us all to believe — was now his homeland again. And it didn't seem to bother him one bit.

He'd been in Pakistan just about a year when I finally confessed I was almost finished with a book in which I wrote it out — what had happened to him and her and to me in our American journeys. I was surprised how lackadaisically he took the news. There was no entreaty to deal with him justly, no admonition to strike a fair balance about my American homeland. Instead, he had this to add about his own experience and suggested I might not want to leave it out: That when he thought of the place now, America, he found it hard to believe he'd spent so much of his life there. As much as he'd always wanted to think of himself as American, the truth was he'd only ever aspired to the condition. Looking back, he said, he realized he'd been playing a role so much of that time, a role he'd taken for real. There was no harm in it; he'd just gotten tired of playing the part. "I had a good life there, so many good years. I'm grateful to America. It gave me you! But I'm glad to be back in Pakistan, *beta*. I'm glad to be home."

FREE SPEECH: A CODA

When the theatricality, the entertainment
value, the marketing of life is complete,
we will find ourselves living not in a nation
but in a consortium of industries, and
wholly unintelligible to ourselves except
for what we see as through a screen
darkly.

— Toni Morrison

The trouble on campus began before I got
there: someone at the college's Muslim
student union had a cousin who had had
what he called a "run-in" with me. I recalled
the episode well: on a cigarette break during an afternoon seminar on my work at a
community college in Southern California,
a young Pakistani-American man shared
with me his recent forays into online activ-
ism. He and a cohort had used Reddit to
crowdfund the production of a porn scene
in which a well-endowed Pakistani-

American male — played by a fellow student whose member fit the bill — had graphic sex with a blond white bombshell. (They'd been able to raise enough money to hire a professional porn star for the shoot.) The video was their counterattack on a group of 4chan bullies who were well known for mocking South Asians about their penis sizes on that anonymous internet image board. The video turned out to be a great success. It went viral, and the resulting deluge of outraged 4chan threads, the young man explained to me — not only without a hint of irony but also, apparently, with every expectation I would find all this admirable — had been truly "life-changing." Which is to say: I had more than an inkling he might not take well to my asking just why it was he cared what anyone thought about his penis size.

The young man in question didn't come back to class after the break, and a few days later, while rummaging about through the 4chan threads surrounding his video, I came across a thread he'd written describing his encounter with me, in which he called me an "arrogant asshole who apparently thinks writing stories about Muslims beating white women instead of giving them a good fuck" was "original." He went on to say that he hoped, on my next trip back to Pakistan, somebody finally gave me what I deserved, namely, a "bullet in the head." The thread ended with three face-with-tears-of-joy emojis followed by a half dozen exclamation points. My heart raced as I read it, but not because I was worried. It wasn't the first time I'd encountered this sentiment about me online. I doubted it would be the last.

The young pornographer in training had a cousin who was a student at the liberal arts college in Iowa where Mary Moroni was now teaching — having left my alma mater a few years after I'd graduated for a position that gave both her and her partner tenure-track jobs. I'd been to visit her there amid the cornfields twice before, once for dinner while driving through, once at her invitation to give a reading. She'd invited me to campus again, this time to spend a day with her spring seminar students. After I accepted, she reached out to the religion department, a student theater group, and the Muslim student union. Two days later, the latter's student president wrote her an email explaining that the Muslim students on campus found my work offensive and demeaning, and, as far as their organization was concerned, I would be considered an "unsafe" presence on campus. The email

549

encouraged Mary to rescind the invitation and ended by threatening protests of any and all events associated with me if she didn't.

In the four years since I'd seen her last, Mary's feelings about teaching had changed. Back then, she spoke of her students with a frustration that surprised me. She had just come off a semester of trouble with her course on social issues in the nineteenth-century American novel when, for the first time in her career as a teacher, a group of students refused an assignment. Objecting to the presence on the syllabus of the author of *Adventures of Huckleberry Finn,* they refused to read *The Gilded Age.* It was only the most outrageous example of a new self-righteousness in the classroom Mary had been dealing with for some time. She'd had some trouble with the matter of the third-person pronoun being used for an individual — she was an English teacher, after all, she tried to explain — but eventually got used to it. Then there was the semester she came under attack for teaching Emerson and Whitman. A pair of students did their presentations on both writers' racist views, culling racist comments both made in lesser-known writings. A larger group canvassed her to replace upcoming readings in both authors' work with other, less objectionable authors. She was reluctant to go that far, explaining that she knew Whitman had racist views; Abraham Lincoln did, too. One needed to be cautious about applying today's standards to the past. Even the most progressive white abolitionists of that time had opinions about race anyone today would consider racist. When Mary refused to drop the writers from the syllabus, four of her students dropped the class in protest.

I remember sitting with her in her office shortly after the ruckus about Twain, listening to her complain about the students' growing intolerance for difficult ideas. "It's feeling more and more to me like cover for their laziness," she said; there was more gray in her hair and a few more pounds to her, but even anxious, she still looked like an angel in a Renaissance fresco. "They take the class because they want to be writers, but they don't want to read. Instead of owning it, they slap you with moral rhetoric about why you're wrong to make them do something they don't want to do. And don't get me started on grades. If you don't give them grades they think they deserve, you get reported." She paused. "The worst part of it? I can't give them the best of what I have. They don't even know if they have the interest, because they're not willing to know what they're made of. I think back on some of what we did together. The work on your dreams? Suggesting something like *that* these days is career suicide. It's disheartening enough to make me wonder if I shouldn't be doing something else with myself entirely."

Four years later, though, her frustration had given way to compassion. Most of her students, she now recognized, were dealing with some very real form of anxiety or depression — or both. They trusted no one and expected that everyone and everything was taking advantage of them. As Mary saw it, they weren't wrong. The university was a case in point: Tuition had risen another 4 percent the year prior. Inflation was below 2 percent. Why the gap? Because the college had taken on more debt to build a new gym and renovate the faculty club. Better facilities attracted better teachers and students, justifying higher tuitions; more cash flow meant the college had an excuse to take on more debt. This vicious cycle was being passed on to the students: the cost of coming to campus had just broken $70,000. Her students were carrying more debt than she thought many would ever be able to repay. It made sense that they didn't want to work for their educations anymore. They were paying more than most Americans made in a year; wasn't that work enough? College was now a customer experience, not a pedagogical one; and what the college customer wanted was only what had been advertised to lure them: physical comforts, moral reassurance, unceasing approbation. Mary believed deep down they knew it was a con, knew they were marks, knew not to trust a world that was now nothing more than a marketplace — but no trust in the world meant they had no basis for trusting themselves. Her students spent so much of their time in class — when they weren't on their phones — wondering what was real that it was hard to arrive at a discussion of anything substantial. Platitudes and pornography commanded their days. As she saw it, much of her work now was about teaching them cognitive basics: how to recognize what was worth paying attention to; how to suffer through boredom; how to discern rhetoric from reality, discomfort from defense.

All this came up in the conversation we had at her six-acre homestead twenty minutes outside of campus, where I showed up on an unseasonably warm morning in March of 2019 and found her in the vegetable garden, tending to the soil. Her work in the garden was like meditation, she said as we headed for the house, which was something else she was making more time for every day. "And I finally got rid of my smartphone. Strictly a flip phone for me now."

"Hard to text on those, isn't it?"

"Small price to pay for my brain," she said, holding open the door to a mudroom filled with gardening tools. In the kitchen, as she filled the kettle for tea, she shared the latest news from the Muslim student union: I was already aware she'd visited with some of the students there, aware she'd discovered none of them knew much about me or my work other than what they'd been told by the young pornographer in training's cousin. I was also already aware that Mary encouraged them to read some of my writing and, if they still had issues, to pen a letter she would deliver to me, which I'd agreed to respond to in public. What was new was that the letter hadn't yet arrived because something else just happened: overnight, posters depicting me against a photograph of the burning towers appeared around campus. Mary believed they were inspired by a similar poster depicting Representative Ilhan Omar that had gone up in

West Virginia a few weeks earlier; she pulled open a kitchen drawer and laid a crinkled eight-by-ten color image on the table between us. She was right: it was more or less the same image used in the Omar poster — a photo of me, seated, superimposed awkwardly beneath the image of the towers on fire. The caption along the bottom read: PROUD OF 9/11.

I couldn't hide my shock. "How many of them are up on campus?" I asked.

"We don't know exactly, but the kids from the Muslim student union went around, found a dozen or so, took them all down. Now that this is happening, they're getting behind you."

"Jesus."

"I spoke to the dean this morning. We'll have security with us today and tomorrow morning for our talk."

"I doubt that's necessary."

"Maybe not, but I don't want to take any chances."

That afternoon, I sat in on Mary's senior seminar while two security officers stood guard outside the classroom door. Inside, a dozen of her students led a discussion about that week's reading assignment: Whitman's *Democratic Vistas.* They were all startled that the poet's portrait of the nation 150 years ago was one they still recognized, a country of endless energy, enterprise, and breadth — both natural and human — but ensnared in a materialism from which it couldn't seem to escape. Back then, Whitman worried America's preoccupation with the business of making money would lead to the failure of its historic political mission. On his remedy, the students were less agreed. Most thought Whitman naive to believe that future American poets and writers could inspire the nation to a nobler idea than money, something higher that could inspire us all to put our material abundance to more generous use. Some of the students did not believe there was a remedy; for them, the die was cast; remunerative individualism was our national character; we would never overcome it. For others, the looming climate crisis would provide the necessary larger idea. Change was coming to the system because it would have to. Only Mary still believed that art would play an essential part. I found the session engaging and invigorating, and when it was over, I told Mary I didn't recognize the students she was so worried about in that classroom. An embarrassed smile crept across her lips: "I don't want to take too much credit. But

I have had all of them for at least two semesters before they take that seminar. We've had time to get into the practice of *thinking*."

Over dinner that night at the local pasta place, Mary asked about my father. She knew he'd left the country; I'd written her about it. I told her he was struggling with his health, which wasn't great, and so a trip back to see me wasn't likely.

"You can go see him, though, right?"

"They won't give me a visa."

"Who won't?"

"Pakistani consulate. I was in Israel last year. I don't have the stamp on my passport, but somehow they've got a record of it. So no visa. 'Are you a Jew lover?' was what someone there asked me."

"What did you say?"

"What I've always said to it: Muhammad loved them; why shouldn't I?" Mary laughed. "As much as I want to see my father, it's probably for the best. I've been seeing a woman who has an uncle high up in Pakistani intelligence. He told her I shouldn't go. They've got a file on me, and someone's decided my work violates the country's blasphemy laws. Which means they could make my life very difficult if they wanted to."

"Exile's hard."

"Exile?"

"One way or the other. Right?"

It took me a moment to realize what she meant. I lifted my glass. "To exile," I said with a smile.

"To exile," she said. We drank.

That night, I couldn't sleep and found myself on my computer, browsing 4chan well past midnight. It didn't take me long to discover a new video posted by the young pornographer in training. It was called "Long Tom" and featured the same well-endowed South Asian fellow, but now with a different naked white woman. She was fellating him in what looked like a museum lobby — in front of a statue of Thomas Jefferson. The edit alternated a series of Dutch angles of the oral sex in the museum with images of the Constitution, all to the beat of a fife-and-drum march that served as the video's musical score. It was hard to tell how ironically any of this was meant, which was maybe the reason it was hard not to laugh. I wasn't alone in finding it amusing: the post had over twenty-five thousand replies.

I doubt there were even twenty-five people in the auditorium the next morning to hear

Mary and me speak. Most of her students from the seminar were there; a half dozen from the Muslim student union; and a handful of aging "townies" who, I was told, showed up to everything like this on campus. The same two security guards checked everyone's coats and bags at the door, then stood in back scrolling on their smartphones as Mary and I conversed for an hour, mostly about capitalism, the collapse of our national politics, and what part (if any) an artist could play in helping shape the world anew. As usual, I was dour on that subject. America had always evinced deep strains of anti-intellectualism; life had never been easy here for artists and thinkers of any conviction. I quoted Emerson, who bemoaned, in the 1830s, that he couldn't sit down to think in this country without someone asking if he had a headache. There were chuckles. Mary knew the passage — she'd been the one to point it out to me a quarter century earlier. She accepted that there were challenges but believed there was reason for hope. After all, here we were, still quoting Emerson. She proceeded with an eloquent defense of the imagination and its uses that inspired more than a few of us in that room.

During the Q&A that followed, an older white man stood up in the back row and

ACKNOWLEDGMENTS

I want to thank: Judy Clain, Sabrina Calla-han, and the entire team at Little, Brown; Julie Barer, Michael Taeckens, Mark Warren, Mary Cappello, Shahzia Sikander, Marc Glick, Chris Till, Martha Harrell, Mike Pol-lard, Matt Decker, Lisa Timmel, Oren Mov-erman, John Landgraf, Daniel Kehlmann, Jennifer Egan, John Burnham Schwartz, Laquat Ahamed, Nimitt Mankad, Shazad Akhtar, Andre Bishop, Jim Nicola, Oskar Eustis, Indhu Rubasingham, Chris Ashley, Donna Bagdasarian, Don Shaw, Melis Aker, Chris Campbell-Orrock, John Ochsendorf, Mark Robbins, and the American Academy in Rome — and always and for everything, Annika Boras.

The employees of Thorndike Press hope you have enjoyed this Large Print book. All our Thorndike, Wheeler, and Kennebec Large Print titles are designed for easy reading, and all our books are made to last. Other Thorndike Press Large Print books are available at your library, through selected bookstores, or directly from us.

For information about titles, please call:
(800) 223-1244

or visit our website at:
gale.com/thorndike

To share your comments, please write:
Publisher
Thorndike Press
10 Water St., Suite 310
Waterville, ME 04901